PRAISE FOR
SUE MARGOLIS'S NOVELS

BEST SUPPORTING ROLE

"Delightfully funny, deliciously naughty, and compulsively read-able. I'll never wear the wrong size bra again!"

—Susie Essman, actress, *Curb Your Enthusiasm*, and author of *What Would Susie Say?*

A CATERED AFFAIR

"Wickedly funny. . . . I laughed until I hurt while reading *A Catered Affair*. It's a delightful romp with a theme lots of women can empa-thize with, but it's got a lovely message, too."　　—Popcorn Reads

"A guilty pleasure . . . bawdy and fun."　　—The Romance Reader

"British chick lit at its finest. Sharp-witted humor with warm, breathing characters . . . [a] unique love story."　　—*RT Book Reviews*

"A romping-good English chick lit tale that will keep the reader in stitches."　　　　　　　　　　　　　　　　　—*Booklist*

PERFECT BLEND

"A fun story full of an eccentric cast of characters. . . . Amy is an endearing heroine."　　　　　—*News and Sentinel* (Parkersburg, WV)

"Laugh-out-loud funny, passionate, sexy, mysterious, and truly un-expected. Sue Margolis has created the 'perfect blend' of characters, romance, and mystery. Read it!"　　　　　　—Romance Junkies

"A fun, sassy read. . . . The romance blooms and the sex sizzles. This is a hilarious and engaging tale. Sue Margolis has whipped up a winner."　　　　　　　　　　　　—Romance Reviews Today

continued . . .

FORGET ME KNOT

"A perfect beach read, with a warm heroine."
—*News and Sentinel* (Parkersburg, WV)

"Amusing . . . the story line is fun and breezy."
—Genre Go Round Reviews

"A wonderful glimpse into British life with humor and a unique sense of style. . . . If you're looking for a lighthearted romance with original characters and lots of fun, look no further. . . . This is one British author that I'm glad made it across the pond, and I will definitely be looking for more of her books."   —Night Owl Romance

PRAISE FOR OTHER NOVELS
BY SUE MARGOLIS

"[A] sexy British romp. . . . Margolis's characters have a candor and self-deprecation that lead to furiously funny moments . . . a riotous, ribald escapade sure to leave readers chuckling to the very end of this saucy adventure."   —*USA Today*

"[Margolis's] language . . . is fresh and original. . . . [This] is a fast, fun read."   —*Chicago Sun-Times*

"Another laugh-out-loud funny, occasionally clever, and perfectly polished charmer."   —*Contra Costa Times*

"Has something for everyone—humor, good dialogue, hot love scenes, and lots of dilemmas."   —*Rendezvous*

ALSO BY SUE MARGOLIS

Neurotica

Spin Cycle

Apocalipstick

Breakfast at Stephanie's

Original Cyn

Gucci Gucci Coo

Forget Me Knot

Perfect Blend

A Catered Affair

Coming Clean

best

supporting

role

Sue Margolis

NEW AMERICAN LIBRARY

New American Library
Published by the Penguin Group
Penguin Group (USA) LLC, 375 Hudson Street,
New York, New York 10014

USA | Canada | UK | Ireland | Australia | New Zealand | India | South Africa | China
penguin.com
A Penguin Random House Company

First published by New American Library,
a division of Penguin Group (USA) LLC

First Printing, July 2014

 REGISTERED TRADEMARK—MARCA REGISTRADA

LIBRARY OF CONGRESS CATALOGING-IN-PUBLICATION DATA:

Margolis, Sue.
   Best supporting role/Sue Margolis.
      pages cm
   ISBN 978-0-451-24013-2 (pbk.)
   1. Widows—Fiction. 2. Businesswomen—Fiction 3. Man-woman relationships—Fiction.
I. Title.
   PR6063.A635B48 2014
   823'.914—dc23   2014000826

Printed in the United States of America
10   9   8   7   6   5   4   3   2   1

Set in Spectrum MT Std.
Designed by Alissa Theodor

best

supporting

role

Chapter 1

*B*arbara, the addiction counselor, took off her spectacles, brought one of the tortoiseshell arms to her lips and looked carefully at my husband. "Well, Mike, after what you've told me, I think there's a good chance that I can help you with your gambling problem."

Mike grinned. "So what are you saying? That there's an even chance? Less than even? Don't suppose you'd care to make it interesting . . ."

Barbara winced. I sat shaking my head. "I can't believe you just said that. Jesus Christ, Mike, we're about to lose the house because of your gambling. Do you mind telling me when you're going to stop making pathetic jokes and start facing up to what you've done—to the misery you've caused?"

Eight years I'd been married to Mike. He'd been gambling for six of them. Only now that I was threatening to leave him and take the kids with me had he agreed to get help.

He looked down at his hands.

"I am facing up to it. I make jokes because that's what I do. I don't know how else to cope."

Mike had always been a comedian. It was what attracted me to him. That and the fact that he was six-three and built like a tank—only more cuddly. He said he fell for me because I looked like a Jewish princess. He was quick to point out that he meant this in the sister of Moses, biblical sense and not in the JAP, plastic nose and boobs sense.

We met at the Red Cow in Shoreditch. I was with my flatmates Zoe and Belinda and the rest of our gang. We were celebrating Zoe's thirtieth and watching Real Madrid massacre Manchester United in the European Cup. At halftime I went to fetch a round of drinks. Mike was propping up the bar with a mate, telling him how the night before he'd had this really horny dream about Kate Winslet.

"So of course you shagged her," the mate said.

"Nah, she turned me down."

"She turned you down—in your own erotic dream? How could you let that happen?"

"Dunno. I guess I didn't hit her with my best stuff."

The laughter burst out of me. Then I stopped. I mean, what if Mr. Gorgeous wasn't joking and he really was some pathetic loser?

"See, that woman over there thinks it's funny," the mate said, nodding in my direction. "I told you it worked."

I must have looked confused.

"We're TV joke writers," Mike said.

"Oh. Right."

"*Aspiring* TV joke writers," the mate corrected him. "As yet, we haven't actually sold a single joke."

Mike looked at me. "He's such a miserable git. He thinks if success doesn't happen instantly, it'll never happen."

"What d'you mean *instantly*? It's been eighteen sodding months."

"Well, that gag really worked," I said, eyes fixed on Mike. "I think you could be about to have your first success." He had dark stubble and messy, slept-on hair. The slogan on his T-shirt read: *The problem with real life is there's no danger music.*

"I'm Sarah, by the way."

"Mike . . . and this is Rob, a lapsed mathematician who lives with a transsexual cat. . . . So, can I buy you a drink?"

*W*e started dating. Meanwhile, Mike and Rob sold the Kate Winslet joke to a radio sketch show, along with a couple of others. As the months went by, they even managed to sell a couple of entire sketches. The money was lousy, though. They earned nothing like enough to live on. Since neither of them could afford to sit it out until they hit the big time—and as Eeyore Rob kept reminding him, there was no guarantee that was ever going to happen—they quit. Mike swapped his T-shirts for sharp suits and went into advertising. Rob went back to researching patterns in probabilistic number theory.

Mike found the transition from joke writing to copy writing easy. Punch lines, taglines—the way he saw it, there wasn't much in it. But becoming an adman didn't sit well with him. He felt he should be contributing something to the world, not boosting the profits of the burger giants and soft-drink companies. The problem was, he was good at it. He eased his social conscience by working for agencies that took on pro bono work for charities.

Mike's talent didn't go unnoticed. It wasn't long before the big guns started coming after him. Once he was earning a decent salary, we got married. After a couple of years Dan arrived, followed by Ella.

The children were toddlers when Mike was headhunted by Althorp Baggot Tate. He quit his job and joined them as a senior copywriter. ABT was the highest-paying agency in London—and they did work for several children's charities. He chose to ignore the fact that they also had the highest staff turnover of any agency in London. This was down to its chairman, advertising wunderkind Louis Liebowitz, operating a zero-tolerance policy towards imperfection. (There was no Althorp, Baggot or Tate. According to ABT legend, Liebowitz invented the names so that the company would sound less like a purveyor of kosher brisket.)

Liebowitz's talent was undeniable. His career took off in the late eighties with his *Stub it out before it stubs you out* antismoking campaign, which was famously illustrated by a cigarette butt melting a man's face, and it earned him a heap of plaudits and prizes. Thirty years later, Louis Liebowitz was still hailed as a creative colossus, but as a boss he was a tyrant.

A copywriter or creative director whose work didn't cut it with LL was out. In the end, most people couldn't handle living in constant fear and didn't wait around to be sacked. Those who chose to hang on self-medicated with booze and class A drugs. Mike wasn't really into drinking. He enjoyed going to the pub and having a few beers, but, like most Jews, he preferred food. He'd tried weed once, but it gave him palpitations.

He dealt with the stress by gambling—occasionally on the horses—mainly at the Golden Nugget in Leicester Square, never online. He said he enjoyed the company you got at the casino. I'd been to the Golden Nugget once on a hen night. The place looked like it had been "interiored" by Liberace and Tutankhamen. It was full of tourists and groups of bombed businessmen, some of whom had gotten lucky and were draped over women in sparkly boob tubes. A few blokes sat at the roulette table, focused and alone, nursing drinks. The addicts, I assumed. Mike loved the so-tacky-it's-cool atmosphere and called me a snob for sneering at it.

He never referred to his Golden Nugget activities as gambling. For him it was nothing more than a bit of lighthearted fun. Plus he was only going a couple of times a month and always with guys from the office. It was a harmless lads' night out.

Back then he could afford to fund his "lads' nights." He was one of ABT's rising stars. He'd even won a couple of awards. Ever wondered who was responsible for the Nike "Da Do Run Run" ads? His reward was a salary that ran well into six figures.

This meant that we'd had no trouble taking out a huge mortgage on a three-story Victorian fixer-upper overlooking one of the prettiest commons in London. The moment I set eyes on the house, I knew it was the one. It had marble fireplaces, original shutters at all the windows, coving and cornices galore. I couldn't wait to get started on the renovations.

Because Mike was so busy, he was forced to take a step back from day-to-day decisions about the building work, but I was in my element. Giving up control wasn't easy for him. On top of that, he wasn't sure he trusted me. I'd majored in fashion rather than interior design at art school, but once I'd convinced him that I knew my fenestrations from my finials, he was happy to let me get on with it.

For months there was a cement mixer in the living room and we were reduced to living in two bedrooms and washing the dishes in the bath.

Most mornings, having debriefed the builders and dropped the children at kindergarten, I would abandon the chaos for a couple of hours and meet up with some of the other mums for a latte, a gossip and a moan.

Project managing house renovations and small children wore me out, but I remember feeling happy and hopeful and excited about the future. With so much to occupy me, I barely gave a thought to Mike's gambling.

*T*hen he started going to the Golden Nugget more often—twice a week maybe. On his own. Now I was worried. I Googled "gambling addiction—signs." Top of the list of things to look out for were emotional withdrawal, secrecy and lying. None of these applied to Mike. He was as loving as ever and always perfectly open about where he was going. Whenever I confronted him, his response was the same: "Sarah, lighten up. You're overreacting. I'm totally in control. The Golden Nugget helps me unwind, that's all. And so what if I lose a couple of hundred quid here and there? It's not like we can't afford it."

Then he would take me in his arms. "You know, there are two things I adore about you. Sometimes I still can't believe these are all for me." By now his face would be buried in my breasts, aka Wilma and Betty.

"Behave, Mike. This is serious. You worry me."

Then it occurred to me that maybe he was right. Maybe I was

being too hard on him. I knew that working for Liebowitz was like working for Hitler with low blood sugar. The casino was Mike's outlet of choice. And there were so many good things about our life. A day never went by when my husband didn't tell me he loved me. He still sent me sexy texts from work telling me what he wanted to do with me when he got home. On top of that, he was a loving, hands-on father. He adored Dan and Ella and they adored him back. Their giant bear of a dad would walk in each night, scoop them up, make mouth farts on their tummies and tell them how much he'd missed them. Daddy made everything OK. He made their world safe.

It was easy to feel safe in Mike's arms. His bulk, his physical strength, made him seem invincible.

Much as I tried to back off, I couldn't. I asked him again if he was gambling online as well, but he still denied it. He said that even when he went alone, he had a laugh at the Golden Nugget. By now he knew most of the people who worked there. He insisted that sneaking off with his laptop to the garden shed didn't have quite the same appeal. He also made the point that he wasn't coming home drunk or seeing other women. End of discussion.

Despite his assurances that he wasn't cheating, I couldn't help wondering if he was picking up the occasional boob-tube woman at the casino. I went through a stage of checking his texts and e-mails and going through his pockets, but his missives were either to me, his guy friends or work colleagues. His pockets were stuffed with gambling chips, betting slips and antacid tablets.

As Dan and Ella got older, they started missing him on the nights he wasn't there to read them a bedtime story. I was quick to point this out to him. I felt bad, using the kids to guilt-trip him, but it clearly hit a nerve. He did an instant about-turn. Suddenly he was getting back each night for bath time. The downside was, he brought work home with him. I would go to bed and leave him sitting at the kitchen table, staring into his laptop. Then one night, in the early hours, I came downstairs for a glass of water. Mike was in the loo. His laptop was lying open on the kitchen counter. He'd been playing online poker.

"So, how long has this been going on?" I said, arms folded under my bosom, like some old battle-axe.

"This is the first time."

"Yeah, right."

"I am not lying. I promise you, this is the first time." Then he did what he always did and tried to schmooze me. "Come on," he said, wrapping his arms around me. "This Procter and Gamble campaign is really stressing me out. Liebowitz is constantly on my case. If I can't go to the casino 'cos you want me home each night, then this is all I've got."

"So you're saying this is my fault?"

He closed the lid on his laptop. "No, it's not your fault, but the fact is I need an outlet."

"Mike, has it ever occurred to you to get another job?"

"Where would I go? ABT is one of the top ad agencies in the world. They employ the most talented people. And over the years, I've become one of them. Yes, it's stressful and yes, I have moral issues around advertising, but I need to keep stretching and challenging myself. I enjoy being at the top. It's who I am." He started nibbling my earlobe. "Tell you what—why don't we go away for a few days? Just the two of us. What about Venice? I'll see if I can get us into the Gritti Palace."

"But that's, like, a seven-star hotel."

"So what? We can afford it."

We did the usual touristy things, drank the best hot chocolate on the planet at Caffè Florian, people watched at Harry's Bar, smooched in the back of a gondola. We ate and made love with equal passion. We also laughed. This was down to Mike's repeated observation that in the whole of Venice, there didn't appear to be a single venetian blind. One night, after a boozy dinner, he insisted we go on a venetian blind hunt.

We got back to London and for a while I stopped nagging him about the Golden Nugget.

But eventually, the worry and fear built up again. A pattern emerged. Every few months I would confront him and accuse him of being an addict and he would convince me that I was worrying about nothing. Then he would start kissing me. In between he'd say something daft like, "Do you think Satan had a last name?" Or "I tell you what's a dangerous insect—that hepatitis bee." I could never resist him for long. His ridiculous one-liners, the way he swallowed me up in his arms, convinced me that he would never let anything bad happen.

But he did. It started with my debit card being declined in stores. Then it was the ATM. More often than not, it spat back my card and laughed: "Two hundred quid? Yeah, right, lady. In your dreams." On the few occasions the damn thing relented, I swear I could hear violins playing and bluebirds singing. I decided that the sweetest words in the English language were, "Your cash is being counted."

Mike always had an excuse: a load of direct debits had left our account at the same time; his salary had been paid late that month.

Then I found a stack of unpaid bills. I'd been rooting around Mike's desk looking for a stapler. There were a dozen or more—all unopened. Heart hammering, I gathered them up. It took me a full ten minutes to pluck up the courage to start opening the envelopes. Finally I ripped into them. The utilities companies were threatening to cut us off. The credit card companies were about to take us to court. The letter from a firm of bailiffs was particularly menacing. If we didn't pay what we owed in thirty days, they would distrain on our goods and property.

It got worse. There was a letter from the bursar at the children's posh school saying that unless we paid the three thousand pounds we owed, he would have no choice but to ask us to withdraw Dan and Ella.

The final letter was from the mortgage company. We hadn't made a payment in nine months and they were threatening to re-possess the house. I felt the blood drain from my head. I just managed to get to the loo before I threw up.

I blamed Mike. I also blamed myself for all the times I'd allowed him to get round me and convince me that he wasn't an addict. Yes, I'd been on his case, but while we had money, my attempts had only ever been halfhearted. Instead, I'd been too busy having fun spending a fortune on granite worktops and fancy German showerheads. Instead of insisting Mike get help, instead of checking how much money was going out of our bank account and scrutinizing it daily, making sure that bills were being dealt with, that our mortgage payments were going out, I had allowed him to remain in charge of our finances. I had let myself be drawn into his insane fantasy that everything was under control. To say I'd been naive was an understatement. I was the mother of two small children. I should have been doing everything in my power to protect them. And what had I done? Sod all.

I dealt with my guilt by yelling at him.

"Sarah, you have to calm down. This isn't as bad as you think. I'm sorting it. OK?"

"No, it's not bloody OK! You need help. We need financial advice. We have to speak to the building society—see if we can make some kind of a deal which would enable us to keep the house. Please. I'm begging you. We have to do something. We can't go on like this."

Screaming at him did no good. He simply walked away. I didn't know where to turn. I wasn't sleeping. I wasn't eating. I was losing my temper with the kids. I was fearful that any minute they were going to be tossed out of school and that the bailiffs would arrive and turn us out onto the street. Where would we go? What would I tell Dan and Ella?

In the end, I did something I should have done years ago. I called Gamblers Anonymous. I was put through to one of their counselors. Her name was Kathy. Up to this point, I hadn't told a soul about Mike's addiction and our financial problems. I was too ashamed. Now, as this kind, soft-spoken woman urged me to tell her what was going on, everything came spilling out. Words tumbled over one another. I told Kathy how scared I was that we were going to lose the house, how furious I was with Mike. How furious I was with myself. I'd been weak, a coward, a bad mother. I should have listened to my instincts, taken control, and I hadn't. I would never forgive myself.

Kathy told me not to be so hard on myself. She said that she'd lived with a gambling addict for thirty years. "I loved my husband and I wanted to trust him. I also knew that if I couldn't trust him, our marriage would be over. I had a choice: end it or live in denial. I had young children who loved their father. Since I couldn't face destroying my family, I chose denial."

"You've just described me," I said.

Kathy suggested I call the Citizens Advice Bureau, who would be able to offer me financial guidance. She also said that I should try to persuade Mike to start going to GA meetings. I told her that was never going to happen. First, Mike didn't see himself as an addict. Second, he wasn't a joiner. He didn't "do" groups.

"OK . . . Do you think he might agree to see a counselor?"

"I don't know. Maybe."

She gave me Barbara the therapist's number. As we said our good-byes, Kathy wished me good luck. I put down the phone. I felt lighter—how I imagined Catholics felt after going to confession.

That night I gave Mike an ultimatum. He either phoned this Barbara woman or I was leaving him and taking the kids. "I have to get them out of this atmosphere."

"What atmosphere? We never discuss any of this in front of the kids. They're fine."

"For now, maybe. But how long before they start picking up on my anxiety—on the tension between us?"

He didn't say anything.

"Get help, Mike. Or I will leave."

"Come on. You don't mean that." He tried to put his arms around me.

"Don't touch me! I do mean it. You have until the morning to make up your mind about where we take it from here."

"But I'm doing my best. Look, I've paid the kids' school fees." He produced the receipt from his pocket and waved it in front of me.

Relieved—not to say shocked—as I was, I wasn't about to let him off the hook.

"What do you expect me to do, fall to my knees in gratitude? The school fees are a drop in the ocean. What about all our other debts? We owe tens of thousands. Like I said, you have until the morning."

With that I walked out. I had forty quid in my purse. I bought a bottle of cheap Chardonnay and booked a room at the local Travelodge. I sat on the bed, drinking wine out of a plastic mug, wondering what I would do if Mike refused to make the call. I still wasn't sure that I had the courage to leave him—to break all our hearts.

The next morning, I made sure I was home before the children woke up. Mike was getting ready for work. The sheer arrogance of it: assuming that I would be back before he needed to leave. When I asked him if he'd made up his mind about calling Barbara, all I got was: "I'm running late. I've got to go." I didn't push it. Then, around midday, he texted me to say he'd just spoken to her. My threat had worked. I had finally managed to get through to him. That night, when he got home, he told me that Barbara had suggested I come along to the first session. It seemed clear that she wanted him to start listening to me and take responsibility for the chaos he was causing. For the first time in years, I felt a surge of hope.

At Barbara's suggestion, I carried on going to Mike's sessions. I liked Barbara. She was a middle-aged, mothering soul and easy to open up to. Mike wasn't so keen on her. Despite the compassion she clearly had for him, she refused to let him off the hook.

"Stress at work may have caused you to start gambling," she said, "but it isn't the reason you've carried on. You carry on because you're an addict."

Mike winced as she said the word.

Time and again, Barbara tried to make him look at himself and face up to the damage he was causing.

He accused her of overreacting, just like he accused me. He parried her remarks with jokes and one-liners. Occasionally, though, the jokes would dry up. When they did, he wept. And so did I. I cried for him. For me. For all of it. Barbara said he was making progress.

After a couple of months our joint sessions ended. Barbara felt that we'd sufficiently explored the effect Mike's addiction was having on our marriage. Now it was time for him to do the real work and get clean. He would see her once a week—on his own. Barbara was anxious that I didn't feel abandoned and unsupported, so we agreed that once a month I should see her on my own.

During our first one-on-one meeting, Barbara registered surprise that I hadn't discussed Mike's gambling with a close friend. She said that bottling it up could only be adding to my stress.

"I just feel so ashamed."

"But what on earth do you have to feel ashamed about?"

I shrugged. "Mike's my husband. It's shame by association."

I explained that the shame had caused me to become less sociable. "There used to be this group of women I hung out with for coffee when the children were at kindergarten, but these days I hardly ever see them."

"But now the children are at elementary school. Surely you've made friends with other mothers."

"I did, but when Mike's gambling got really bad and we had no money, I started to pull back. My children are at a snotty private school. Can you imagine how those women would judge me?"

"But there must be somebody close to you that you can confide in."

Once there had been Zoe and Belinda. Five years we'd lived together in that grotty flat in Shoreditch. We'd shared everything—hopes, dreams—even packets of condoms were kept in a communal bowl in the bathroom. I thought we'd be best friends forever. I used to joke about the three of us meeting up as old ladies on walkers with pee trickling down our legs. Then Zoe met Ken, who had a beard and no mustache, and the pair of them got born again. The last I heard, they were speaking in tongues in North Devon.

Belinda, who was a doctor, had got a job as a pediatric consultant at a hospital in Sydney. She was married now, living in the Eastern Suburbs and up to her eyes in toddlers. With ten thousand miles and several time zones between us, we weren't part of each other's lives anymore. Over time, our e-mails had fizzled out.

"No, there's nobody else," I said in answer to Barbara's question.

"OK . . . What about telling your parents?"

"You have to be kidding. There is no way I'm telling Mum and Dad."

I explained to my therapist that neurotic Jewish parents didn't do well under stress. I said that I wasn't sure if I could deal with their weeping and garment rending as well as my own emotions.

Barbara said she took the point. "But in my experience, when the going gets really tough, the most unlikely people often find inner resources. Your parents might surprise you."

I said that I doubted it.

------

*G*radually Mike started to wean himself off the Golden Nugget. We also had a meeting with Steve, the financial advisor. His name was always being bandied about on the school playground. If you needed advice on natty tax avoidance schemes or how to boost your investment portfolio, Steve Milligan was your man. It took me ages to find the courage to call him. I expected him to tell me to go away—that his clients were loaded bankers, not pathetic, gambling-addicted losers. But he didn't. Nor did he attempt to judge or point the finger. Instead he said that his specialty was helping people avoid bankruptcy and that we should come in for a chat.

"Remember what Steve said about the possibility of making a debt repayment deal with all our creditors. You earn a fortune and if you can prove you've stopped gambling, they're bound to go for it. Why make us bankrupt when they can get the money back?"

"Good old Steve. He's got it all worked out."

"Actually, yes, he has. What's more, he's trying to help us. I don't understand what you have against him."

"He wears boring gray suits and he parts his hair like a Mormon."

"That's it? You find his clothes and hairstyle uncomfortably conservative?"

I wasn't about to say that I thought Steve was rather attractive. To me, his Mormon look conveyed solid reliability. These days I couldn't help finding that rather sexy. Plus he had beautiful eyes. Windex blue, my mother would have called them.

I understood perfectly well what Mike had against Steve, and it had nothing to do with the man's hair parting or his gray suits. It had to do with Mike's ego and pride. Here he was, being made to come face-to-face with a stable, financially competent guy his own age and admit that he was an addict and a failure. Penis-shrinking stuff.

"You know what?" Mike said, starting to get angry. "Maybe you're right and I am finding it too painful. Maybe I don't need Steve the Mormon's advice or that shrink woman reminding me time after time what I've done and what a shitty person I am. I'd rather buy a few books and sort myself out."

"Mike . . . please . . . don't do this. I know it's hard, but you're getting there. Don't give up now."

"It's not up for debate. I've made up my mind. I'll carry on seeing Steve because we need to sort out the mess I've got us into, but I'm absolutely not going back to therapy."

I knew there was no point in coming at him with more threats and ultimatums. It was down to me now. I had to decide once and for all whether to leave.

In the end the decision was made for me.

It was a few days before Christmas. I needed cash to buy presents for the kids, plus all the holiday groceries—the turkey, smoked salmon, booze, the posh fruitcake with Partridge in a Pear Tree icing.

*M*ike assured me his Christmas bonus had been paid into our account and that he had the holidays covered. But when I tried to get cash out of the ATM in the high street, it just gave me its usual sneering laugh. I brought my fist down on the keypad. "Mike, please . . . don't do this to me now. Not at fucking Christmas."

I called him at work. I was sobbing. "Mike, tell me you haven't been back to the Golden Nugget and gambled away the money we need for food and presents for Dan and Ella."

"OK, I fell off the wagon, but it's not serious. I'll sort it." There was panic in his voice. That was a first. "Don't worry. I'll think of something."

"What?"

"I don't know, but I'll get hold of some cash somehow. Just give me a few hours."

I could have shouted and sworn at him—asked him if he'd given a thought to the children before he gambled away his bonus—but there seemed little point. I'd wasted my breath too many times. Instead I hung up. Furious and fearful—tears streaming down my face—I headed back to the car. I didn't weigh it up or consider the consequences—I just started driving to Mum and Dad's.

So far, I'd disregarded Barbara's advice to tell my parents about Mike's gambling and the debt we were in, but I couldn't hold out any longer. I was in trouble and I needed them. I called to check they were in. Dad picked up.

My timing was perfect, apparently. They'd been Christmas shopping in Oxford Street and had just got back. "You should see it out there. It's a madhouse. And do you mind telling me why they have to play pop music so loud in the shops? It was so bad it's brought my tinnitus back. Your mother's in the kitchen. Shall I pass you over?"

"No, just tell her I'll be there in fifteen."

I hit the gas and made it in ten.

Mum opened the door, a duster in her hand. "Hello darling. What, no Dan and Ella?"

"Playdates . . ." I gave her a hello kiss. "Listen, can we sit down? There's something I need to talk to you and Dad about."

"What's the matter? Has something happened? . . . Omigod, look at you. You've been crying. Is somebody ill?"

"Nobody's ill. We're all fine."

"You sure?"

"Positive."

"So what is it?"

"I need to speak to both of you. Where's Dad?"

"Watching TV." I followed along the hall. She stopped to wipe some dirt off the hall mirror.

Dad was sitting on the sofa, grimacing at horrific color footage of the Siege of Leningrad. He'd been retired a year. After spending fifty years driving a cab, he'd replaced being behind the wheel with being in front of the TV. He watched documentaries mainly. He loved anything to do with Hitler or health.

"Twenty million, the Russians lost," he said by way of greeting. "Did you know that? Twenty million. Slaughtered."

"Actually, I did." I gave him a hello kiss. As I sat down next to him, he began rolling up his shirtsleeve. Then he reached onto the coffee table for his new blood pressure monitor. Unlike his old device, this one was capable of storing hundreds of readings and presenting them as an on-screen graph. I watched as he secured the cuff.

Mum rolled her eyes. "Third time since we got back from shopping," she said, shoving the duster into the pocket of her *Dinner is ready when the smoke alarm goes off* apron.

"So, Dad, I thought it was your tinnitus you were having trouble with."

"It was, but while we were out, I started to feel this pressure building up in my head."

Mum came over and looked at the readout. "A hundred and thirty over eighty. That's perfect for a man your age."

He grunted—clearly disappointed—and ripped off the Velcro cuff. "Well, I've still got the ringing in my ears."

"Idiot! It's the oven timer. My lokschen pudding's ready." Despite the slogan on her apron, Mum was an excellent cook who had never been known to serve burnt offerings. She disappeared into the kitchen. Dad picked up the remote and switched off the TV.

"So . . . no children?"

"Previous engagement."

"I can't believe the social lives kids have these days," he said, rolling down his sleeve. "What did my generation do at their age? We didn't have playdates. We played in the street. . . ."

By now Mum had reappeared. "Faye—isn't that right? When we were kids, we used to play in the street."

"You may have. My mother thought playing in the street was common."

Dad waved his hand in front of him. "This from the woman who used to take her dentures out in public."

"Sam, that's enough. Sarah has something important she needs to talk to us about." She sat down in the armchair and pushed her red, white and blue Jubilee cushion into the small of her back.

"I know," Dad said. "You're expecting!"

"Stoppit. Of course she's not expecting."

"Why shouldn't she be expecting?"

"Because if she was expecting, she'd tell me first."

"Why?"

"Because I'm her mother. A daughter shares that sort of news with her mother first."

Dad shrugged.

"I'm not pregnant."

"Told you," Mum said.

"It's something else."

Mum and Dad had always adored Mike. To them he was the perfect son-in-law: a loving husband, a great dad and, more to the point, an excellent provider. Bursting their bubble wasn't going to be easy.

"It's about Mike . . . and no, he's not ill. . . ." I'd barely begun and already I was crying. I told the story as best I could. Mum interrupted with a couple of muttered oh-my-Gods and I-can't-believe-its. At one point she took the duster out of her pocket and rubbed an invisible mark on the coffee table. Dad sat holding my hand, looking grim-faced. He rubbed the back of his head a couple of times. The pressure was clearly building up again.

When I'd finished, Mum came over and wrapped me in her arms. By now I was sobbing and there was snot running from my nose.

"Sam. Handkerchief."

Dad obliged and Mum wiped away the snot. "Everything's going to be all right now. Your dad and I are here. You and the children will always have a home with us."

Dad didn't say anything. He carried on sitting there—his mouth a thin line.

"Right. I think we could all do with a drink," he said eventually. Even though it was only four in the afternoon, he poured us all a

Scotch. Mum, who rarely drank more than the occasional glass of Chardonnay, downed hers in a couple of gulps.

"You think you know somebody . . . ," she said, shaking her head.

"No-goodnik bastard," Dad muttered.

Of course, they were both cross with me for not saying anything before now.

"I can't believe you've been going through all this for so long and not a word to us," Mum said. "Why would you shut us out like that?"

"I didn't want to upset you. I know how you worry."

"Of course we would have worried, but if you'd come to us, we could have helped."

"Your mother's right. I could have spoken to my cousin Maury— he's a financial advisor."

"We're seeing a financial advisor. Mike just sees him as a threat." As I took a slug of Scotch, I watched Dad's hand form a fist.

"He's a pathetic, wretched excuse for a husband and father, that's what he is."

"The thing is," I said, "I still love him."

Dad's hand went to his forehead. "Now I've heard everything. How can you still love him after the way he's treated you?"

"Be quiet, Sam. You're a man. Men know nothing about feelings."

"Apparently not."

"So what will you do?" Mum said to me.

"What can I do? I guess I have to face the fact that Mike and I are done."

"Are you absolutely sure? I mean you could go back into counseling."

"No. It's over."

Mum nodded. "As my mother used to say . . . it's time to ask for the bill."

I said that I would tell him tonight. "I might as well get it over with."

"After everything you've told us," Mum said, "I think that might be for the best."

"But it's Christmas. I can't throw him out of the house at Christmas. Would it be OK for the kids and me to come and stay with you for a while?"

"I've told you there will always be a home for you here," she said. "Just pack a bag and come."

I put my arms around her and kissed her. "Thank you."

"Oh, sweetie, you don't have to thank me. I'm your mother. It's what I'm for."

I realized that Dad had disappeared. He returned and shoved four fifty-pound notes into my hand. "Something to tide you over for a bit."

"What? No! I didn't come here to beg for money."

"Of course I know you didn't come here for money."

"Buy the kids some Christmas presents," Mum said.

"I don't know what to say. Thank you. Thank you both."

I got up to go. Mum said she would give the oven a clean while it was still warm.

On the way home, I decided to stop off at the supermarket. I would dip into Mum and Dad's money and buy a piece of beef. A roast. I hadn't done one in ages.

An hour or so later, having bought supper ingredients and picked up Dan and Ella, I was in the kitchen, peeling potatoes.

I had tonight all planned. I would feed the kids, get them bathed and in bed. Then, when they were asleep, I would tell Mike that after what had happened today, I couldn't go on living with him and that I wanted a divorce. I wasn't scared or nervous. I was too angry.

If I was worried about anything, it was the children waking up and hearing all the fighting and yelling that was bound to erupt— particularly on Mike's part. The last thing I wanted was two sobbing, traumatized kids on my hands. I realized how stupid I'd been. In- stead of bringing them home after their playdates, I should have taken them straight to Mum and Dad's. I would take them now.

Tomorrow, I would find a way to tell them that their father and I weren't getting along, that we were splitting up and they would be living with me. Dan was seven. Ella was five. Babies. I could hear the sobbing, the questions: "So, Mummy, don't you love Daddy any- more? . . . Why can't you just make up and be friends again? . . . But it's Christmas. We can't leave Daddy at Christmas."

There were going to be costs and consequences. If I knew one thing for sure, it was that kids rarely came through divorce un- scathed. On the other hand, if I stayed, they would acquire different scars: ones you got from living with an addict father and a mother who screamed at him from morning to night because she couldn't afford to put food on the table.

I was about to call Mum and Dad to ask if I could bring the chil- dren round later, when the doorbell rang. I decided to ignore it. I knew it would be carol singers collecting and, apart from the money Dad gave me, I didn't have more than a few coppers in my purse. The bell kept on ringing. I called out to the kids not to answer it, but I was too late.

"Mum," Ella yelled. "It's two policemans. They want to speak to you."

I guessed what it was about. A few days ago, a gang had broken into the Forrester house down the road. Joan and Cyril Forrester were in their eighties and frail, but the thugs had shown no pity. They had tied them up and slapped them around while they ransacked the place. The house was empty, so I assumed the Forresters were still in hospital. Since yesterday, the police had been interviewing everybody in the neighborhood to find out if they'd seen anything.

Two uniformed officers—a man and a woman—stood on the doorstep.

"Mrs. Green?" the woman officer said.

"Yes?"

"I'm Sergeant Brooks." She produced her badge. "And this is my colleague Constable Wilson."

"If this is about what happened down the road, I'm afraid we didn't hear or see anything. We were sound asleep. How are Joan and Cyril doing? Are they going to be OK?"

"As far as we know, they're fine," Sergeant Brooks said. "They're spending Christmas with relatives."

"Oh, that's wonderful news. Thank heavens they weren't too badly hurt. But I have to say, the whole neighborhood is in a panic about these louts coming back."

"I know, it is a worry, but we've got a car doing regular patrols."

"That's good to know."

"Actually we're not here about the burglary. May we come in?" Sergeant Brooks looked uneasy—as if she would have paid good money not to be here.

They both took off their caps. Constable Wilson, who despite his impressive height looked about seventeen, wiped his feet several times on the mat.

"Have you got handcuffs?" Dan piped up, addressing himself to Constable Wilson.

"As it happens, I have," he said, offering my son a smile.

"Really? Can I see?"

"Tell you what," Sergeant Brooks said. "Why don't you and your sister go into the living room with the constable, and he'll show you his handcuffs. He might even let you try them on."

"Cool. Have you got a truncheon as well?"

"Yep."

"Have you ever hit baddies with it?"

"Er . . . once or twice."

Ella announced that handcuffs and truncheons were boring. She was going up to her room to play with her princess doll's house. The sergeant crouched down so that she was level with her. "You know what, sweetheart?" she said, giving the top of Ella's arm a gentle rub, "I think it might be best if you go with the constable while I talk to your mum."

There was a solemnness about this woman that scared me.

Ella nodded. She wasn't about to argue with a police officer.

I led the sergeant into the kitchen. I was about to offer her a seat, but instead she asked me to sit down.

I felt my heart pounding. "What's happened? It's Mike, isn't it?"

26

Sergeant Brooks said that according to witness reports it was all over in seconds. A man had leaped from a thirty-foot-high ledge in what the police believed was a suicide attempt. Mike, who had been walking back to the office after apparently visiting a local betting shop—they knew this because he had a betting slip and several hundred pounds in cash on him—was simply in the wrong place at the wrong time. The jumper landed directly on top of him. Mike died instantly. The jumper survived.

The room started to spin and turn green. Sergeant Brooks got me to put my head between my knees. Then she asked if there was anybody she should call.

Chapter 2

"*L*ooks like the rain's stopping," Mum said, buttering another half of a bagel and passing it to me to top with chopped herring and a cocktail olive. "We should get a decent turnout." In Mum's world, the size of a funeral correlated directly with the weather conditions. "You know, I'm starting to wonder if maybe I should have ordered more bagels."

I said we had enough bagels to feed half of Africa.

Just then Dad appeared, fiddling with his cuff links. "I just had your uncle Barnet on the phone. He says he needs a lift to the cemetery and could our limo go via his care home and pick him up."

Mum stopped buttering. "What? He actually expects the chief mourners to chauffeur him to the funeral? Bloody cheek. What did you tell him?"

"I told him to get a taxi."

"What did he say?"

"That he'd ring round and get some quotes, but we shouldn't rely on him being there."

"Like I care . . . but he'll be there—see if he isn't. When have you ever known that man to turn his back on free food?"

*I*t was more than three weeks before Mike's body was released. First there was a postmortem. This was followed by an inquest, where the coroner recorded a verdict of death by misadventure. Some misadventure, but I couldn't help thinking that the suicide guy surviving was the kind of ironic punch line that Mike would have appreciated.

The death-by-misadventure verdict meant that no charges were brought against the suicide jumper. Psychiatric reports concluded that he was suffering from severe schizophrenia and, the last thing I heard, he'd been placed in a secure psychiatric hospital.

If I hadn't had Mum and Dad, I'm not sure how I would have coped. They came tearing over the moment they got Sergeant Brooks' call. In the days that followed, as I veered between disbelief, numbness and raw, howling emotion, they barely left my side.

When they weren't comforting me, they were tending to Dan and Ella—holding one, gently rocking or shushing the other. The only thing that seemed to soothe them was watching an old tape of *Annie*—I think it had been mine when I was a kid. When I asked them why, they said because it was about children who didn't have mummies or daddies. "But then it ends happily," Ella said. "And Annie gets a daddy and a mummy. Will me and Dan ever get a daddy again?"

From time to time, Dad escaped to the bedroom to watch a Hitler documentary on the History Channel and, I'm guessing, check his blood pressure. Mum turned out my kitchen cupboards, mopped the floors and took charge of the laundry—anything to keep busy. "OK, I'm doing a white wash. If anybody's got light-colored underpants on—take them off now and hand them over." She also baked. One day it was a gloriously puffy Victoria sponge; the next, pineapple upside-down cake. None of us had much of an appetite for proper food—in fact Ella was refusing all meals unless I fed her with a spoon—but we demolished the cakes.

The day after the inquest, reports of Mike's death appeared in the newspapers. We kept getting calls from the *Sun* and the *Daily Star*, eager to get a quote from the grieving widow. Dad told them "no comment," but the story appeared anyway. The headline in the *Sun* read: SUICIDE JUMPER CRUSHES DAD TO DEATH. At the end of the article, there was one of those fact boxes you get in the tabloids. This contained a list of other tragicomic fatalities. It seemed that Mike had joined a hall of fame that included a bloke who departed this world while peeing onto an electrical fence, somebody who set a time bomb but blew himself up because he hadn't accounted for daylight saving and a German spy who choked to death on a cyanide pill.

I was in too much pain to bother about nonsense in the tabloids.

"It will get easier," Mum said one night when I couldn't face going to bed. "You have to believe me."

"How do you know? You've never lost a husband. And anyway, you don't understand."

"What don't I understand?"

I paused. "You don't understand . . ."

"What . . . ?"

I shook my head. I couldn't bring myself to say it out loud.

"Come on, sweetie. . . . Tell me."

I hesitated for a few more seconds. "OK . . . Part of me is glad Mike's dead."

"I get that."

"I'm glad he's dead because I won't have to deal with his addiction anymore. Jesus Christ—what sort of a person is glad that her husband, the father of her children, is dead?"

"How's about one who has lived with the kind of stress and anxiety that you have."

"I know, but . . ."

"No buts. Listen to me. I am your mother and I know what a good person you are. Mike put you through hell."

"I should have done more. I should have been on his case right from the start instead of being so preoccupied with the kids and doing up this bloody house."

"Sarah, you were a good wife. Take it from me, you have nothing to feel guilty about. Nothing."

By now Dad had appeared with a tray of tea. "Your mother's right. You did your best. You have absolutely nothing to reproach yourself for."

"See, for once even your dad agrees with me. Now come on, drink your tea while it's hot."

*D*an reacted to his father's death by withdrawing. If he wasn't on the sofa with Ella watching *Annie*, he was in his room on his PlayStation. Ella was still asking if she would get a new daddy one day and then in the same breath she wanted to know when her daddy would come back to life. Aged five, she had a Cartoon Network, Wile E. Coyote take on death. The vision of her little face crumpling in anguish as I explained that her beloved daddy wouldn't be coming home broke my heart.

Mum and Dad were adamant that the children shouldn't go to the funeral. The way they saw it, the kids had been through enough trauma. Watching their father being buried would only add to it and give them nightmares. It could scar them for years to come.

What they said made sense, but my instinct was to let them go. By now I'd been onto Amazon and bought several books on helping children cope with grief. The authors—all child shrinks—were unanimous. Even young children needed a chance to say good-bye to a parent. If I excluded them from the funeral, they might feel left out and abandoned. When they were older, they could become resentful and angry. I ignored my parents and went with the shrinks—and my own instinct.

The day before, I sat the kids down and we had the funeral talk. I explained that grown-ups often got very upset at funerals. "Some of them might be crying, but don't be frightened. It's perfectly normal." They were nodding and taking it all in and I was congratulating myself for making a halfway decent go of this when Ella asked what a grave was. Even before I'd finished explaining, she became distraught. How could I bury her daddy in a deep, dark hole full of creepy-crawlies? I was the cruelest person in the whole world and she hated me. Oddly, it was Dan who managed to calm her down.

"When we buried Jeffrey, our class hamster, Mrs. Willoughby explained that he couldn't see or feel anything anymore and that he'd be fine and wouldn't be frightened."

"Dan's absolutely right," I said. "Daddy can't feel anything. He won't be scared."

"You promise?"

"I promise."

Telling the kids about sex was going to be a breeze after this.

When I tried to persuade Ella to wrap up warm and wear trousers and a sweater to the funeral, she virtually threw a tantrum. "No! I'm saying good-bye to my daddy today. Trousers are ugly. I want to look pretty." She insisted on wearing her pink fairy dress under her winter coat.

Unlike Ella, I didn't look pretty. Grief plays havoc with the complexion. My skin was gray. It was also chapped and dry from all the tears and nose blowing. Foundation and a bit of mascara would have brightened me up, but I hadn't bothered on the grounds that it was only going to get washed away and leave me with streaks and panda eyes.

I hadn't bothered much with my funeral outfit either. That was partly due to grief, but it was also because I had no money. The poorer Mike and I had become, the less interest I took in what I wore. Back when I was studying fashion at art school, all my outfits had been meticulously planned. In a week I could go from emo (black everything, multicolored stripes in my hair) to grunge (ripped tights, Doc Martens) to vintage (1940s shirtwaister dresses with shoulder pads.) These days I lived in leggings and jeans. I always managed to scrape together the money for a decent haircut, though—usually by eBaying some fancy objet I'd bought when we were doing up the house.

Mum wanted to take me out and buy me a dress for the funeral. She had in mind a black shift dress, lifted with a long string of pearls and topped off with a chic little hat—nothing too overstated. Jackie Kennedy was the widow to beat. I said thanks but no thanks and opted for black leggings, a woolen tunic top and boots. To her credit, my mother, who wasn't known for her tact, had the sense not to say anything.

Mum's prediction had been right. We did get a decent turnout. Over a hundred people showed up. Mike's work colleagues came—although I'd sent a message saying that I didn't want Louis Liebowitz there. Rightly or wrongly, I blamed him for Mike's addiction, and by extension—ludicrous as it may have seemed—there was part of me that blamed him for Mike's death. I'd never truly hated anybody in my life, but my feelings for Louis Liebowitz came close.

There were relatives at the funeral I hadn't seen since our wedding. Uncle Barnet was there. He'd clearly managed to get a reasonable quote from a cab company. There were other oldies, too, who had come—according to my mother—because a funeral made a day out and, like Uncle Barnet, they could never turn down a free bagel brunch.

Glad as I was to be surrounded and supported by all these people, part of me wished they weren't there. It was no comfort to hear how shocked and "utterly devastated" *they* were. My dad's sister Gloria couldn't stop talking about her devastation. "Me and your uncle Jerry were on holiday in Tenerife when we heard. There we were, just sitting by the pool reading *Fifty Shades of Grey*. I thought I was going to pass out from the shock. But thank God there was a doctor sitting next to us—lovely man—retired gastroenterologist . . . American . . .

from Englewood, New Jersey. . . . We have cousins there—the Bermans—but he didn't know them. . . . Anyway he got me to put my head between my knees. . . ."

Even though they meant well, it was no consolation to hear from Mike's workmates what a great, laugh-a-minute guy he'd been. Several told me that before he'd left the office that day to place his final bet, his parting words had been, "Napoleon . . . small bloke or just a long way away?" I wanted to yell at them. "Yes, he made everybody laugh, but you don't know what he was really like. If you only knew . . ."

Standing at the graveside in the frigid air, a silent, bewildered child on each hand, I was grateful for one thing. I thanked God that Mike's parents hadn't lived to see their son's coffin being lowered into the ground. He'd always complained about having elderly parents. In the end it turned out to be a blessing.

O n the way home in the limo I sat between the children, an arm around each of them.

"So, is Daddy in Kevin yet?" Ella said. "And how do you get to Kevin?"

"It's not *Kevin*, dummy," her brother came back. "It's *heaven*. Angels come to collect you and you fly up into the clouds and you get to meet God."

"Can we meet God?" Ella continued. "Do you think Daddy would let us come for a sleepover?"

Dan opened his mouth, clearly about to deliver another put-down, but I shushed him. "That's a great idea." I said to Ella, "And

I'm sure Daddy would love to have you come visit, but unfortunately only people who have died get to go to heaven."

"That's not fair." She started crying.

"Oh, sweetie," I said, pulling her to me. "I know it isn't fair. It couldn't be less fair if it tried."

It seemed that telling my five-year-old daughter that her daddy was up in heaven being looked after by this kind grandfatherly God hadn't softened the blow. It had simply left her with abandonment issues.

"You know," Dan said, "I still can't believe Dad's actually dead." He was drawing a stick man in the condensation on the car window. "I keep thinking he's away somewhere and in a few days he'll be home."

"Me, too," I said, giving him a squeeze. Part of me thought that Mike would be waiting for us when we got back to the house. "Hey— what's with all the herrings and hard-boiled eggs? Has somebody died?"

Dan rubbed out his stick man. "Mum . . . you know how God lets people die and then he has to make new ones?"

"Uh-huh."

"Well, why doesn't he make do with the people he's already got? If he did, then Dad wouldn't have had to die."

"Well, I guess people have to die when they get really old."

"Yes, but Dad was only a bit old. God shouldn't let people die who are only a bit old. It's a waste."

A few days after the funeral, the children went back to school. I had been expecting protests and tears, but they went without a fuss. It occurred to me that they were glad that things were returning vaguely to normal.

I stood watching as they were greeted with hugs and homemade cards from their friends. Having lost their dad, they were suddenly the center of attention. Maybe in a weird kind of a way they were about to become the cool kids to hang out with.

There were condolences and hugs for me, too. Mothers I knew, and some that I didn't, came up to me and said if there was anything I needed, I should just pick up the phone. Oh, and Jim/Tom/Dave was great with a wrench. If I needed any jobs doing around the house, he would be more than happy to oblige.

Some of the mums said that they were heading down the road to the coffee shop. Why didn't I come along? It would do me good. I thanked them for all their kindness and declined. I was too immersed in grief to socialize. I wanted to get home. Back to my cocoon, where I didn't have to pretend that everything was OK.

I was heading back to the car when I saw Imogen Stagge striding towards me. Was she wearing pj's under her raincoat?

"Sarah . . . I've only just heard." Imogen made the Queen sound like Eliza Doolittle. Her hug involved much vigorous back rubbing. I felt like a forlorn Labrador being greeted by its mistress. As she released me, I could see that she was indeed wearing pajamas. Tartan flannel. The trousers were tucked into a pair of dog-eared Ugg boots. "Dreadful news. Just dreadful. How *are* you? And how are the children coping? They must be devastated, poor little mites. I think if anything happened to Oliver, I'd completely fall to pieces."

"We're bearing up," I said.

"Good for you . . . Doesn't help to wallow. Now then . . . it occurs to me that what you need is something to keep you occupied. And in my role as chair of the PTA, I have been put in charge of organizing the spring bring-and-buy sale and I'm on the hunt for people to man the barricades."

Mike had loathed Imogen, on the grounds that she was bossy, condescending and most of all—posh. "And as for that disingenuous charm, they're taught it at school—how to engage the lower orders in conversation and make them feel like nobody else in the room matters. Five minutes later they can't remember who the fuck you are."

It was well-known that Imogen came from a titled family and was in fact the Honourable Imogen Stagge.

I rather liked her. I admired her self-confidence—the fact that she said what was on her mind. I knew this was mainly down to class. The highborn tended not to go in for self-doubt, but it occurred to me that her assurance was also born of age. Having been delivered of the Honourable Arthur (her second son) in her midforties, Imogen was now over fifty and by her own admission had reached the stage in her life when, "Quite frankly, I don't give a flying fart what anybody thinks of me."

"I know it's only January," Imogen was saying now, "but the sale will be upon us in no time. What do you say?"

"Well, actually . . ."

"First planning meeting is next week. I'll put you down, shall I?"

"I don't know. . . . You see, things are still pretty . . ."

"Come on. . . . It'll take you out of yourself."

"Maybe."

"Good girl. That's the ticket."

She patted my arm and urged me to keep my chin up, before striding off again.

*I*t was a few more days before I could persuade Mum and Dad that I was strong enough to be on my own and that they could go home. So far I hadn't had the luxury of being able to grieve alone. I needed that. They went, but not without a fight and not without making sure my fridge and all my food cupboards were full to bursting. Even then, Mum popped in every day with a chicken casserole or some chopped liver—"To keep your iron up."

As the weeks passed, the nature of my grief changed. I started to feel angry. It hit me at the oddest times—while I was emptying the trash or loading the dishwasher. I would look up at the ceiling and rage: "How dare you bloody die and leave me alone and broke with two children to bring up." Then I would call Mike a bastard son of a bitch and collapse in tears at the kitchen table.

Steve, the financial advisor we'd consulted before Mike died, broke it to me—not that I needed telling—that now that I was without Mike's income, there was no chance of negotiating a debt payment plan with the mortgage company or any of our other creditors. If I wanted to avoid bankruptcy, my only option was to sell the house. The equity wasn't huge, so there wouldn't be much money left after the sale—certainly not enough for a deposit on a new place. I would have to rent.

"Tell you what I'll do, though," he said. "I'll try to buy you some time. I'll write to all your creditors and let them know that the house is for sale. I'll also explain that you've been recently widowed and that there are young children. If I appeal to their better nature, they might give you some breathing space and stop hounding you for payments. But you have to understand, I can't promise anything."

When Steve called a couple of weeks later to tell me we had a deal, I burst into tears.

"Steve, that's amazing. I don't know what to say. Thank you . . . thank you so much."

"You're welcome." He paused. "Oh, and . . . regarding my bill."

"Don't worry. Just invoice me for what I owe. I need to find a job soon, so I'll pay you in installments if that's all right."

"No . . . sorry . . . you misunderstand. I wasn't remotely hassling you for money. I was going to say that I don't want paying."

"What? No . . . That's ridiculous. I won't have you treating me like a charity case."

"Well, I'm not taking any money from you and that's final."

"Look, I know you mean well, but for my own self-respect, I have to pay you what I owe."

He let out a sigh. "OK . . . I've got another idea. Get yourself back on track financially and then pay me. It doesn't matter if it's five years from now."

"No. I need to pay you now."

"Sorry, but that's my best offer. I refuse to take money from you when you don't have it."

"OK . . . it would seem that I have no option."

"You don't. So do we have a deal?"

"I guess we do. And thank you. I really appreciate your generosity. But be in no doubt. I'll be paying you back . . . with interest."

"We'll talk about that when the time comes."

Steve wished me all the best, and a few days later I sent him a bottle of posh Scotch to thank him for his kindness.

*I*t wasn't long before the dinner invitations started to arrive—mainly from people I knew at ABT. They were concerned that I was at home moping and getting depressed—which I was—and that I needed to get out of myself—which, according to my mother, I definitely did. I'd always enjoyed getting together with Mike's workmates. They were a hard-drinking bunch, but they were funny and irreverent and great company. I was so touched that they'd thought of me that I said yes to all the invites. Mum and Dad came to babysit and I attempted to find my way to houses and flats on the other side of London. Lost in the wilds of Streatham or Deptford, cursing myself for having been one of those ditzy, oh-it's-all-too-complicated-for-me women who always let their husband take charge of the GPS, I'd never felt so alone.

I was surprised to discover that being surrounded by people, couples in particular, did little to make the feeling go away. I wasn't ready for the "Oh, *we* love that show. . . . No, *we* hated the food there. . . . *We* always pop a Valium before we have a long flight." I hated their smug mutualness. I hated *them*.

When I wasn't busy being bitter and jealous, I was doing my best to cope with the children's emotions. Soon after the funeral, Ella started wetting the bed. Both children insisted on sleeping with me. On top of that, they required constant cuddles and assurance that I wasn't about to die.

"In *Annie*, the children are orphans," Ella said—she was practically watching the movie on a loop. "That means they don't have a daddy or a mummy. What would happen if you died? Who would look after us? Would me and Dan go into a orph-nige?"

I spent hours trying to reassure her that I had no plans to die until I was very, very old and that if by some chance I did happen to die while she and Dan were still children, then Grandma and Grand-dad would look after them.

"But they're old and they could die."

She was right. They could. I had no idea how to reassure her. In the end all I could do was take her in my arms and promise her faithfully that nobody else was going to die.

Then there were the outbursts of anger. They never acted out at school. They saved it for home.

My failure to produce the right flavor of potato chips or yogurt could result in toys being thrown, kicked and trodden on. Once when I suggested to Dan that he might think about tidying his room as the floor had pretty much disappeared, he started screaming and punching me. "I hate you. I hate you. I don't want you. I want my dad."

They were blaming me for Mike's death. Judy the grief therapist (who I'd found through Barbara the addiction counselor) told me what she always told me, that they were exhibiting textbook behavior and it was to be expected.

"I don't care if it's bloody textbook. It's driving me insane."

"I know, but try to understand. Mike was snatched away from them in the most brutal way. Of course they're going to be angry. And who else are they going to take it out on? Children see their mothers as protectors. According to their logic, you should have been there to save Mike." She promised me it was just another stage in their grieving process and that their anger—and mine, come to that—would eventually subside. Meanwhile I had to stay calm, grit my teeth and wait for the storm to pass.

"So once I've worked through all my bad feelings," I said, "what do I get left with?"

Judy smiled. "I can't tell you that. People's experiences vary depending on what sort of relationship they had with the dead person. All I will say is that you don't get over the death of a loved one—or even an unloved one. With time, the feelings of grief become less intense, but they never go away. You simply learn to live alongside them."

So, a peace of sorts awaited me. I wondered how long it would take to reach it. For the time being, though, I had to put my search for serenity on hold and find a job. I was getting by on my state widow's pension and the money I'd made from selling the Range Rover. (I'd begged Mike to sell it, but he always refused. The car and the house were outward displays of his success. Like he would be seen dead driving some old banger.) On top of my pension and the car money, there was a small pension from ABT. Had the contributions not been deducted automatically from Mike's salary, he would have spent the money and left me with nothing.

I planned to spend the Range Rover money on school fees. I could live with being seen driving a '97 Fiat hatchback. I couldn't live with the children being forced to leave the school they loved and all their friends.

Finding a job in a recession was easier said than done. It didn't help that I'd been out of the workplace since Dan was born. In that time I had developed excellent multitasking skills, but I doubted that any employer was going to pay me to rustle up a spag bol at the same time as building a Lego fort, unloading the dishwasher and breast-feeding.

When Mike and I first met, I'd just set myself up in business designing and making rockabilly party frocks—halter-necks, huge petticoats under polka-dot skirts. I rented a grotty, airless cellar beneath a bagel bakery in the East End and worked on my hipster image—cropped, sexually ambiguous red hair, Rosie the Riveter head scarves and vintage twinsets.

After Mike and I got married, the business took off. My ancient Singer sewing machine and I were making a living. It was then that I started schlepping dress samples around the trendy boutiques and West End stores, begging for a few moments' face time with one of their buyers. Mostly they showed me the door. Buyers were either in meetings, on conference calls, off sick or at lunch—at four in the afternoon. I would ask if I could leave my card and a couple of samples. People tended to say yes, just to get rid of me. When I heard nothing after a few weeks, I would go back to the shop to retrieve the samples. Occasionally they had been kept. More often than not, they'd been trashed.

One day, I'd been about to go back to Threads, a boutique on Carnaby Street, to collect my samples, when I got a call from the owner to say he was prepared to offer me a contract. I almost blew it because I assumed it was Mike on the phone, camping it up, and told him to bugger off. It took the guy a full five minutes to convince me that he was genuine, after which I spent another five minutes apologizing.

The order from Threads wasn't huge—just a dozen dresses—but it was a start, and each dress would carry the Sarah Green label.

There was a second and a third order, each slightly bigger than the last. By now I'd hired two seamstresses to help manage the workload. I was high on the thrill of it.

Then I got pregnant with Dan. I realized that if the dressmaking business was to carry on growing, I needed to go straight back to work after he was born. I convinced myself that I could hand him over to a nanny, but in the end I couldn't. Just the thought of being parted from him reduced me to tears. When Evie Sparrow, the Shoreditch hipster fashionista, invited me in for a meeting to discuss a possible contract to supply her shop, I explained that I was on maternity leave. She said that I should get in touch when I was back at work, but soon I was pregnant with Ella.

The Singer lived hidden behind my shoes at the bottom of the wardrobe—abandoned along with my hipster image. Occasionally I would get it out because a girlfriend had begged me to make her a dress for a party or a wedding. Then I would be reminded of all the hope and excitement I'd felt setting up my own business and later getting that order from Threads in Carnaby Street. Life had been about possibilities. Those memories always made me feel sad and homesick. I spent a lot of time lost in my thoughts, imagining what might have been. I was disappointed in myself. I should have grappled harder with my emotions, found a way to combine being a good mother with pursuing my dream.

Now that I needed money, my first thought was to go back to dressmaking. With the children at school, I could easily work from home, but these days I had no reputation. It took years to build one.

I traipsed round town handing my scant CV to every restaurant, bar and shop. When I wasn't traipsing, I wrote application letters and e-mails. I made follow-up phone calls and spent hours on hold listening to Vivaldi's *Spring*. The message was always the same: no experience.

In the end, the police came to my rescue. A nonemergency crime helpline was being set up at the local police station and they were looking for people to man it. The only requirements were good communication skills and lack of a criminal record.

I applied and got an interview. The first question the sergeant asked me was: "So how would you respond in a hostage situation?"

What? They were expecting terrorists to burst in and take control of the nonemergency crime helpline?

"Oh, I'd definitely call Jack Bauer."

The sergeant, stony faced, looked at me and wrote something on his notepad. I'm guessing it was "candidate displays inappropriate use of humor." I'd clearly blown it.

"So, if you had to list your strengths, what would they be?" He was just going through the motions now.

"Well . . . for eleven years I was married to a gambling addict. Coping with that as well as raising two children took a huge strength. A few months ago my husband was killed in an accident. He left me with massive debts, so things haven't been easy, but I'm working hard to get my finances back on track as well as give my children the care and emotional support they need."

I thought I detected a flicker of approval.

Ten days later I received a letter telling me that I had the job, subject to police checks. I also had to attend a race, disability and gender awareness course. Three weeks later, I started work at the police station. The kids were convinced I'd be given a uniform and handcuffs. They were seriously put out when I wasn't.

The nonemergency crimes the public were encouraged to report included car theft, damage to property and drug dealing. The non-emergency crimes they actually reported were very different.

"Hello, is that the police? I'm at Burger King and they've run out of Diet Coke." Or: "Can you tell me how to defrost a turkey—do I take the giblets out?" Or: "I've don't have any bus fare, can the police give me a lift home?" Or: "My boyfriend wants me to do anal. That's a crime, right?"

There were four of us manning the helpline. Everybody except me was retired. Don, our team leader, had owned a hardware store. Maureen and Glenys had been nurses at the local hospital. Tony had sold cars for fifty years and thought all immigrants should be repatriated—not that he was racist, mind you. Don called him Tony the Fascist to his face. He said it was the first time in his life he'd been given a nickname and seemed to rather relish it, so we all joined in. Every Friday, Maureen brought in one of her homemade cakes. Don was always highly complimentary about her baking. In fact he was highly complimentary about Maureen in general. It was pretty clear that it wasn't just her Victoria sponge he was after. When the phones were quiet, we drank tea and joked about the stupid callers. "IQs lower than their shoe size," was Tony's favorite line. He put their lack of intelligence down to too much cross-pollinating with undesirables.

Don would react by calling Tony a fascist prat. Tony would call Don a commie and then we'd all have another cup of tea. Nobody could get really angry with Tony. He was knocking on seventy. His wife had just died and he had no family. Deep down we all felt sorry for him.

Sometimes Glenys and Maureen would tell us grisly hospital stories . . . corpses that sat up, the man who came into the ER and announced he had *gentile* warts, the surgeon who shouted at Maureen, "Here, nurse, catch," and threw her a leg he'd just amputated—which she of course dropped.

Being a nonemergency helpline operator was an OK job, but it was hardly a career.

Mum said that with a million people out of work, I should be grateful for a job, even if it did mean talking on the phone all day to idiots.

"I am grateful. But I need more. The thought of doing this for the next thirty years fills me with absolute dread. I mean . . . suppose this is it. . . ."

"Sarah, God knows you have been through hell, but you have to stop feeling sorry for yourself and stay positive. You're thirty-six—a young woman. You will turn your life around. I mean . . . look at Erin Brockovich."

So, according to my mother, in order to give my life new meaning, I had to start wearing boob tubes and skirts up to my navel, find a gas company dumping toxic waste and sue them. Why hadn't I thought of that?

Chapter 3

Spring the Following Year

"... So, after the Big Bad Wolf huffed and puffed and blew the little pigs' house down, the little pigs decided to make a house of bricks, but there were problems at the brick factory and they had to wait weeks and weeks for the bricks to arrive...."

"That's not how the story goes," Dan declared. "Plus the way you're telling it is boring."

"I know," I said. "Bedtime stories are meant to be boring so that they'll send you to sleep."

"And I'm too old for the 'three pigs' story. It's for babies."

"I like it," Ella shot back. "And I'm not a baby."

"Yes, you are."

"I ... am ... not. You're a baby."

"No. You are."

"OK—enough," I said. "Nobody's a baby. Now can I please carry on with the story?"

At this point, Dan threw back his duvet and began jumping on the bed.

"Dan, stop that! You're going to damage the springs. Come on . . . settle down, both of you. It's way past bedtime."

Dan carried on jumping. "So, Mum . . . is Dad a skeleton yet?"

"What?"

Judy, the grief therapist, had warned me that one of the ways children cope with death and try to make sense of it is to gather information. As the months passed, I should be prepared for more rather than fewer questions on the subject. "And don't be surprised if they become a bit obsessed—particularly with the more macabre aspects. Ghosts, the devil and hell might well become hot topics."

We'd had the occasional discussion about ghosts and whether Mike might come back as one. Dan pretended to be intrigued by the idea, but I could tell that it scared him. My response was unequivocal. There were no such things as ghosts.

Dan wondered if there was TV in heaven. If there was, did Dad get to watch football? And did they get earth news or heaven news? He decided they probably got both.

Neither of the kids had mentioned cadavers. Until now. "So, is Dad a skeleton?" Dan repeated the words slowly—in case I hadn't heard the first time.

"I don't know. . . . Dan, will you *please* stop jumping."

"Mum, tell Dan to shut up. My daddy's not a skeleton."

"Maybe not yet," Dan came back, landing hard on his rear. "But he will be once his body has rotted. That takes ages. He's most likely still got worms and maggots crawling inside him, eating his flesh."

Ella burst into tears and started howling. I got up from Dan's bed, moved across to hers and pulled her onto my lap.

"Dan, that's enough. If you want to talk about this, come to me. But I will not have you upsetting your sister, and especially not at bedtime."

"I want my own room," Ella sobbed. "I hate Dan. I hate him. I had my own room in the old house."

"I know, hon, but for the time being you two are going to have to get used to sharing."

"But why do we have to share? Why did we have to leave the old house?"

"You know why. Now that Daddy isn't here anymore, there isn't as much money coming in as there used to be." The children still knew nothing about Mike's gambling or all the debt he'd left, and while they were young, I intended for it to stay that way.

"So we're poor and we're going to starve like Bob Cratchit and all the people in Africa. . . ."

"What? No. Dad's been gone for months—have we starved so far? I've got my job, so we're going to be absolutely fine. I don't want either of you worrying."

This was our second night in the new rented house. It had taken over a year to sell the old one. It wasn't that there had been no interest. There had been plenty. I must have had a dozen offers, but these days the mortgage companies weren't lending the huge amounts that London buyers required, so people pulled out. The couple who finally bought it were in the music business. She had a sleeve of tattoos. He had a Hitler Youth haircut and said the house had a real Velvet Underground vibe. They paid cash.

I'd driven past a couple of times since they moved in and seen their Mercedes Sport in the drive. Meanwhile, the kids and I had moved into a two-bedroom Victorian terrace on the wrong side of the tracks. Literally. The Reading-to-Waterloo line was a couple of hundred yards beyond the back garden. At the end of the street was the level crossing, the border post between our new scruffy neighborhood and our old swanky one.

"What a difference a mile makes," Mum had said when I took her with me to view the house. I watched her shudder as she took in the greasy pavement covered in gray disks of gum, the corner shop with sheets of security mesh protecting its windows.

"Mum, this is all I can afford. And anyway, I quite like it."

"Don't be ridiculous. What can you possibly like about it? The dirt? The homeless? The fact that you're practically living on the railway line?" Then she got upset because she and Dad didn't have the money to help me buy a house in our old neighborhood.

I insisted that the trains weren't a problem. "You can hardly hear them—particularly if the wind's in the right direction." Then I launched into my spiel about how good it would be for Dan and Ella to be raised in a neighborhood where the kids weren't ferried to school in the nanny's Jeep Cherokee. "Plus there's real cultural diversity here. They need to know that the world isn't made up of rich white people."

"Fine. Let them watch *Roots* or *Gandhi*."

"Oh, so it's OK for them to learn about ethnic minorities, but not to live among them."

"You know I didn't mean it like that. I may be a lot of things, but I'm not a racist."

"No. Just a snob."

"Sarah, you and my grandchildren are living in a poor, deprived, crime-ridden neighborhood. Are you telling me I shouldn't be worried?"

I informed her that I had done my research and discovered that the crime figures were a fraction of what they used to be. "This is an up-and-coming neighborhood."

"Who told you that? The estate agent?"

"No. I know for a fact that several of the kids' teachers lived here. There's an Italian deli just opened, a great new coffee shop, and the church hall holds judo and gymnastics classes for the kids. There's even a gospel choir that invites people to join them for a sing-along once a week."

Mum threw up her hands. "A gospel choir! I take it all back. What more could a Jewish girl want?"

The estate agent's blurb had described the house as bijou. Mum said "bijou" was code for "suitable for contortionist with growth hormone deficiency." "Compact" was even worse. That meant you could wash the dishes, watch TV and answer the front door without getting up from the toilet.

Despite Mum's misgivings about the area, she agreed that the house had a lot going for it. The young couple letting it (while they went traveling) had spent the last two years renovating the place. They'd restored the cast-iron fireplaces, stripped the floors, put in a new kitchen and bathroom. There was only one downside. It was rather more bijou than I had imagined. The entire ground floor was about the size of the kitchen in the old house. I'd looked at umpteen bigger places, but they were shabby student houses. This house was a little gem. It would be perfect—for the time being at least.

Back in the kids' bedroom, I turned to my son. "So are we agreed? There's to be no more talk of skeletons and maggots in front of your sister."

Dan shrugged. "I'm only giving her the facts. Tom in my class told me how bodies rot. He found out from his cousin who's twelve. He looked it up on the Internet."

Clearly playdates chez Tom—Dan's best friend—weren't the innocent affairs they'd once been. "That's a mean, cruel thing to do. He knows your dad died and he's trying to scare you."

"He didn't scare me."

The child was eight. Of course he was scared. Petrified, probably. And now he was paying it forward, bullying his sister the way this older child had bullied him.

"But Ella *is* scared," I said. "You have to stop. I don't want any more arguments."

Dan shrugged. "OK."

"My daddy's not a skeleton," Ella was saying now. "He's in heaven. He's with his mummy and daddy and all the angels." She looked at me. "Do you think he's still making TV ads in heaven?"

"Oh, I would think so."

"And what about if he meets the devil? The devil could take him to hell, where it's really hot like in Majorca."

I decided it was time for some light relief. I reached for the scruffy copy of *The Twits*, which was lying on the floor. The description of Mr. Twit's beard and the bits of old breakfasts, lunches and dinners that clung to it always had them shrieking with laughter.

"OK, *Twits* time," I said. "But only if you both get back into bed and lie down."

They did as I asked. I thought Ella might get upset again when we got to the bit where Mrs. Twit serves Mr. Twit worm spaghetti, but she laughed as usual. Twenty minutes later I kissed them both good night, turned off the light. As I headed downstairs, I could hear them giggling.

"Night-night, Mummy Twit," Ella called out.

"Night-night, Daughter Twit."

More giggles.

*M*um was in the kitchen getting up off her hands and knees. She made an oo-phing sound as she went. "Right, that's the floor done. It took three goes, but it's finally come up OK."

"Three goes? It looked pretty clean to me."

"Believe me, it wasn't. I had to get between the floorboards with Q-tips. You should have seen the muck that came up."

Mum and Dad had insisted on helping me move in. Yesterday and today, Dad and I had arranged furniture and unpacked boxes. Mum had scrubbed, scoured and dusted. The place reeked of ammonia and bleach.

"You know," Mum said, rinsing her cloth under the tap, "that sofa's far too big for the living room."

"I know, but it reminds the kids of the old house." I'd been forced to sell all our old furniture because there wasn't space for it here. I couldn't face parting with the sofa.

Just then Dad walked in carrying a bag of Chinese food.

"Did you tip the delivery guy?" Mum said.

"No."

"Why on earth not?"

"He was Chinese. I figured he owned the business. I only tip the Poles."

"But even if he was the boss, he's still driven out on a cold night. Doesn't he deserve a tip?"

"You never tip the owner. They find it demeaning. Tell me something. If Hyatt took your luggage up to your room, would you tip him?"

"What? We're not talking about Hyatt. We're talking about the guy who owns the China Garden."

"The principle's the same."

"Of course it's not. Hyatt—if there even is a Hyatt, which I doubt—is a billionaire. The bloke from the China Garden probably drives a fifteen-year-old Nissan."

"Guys, fascinating as this debate is, do you think we could eat? The food's getting cold."

"I still can't believe you didn't tip the guy," my mother mumbled.

After we'd eaten, I insisted Mum and Dad call it a day. "You've done enough and you both look exhausted."

"Fine," Mum said, "but just let me load the dishwasher and wipe over the dishwasher liquid bottle."

"What?"

"I noticed it's a bit gloopy, that's all."

Dad tapped my arm. "Best just let her get on with it," he whispered. "Tends to be quicker in the long run."

"Guess you're right." I glanced at my mother. She looked pale and she'd lost weight. "Mum . . . come on . . . go home. You need some rest."

"I'll rest in the next world. Funnily enough, being here with you and the children has taken my mind off everything."

By "everything," she meant her sister, Shirley. Shirley was dying. Having found a lump in her breast, she'd put off going to the doctor. A few weeks after Mike died, Mum finally persuaded her to get the lump checked out. It was cancer. What's more, it had spread to her lymph nodes. Now, despite a double mastectomy and several rounds of chemo, the disease had traveled to her spine.

"You know, I blame myself," Mum said. "I should have got her to the doctor earlier."

"What are you talking about?" Dad came back. "You didn't know earlier. She had the lump for nearly a year before she told you about it."

"I know, but I sensed something was wrong. I should have made more of an effort to find out. I look at her lying in that bed and I feel so guilty. . . ." Mum's eyes filled with tears. "My big sister . . . what will I do without her?"

I put my arms around my mother. "Come on, Mum, you've got me and Dad and the kids. We all love you."

"I know. And I shouldn't be upsetting you . . . not after what you've been through. I'm sorry." She wiped her eyes with the back of her hand.

"I'm so fed up with this family," I said. "Everybody dying. It has to stop."

"She'll be out of pain, which will be a blessing," Dad said.

"Tell you what," I said. "I finish my shift at three tomorrow and the kids have got playdates after school. Why don't I pop in and see her?"

"She'd like that," Mum said. She folded her cloth and put it in the cupboard under the sink.

Once Mum and Dad had gone, I began collapsing the last of the cardboard packing cases. I'd just added the last one to the pile when the doorbell rang. I peered through the spy hole—which, since I lived in such a lawless neighborhood, Mum had insisted I have fitted—and opened the door.

"Your financial advisor wishes to present his compliments," Steve said. Then he handed me a bottle of champagne. "House-warming present."

"Aw, you really are a sweetie. You shouldn't have, but I'm glad you did. I can't remember the last time I had champagne."

It had taken Steve nine months to ask me out. After that awkward conversation about his bill, he'd started calling every so often, "just to check how you're getting on." His manner was always professional: he was glad to hear I was doing well and if he could be of any further assistance, I should let him know. I guessed he had a soft spot for me, but he didn't push it. He clearly sensed that my emotions were pretty raw and that dating was the last thing on my mind.

Then, in October we erected Mike's headstone. There was a religious service, which was pretty much a rerun of the funeral—only without a casket and with fewer people. I blamed the so-so attendance on people feeling that they had paid their respects once and that doing it a second time seemed over the top. My mother blamed the rain, which had fallen in lumps.

The stone setting stirred up so many emotions in me—as I knew it would. In the days that followed, I felt pretty low. When Steve called for one of his regular chats, I found myself blubbing and telling him how miserable I was. He didn't say as much, but he left me in no doubt that if I needed a shoulder to cry on, his was ready and waiting. The following week we met for coffee and I availed myself of his shoulder—with far greater zeal than I intended. Afterwards, I convinced myself that all my tears and soul baring had blown our friendship. But it hadn't. Coffee led to dinner, which led to more dinners, which led to us dating.

"I know you weren't expecting me until tomorrow," he said as he stepped into the hall, "but I wanted to see how you were doing and check you were OK. I'm so sorry I wasn't around to help you move in. I almost never have to work weekends. . . ."

"It's been fine, honest. Mum and Dad have been great and we coped brilliantly." I led him into the kitchen and put the champagne bottle down on the worktop. "So, what do you think of the place?"

He stood taking it in. "Very nice. Somebody's done a really great renovation job."

I went to find some glasses.

"So, what are you doing about security? In this neighborhood you need to be careful. Have you got window locks? What about an alarm system?"

"You sound like my mother. Yes, there are window locks and yes, there's an alarm system. . . . Stop panicking."

"I'm sorry. I worry about you, that's all.

"Oh, and I have another small gift," he was saying now. "Check your e-mail."

"Another one? Honestly, the champagne was more than enough."

On the other hand, a voucher for a full-body massage at the Sanctuary would be more than welcome. Right now my shoulders ached so much from all the lifting and lugging, I thought my arms might fall off. I picked my laptop up off the coffee table, went into my e-mail and clicked on the attachment Steve had sent. It took me a second or two to process what I was looking at. "Wow—you downloaded me an Excel Household Budget spreadsheet."

"Yeah, when we've had a drink, I'll show you how to use it."

"You know, Steve, this is really thoughtful of you, but I'm not sure I need help budgeting. I've been doing fine since Mike died. I know you mean well, but it wasn't me who got us into debt—Mike did."

"True, but for a long time you chose to turn a blind eye."

"I did, but my eye is very much on the ball now."

"So you clip coupons, right?"

"Oh, come on . . . who can be bothered? Plus I can't stand those people who hold up the queue in the supermarket while the checker goes through their two hundred coupons."

"What about looking for offers and deals at the supermarkets?"

"I have a life."

"But there's so much you can do to save money."

"I'm sure there is. I could save on laundry bills by declaring Wednesday Nude Day. Instead of turning on the lights, I could save on electricity by wearing night vision goggles. I could start haggling at the supermarket."

He started laughing. "OK, I hear you. I'm being patronizing. I apologize."

"Look, don't get me wrong, after everything I went through with

Mike, it's good having somebody worry about me for once, but I don't need you hovering over me all the time."

"Point taken. It's just my way of showing that I care, that's all."

"I know." I went over and gave him a hug. "Come on, let's open that bottle."

We took our drinks to the sofa. Steve put his arm around me and pulled me close. Affection, physical contact that didn't come from my parents or the kids, was something else I was enjoying.

"If you like," he said, "I could stay over tonight. I'd be gone before the kids woke up."

I looked up at him. "I don't know. . . . I'm still not sure I'm ready. I know it's been over a year since Mike died, but . . ."

"Don't worry. It's OK. Take as long as you need. I'm not going anywhere." He gave me a squeeze.

"And what if the kids woke up in the night and found you in bed with me? Can you imagine the effect that would have on them? They haven't even met you yet."

"You're right. I wasn't thinking. But what I don't understand . . ."

"Is why I'm finding it so hard to move on?"

"Yes . . . after all, Mike put you through hell."

"I'm not sure I understand it myself. All I know is that grieving is a long and complicated process."

I couldn't tell him that, despite everything Mike had done and even though I'd been planning to ask him for a divorce, I'd never stopped loving him. I still loved him, and when you loved a person, you didn't cheat on them.

———

*S*hirley's nurse, Denise, told me to go on up. "She seems to have got some of her mojo back . . . been giving me hell since seven o'clock this morning. Her soft-boiled egg was too soft. . . . I forgot to cut her toast into soldiers. . . ."

"Oh God, I'm sorry."

"Don't worry, I'm used to it. She'll apologize later like she always does. And it's a good sign. Your aunty Shirley may not be long for this world, but she's putting up one hell of a fight."

As I climbed the stairs to the bedroom, I could hear the sound of the Aussie soap *Neighbours*. Shirley loved the daft plotlines and wobbly sets.

I poked my head round the door. Shirley, wasted and pale, was lying in bed, propped up by a stack of pillows.

"Hey, Aunty Shirl."

I made her jump. "Sahara! My favorite niece. What a wonderful surprise." Her bony hand picked up the remote and zapped the TV. "Load of rubbish. Gets worse. Don't know why I watch it."

"So how are you?" I said as I reached the bed.

A shrug. "I'm dying. How should I be?" For a dying person, her voice was still pretty strong.

With an almighty effort, Shirley heaved herself off the pillows and gave me a kiss. I felt her cheekbone against mine, protruding through tight parchment skin. As she fell back onto the pillows, her blond, big-hair wig slipped and I caught a glimpse of the sparse, post-chemo regrowth underneath. It wasn't the cancer that had caused Aunty Shirley to start wearing wigs. She'd worn them ever since I could remember. She owned several. They all had names. Today she was wearing her Alexis. Her Tina and her Dolly were draped over wig stands on her dressing table.

"Denise says you're having a pretty good day today," I said.

Aunty Shirley finished adjusting her wig. "Ach. What does she know?"

I was used to seeing Shirley in her false eyelashes and thick orange foundation. These days—although she still insisted on wearing her wigs—she couldn't be bothered with makeup. I understood why she used to call it her "war paint." Her lack of lippy and liner, not to mention her sallow, sickly face, made her look defenseless.

"Denise said that you ate breakfast. That's good. You need to keep your energy up."

"Since when did you need energy to die?"

What did you say to that?

"So, Sahara, still not wearing a decent bra, I see."

"Again with the bra . . . You know, when somebody comes to visit, it's customary to indulge in a little polite chitchat—at least for the first few minutes."

"What is this, *Pride and Prejudice*? Plus as a dying person, I don't have time for chitchat."

"What's meant to be wrong with my bra? I just bought a new one."

"I'll tell you what's wrong with it. Even with your clothes on, I can see it doesn't fit. Tell me, what size do you think you are?"

"This one's a thirty-eight D."

Shirley rolled her eyes. "I get so cross with you. Why will you never do as I ask and come to the shop for a proper fitting?"

Aunty Shirley was directrice of Shirley Feldman Exclusive Foundation Garments. The shop, around the corner from Selfridges, was her whole world, the child she never had.

"Because whenever I come, you shout at me and tell me off."

"Nonsense. When have you ever known me to shout?"

I gave her a look. "This from the woman who yelled at Princess Grace of Monaco."

"She deserved it. The woman was such a diva . . . always changing her mind."

"Then you fell out with Sophia Loren."

"That was a misunderstanding. I still get a Christmas card. . . . So, are you done accusing me? . . . Good. Now listen. There is no way you are a thirty-eight. Looking at you, I'd say you're a thirty-four, tops. . . . Your back is narrow. But your cup size . . . different matter. F to double F, depending on the make of bra."

"Double F? That's humongous. I'm never a double F."

"I'm telling you that you are."

"But how do you know? You haven't even measured me."

"Tape measures are for amateurs. I can take one look at a woman and tell her bra size—even when she's wearing a coat."

"But the one I'm wearing feels perfectly OK."

"Sahara, you don't get it. . . . A bra isn't meant to feel just OK. It's meant to feel wonderful. In fact if you're wearing the proper-size bra, you shouldn't be aware of it at all. Now then, take off your top."

"What?"

"Oh, come on, it's only us girls. Take off your top."

I took it off. Shirley told me to go and stand in front of the full-length mirror.

"Now take a look at your bust. How many breasts have you got?"

"Er . . . that would be two?"

"Wrong. Try six."

"What? Where?"

"You've got the two you were born with. Then you've got two more spilling over the top of your bra and two more spilling out at the armpits. That makes six. Women like you, with large breasts, always make the mistake of buying bras that are too big in the back, when in fact what they need is a larger cup."

I looked. She was right. I was spilling out of the bra. And maybe it did feel a bit loose at the back.

"Now then, stretch—like you're reaching up to a high shelf."

I stretched. "OK, you win. It's riding up."

"Huh! Of course it is. OK, now take a look under the bed."

"What? Why do you want me to look under the bed?"

"You'll see. Just take a look."

I bent down. There must have been half a dozen clear plastic crates, packed with bras.

"It's surplus stock from the shop. There isn't room to store it all. Right, look in the box marked *Ophelia* and see how many thirty-four double Fs you can find."

I rummaged through the box of black and white lace bras and found three.

"OK, let's try one on. Take off your bra."

I hesitated.

"Oh, come on. Get on with it. I'm dying here."

I did as she barked.

"Right—put the straps over your shoulders and let your breasts fall into the cups. That's the correct way to put on a bra. Now fasten it. What do you think?"

I adjusted the straps and went to look in the mirror again. My breasts were fully enclosed and supported. "Blimey. I don't know what to say. That's amazing. And it's really comfortable." I began moving and stretching. The bra didn't budge.

"What did I tell you? So how many breasts do you have now?"

"Just the regulation two."

Aunty Shirley said I should keep the three bras.

"And don't you dare start offering to pay for them. Think of them as your inheritance," she said.

I pulled on my top; then I went over and gave her a hug.

"Thanks, Aunty Shirl. I don't know what to say. That's really generous of you."

She harrumphed and said she was still cross with me for never letting her fit me before.

"So . . . look at me," she went on. "What do you think? I finally made it to a size zero. That's the one good thing about cancer—the weight loss. You remember how fat I was before I got ill? I used to sit in the bath and the water level would rise in the toilet."

I sat back down on the bed and took her hand. "How do you manage to keep laughing?"

"I've done my crying. I'm nearly eighty. I've had a good life and now I'm ready to meet the guy upstairs. The question is . . . is he ready to meet me?"

"Possibly not," I said.

"Do you think God speaks English? 'Cos I'm telling you, if I get to heaven and find I have to point at pictures on menus, I'm going to be seriously pissed off."

Now we were both laughing. "You know what?" I said. "I think I can safely say I've never had this much fun talking to a dying person."

"I wish I could joke around like this with your mother. She just weeps and wrings her hands the whole time."

"She doesn't want to lose you."

"I get that, but it's not like I have any say in the matter." She paused and started to look thoughtful. "Sahara, I'm glad you came, because I want to talk to you about the shop."

"What about it?"

"As you know, it hasn't been doing so well these last few years."

The truth was it hadn't been doing well these last few decades. The heyday it had enjoyed while it was being patronized by Hollywood royalty, not to mention actual royalty, had ended in 1992. In March that year, Clementine Montecute, a young lingerie designer, who just happened to be the Queen's third cousin, returned from Paris—where she had been designing bras and corsets for the likes of Chantelle and Pérèle—to open her own Mayfair atelier. *Vogue*, *Tatler* and *Elle* attended the launch along with dozens of A-listers and a sprinkling of minor royals. Claudia Schiffer cut the satin ribbon. Shirley Feldman's reign as queen of British lingerie was over.

It was the theater and opera companies that kept the business afloat. Period costumes required the correct foundation garments and Shirley's "girls"—the corsetieres and bra makers who worked for her—were experts at creating the perfect Edwardian S-shaped corsets and bust bodices. But since the recession, theaters couldn't afford to put on lavish, costume-heavy productions and orders were falling off.

"The thing is, I'm worried about the girls. I don't know what's going to happen to them when I'm gone. They're pushing seventy.

They're both widows. They depend on me for their income. Who's going to take them on? I can't leave them high and dry. I just can't."

I'd known Aunty Shirley's "girls" since forever. When Mum needed new bras, she would always drag me along to the shop. "One day you'll be a woman and have boobies like Mummy. For a while they will be firm and perky, but then after you have babies, they'll sag and move independently and you'll need a really decent bra that lifts and supports."

This was how my mother bonded with me at age six.

When we arrived at the shop, Shirley would be standing behind the counter looking glamorous in her red nails and big blond do. (Back then I didn't know it was a wig.) She would call down to the workroom. "Girls . . . Faye and Sahara are here. Come and say hello."

My mum and the "girls" would exchange kisses and do the "look at you—you've lost so much weight" thing, after which Mum would prod me. "Sarah, come on—say hello to Aunty Sylvia and Aunty Bimla."

I knew that Aunty Bimla in particular couldn't be my aunty. She spoke with a strange accent and wore pajamas.

"Hi, Aunty Bimla."

"Sarah, my poppet. My, how you've shot up. And look at you—so beautiful. Just like your mother. You are two peas in a pod."

Aunty Bimla came from Pakistan. That's why she spoke with a strange accent. Once I asked Dad where Pakistan was and he showed me on my globe that lit up. It was even farther away than Majorca—where we always went on holiday.

"Hi, Aunty Sylvia."

"Bubbie!" She would pinch my cheek. "Isn't she gorgeous? Couldn't you just eat her?"

Even though Aunty Sylvia called me "Bubbie" and wanted to eat me, just like both my grandmothers, I knew that she couldn't be my real aunty either. She never came to family teas at our house or to those big parties held in halls and hotels that my mother called *affairs*.

I remember asking Mum why I had to call Aunty Sylvia and Aunty Bimla "aunty," when they weren't really my aunties.

Mum said that they thought the world of me and it was a way of returning their affection. I thought about this and realized that I was rather fond of these women who called me pet names and hugged me until I could barely breathe. Plus Aunty Sylvia fed me Fox's Glacier Mints, which she kept in the pocket of her nylon smock alongside the bra cups and underwire. With Aunty Bimla it was carrot halva, which I adored even though it was rich and made me feel sick if I ate too much. I agreed to carry on calling them Aunty.

Aunty Bimla and Aunty Sylvia had worked for Shirley for more than forty years. While Shirley ran the shop, fitting customers with ready-made bras, the aunties did alterations and created made-to-measure pieces. All week they sat at their sewing machines, in their cubbyhole of a workroom, stitching bras, basques and corsets for period stage productions or for the few individual clients who hadn't deserted them for the upstart Montecute.

When Shirley got ill, Aunty Bimla and Aunty Sylvia took turns working upstairs in the shop.

———

"But, Aunty Shirl, this house is huge," I was saying now. "It must be worth a fortune. Surely you can leave Aunty Sylvia and Aunty Bimla some money."

Shirley explained that on her death the house would go to her stepchildren. She had married her late husband, Harry, in her fifties. He had been a widower with grown children. After the wedding, she moved into the house that he had bought with his first wife. Shirley and Harry agreed that if he died first, she would be allowed to carry on living in the house. On her death, his children would inherit the property.

"OK, so maybe you could sell the business and give the aunties something from the proceeds."

She laughed. "You're joking. The business itself is worth zip. The premises I rent."

"But surely the aunties must have family who can help them financially."

"Actually they don't. Sylvia's only relative is that dotty daughter of hers. The last I heard, she's still in LA trying to break into movies. A few years back she got a bit part in a soap on some cable channel, but it got canceled and since then she's worked in Target. Bimla's family are all in Pakistan. The only person she has over here is this wheeler-dealer nephew. She always refers to him as 'my nephew the property tycoon.' I've met him. Drives a flashy Italian sports car, usually got some blonde draped over him. He's always after Bimla for money to help finance this or that new project. He's clearly some cheap huckster, but she won't hear a word against him."

Shirley picked up a glass of water from the nightstand. As she took a sip, her hand shook. "Tell me, Sahara, are you happy in your job with the police?"

"I wouldn't say I'm happy exactly, but it pays the bills."

"So you don't see yourself doing it forever?"

"God no. That's a really depressing thought. At some stage I'd like to get back into fashion and run my own business again."

"Why not do it sooner rather than later?"

"Because I have no start-up cash and no reputation to build on. It could take years before I turned a profit."

She nodded. "I can see how that would be a problem. . . . But I've had an idea. How would you feel about taking over the shop?"

She handed me the water glass and I put it back on the nightstand.

"Are you serious? Me? Running a bra shop? You just spent ten minutes telling me I know nothing about bras."

"Maybe not, but you could learn. You trained in fashion. And remind me, you graduated where?"

"Top of my class, but that doesn't mean anything."

"Of course it does. It means you have huge potential. And you proved it. Before you married Mike, you were selling your dresses to that place in Carnaby Street. Later on you had Evie Sparrow chasing you. You're a gifted young woman. You also need a new start."

"But the shop is on the verge of collapse."

"So rebuild it."

"But how? You've worked yourself into the ground trying to compete with Clementine Montecute. What makes you think I could do any better?"

"Simple. You're younger and more talented than me. And you would have the girls to help you. Not only do they know the lingerie business inside out—they are the best bra and corset makers in London. They're in a different class from anybody that Montecute woman has working for her. I owe the girls so much. When Harry was dying and I needed to be with him, they took over the running of the shop. Without them, the business would have gone under. I can't bear the thought of them being left high and dry after I'm gone."

"I get that, but if I tried to rebuild it, where would I start?"

"Honestly? I don't know, but I suspect you're more resourceful than you give yourself credit for. After all, you've had experience running a business."

"Hardly. Mine was tiny and I only ran it for a couple of years."

"You will have learned a hell of a lot more than you think. Come on. What do you say?"

"I'm sorry . . . I have to say no."

"But I'm a dying woman," she said, full of mock indignation. "You can't refuse a dying woman."

This was so difficult. "Shirley, please try to understand. I don't want to say no, but I have to. I've got my kids to think about. Mike pretty much bankrupted us because of his gambling. Now you're asking me to take a huge gamble on the shop. I can't do it."

"It's not a gamble. It's a risk—a calculated risk."

"Risk, gamble, whatever. I can't do it. You're asking too much of me."

"I'm not sure I am. I admit that this will be the toughest challenge you've ever taken on, but I believe that I'm offering you an opportunity. What you see as a millstone could turn out to be my legacy to you. At least think about it. Please, Sahara—don't just walk away from this."

What could I say? Like she said, she was a dying woman. I said that I would think about it—but only to placate her.

"Good girl. That's all I wanted to hear. I'd hate to think of you turning down this chance and living to regret it. Regret is a terrible thing."

"You have regrets?"

"Of course I do. Who doesn't? There's one in particular."

"You want to talk about it?"

She shook her head. "I'm too tired and it was a long time ago, but let's just say that there were things I should have put right and I didn't. I lost a very dear friend because of it."

"I'm sorry."

"Don't be. It was my own stupid fault." Her face brightened. "Now then, how are those beautiful children of yours? I hope you brought pictures."

I took out my phone and flicked through the latest snaps. I could see Shirley's eyes filling with tears. I wondered, not for the first time, if she regretted not having children of her own.

"Couldn't you just eat them?" she said.

Suddenly her eyes were looking heavy. She needed to sleep. When I said that maybe it was time for me to go, she didn't object.

I kissed her good-bye.

"You always were my favorite niece, you know."

"What do you mean? I'm your only niece."

"Really? You sure?"

"Of course I'm sure."

Shirley started laughing. "Love you, Sahara."

"Love you, too, Aunty Shirl."

I was up all night fretting and feeling guilty about having to refuse Aunty Shirley her dying wish. There was no doubt that part of me yearned for a fresh start. I was in a job without prospects. Running my own business would give me the excitement and challenge I needed. I thought back to when I'd been making and designing dresses. I'd felt happy and fulfilled. I was always making plans and looking to the future. These days I thought about my children's future rather than my own.

But taking over the bra shop was a no-brainer. I didn't have the tens of thousands needed to get it back on its feet and even if I had, I knew nothing about the lingerie business, nothing about bra making. How could I even think of competing with Clementine Montecute? It was crazy. Aunty Shirley was crazy. Even so, telling her that my answer was still no would feel like the cruelest thing I'd ever done.

The next morning, as I was kissing Dan and Ella good-bye in the school playground, my cell rang.

"Sarah, it's Dad." I got him to hang on while I shooed the kids into school. "Have a good day, you two. See you later . . . Hey Dad. You OK? You sound a bit down."

"Sweetie, I'm afraid I have some bad news."

Aunty Shirley had died in the night.

I lowered myself onto a playground bench. "I don't believe it.

When I saw her yesterday, she was weak, but I'd have said she had weeks or even months left in her."

"Seems like she took an overdose of sleeping pills."

"What? But she was in really good spirits. She was cracking jokes, demanding to see pictures of the kids. She even had this mad plan for me to take over the shop. She said I should go away and think about it and let her know my decision. Why would she end it before I got a chance to tell her?"

Dad let out a half laugh. "Maybe because she knew you'd tell her the idea was crazy and she didn't want to hear it."

"Maybe . . . Jeez, I feel so bad that none of us realized how depressed she was."

"I'm not sure she was depressed. I think dying made her feel out of control."

Dad read me Aunty Shirley's suicide note. *"Dear God—I'm not prepared to wait around while you decide when to sack me, so I quit."*

I couldn't help smiling. "That's so Aunty Shirley—always in the driving seat. Part of me wants to say 'good for her.' . . . So, how's Mum taken it? She must be in pieces."

Dad said that she was actually doing OK. Better than he'd expected. I offered to come straight over, but Dad said that so long as I felt up to it, I should go to work.

"You haven't been in this job long. You can't start taking time off."

"OK, but only if you're sure. Tell Mum I'll pop over later with the kids."

When I got there, Mum and I fell into each other's arms and sobbed. "Yesterday she fitted me with this amazing bra," I said, blubbing. "Now I only have two breasts instead of six."

Mum managed to laugh through her tears. "I can still see her shaking her finger at me. 'Faye, God gave you two breasts for a reason. Don't challenge his wisdom.'"

Once we were all cried out, Mum handed me an envelope with my name on it. Apparently it had been on the nightstand, next to Shirley's suicide note.

My darling Sahara,

Re our discussion today: Your mother has a copy of my will, which, anticipating that you would agree to my proposal, I drew up months ago. The business is now yours. Be brave and have faith in the talent and ingenuity which you have in spades. I know you will rise to this challenge. I swear I'll haunt you if you don't.

Your devoted Aunty Shirl xx

PS . . . Check with your mother, but I'm pretty sure I have a great-niece in Ontario.

Chapter 4

*T*he Honourable Imogen Stagge, breathless and red of face, lowered herself onto the child-size school chair. "Sorry I'm late, chapesses. Bloody au pair's got thrush."

Tara, Charlotte and I chose not to inquire how precisely Imogen's au pair's yeast infection had contributed to her tardy arrival at the inaugural summer fair planning meeting.

"Hang on—where's everybody else?" Imogen said. "I worked so hard rounding people up. Please don't tell me it's just going to be the four of us."

Tara reminded her that the kids who went to Mandarin Club after school didn't finish until six, so a lot of the mothers would be late. "I only made it because the nanny offered to stay late to pick up Cressida and Mungo."

And I was only there because I felt so guilty about not lending a hand at last year's bring-and-buy sale that when Imogen launched herself at me in the playground earlier that week, I promised faithfully that this time I would do my bit. Plus I needed to get out. After Aunty Shirley's funeral, Mum sat shiva for the entire week. Dad had tried to persuade her that since none of the family—Shirley in particular—was religious, one day of official mourning, possibly two, would suffice, but Mum put her foot down. "No. I want to do this properly. It's the least I can do for her."

I could see Dad was worried about her. We both were. It wasn't just that she'd lost even more weight. Her face looked gray and drawn. "She's exhausted," he said to me the night after the funeral. We were in the kitchen. The kids were asleep upstairs and I was making the rest of us bedtime cocoa. "She needs a rest." He was right. Mum had worked herself into the ground this year looking after me and the kids and Aunty Shirley.

"I feel so guilty," I said.

"You? What on earth have you got to feel guilty about? Good Lord, it's hardly your fault that Mike died." Dad pulled me to him and gave me a hug. "Stop it. I won't hear any more of this nonsense. None of this is your fault. I'll sort your mother out. Leave it to me."

I blinked away my tears and nodded. "Dad—there's something else . . . about the shop. I keep going over and over Aunty Shirley's letter. Every time I read it, I start crying. She had such faith in me. Selling the business seems so unkind and disloyal."

"Sarah, we've been over this. It would be madness to even think about getting the shop up and running."

Just then Mum appeared. She'd changed out of her black suit and into her dressing gown. "Lord—not this again. Sarah, you can't possibly give up a decent salary to take that kind of risk—and especially not with two children to think about. Haven't you had your fill of gambling?"

"Of course I have. But has it occurred to you that one of the reasons Aunty Shirley wanted me to take it over was that she couldn't bear the thought of the business dying with her? She had no children of her own, no investment in the future. I think she wanted something of her to live on after she'd gone. She was depending on me to make that happen and now I'm going to let her down."

"And has it occurred to you—bearing in mind the state of the business—that she had no right to ask that of you?"

*T*he shiva was held at Mum and Dad's. As Jewish tradition demanded, Mum covered all the mirrors. This included the shaving mirror in the bathroom.

"Let me get this straight," Dad said. "We're in mourning for your sister, so, according to Jewish law, I am required to cut my throat shaving?"

"But the whole point is that when you're in mourning, you turn your back on vanity and stop shaving."

Dad said he wasn't about to endure an itchy face for a week—even for Shirley. He uncovered the mirror.

As mourner in chief, Mum spent each day perched on a low wooden chair supplied by the synagogue. From here—pale and weary—she received visitors who came to pay their respects. First thing every morning she dispatched Dad to the Jewish baker's to stock up on miniature cheese Danish and babka: "Get the chocolate as well as the cinnamon. People like a choice."

I took the week off work to be with Mum and help with the catering, which went on all day. Relatives—mainly the elderly who didn't have jobs to go to—would start arriving around eleven—just in time for coffee. While Mum and her old aunts, uncles and cousins sat making maudlin conversation, Dad and I topped up their cups and kept the babka and Danish flowing.

At some stage a bony hand would reach out for mine. Sit down, darling. Now, tell me. How are you? A widow at your age, a person shouldn't know of it. Such a tragedy, a young, talented man like Mike, struck down in the prime of life. What a thing. Still, these things happen and you're young. Please God one day you'll find somebody else.

Around three, I would nip out to collect Dan and Ella from school. I'd take them for ice cream or a soda so that we could have some "us" time and then bring them back to Mum and Dad's. Later on, when the rabbi and mourners arrived for evening prayers, I shooed the kids upstairs to watch TV.

"So now that Aunty Shirley's in heaven," Ella said, "Daddy will have some company."

"Maybe he could even marry her," Dan piped up.

"There's a thought," I said.

By eight o'clock the living room would be full and Dad and I would be handing out prayer books.

Shirley's "girls"—my "aunties"—came each night and were beside themselves, as they had been at the funeral. I hadn't seen them for what—five years? Aunty Bimla's hair was entirely gray now, but she still tied it in a long girlish plait that hung down her back. The chunky pink cardigan she wore over her *salwar kameez* probably wasn't the same pink cardigan I remembered from my childhood, but it might as well have been. Sylvia appeared to have shrunk with age—both in height and substance. She'd always been tiny, but now she looked positively birdlike. The effect was to make her frizzy hair, which she dyed red and referred to as her Jew-fro, seem bigger than ever.

Once the prayers were over, they would follow me into the kitchen and help with the tea. Before we got started, they would take it in turns to pull me to their bosoms.

"Bubbie. We should only meet at celebrations."

"Poppet. What a fine kettle of fish. We are so down in the dumps." I'd always loved the way Aunty Bimla spoke—like she'd swallowed the *Oxford English Dictionary of Sayings, Maxims, and Proverbs.*

"When my Gerald got ill with his prostate," Aunty Sylvia said one night as the three of us buttered bagels and arranged slices of cake, "Shirley was on the phone every day. She was more like a friend than an employer."

"Well, to me she was more like a sister. The day Parvez died, she dropped everything to come and be with me."

Aunty Sylvia shook her head. "She didn't deserve what happened to her . . . the cancer . . . that bloody Montecute woman stealing all her business."

"It was the worst possible tragedy. Most definitely."

I wondered if Aunty Shirley had told the aunties about her plan for me to take over the shop. I wouldn't have put it past her, bearing in mind she'd seemed so certain that I would agree to it.

"By the way, did Shirley . . . ?"

"So, poppet, what will you do with the shop, now it is yours?"

"Ah, so she did tell you she was leaving it to me."

"She talked about little else," Aunty Sylvia said. "How gifted you are, what faith she had in you, how she knew that you were the one who could turn the business around." She touched my arm. "Look,

Sarah . . . don't take this the wrong way. . . . We don't doubt that you are an extremely talented young woman, but the shop is on its knees. While that bloody Montecute woman remains the toast of the town, nobody can compete. You wouldn't stand a chance."

"But if I close it down, the two of you will be out of a job."

"We'll be fine," Aunty Sylvia said. "We've got our pensions and once Roxanne hits the big time in LA, I'll have nothing to worry about. It won't be long now. Yesterday, she phoned to tell me that she's doing breakfast with this hotshot Hollywood producer who wants to make a film about a haunted refrigerator."

"And my nephew Sanjeev is about to sign a huge deal with a man from Paraguay. Please don't worry about us, poppet."

Like that was going to happen.

It was only going out to do the school run and chatting to Steve on the phone each night when the kids and I finally got home that stopped me going stir-crazy. By the end of the week I was actually excited about going to the summer fair planning meeting.

*B*ack in the classroom, Tara turned to me. "You know, Sarah, you really should encourage Dan and Ella to start Mandarin Club. Cressida and Mungo love it and, as I keep telling them, businesspeople who speak Mandarin have such an advantage when it comes to tapping into the Chinese market."

"Actually," Charlotte ventured—she wasn't nearly as self-assured as Tara—"I think learning the classics is just as important. So much of the English language is based on Latin and Greek. Ottilie has a tutor who comes in on a Saturday morning to teach her Latin."

"Really?" I said, for want of anything else to say. On the one hand I thought that women like Tara and Charlotte, who thought they could buy talent and intelligence for their children the same way they could buy a Mulberry tote, were idiots whose pushiness would come back to bite them on the ass when their kids burned out in their teenage years and developed eating disorders. On the other hand I was jealous that these wealthy women, like dozens of others in the school, could afford all these extra activities and I couldn't.

"Well," Imogen said, "I'm afraid Archie spends his Saturday mornings sprawled on the floor in his pj's watching cartoons. I did all that pushy parenting stuff with his older brother. What people don't realize is that no matter what you do, one's progeny still grow into moody, monosyllabic teenagers who lie in bed all day smoking marijuana and masturbating."

You couldn't not love Imogen.

Tara and Charlotte managed thin smiles. I don't know what horrified them more, the thought of their children doing drugs or jerking off.

"Good Lord," Imogen was saying now. "Is it me or is it hot in here?" She reached into her bag, took out the Tommy Padstow spring catalog and began fanning herself. She was wearing the plum wrap dress featured on the front cover. The only difference being that hers was a size sixteen and dusted in dog hair.

"I think it's you," Tara said to Imogen. "Before you arrived, we were all saying how cold it is in here. The caretaker must have turned off the heating."

"Must be a hot flush, then. I'm getting them all the time. If it's not hot flushes, it's mood swings. Not to put too fine a point on it, but I have recently been visited by the menopause dwarves—Bitchy, Moody, Sleepy and Sweaty."

Charlotte squirmed, as if menopause could be catching. "My mother's about your age," she said. "She swears by black cohosh."

"Thanks for the tip," Imogen replied, apparently unaware that she had been insulted. "Perhaps I'll give it a go." She stood up. "Right, while we're waiting for the stragglers, I think I'll pop to the loo. Stress incontinence—that's another of nature's delights you have to look forward to. Instead of buying condoms you start bulk buying adult diapers."

With that she strode off.

Tara watched her go. "I do wish Imogen wasn't quite so *toilety*."

"By the way," I said. "I just wanted to thank you both for having Dan and Ella over for so many playdates lately. I think it really is time for me to reciprocate. How are your lot fixed for next week? I thought I'd have all the kids at my place."

I saw a look pass between Tara and Charlotte.

"That would be lovely," Charlotte said, clearly forcing a smile. "But maybe we should wait a while . . . until it gets a bit lighter."

Tara nodded. "Yes, I think that would be for the best."

"Sorry. I'm not with you. How do you mean, 'until it gets lighter'?"

They both appeared to be scrambling for the right words.

"It's the streets. . . ."

"Yes . . . very dark . . . and you never know. . . ."

Ah. The penny dropped.

"Do you mean the streets in general or just the streets where I live?"

"Look, Tara and I don't mean to be rude and clearly things haven't been easy for you since Mike died and we do sympathize, but . . ."

"At the same time you don't know if you're going to get mugged as you walk the six feet from the curb to my house. Or maybe some hoodie will stick a petrol bomb through the letter box while the kids are having tea? It's OK. I get it."

"You must think we're terrible snobs," Tara said, running her hands through her five-hundred-quid highlights. "But we have to think about our children."

"Meaning that I don't think about mine?"

"No . . . of course you do. We didn't mean that. . . ."

By now Imogen had returned, followed by a gaggle of latecomers.

"OK, chapesses, if you could all pull up a chair and make a circle, then we can get started."

Fiona—mother of Grace, who was in Ella's year, and Tom, who had been telling Dan how dead bodies rot—arrived a few seconds behind the other mothers. She saw me, waved and came bounding over.

"So, how are you doing?" she said, giving me a hug, followed by one of her pity looks.

I responded to the look by switching my face onto full beam. "Not too bad, actually."

"Really?" She either didn't believe me or chose not to. "I think you're being ever so brave." She took my hand in both of hers. "I was wondering—have you considered Zumba?"

"Zumba?" I said, extricating my hand.

"Yes. It helps with grief, apparently. Takes you out of yourself. I read this marvelous piece in the *Daily Mail* on learning to live again after the death of a spouse. A couple of women interviewed spoke really highly of Zumba classes."

"Thanks, I'll bear that in mind. But you know it's been over a year since Mike died and I'm doing much better."

"Well, good for you." Another pity look. "Take care. And remember if you ever need a shoulder, I'm here for you."

"Thanks, Fi. That's good to know."

She rubbed the top of my arm and went in search of a chair. After she'd gone, Tara turned to me. "I can't stand that woman. She hates it if she hasn't got some lame dog to cluck over. It's a power trip. Patronizing the rest of us makes her feel superior."

Before I had a chance to say I was sure that deep down Fiona probably meant well, Tara spied one of her cronies. "Emma—long time no CC. How *are* you?" Double kisses.

"Not good. Freddie is stressing me out like you wouldn't believe. He's reacting really badly to the two-story glass conservatory we're building on the back of the house. He says he doesn't want the house to look different. I've told his therapist that I think change is a huge issue for him. Plus I've been keeping a log of how many playdates he's had this term. I'm convinced he's not as popular as he was last year."

"Oh, stop it," Tara soothed. "Freddie's a great kid. I'm sure you're overreacting. What about the twins? How are they doing?"

"They're fine, but I still haven't got over what happened to the poor little mites at Christmas. The girls are identical. What sort of a teacher gives the part of Mary to one and asks the other to be a sheep?"

Just then I saw Louise Warburton started waving at me. I returned the gesture. "Hey Lou . . . haven't seen you lately."

"Dom and I have been at the house in France. Left the boys with my mother." Louise and her husband had just bought a wreck of a farmhouse in the Auvergne. It came with a dairy and Louise had decided to try her hand at making cheese. Her Fourme d'Ambert had gone down really well with the locals, but now she was working on that difficult second cheese. "All a bit of a struggle, but I'm sure I'll get there in the end."

"Come on, everybody," Imogen's voice boomed above the chatter. "Do let's settle down. *Tempus fugit* and all that."

"Better do as Imo says," Louise said, grinning. "We don't want to risk getting detention."

Once Louise had disappeared, Tara turned back to me. "What does Louise look like in that daisy smock? She used to be so chic—now she's turned into Padstow Woman. I have to say I've never understood the whole Padstow thing. It's so unspeakably dull and middle England. Last summer when we were in Cornwall, you practically had to wade through all the Breton tees and preppy polo shirts."

I suggested that one of the reasons people bought the tops and T-shirts was that they were practical.

Tara shuddered. "The day I buy clothes because they're practical is the day I die." She crossed her legs and then, as if to emphasize her point, waved a foot clad in an impossibly high platform ankle boot.

"I know, darling," Charlotte said. "You'd go trekking in the Himalayas in a Hervé Léger bandage dress."

The two of them fell about laughing.

I wasn't about to tell Tara and Charlotte that these days part of me longed to be a Padstow woman. It wasn't so much the splashy prints and chirpy chinos that I coveted as the lifestyle they represented. Padstow women were married to chaps called James or Alistair, solid reliable types who worked in the City or at the BBC. They raised their children without resorting to TV or sugar and fretted about when was the right time to have the big conversations about death and war. On the weekends, Padstow mummies and daddies hit the farmers' markets with their big goofy dogs and children in their cozy gilets. The daddies filled their burlap bags with organic radish pods, artisan breads and pâté. Afterwards they all went home to their houses on the right side of the tracks to toast halloumi over an open fire.

Padstow men didn't gamble, or if they did, it was only once a year on one of the big races like the Grand National. If they happened to die prematurely—a rare event since they cycled to work and watched their carbs and cholesterol—they didn't leave their wives on the verge of bankruptcy. This was on account of the substantial life insurance policies they took out the moment their wives got pregnant with their first child. If Padstow was dull, I didn't care. I yearned for dull. I craved dull.

I was so lost in my reverie that I was only vaguely aware that the meeting had started.

"Right—first item on the agenda . . . ," Imogen was saying. "I'm looking for people to run stalls. A few of you have already volunteered. . . . So far the tombola, face painting and hoopla are covered, but more bodies are needed. If you're prepared to help— even for a couple of hours—then please sign up at the end of the meeting. OK . . . moving swiftly on. The auction. The plan is to hold it after the principal announces the results of the cake-making competition. I'm looking for items to go under the hammer. Any thoughts?"

Cheryl—nickname Cheryl Tan—who owned a chain of spas with her husband, a part-time male model, said she would donate three "spa day, pamper yourself" experiences.

"If that woman's makeup fell off," Tara hissed, "I swear it would be heavy enough to kill the cat."

Cheryl's friend, whose name I didn't know, but who was wearing the biggest diamond crucifix you ever saw, said that her husband was part of the Stones' management and that she had six tickets for the band's August gig at the O2.

A Padstow woman whose husband was a City lawyer volunteered him for twelve hours' legal advice. Somebody who ran her own catering business said she would auction her services and prepare a dinner party for six.

Charlotte, who was PA to the director of a swanky interior design company that had done work for the likes of Madonna and the Paltrow-Martins, announced that her boss was prepared to offer a one-hour Skype consultation. Not to be outdone, Tara, who worked for the company that handled Marc Jacobs' PR, said that a couple of his evening dresses—unworn and with the tags on—had recently come her way and that she was more than happy to auction them. Charlotte asked her why on earth she didn't want them.

"Darling—a size six simply swims on me."

By now my thoughts were drifting back to Aunty Shirley's proposal. If making ends meet weren't an issue, if I didn't have Dan and Ella to think about, maybe I could have risen to the challenge and had a go at getting Aunty Shirley's business back on its feet. But these days I was done with gambling. I wanted to keep life uncomplicated, worry free and predictable. Like I said, I craved dull.

"Right, I think that's pretty much it," Imogen was saying. "Apart from one thing. We don't have anybody to open the fair. We were so lucky to have Ewan McGregor last year—thanks to his cousin Morag, who sits on the board of governors. I'm thinking perhaps another star of stage and screen."

Cheryl Tan raised her hand. "Kim and Kourtney both come to the spa when they're in town. I have their e-mail."

Imogen frowned. "Kim and Kourtney?"

"Kardashian."

"I'm not with you, I'm afraid. It sounds like something Armenians would serve as a starter."

There were a few titters.

"The American reality show?" Cheryl persisted. "The Kardashians?"

"Nope. Sorry, means nothing to me."

"Plus they're totally naff," one of the Padstow women sniffed. There was a chorus of hear-hears.

"Surely somebody must have some ideas. Sarah, you've been quiet. Anybody spring to mind?" Imogen was getting hot and bothered and had begun fanning herself again with the Tommy Padstow catalog.

All eyes were on me.

"Er . . . I'm not sure. . . ."

"Come on—Mike worked in advertising and what with so many celebs doing voice-overs, you must have rubbed shoulders with a few of them."

"Not really."

"I suppose I could give Marc a call," Tara said. "But he lives in Paris and his schedule is always totally manic. I'm not sure. . . ."

Charlotte offered to call Gwyneth. "But I know she's really up against it trying to finish her new cookbook. Or maybe I could try Catherine. I heard she's going to be over again in the summer, but it's such a huge ask, dragging her all the way from Wales."

"My hairdresser does P. Diddy when he's in town." It was the crucifix woman.

"P. Diddy," Imogen said, frowning. "Isn't he that rapper chappie? Rather tacky, don't you think?" She lowered the catalog to her cleavage.

"There is one person who springs to mind," said Louise in the daisy smock.

"Who?"

"What about Tommy Padstow?"

There were actual squeals of delight. These drowned out the groans from Tara and Charlotte.

"Oh, I a-dore Tommy Padstow," Imogen said. "The man leaves me quite weak at the knees."

There were cries of "me, too." Everybody agreed it was because he bore more than a passing resemblance to Damian Lewis.

"I've never understood the whole Damian Lewis thing," Tara said. "If you ask me, the man looks like a duck."

There was loud indignation. Damian Lewis looked nothing like a duck. How could she possibly say such a thing? Imogen was forced to shush everybody.

"Anyway, I know for a fact that Tommy Padstow wouldn't be able to do it," Charlotte announced.

"Why not?"

"Our neighbors are friends with the Padstows and they're all off to a villa in the Algarve for the summer."

"Pooh," said Imogen.

"I know," Tara piped up. "What about Greg Myers?"

"Now you're talking," Charlotte said. "He's *really* hot."

People were oohing in agreement.

"Remind me who he is again," Imogen said.

Tara rolled her eyes. "*The Sleeper*? It's the biggest thing since *Homeland*?"

"Oh yes, of course. He is rather dashing. He was in *Jane Eyre* a few years back. I adored his Mr. Rochester. . . . But doesn't he live in LA these days?"

Tara said she'd read that he was about to start a West End run in *Death of a Salesman*. "I'd say it's definitely worth asking him. Apparently he was born round here, so he could well be up for opening the fair."

"And it just so happens," I heard myself say, "that I have a way of getting to Mr. Myers."

What? No I didn't. What the hell was I doing? Bigging myself up, that's what. I'd had enough of Tara and Charlotte making me feel like a worm. First they'd informed me that my neighborhood was too ghetto for their brats. Then I'd had to listen to them bragging about their fashion and showbiz contacts.

"Goodness," Imogen said. "This just gets better."

Tara was looking distinctly sniffy. "You can get to Greg Myers? How?"

"My cousin Rupert was at Eton with him."

Chapter 5

"*S*o after the meeting, Tara collars me and she's like, 'Sarah, I had no idea your family was posh. I thought you told me your family were in the rag trade, and didn't your father used to drive a cab?' "

Steve reached for the wine bottle and topped up my glass. "This woman sounds like a real piece of work."

"You can say that again."

"So what did you say?"

"I told her that Rupert's dad was an international lawyer. I'm not sure if she bought it, though."

"What does he actually do?"

"Uncle Bernie? He's in buttons and trimmings."

Steve laughed. "And I take it he doesn't have a son called Rupert."

"You take it correctly. I cannot tell you the extent to which no Jewish man is called Rupert. It was the first posh name I could think of. His real name's Bradley."

Steve had dropped by for a drink on his way to the Chartered Institute of Accountants' Annual Professional Development Dinner. (The children had gone to Mum and Dad's for Friday night dinner and were staying the weekend.) I'd offered to be his plus one, but he said it wasn't a plus-one kind of do. He explained that Chartered Institute of Accountants' Annual Professional Development Dinners involved five hundred accountants sitting down to eat rubber chicken and dessert topped in aerosol cream while they listened to long, dreary speeches on professional development.

"OK," Steve was saying now. "I understand that these women made you feel like a worm and that's why you made up the Rupert story, but you have to come clean. Carrying on with this charade is only going to end in tears."

"So you're saying that I have to admit that I lied? No way. Why would I humiliate myself like that?"

"You don't need to go as far as admitting you lied. You just say that you e-mailed Greg Myers and discovered he's going to be out of the country on the day of the fair."

"I'd still look like a pathetic loser. Then Tara would call Marc Jacobs and save the day and people would be all over her." I paused. "I know you think I'm making too much of this, but I can't help it. Tara and Charlotte and the rest of their cronies are just so vile."

"So what's your plan?"

"I don't have one."

"Great."

I sat raking my fingers through my hair. "OK . . . what about starting with the obvious? I'll e-mail Greg Myers' agent and ask if by any chance he's available."

"Fine, but you won't get anywhere."

"You don't know that."

"Actually, I do," he said.

"Has anybody ever told you that you can be really self-righteous and pompous?"

"Frequently," he said, grinning.

"And if I don't get anywhere with his agent, I'll ambush him one night as he leaves the theater. Then I'll cry and beg."

"And end up with a restraining order. Good thinking." He paused. "Sarah, please just do the sensible thing."

"I've told you, that isn't happening."

"Your funeral," he said.

"Thanks for the vote of confidence."

"I'm just being realistic. You need to approach this problem rationally and sensibly."

"I do wish you'd stop underestimating me. I can't wait to see your face when I pull this thing off."

The corners of his lips were twitching. "You really are the most obstinate woman."

"Only when it comes to Tara and Charlotte."

"So," he said. "What's happening with the shop? Have you told the landlord you're shutting it down?"

"No, but I will. It's just that it feels so final."

"Are you sure that isn't guilt talking?"

"Probably . . . But surely my decision to close it down should be based on hard financial facts?"

"What are you talking about? Your decision *is* based on hard financial facts. The shop is practically bankrupt."

"But I don't know that for certain. I haven't had anybody go over the books."

Steve rolled his eyes. "Sarah, I know how upset you are about having to let the shop go, but if there was even the remotest hint that the business was anything other than on the skids, don't you think your aunty Shirley would have told you?"

"I guess."

"OK, tell you what. Why don't I take a look at the accounts? Would that make you feel better?"

"Yes, but you've done enough pro bono work for me. I can't let you do more."

"Sarah, I'm seriously not counting. The most important thing is that you get it into your head once and for all that the shop has no future and move on."

I told him that I was planning to go to the shop the following afternoon. I wanted to look around, just for old times' sake. "Aunty Shirley kept all her files and documents there, in the safe—you fancy coming with me?"

"Absolutely. The sooner we get this done, the better."

"You know, even if the shop is a no go, I've realized I'm in dire need of a new challenge. I can't stay at the nonemergency helpline any longer. I'm bored out of my brain."

"What would you do?"

"Well, it has to be something arty and creative. You know, it wasn't until I gave up the dressmaking business that I realized how happy I'd been."

"Well, trying to start your own business in a recession would be madness. And what would you do for capital? I could lend you a bit, but . . ."

"Steve, that's really kind, but there's no way I'd take money from you. Or Mum and Dad. There are all these government grants available for people trying to start new businesses. I've been reading about them."

"Yes, but if you're not gay, disabled or an ethnic minority, you don't stand a hope of getting one. Take it from me, you need to abandon these daft notions of running a business and get a job that will stand you in good stead until retirement—something with a good pension. What about the civil service or local government? I know for a fact that your local health department has a couple of junior vacancies—I saw the ad in the *Standard*. Apparently they train you on the job."

"Steve, have you met me? I have a degree in fashion design. I ran my own business selling rockabilly dresses."

"Fine. Do it as a hobby. Tell you what, I'll see if I can dig out the health department ad and send you the link."

"Steve . . . look at me. There is no way I am ever going to work in local government. I would rather be pecked to death by a flock of starlings."

"Suit yourself."

"I will."

"You know your problem, Sarah—you're absurdly unrealistic. You need to get yourself grounded, make contact with planet earth before it's too late. I'd have thought that after everything you'd been through, that would have been obvious."

"So because I'm a struggling widow, I have to give up on all my hopes and dreams?"

"Hopes and dreams are for romantics. In the end they get you nowhere. It's why so many creative types go bust. No grip on reality. I see it time and again. If life has taught me one thing, it's that in order to survive, you have to make safe, sensible choices. Only the wealthy can afford to take risks."

"So the rest of us have to live our lives bored to death."

"I'd rather be bored than bankrupt."

He looked at his watch. "Jeez . . . I need to get going. . . . You sure I look OK and not too much like a dork?" He got up from the sofa and presented himself for inspection.

I gave his black bow tie a tiny tweak. "You don't look remotely like a dork. You look great."

I kissed him on the lips and he kissed me back. Afterwards we stood there, eyes fixed on each other. My cue to suggest that after the professional development do, he come back here for the night.

"See you tomorrow, then," I heard myself say.

I could see the hurt and disappointment on his face. "Sure," he said. "I'll pick you up around half three."

He gave me a quick peck on the cheek and was gone.

I should have invited him back. It was time. I felt bad about being so mean, but Mike and the mess of feelings I had for him were still getting in the way. In my head I knew that he was gone, that he wasn't coming back and that I needed to get on and live my life. But my heart wouldn't let go.

I shoved a frozen lasagna in the oven and went back to the sofa. I lay there mulling. Steve was good for me. He was grounded, trust-worthy, dependable. OK, he could be a bit pompous and he was cau-tious to the point of irritation. On the other hand, I'd seen where Mike's contempt for caution had got him. Steve was what I needed. Plus he looked seriously sexy in a tux. He was doing his best to pull back and not pressure me into sleeping with him, but he wasn't going to wait forever. If I carried on pushing him away, I would lose him. I needed to lay Mike to rest, learn to live alongside my feelings for him—the loving ones and the not so loving—instead of letting them dominate my life.

The oven pinged.

The supermarket lasagna was runny and tasteless. I washed it down with another glass of wine. When I'd finished, I filled the sink with soapy water and washed up my plate along with the glasses and cereal bowls left over from breakfast. I could have put them in the dishwasher, but that would have meant unloading it first and putting everything away. I couldn't be bothered. As I placed the last bowl on the drying rack, I made a decision. Tomorrow, after Steve and I had been to the shop, I would invite him back for dinner. Then, while we were on the sofa watching a movie and making out, I would suggest he stay over.

I took the plug out of the sink and pulled off my rubber gloves. The greasy water refused to drain. It was thick with this morning's Coco Pops, which had risen to the surface. Fabulous. The sink was blocked again. It was my fault. Whenever I washed up by hand, my plate scraping was never more than cursory. Sometimes I didn't bother at all. This meant that I always ended up massaging bits of food down the plughole. When the waste pipe could take no more, it went on strike. It had been the same at the old house. It used to drive Mike mad.

I opened the cupboard under the sink and went in search of a bottle of Drano—I bought them six at a time. I used to own a plunger, but I'd managed to lose it in the move.

I looked at the kitchen clock. It was a quarter to nine. If I was going to start knocking on neighbors' doors asking to borrow sink plungers, I needed to get on with it. Nine was definitely the cutoff for unsolicited house calls. Then again, the only neighbors I'd met so far were Betty from across the street, who had to be in her seventies and probably didn't answer the door after dark, and the students from several doors down. They seemed a jolly enough bunch and, since they probably hadn't got up until midafternoon, weren't going to have a problem with me calling on them. On the other hand, being students, they probably lived in a pit. It was unlikely they owned a broom, let alone a plunger.

I had no next-door neighbors. The house on one side was empty and for sale. The place on the other side was also unoccupied, but since the mailman was delivering letters, I assumed the owner's absence was temporary. Betty, who despite her advanced years appeared to have no trouble keeping track of all the comings and goings in the street, confirmed this. She told me that the woman who lived there had recently had a baby and gone to stay with her sister. "No husband from what I can make out," she'd said, lowering her voice. "Her at number forty—she's the worst. Men coming and going in the middle of the night. Not that I'm spying, you understand. I'm not one of those curtain twitchers. I just happen to see them sometimes when I get up in the early hours to make myself a cup of hot milk. She's got three kiddies, that one—all by different men. Of course these days there's no shame in being a single mother. In my day you kept both legs in one stocking. You young women—you're so brazen." I assumed this was a dig at me.

"Actually, Betty, my husband died."

"Oh, I know! Terrible thing. Your mum and I had a lovely chat the other day and she told me all about your poor, tragic husband.

Believe me, I know what you're going through. My poor Donald dropped dead of a stroke at forty-three. My life ended that day. Take it from me, you never recover from something like that. It might have been easier if we'd had children. It wasn't for the want of trying, mind you, but it wasn't to be. Sad . . . I was always good with kiddies. They seemed to take to me. Heaven alone knows why."

I picked up my keys and went outside to see if by any chance there was a light on in Betty's house. There wasn't. It was then that I noticed that my absentee next-door neighbor appeared to be back. The venetian blinds were open. I could see tea lights flickering on the coffee table. I climbed over the low hedge that separated our garden paths and rang the bell. Nothing. I waited a few seconds and rang again. Finally—the sound of footsteps. "Hang on. . . . Coming."

The woman who answered the door had her cell wedged between her chin and her shoulder. Her T-shirt was rolled up on one side, exposing a plentiful breast to which a newborn baby was clamped. "With you in a tick," she mouthed, holding up an index finger. "Of course I'm still here, big boy," she purred into the phone.

Big boy? She clearly wasn't on the phone to the gas company.

She smiled and beckoned me inside, which I thought was odd since it was after dark and she had no idea who I was.

She led me down the hallway. "Oh . . . I am so hot and wet for you, big boy. . . . Are you hard for me?" The baby carried on sucking. "I want to hear you say you're hard. Go on . . . say it."

OK, this was beyond awkward.

"You know what?" I said, following her into the living room. "I think I should go. I can see this isn't a good time. It isn't urgent. I'll come back. . . ."

But she was shaking her head. "Literally one minute," she whispered. "Ooh, that's it. Now I can feel how hard you are. Come on, fuck me. That's it. Let me feel you inside me."

Oh, God.

"No, really. I shouldn't stay. Another time, maybe."

"Oh, oh! That's it. Harder. Faster. That feels so good." I watched as she eased the now sleeping baby off her nipple.

I turned to go.

"No, please stay," she whispered, pulling down her T-shirt. "I'm almost done."

"But it really isn't important. I was just wondering if you had a sink plunger I could borrow."

"Oh . . . Yess . . . yess . . . I can feel you coming. That's it. Do it for me, baby."

She nodded and gave me the thumbs-up. I wasn't sure if this was because the guy on the end of the phone was coming or because she had a plunger I could borrow.

"I've just moved in next door and my sink's blocked."

"Wow . . . Yess . . . Oh. Oh. I really felt that."

"My fault. I'm terrible. I'm really bad about scraping plates."

"Oh, that was so good. How was it for you, big boy?"

She pointed to the phone and rolled her eyes. It was then that I noticed how striking she was. There weren't too many women who could carry off the baggy-sweats, slept-in hair and nude-face look, but this woman was one of them. Her gorgeousness shone through the grunge. She had it all: the height, the figure, the pouty lips, the green eyes that made Angelina Jolie's look meh. And she had big tits. Fair enough, most breast-feeding mothers did, but unlike those of most of the other breast-feeding mothers I had known (myself included), hers were firm and perky and definitely not careening towards her knicker elastic. Whereas my boobs had moved independently—and still did—just as my mother had predicted, giving me the nipple equivalent of a lazy eye, hers were round and plump and perfect. She was one of those women that other women either loathed on sight or joked about turning gay for.

"So, will that be credit card or account? . . . Account. Fine."

Ah . . . So big boy wasn't her boyfriend. My next-door neighbor was a hooker. Fabulous.

"OK, Pete, I hope to hear from you again very soon. Bye for now." She let out a lengthy sigh and put her phone down on the coffee table. "God, I wish that man would stop calling me honey tits. It's so demeaning. . . . And in case you're wondering, I'm not a hooker."

"You're not? . . . I mean . . . sure, whatever. Look, it's none of my business. . . ."

"What I do is strictly verbal masturbation."

"Right. Excellent."

"There is never any physical contact. Nobody gets invited here. Ever. A friend of mine runs an agency and I do twenty hours a week. For the time being it puts food on the table and I get to work from home."

"Cool. In fact it's more than cool. It couldn't be cooler."

"Great. I didn't want you to get the wrong idea. . . . I'm Rosie, by the way."

"Sarah. I'm your new neighbor."

"I know. I was putting out the trash earlier and I saw you getting out of your car. And this little chap is Will. He's eight weeks."

Before I had a chance to coo over the baby, she was apologizing for taking so long on the phone. "But you can't rush these men or they complain they're not getting value for money." She lowered the baby into a Moses basket and planted a kiss on his forehead. "Sleep tight, noodle. . . ."

"But doesn't it turn your stomach—talking dirty like that?"

"Not really. It's all done from a script—a bit like working in a call center. OK, you have to improvise, but essentially, you learn the spiel, recite it and switch off. It's the only way."

"And they never ask to see you?"

"Of course they do, but I'm very clear that it's not an option. And they don't have my landline number, so they can't find me."

I didn't know what to think. This woman could easily be lying when she said that her services were limited to verbal masturbation. She could still be a hooker. On the other hand her living room couldn't have looked less brothel-like. (Not that I'd ever had cause to visit a brothel, but the ones on those BBC 2 documentaries always had shiny silver wallpaper and lava lamps.) I took in the painted white floorboards and matching sofas, the fresh tulips in those edgy stainless steel vases you got in Ikea, the copy of the *Guardian* on the glass coffee table. Then there was the baby stuff: the muslins, the bunnies and rattles, the Moses basket. Of course she could have been some upmarket, two-grand-a-shag call girl who worked in posh hotels, but if she were, then she wouldn't be breast-feeding (I doubted that many guys were into the lactation option), plus she would have been able to afford a damn sight more than a terraced house in a scruffy street in SW21. No, if this woman was a hooker, I was the king of Luxembourg.

"Look, it's none of my business, but don't you worry about people finding out what you do? I mean how do you know I'm not going to start gossiping to the entire neighborhood?"

She shrugged. "I'm past caring what people think of me. The only thing I'm concerned about is keeping a roof over my child's head and I will do whatever it takes. And for the record, social services have already paid me a visit. I made the mistake of telling my ex what I was doing and he decided to report me as an unfit mother. The social worker disagreed."

"Really?"

"Yeah. She thought it was all pretty harmless, particularly when I explained that I had no intention of carrying on once Will learns to speak. There is no way on this earth that 'come' is going to be my son's first word. I even ended up giving her the number of the phone sex agency. She said she was getting married next year and that she was desperate for some extra cash to pay for the wedding reception."

Will let out what sounded like the beginning of a cry. Rosie leaned over the Moses basket and started stroking his cheek. "Ssh . . . Come on, noodle. Time for some shut-eye."

I went over and peeked into the crib. He was a chunky little fellow with the prettiest Cupid's bow lips and a mass of hair the same shade of blond as his mother's. "Aw, he is such a cutie." I watched as he found his two middle fingers and began sucking. After a few moments, he dropped off again. "And that is a great outfit." He was wearing a black-and-white striped romper suit. Across the chest it read: *Been inside for nine months.*

"Yeah, it always makes people laugh. My son, on the other hand, is less than amusing. Before you arrived, he'd been screaming nonstop for five hours. And he's like that most evenings. He starts around four and it can go on until midnight."

"Ah, the colic months," I said. "I remember them well."

"You have kids?" she said.

"Two." I assured her that Will would grow out of the screaming phase in another month or so, but she didn't seem convinced.

We sat down and she asked me about Dan and Ella, what I thought of the neighborhood, had I met Betty yet.

"Oh yes. I've met her."

"Did she tell you what a disgrace I am—being a single mother? God knows what she'd say if she knew what I did for a living. In fact one day I might just tell her, just to see the expression on her face."

I started laughing. "Be careful. The shock might kill her."

"Nah—she's a tough old bird. It would take more than that to see her off. The thing is, I've explained several times that Will's dad and I were married, but she either forgets or she chooses not to remember."

I said that it was probably the latter. "So you're divorced?"

"Not quite. It's still going through."

I wasn't sure if she wanted to elaborate, so I decided not to press her on the subject.

"I threw the bastard out when I was three months pregnant," Rosie said, clearly more than happy to elaborate.

"Wow. That can't have been easy."

She shrugged. "I had no choice."

She said that when Simon wasn't chasing other women, he was lying on the sofa, smoking weed. "He thought he could make it as a screenwriter, but no matter how much I tried to drum it into him, he never understood there was more to writing than sitting with his MacBook in Starbucks."

These days he was living on a houseboat in Chelsea that belonged to his rich actress-slash-model girlfriend. Rosie had no idea if he was writing or earning any money, but she was going after him in the courts for child support anyway. "Suffice it to say that so far I haven't seen a penny."

"Bloody hell. Can't be easy."

"It isn't. Money's been a real issue for me since Will came along, hence the phone sex. It pays way better than an office job and like I said, I can do it from home." She paused. "Why don't I make us something to drink? I'm on the wagon while I'm breast-feeding, but I do a pretty decent hot chocolate. None of your powdered rubbish—I'm talking melted Green and Blacks and cream. I think I might even have some marshmallows somewhere."

I said that sounded great. Rosie went off into the kitchen while I watched Will. Ten minutes later she was back with two mugs of thick, dark chocolate and a plate of marshmallows on cocktail sticks. Under her arm was an industrial-size sink plunger.

"The Clog Sucker should sort you out," she said. Apparently, Clog Sucker was its real name.

We sat for a few moments sipping and dunking, me telling her how heavenly the hot chocolate was.

"Well," I said, helping myself to my third marshmallow. "I certainly know how it feels to be hard up."

I told her about Mike's gambling and how it had pretty much bankrupted us. How long had I known this woman? Ten minutes? And I was already telling her my life story. But there were some people you just clicked with from the get-go. It had been like that with Mike. When I described how Mike had died, her eyes filled up.

"I can't imagine what that must have been like. How on earth did you cope?"

I said what I always said, that you just find the strength—especially when you've got kids. "Counseling helped. My emotions were all over the place. The problem was that after Mike died, I had such mixed feelings. I was overwhelmed with grief, but at the same time part of me was relieved that he'd gone."

"And you hated yourself for feeling that."

"You've got it. The guilt was unbearable."

I realized that I was talking about stuff that I'd only discussed with my mother and Judy the grief therapist. I hadn't talked to Steve about my conflicting emotions after Mike died because I wasn't sure that he'd understand. But Rosie understood. Talking to somebody who had also been in a lousy marriage was a bit like group therapy. We carried on chatting about Mike's death, me telling her how it had affected the children and how I'd been forced to sell the house.

"Wow, so you lived in one of those amazing houses on the *other side*," she said, emphasizing the last two words.

I asked her about Simon.

"Not much more to tell. Like I said, he was an idle, philandering bastard. I threw him out. End of story."

"Fair enough, but what I don't understand is why he would want to play around when he was married to a woman as beautiful as you."

Rosie turned pink, which surprised me. She didn't come across as the type who was easily embarrassed. "I don't know about that," she said.

"Oh, come on. You could easily be a model. You've got the figure, the face . . . the . . ."

"Big tits?"

"Well, yes, now that you've said it."

"It's not just the breast-feeding. I've always had them."

"Me, too. But you're lucky. I couldn't help noticing that yours are still perky."

"They are. People tell me that's quite unusual."

"You bet it is. I can practically throw mine over my shoulder. You do realize this means I shall have to kill you."

"Oh, please don't. If it helps, I have stretch marks on my stomach."

"Above the panty elastic or below?"

"Below."

"Sorry, doesn't count. No, I really do have to kill you."

By now we were snorting with laughter.

"But seriously," I said. "You could have walked into any modeling agency and they would have signed you up on the spot."

"OK, I admit that when I was seventeen or eighteen, I thought about it, but if I'd gone into modeling, my mother would have disowned me."

"Why?"

She told me about her pushy mother, her dad who had walked out when she was four. Her mother had raised her alone, working two jobs in order to send her to a posh girls' school.

"I was meant to be a lawyer."

"What happened?"

She shrugged. "The pressure got too much. I made it to university, but I dropped out. Mum never forgave me. She also never told me I was pretty. Not even once."

"That's so cruel. Why would a mother do that? Jealousy?"

I thought about my own mother, who still occasionally pinched my cheek and referred to me as her "beautiful, almond-eyed baby."

"No, it wasn't jealousy," Rosie said. "She was scared that I would start running after boys, get pregnant, and that would be the end of all her hopes for me."

"But you must have had boys chasing you, girlfriends telling you how beautiful you were?"

"It didn't make any difference what other people said. The damage had been done. All my friends told me to have a go at modeling, but my self-esteem was nonexistent. I felt worthless. I just drifted from one temp job to another. Then I met Simon."

Apparently the attraction had been instant for both of them. "We were both lost souls, black sheep who had disappointed our parents."

She explained that in Simon's case, his dad had been an army major, a bully who expected his son to follow in his footsteps and go to military college. Simon rebelled, dropped out of high school and found a job in a bar.

"When I met him, he was this brooding, wannabe writer living in a crappy flat in Balham. He convinced me that he was a creative genius just waiting to be discovered. I had found my very own struggling artist. How sexy was that? Except this was Balham—not the Left Bank circa 1930. Once we were married and I got pregnant, I saw him for the lazy git he was and it all fell apart."

There were two marshmallows left on the plate. Rosie handed

me one, despite my protestations that it would be my ninth, and took the other for herself.

"Round about the time I met Simon," she said, chewing on her marshmallow, "Mum was diagnosed with colon cancer. They gave her six months. She lasted a year. The closer she got to the end, the more I hoped that she would find it in her to tell me that she was proud of how hard I'd worked as a kid, but she never did."

"That must have hurt."

"Oh yeah. It still does. But on the upside, the money she left me was enough for the deposit on this house."

"That was something, I guess."

I said that I didn't understand why, if she had such low self-esteem, she found the confidence to have phone sex with strangers. It was something I associated with exhibitionists, not shrinking violets.

She laughed. "Believe me, I'm no exhibitionist. But becoming a single mother with no income changed me. When you have a child, you do what you have to do to provide for them. Right now the only thing that matters is Will's welfare and having enough money to live on."

I said I felt exactly the same about Dan and Ella. "But one day wouldn't you like to have a proper career?"

She said that maybe she'd give it some thought when Will started school, but modeling was definitely out. In four years she would be thirty-three, practically geriatric in the modeling world.

"So come on—what do you do?" she said.

I explained how I used to be a fashion designer and that now I did something much less glamorous.

"Hang on," she said after I'd told her what I did. "You gave up running your own company to become an operator on the police nonemergency helpline?"

"I needed to earn money—like you. And it has its moments. Only the other day, a woman rang to complain that the rabbit she'd bought didn't have the floppy ears she'd been promised and what were the police going to do about it."

"What did you say?"

"I referred her to the Sale of Goods Act. After which I attempted to eat my own head."

Rosie burst out laughing. "I'm not surprised. . . . So here we are, both in dead-end jobs with no hope for the future."

"Yep. Here we are."

"Shall I open another packet of marshmallows?"

"Why not?" I said.

"Oh, by the way," I said to Steve as we pulled up at a traffic light a couple of blocks from Selfridges. "I finally got to meet my next-door neighbor—you know the one with the baby, who's been away all this time."

"Yeah? What's she like?"

"Unusual."

"How d'you mean?"

"OK . . . you have to guess what she does for a living."

"I dunno. . . . She breeds badgers."

"Nope."

"She writes the predictions in fortune cookies."

"Nope."

"She's a pet food taster."

"What? No. That's gross."

"OK, I'm bored now. I give up."

"She does phone sex."

Steve blinked. "What? How does that work?"

"You know . . . she gets paid to talk dirty over the phone."

"Nice. And you call that unusual? I call it perverted."

"Oh, stop being such a prude. She's hard up and it pays the mortgage."

"I'm not being a prude. I just happen to think it's not the greatest career choice, that's all. What sort of a role model is she for her child?"

"One that keeps a roof over his head."

"Money isn't everything."

"It is when you don't have it."

"OK, touché," Steve said.

"I really like her. Ever since I lost touch with Belinda in Sydney, I've had a girlfriend vacancy. I think I might just have filled it."

"So you spend a couple of hours with this person and suddenly she's your best friend?"

"I didn't say she was my best friend. I just really like her, that's all."

"Fabulous. My girlfriend's new best friend is a hooker."

"Stop it. She's not my *best* friend." But I knew she would be. Rosie was fun, alive, a bit of a rebel. She couldn't have been less like the conventional conformist Tommy Padstow mothers at school, who, even though I envied them, would never be my friends. I had nothing in common with those women, whereas Rosie and I had loads in common.

"Plus she isn't a hooker," I went on. "It's purely phone sex."

"And you believe her?"

"Actually, I do."

Steve grunted.

"Oh, look, we're here," I said, ignoring the grunt. "Make a left."

Villiers Mews, with its cobblestones, its lopsided antiquarian book-shops dotted among impossibly quaint Georgian cottages, could have provided the template for a Christmas cookie tin.

Shirley Feldman Exclusive Foundation Garments was halfway down the street—the limp, dried-up shop between a swanky cigar shop and Chandrika Crew—Nannies for Discerning Mummies. The bra shop's candy-striped awning—chic circa 1982—was faded and full of holes. As we got closer, I noticed that some letters had fallen off the sign. It now read: SHIRLEY FELDMAN EXCLUSIVE FOUND GARMENTS, which didn't have quite the same cachet.

There was a parking space directly in front of the shop. "Can you believe it?" Steve said, killing the engine. "We've actually found a parking space around the corner from Selfridges on a Saturday." He took his cell out of his pocket and announced that he had to tweet this momentous news.

While he tweeted, I carried on staring at the shop. I could see Aunty Shirley, all red lippy and big do, dressing the window. I could hear her swearing at the mannequins through a mouthful of pins when their arms fell off.

"OK, done," Steve said. "I take it you've remembered the shop keys."

I jingled them in front of his nose.

"OK. I was only asking."

I'd gone round to Aunty Bimla's a few days ago to pick up the keys. She and Aunty Sylvia had been bent over a pair of ancient Viking sewing machines—which they'd set up on the dining room table—working on an order for corsets for a Royal Opera House production of *Così fan tutte*. Now that Shirley was gone, neither of them could face going back to the shop. "I hope you don't mind us working here, poppet," Aunty Bimla said, "but the shop holds too many memories." I told her that I was perfectly happy for them to work from home. I wasn't about to add to their distress by insisting they go back to the shop for the few weeks it would take to finish the order.

We adjourned to the living room and Aunty Bimla served us milky tea and Bombay mix, which we ate in the traditional way, with a spoon. I'd been in this room once before, about ten years ago. Aunty Bimla's husband had just died and Mum and I came to pay our respects. It was the same as I remembered it—the swirly royal blue and gold carpet, the giant color photograph of Mecca over the mantelpiece, the minaret-design sofa pillows.

The aunties asked after Mum and Dad. I asked how the corsets were coming along. They were coming along fine.

"So, poppet," Aunty Bimla said, "you've definitely decided to close down the shop?"

"Pretty much, but first I thought I'd take a look at the books. I just want to check there isn't a bit of extra cash lying around— enough to get the shop going again."

"There's nothing, poppet. We would have known if there was. You are definitely barking up the wrong tree. You mustn't worry about closing the shop. All in all, it's for the best."

Aunty Sylvia put down her china cup. "It's the end of an era, though. Forty years we've worked there. Where did the time go?"

"I haven't the foggiest notion, but all good things come to an end." Aunty Bimla placed her hand on top of Aunty Sylvia's. They both had tears in their eyes.

"I hate doing this after everything you did for Aunty Shirley. She was so grateful and you know she thought the world of both of you."

"It was mutual," Aunty Sylvia said.

"But you must do what is right for you and your children, poppet. Put your best foot forward. Carpe diem—that's what my father used to say. Seize the carp."

I said that I would do my best.

As I drained my teacup, it occurred to me that Aunty Shirley might owe the aunties money. "By the way, when was the last time Shirley paid you?"

"A few days before she died," Aunty Sylvia said.

"Are you sure?"

"Positive." I saw her shoot Aunty Bimla a glance. I knew she wasn't telling the truth.

"Look, you have to tell me if you're owed money. If you are, I'll see you get it."

I would have no choice other than to borrow from Mum and Dad.

"Shirley owes us nothing," Aunty Sylvia said. "Now let that be an end to it."

"I agree," Aunty Bimla said. "We are all square. You mustn't give it another thought."

Easier said than done. When it was time to say good-bye, they both hugged me until I couldn't breathe.

"Thank you," I said. "For everything."

"It has been our pleasure, Bubbie."

"See you soon, poppet, and don't be a stranger."

*W*hile Steve put money in the meter, I stood outside the shop, struggling to unlock the door. There were three keys and it took me a couple of minutes to work out which one fitted which lock.

Inside, envelopes and junk mail were sprawled over the mat. Once I'd gathered them up, I looked around. Jeez. To say the place was in need of a makeover was an understatement. The pale green carpet, which I remembered from my childhood, was worn and stained; ditto the matching green and gold brocade curtains draped across the changing rooms. The fake gilt trim was coming away from the white melamine counter. On the ceiling, the Styrofoam tiles were coming loose. Several had fallen off. I looked back at the counter and to the wall of wooden drawers behind it. They were dark and Dickensian. When I was a child, they had given me the willies. I'd called them "the brown drawers." As I'd got older, I still couldn't bring myself to think of the drawers as beautiful, but I began to appreciate their quality and that they had character. Attached to the drawer fronts were filigree label holders. These were in desperate need of a good going over with some Brasso. The slips of paper inside were yellow and torn. Written on each, in thick italic script, was a bra size. The smallest was 32A. The largest was 46JJ. Mother of God—and I thought I had big boobs.

"You know what this place needs?" Steve said as he walked in.

"What?"

"A flamethrower. How did your aunty Shirley let it get like this?

The seventies will definitely be wanting that till back. And look at those drawers. Where did she find them—Uriah Heep's Dumpster?"

"Well, I think they're rather magnificent. Shirley was always talking about updating, but after Harry died, I think the spirit went out of her. Then, when business started to trail off, there wasn't the money to do it."

Steve carried on looking around. "The place needs total gutting. Have you noticed the ceiling? Look at the gaps where the tiles have fallen off."

I looked up. There were deep cracks in the ceiling.

I suggested we take a look at the workroom. "Through the door and down the stairs."

Steve opened the door. Inside was pitch-black. I fumbled for the switch. The fluorescent strip began to buzz and flicker. As I followed him down the steep, narrow stairway, he warned me to watch my step. "Have you seen how the carpet's coming up? I'm amazed somebody hasn't broken their neck."

The basement was pretty cramped. The only daylight came from a small window at one end. Funny, as a child I'd thought the room was huge. I used to love coming down into this secret cave with its boxes of lace and ribbons, tiny teardrop pearls and dainty satin rosebuds with *actual* diamonds in the center. I knew they were real because the aunties told me. The aunties always let me choose some lace and a length of ribbon to take home.

The first thing I noticed now was the cork floor tiles curling up at the corners. Then I found myself wondering if it had always been this untidy. Piles of boxes, old order books and rolls of satin were stacked against the walls. Two sewing machines, which Aunty Shirley had bought a few years ago to replace the old Vikings (which now lived with Aunty Bimla), sat on a couple of battered postwar utility desks. Every surface, including the floor, was littered with under-wires and trimmings.

Steve began to sneeze. It was the dust. He had sensitive sinuses.

"I'll put the kettle on," I said. There was a tiny alcove kitchen area at one end of the workroom, along with a loo. Steve looked at the tea stains in the sink and pulled a face.

"Don't panic," I said. "The cups are perfectly clean." I picked one up and wiped my finger around the inside. "Bit dusty, that's all. I'll give it a good rinse."

But he wasn't having it. Steve wanted a "decent" espresso and insisted on fetching one from the Italian place a couple of doors down. I made myself a cup of Taylors Yorkshire.

He returned with his coffee and two enormous chocolate éclairs. We sat devouring the éclairs, dripping cream over the workbenches.

"So where's the computer?" Steve said.

"Computer?"

"Yes. Remember . . . I've come to look at Aunty Shirley's accounts. And I'm assuming you know her password."

I carried on chewing. "She didn't have one."

"What? Who in their right mind doesn't have a password?"

"No—I mean she didn't have a computer."

"No computer," he repeated.

"That's right. She was a complete technophobe. She did her accounts the old-fashioned way. If I remember rightly, she kept the books in the safe." I directed him to the cupboard under the sink. "The safe's to your left . . . at the back."

He was kneeling down, his head inside the cupboard. "Christ, I can hardly see it. So what's the combination?"

"She didn't bother. Give the door a tug. It'll be open."

A few moments later he was upright again, clasping three old-fashioned, leather-bound ledgers and brushing a cobweb off his sweater.

I suggested we take the books back to my place and go over them there. "Maybe we could order a curry later and watch a movie." I was putting the first part of my seduction plan into action.

"Or we could go back to mine. I've got a lamb and apricot tagine in the oven."

"Yours it is," I said. "Give me a lamb tagine and I'm anybody's."

"That's always good to know."

Steve had been in his flat just over a year. It was in a brand-new development not far from his office in Tower Bridge. He believed in buying new property because it always came with a ten-year guarantee.

He'd bought the show flat, complete with furniture, because he found decorating a chore. And the beige and cream color scheme was neutral and inoffensive.

"So how's your campaign to snare Greg Myers coming along?" he said as we chatted in the kitchen, me making tea, him checking on the tagine, which smelled divine.

"I haven't gotten around to e-mailing his agent yet, but I will."

"Good luck with that."

"Jeez, why are you being so negative?"

"I'm not being negative. I wished you good luck."

I harrumphed and let it go.

We took our mugs of tea and Aunty Shirley's books to the dining room table. Having run my own business, I wasn't totally clueless when it came to reading a set of accounts, but I decided to leave Steve to it. After all, he was the expert. He ran his fingers over the columns, turned page after page, tutting and muttering as he went.

"I'm assuming it's not looking good," I said.

"It's not just that. Her books are so chaotic. God knows what her accountant made of them."

"Oh, she didn't bother with an accountant."

"That figures."

"So what's the bottom line?"

"Well, Aunty Shirley certainly wasn't making a profit. Judging by her most recent figures, she was barely breaking even, but at least there appears to be no debt, which is something. Looks like she's even paid her rent until the end of this year."

He continued to pore over the pages. Meanwhile I turned my attention to the pile of mail I brought with me from the shop. I threw the junk into the kitchen bin and put the utility bills, invoices and payments in a pile. There was a brown envelope from Her Majesty's Revenue and Customs, which I assumed was another bill, but for some reason I decided to open it.

It took me a moment or two to take in what I was reading. "Blimey. Steve . . . look at this."

"What?"

I handed him the letter. "Is this what I think it is?"

He started reading. "It most certainly is. It would appear that in the financial year twenty eleven to twelve the Inland Revenue overcharged your aunty Shirley to the tune of ten thousand three hundred and fifty-six pounds, thirty-two pence, and she's due a rebate."

"But she's dead. Does that mean they get to keep it?"

"No. It will be paid to her estate. As her sole beneficiary, that means you get it." Steve said that all I had to do was send the letter to her lawyer and he would sort it out.

"So what will you do with the money?"

I was in no doubt. "I'll split it between the aunties. When I saw them, I got the definite impression that they hadn't been paid in a while. Plus Aunty Shirley was desperate to give them something to say thank you for all their years of hard work. At least I'll be doing something to make her happy."

"You and your guilty conscience. You do realize that the money would pay for you to upgrade your car and take the kids on a decent holiday."

"I know, but this is more important."

After we'd eaten Steve's magnificent lamb tagine, we took the wine bottle and our glasses to the sofa. Netflix had just got the latest Coen brothers movie, which had come out a few months ago and we'd both missed. We had started smooching and I was letting things take their course—and rather enjoying it—when something occurred to me.

"Of course you do realize what else I could do with the money?"

"What?" He carried on planting kisses on my neck.

"Well . . . I could give the aunties a couple of grand each to keep them going, use two to spruce up the shop and put the rest in the kitty."

"What kitty?" The kisses stopped.

"Well, I'd need a kitty if I was going to get the business going again."

"Hang on," he said, pulling away. "You're seriously thinking about taking over the shop?"

"I don't know. Maybe ten grand—actually nearly eleven—changes things. Plus you said that Aunty Shirley had paid her rent until the end of the year."

"Sarah, are you out of your mind? Ten or even eleven thousand pounds doesn't even begin to change things. It's nothing. It's a drop in the ocean. It's less than a drop in the ocean. First it would take twenty grand minimum to renovate the shop. It needs rewiring, replastering. God knows what state the plumbing is in. On top of that it needs a complete redesign and refit. Have you any idea what that costs?"

"But Aunty Shirley rented the shop. Surely the landlord is responsible for the upkeep of the actual building."

"I'm sure he is. Sarah, your aunt was no fool. Don't you think she probably tried to get money out of the landlord?"

"Possibly, but what if she didn't try?"

Steve sat shaking his head.

"If I could get the landlord to update the wiring and fix the plasterwork, I could take care of the refit."

"What, you can build units and shelves?"

"Of course not. I'd get somebody in, but I've got a bit of an eye for interior design, so I could plan it all. And I'm thinking that I could do a sort of shabby chic thing, which wouldn't cost too much—lick of paint, some junk shop bits and pieces."

"And you think that hipster chic is going to work in the West End? Please."

"Depends how you do it."

"I can't believe I'm hearing this. Sarah, listen to me. Even if you were able to fund the renovations, what makes you think you'd be able to compete with what's her name . . . the Montecute woman? You've said yourself she's got the market sewn up."

"I know, but maybe we could at least attempt to take her on and then the aunties wouldn't be left high and dry."

"You're not leaving them high and dry. You're giving each of them five thousand pounds. They'll be fine."

"How long do you think they'll last on five grand? These women don't have families to look after them."

"They probably have savings and they own their own homes. They'll have to downgrade. Plenty of people do it."

"You know, sometimes you can be really callous."

"I'm not being callous. I'm being realistic."

"But what if I could make it work?"

By now, Steve was twitching with anger and frustration. He took a deep breath. "OK, let's spool back a bit here. How many times have you insisted to me that all you want from life is financial security? How many times have you said that after living with Mike, all you want is an uncomplicated worry-free life? I've even heard you use the word 'dull.' "

"I know all that, but despite everything, there's this voice inside me that keeps nagging away, telling me that I would be a coward if I didn't at least make an attempt to resurrect the business."

"The only thing nagging you is guilt. It's ridiculous and it has to stop. It's making you behave irrationally."

"It's not just guilt." I reminded him how I had given up my dress-making business and lived to regret it. "I let one opportunity pass me by. Can I let another one go?"

"But this isn't an opportunity. It's a recipe for ruin."

"Maybe, but if it came to it, Mum and Dad would always take me and the children in. We would always have a roof over our heads. And I'd just have to start over and get another job."

"And that's the example you want to set for Dan and Ella? You want them to know that they had not one but two irresponsible parents who gambled away their lives?"

I couldn't believe what I'd just heard. I sat staring at him. Then the anger kicked in. I stood up. "I can't believe you just said that. God knows I made mistakes in the past and I'm not proud of that, but I am doing everything in my power to provide for my kids and be a good mother. That doesn't mean I have to accept my lot and rein in my own ambition."

He was standing in front of me now, his hands resting on the tops of my arms.

"I'm sorry. What I said was cruel. I don't know where it came from." I could see the contrition in his face, but I was furious. Tears of rage were welling up inside me. If he thought I was about to forgive him, he could think again.

"Yes, it was cruel." I gathered up my coat and bag.

"Where are you going?"

"Home," I said. "I need to think."

"What about? The shop?"

"No. Us."

Chapter 6

I was setting the table for dinner. It was Sunday evening and Mum and Dad were due back with the kids any minute and were staying for meat loaf—Dad's favorite. The radio was on in the background. I don't know what program I was listening to, but a group of women were discussing why they'd stayed so long in bad marriages. One woman's story caught my attention. I turned up the volume.

"It took years for the penny to finally drop," she was saying. "But in the end I realized that what I took to be concern for my welfare was actually more about his need to control me. People tend to think of controlling men as angry and violent—and that's why I didn't pick up on it. . . . My husband was always so gentle and kind."

I carried on arranging knives and forks, but I felt unsettled. I was aware that my heart rate had picked up. Then the doorbell rang. The kids. I switched off the radio, switched on a smile and headed to the door.

"Mum, can your lips fall off?" Dan said by way of greeting. He came into the house and dropped his rucksack at my feet.

"And hello to you, too." I picked up the rucksack, thereby reinforcing his belief that I was his personal maid, but I figured that since he was probably tired and wired, it made no sense to get into a fight about it.

"But can they?"

"What? No. Of course your lips can't fall off."

"That's what Grandma said. So it really is true that they can't. You promise?"

"Absolutely."

"Good." Clearly relieved, he ran off, making a beeline for the kitchen. I yelled at him not to fill up on junk, as dinner was almost ready.

"Why on earth would he think his lips could fall off?" I said to my mother, who was next in through the door. Dad was behind her, cradling a sleeping Ella.

"He's been going on about it all weekend," Mum said. "Apparently it's a theory doing the rounds in his class. The things these kids get into their heads."

Dad managed to lean over Ella and give me a quick peck hello. Then he followed us into the living room and laid her down on the sofa. "She dropped off about twenty minutes ago."

"Our fault," Mum said. "We let them stay up last night to watch *E.T.*"

"And Grandma and Granddad let us have gummy bears," Ella mumbled, waking up now.

My mother looked down at her and smiled. "Traitor."

Just then Dan reappeared, his hand deep inside a packet of potato chips.

"Dan, what did I tell you? You'll spoil your appetite."

"No, I won't. I'm starving. Anyway, I've been thinking. . . . When I grow up, I want to be a chameleon . . . you know . . . who tells jokes."

Of course we all burst out laughing. Even Ella joined in—clearly not wanting to be left out. Big mistake. Dan turned bright red and his eyes began to fill up. It was obvious that he felt he'd committed some unforgivable faux pas.

"Stop laughing," he yelled, stamping his foot.

I put my arm around him. "I'm sorry, sweetie. It was wrong of us to laugh. It's just that a chameleon is a lizard that changes color. You remember—we saw them at the zoo. People who tell jokes are called comedians."

"I knew that." He charged upstairs and slammed the bedroom door. I resolved to write out a hundred times "I must never ever humiliate my children."

Mum called after him. "Please come down, darling. We're all really sorry."

I said it was probably best to give him some space and I'd go and talk to him when he'd calmed down.

We left Ella on the sofa watching *Annie*—which she still seemed to find comforting—and wandered into the kitchen. Mum and Dad took off their coats and draped them over kitchen chairs.

"Ooh, something smells good," Dad said, sitting himself down.

"Meat loaf and roast potatoes." I began pouring the wine.

"You look tired," Mum said to me as I handed her a glass. "You feeling OK?"

My parents still didn't know about Steve. Telling them that I was seeing somebody would have only made them worry: Was it serious?

Was I ready? Were the children ready? Telling them that I was seeing somebody, that we'd just had a falling-out and that I'd been up half the night fretting about our future together would have caused them real anxiety.

"I'm fine. I've got a few things on my mind, that's all." One of them was the story I'd heard on the radio. It had definitely touched a nerve.

Mum looked at me. "You're not still thinking about taking over the shop, are you? Sarah, this is becoming an obsession. You have to let it go."

"I would, but the situation has changed." I told them about the tax rebate and how Aunty Shirley appeared to have paid the rent on the shop until the end of the year.

"So what?" Dad said. "Ten grand is nothing. The shop is falling apart. You'd need twice . . . three times that amount."

"But surely the landlord is responsible for structural repairs."

"Shirley was always trying to get money out of him," Mum said. "He didn't give a crap. Sarah, for the last time, you have to let this thing go. It's madness. I'm starting to worry about you."

"I'm sorry, but I can't stop thinking about it."

I told them what I'd told Steve—how I'd lived to regret giving up the dressmaking business.

"I get that," Dad said. "And there's no doubt that you're ready for a new challenge. Just not this one, eh?"

"Your dad's right. I mean let's suppose you did get the place spruced up. That still leaves you with one major obstacle: Clementine Montecute. What are you going to do, tell her this town ain't big enough for the two of you and gun her down?"

Mum patted my hand. "Come on, sweetheart, let it go."

I said that I would try.

"Actually," Dad piped up, "your mother and I have some news. We're going away for a few weeks."

"Wow. That's a fantastic . . . just what you both need."

Mum shot Dad a look. "You see. I said it would be a problem—us not being around to help out with the children. We can't possibly go. Now let that be an end to it."

"But Sarah just said it was a great idea."

"Yes, but she didn't mean it—did you, Sarah?" She looked back at Dad. "Look, Sarah and the kids still need us. We can't leave them and go gallivanting off to Spain."

"Yes, you can. Go. Gallivant. I insist."

"Your uncle Lou has said we can have his flat in Marbella," Dad said. "He hardly uses it since the divorce. It's just sitting there, empty. Seems like too good an opportunity to turn down."

"Of course it is."

"So you don't mind?" Mum said. "Lou said we could come as soon as we like, so we'd probably be leaving in a week or so."

"No problem. Stop worrying. I'll be fine."

And I meant it. Of course I would miss Mum and Dad being around to help with the kids, but Mum in particular needed a rest and maybe I needed some time on my own to work out where my life went from here.

While Mum dished up, I went upstairs to make peace with Dan. "Knock, knock. Can I come in?"

Grunt.

"I'm sorry, hon," I said, perching on the edge of his bed. "We really didn't mean to upset you. We shouldn't have laughed at you. It was stupid and hurtful. Can you forgive us?"

He looked at me over his comic.

"What's for dessert?"

"My homemade apple crumble."

"Is there ice cream?"

I grinned. "Maybe."

"Yess."

All appeared to have been forgiven.

*M*um and Dad left straight after dinner. Mum looked all in. I called to Dan and Ella to say they were leaving. They came thumping down the stairs, thanked their grandparents for having them.

"Our pleasure," Mum said.

"So, let me know as soon as you've decided when you're off to Spain."

"Grandma and Granddad are going to Spain?" Ella said.

"Only for a holiday," Mum said. "We'll be back before you know it."

Yays from both children.

"I'll call you," Mum said.

For once, when I announced that it was bedtime, the children didn't put up a fight. They were both zonked—even Ella, who'd had a nap. Once they were in bed, I read them a few pages of *Matilda*, but they were both struggling to stay awake. As I tucked him in, Dan rallied by asking me what starfish ate. I said I hadn't the foggiest. "Other fish, I guess." I prayed that he wouldn't demand to get up and Google the answer.

"Tell you what, I'll look it up and let you know tomorrow."

" 'K." There was no talk of Googling.

I kissed them good night, but all I got by way of reply were grunts.

As I picked up their dirty socks and underwear and dropped them into the laundry basket, it occurred to me that even though Ella still needed to watch *Annie*, the kids were talking less about death and dying. Judy had said it would happen eventually, but I'd never quite believed her.

I went into the kitchen, made another cup of tea and took it to the sofa. My laptop was lying open on the coffee table. First, I bashed out a letter to Aunty Shirley's lawyer, enclosing the letter from HMRC and asking if he could arrange for the tax rebate to be sent to me. Then I went onto Google to look for Greg Myers' London agent. It turned out to be a company called Marcus Winkworth Featherstone. It wasn't possible to e-mail Marcus, Winkworth or Featherstone in person. Instead I had to e-mail the publicity department. Apparently my request would be passed to the relevant person. I didn't hold out much hope, but I wrote the e-mail anyway. Style-wise, I opted for Imogen Stagge upper-class sychophancy and gush.

Hello—a thousand apologies for contacting you out of the blue, but our school is holding its annual summer fair on Saturday July 16th and since we are all such ardent—dare I say fanatical—Greg Myers fans, we were wondering if he might do us the honor of opening it.

This is the most important fund-raising event of the year. The money goes only partly to the school. We also sponsor an orphanage in India, which is home to some of the most wretched and deprived children in the country.

I realize that Greg must be inundated with similar requests, but if he felt able to give us an hour or two of his time and work our fund-raiser into his hectic schedule, we would be forever in his debt.

After the opening, we would be delighted if he would join us for tea and scones in the main tent.

Yours,
Sarah Green

I read over the e-mail. Perfect. The Honourable Imogen might have written it herself. I hit "send."

In my head I heard Steve reminding me that I was wasting my time and that I was bonkers if I thought I'd hear anything back.

I hadn't realized until last night, as I'd lain awake smarting and furious with him for calling me irresponsible, just how often Steve tried to undermine. Whenever I took him to task about it, he always apologized. Then, just like the husband of the radio woman, he assured me that he only did it because he worried about me and he wanted to look after me. Her account of living with somebody who sold his controlling behavior as kindness was still troubling me. It echoed what I'd been thinking for a while, but hadn't had the courage to articulate.

Now, as I stared at the screen saver blobs floating and morphing,

I was starting to voice my fears—albeit in my head. Although part of me relished having a man around who wanted to take care of me—who wanted to be sure that my new house was fitted with window locks and a burglar alarm, who was prepared to give up his Saturday afternoon to look over Aunty Shirley's accounts—maybe Steve's behavior wasn't as benign and benevolent as I thought. Perhaps he wasn't as concerned for my welfare as he made out. Did he behave the way he did because it was a way of controlling me?

All the time I'd known him, he'd been cagey about his previous relationships with women, but he had admitted to being dumped several times. "I don't know what it is. I just seem to attract these insane women." Maybe he found himself drawn to strong women, but once he was in a relationship with them, he felt threatened and found himself needing to dominate them. They dumped him, not because they were insane, but because they refused to tolerate his behavior.

On the other hand, Steve (not to mention Mum and Dad) was right about the shop. The idea of me taking it over was bonkers. But last night when I tried to explain my reasons for wanting to take over the business and suggested that my life wouldn't end if the venture failed, he'd got so angry. He was furious with me for attempting to defy him. It occurred to me that this was a man who would never stop chipping away at my spirit and determination. I was now prepared to admit that the reason I hadn't had sex with Steve had little to do with my feelings for Mike. The reality was, I didn't trust him.

I wanted to pick up the phone to Judy. "Hey, Judy," I'd say. "Here's the thing: I've been seeing this guy for a while and I thought I really liked him, but now I'm having second thoughts. You see, I heard this woman talking on the radio about her controlling husband and it got me thinking. . . ."

I wished the kids and I hadn't stopped seeing Judy, but in the end it had been one expense too many. Right now, I was really missing having her as a sounding board. I was trying to figure out if my finances could stretch to a one-off session, when there was a tap at the door. It felt late, but a glance at my watch revealed that it was barely half past eight. I went to the door and looked through the spy hole. Rosie.

"Hey," she said, standing in front of me now—her face on full beam. "Don't suppose you feel like joining me in a celebration? Wonder of wonders, I just got a child support check from Simon. Only five hundred quid out of the ten grand he owes me, but it's a start." She was carrying a sleeping Will in his Moses basket. At his feet lay her cell phone and a bottle of prosecco.

"Love to," I said, standing back to let her in. "I could really do with a drink." I was forgetting that I'd knocked back a couple of glasses of wine over dinner. "Not to mention a bit of a natter."

"Sounds ominous. You OK?"

"It's this bloke I've been seeing. . . ."

"Giving you trouble, is he? Fear not, your aunty Rosie's here."

While Rosie sat herself down and checked on Will, I went to fetch some glasses. "I thought you were on the wagon while you were breast-feeding," I said, setting a couple of champagne flutes down on the coffee table.

"I am, but I've decided that one night off can't hurt."

Rosie popped the cork and poured us each a glass. I'd barely taken a sip when the thumping started upstairs.

"Oh, crap," Rosie said. "Your kids must have heard me come in. I'm so sorry."

The children appeared in the living room, bleary-eyed, but curious.

"Who's this?" Ella said.

I did the introductions. Ella was fascinated by Will. "He's so tiny. Does he suck your boobies? Phoebe in my class, her baby sister sucks her mummy's boobies. It's weird. And then she gets sick on the sofa and it's really stinky."

"Yeah, babies can be a bit stinky," Rosie said, grinning.

"Does it hurt when he sucks your boobies?"

"Not really."

"If he sucked really hard," Dan broke in, "could they fall off?"

"Fall off?" Rosie was clearly baffled by the question. "Not really. Boobies tend to be fixed pretty firmly."

"But wouldn't you have preferred a hamster?" he went on. "Or a puppy? You can take them for walks and train them to do tricks."

"I have to admit that Will is a bit lacking in the tricks department. Tell you what, when he's older, I might get him a puppy and then maybe you and Ella could take him for walks."

"Cool." Dan turned to me. "Mum, did you check on the computer to see what starfish eat?"

"Not yet. I'll do it before I go to bed and let you know in the morning."

But he was already sitting at my laptop, tapping the keys. "Wow. Did you know they eat other starfish? That means they're cannonballs. Alfie at school, his brother's got the DVD of this film about people who start eating each other. They're in a plane crash, but only some of them get killed and because they're in the mountains and there's no food, they have to eat the dead bodies."

"Stoppit," Ella cried. "People don't eat other people."

"Yes they do. It's called cannon-ball-ism."

"Mummy—tell Dan to stop teasing."

"I'm not teasing. It's true. Mum, tell her."

Rosie was looking at me, grinning all over her face as if to say, "So how are you going to handle this one?"

"OK," I said. "Under very, very extreme circumstances, which almost never happen, people have been known to eat bits of other people."

"Which bits?" Ella demanded.

"I don't know."

"Bums," Dan said. "Bound to be. That's where there's most meat."

"I wouldn't let you eat my bum."

"Why would anybody want to eat your stinky bum?"

I glanced at Rosie, who by now was struggling to keep a straight face.

"Kids, if I gave you each a packet of Monster Munch, would you forget about cannonballs and go back to bed so that I can chat to Rosie?"

Instead of nodding, they made a joint dash to the cupboard and had a fight about who should have the last packet of salt and vinegar flavor. I told them that if they didn't settle their differences immediately, nobody would get anything. Dan backed down and agreed to have cheese and onion.

"Night, kids," Rosie said.

"Night," Ella said. "Nice to have met you."

"You, too, Ella . . . and you, Dan."

"I have no idea who taught my daughter such good manners," I said after the kids had disappeared upstairs. "My mother, probably. As you can see, I spend most of my time bribing my children with junk food instead of teaching them social etiquette."

Rosie laughed. "That'll be me in a few years." She took a sip of prosecco. "So, come on, dish. What's going on with this bloke of yours?"

"How long have you got?"

"Oh, God . . . as bad as that. Tell you what, if this is going to be a long session, I think I should avail myself of the facilities."

Rosie disappeared to the loo, tiptoeing on the stairs. I peeked into the Moses basket. Will was blowing milky bubbles in his sleep.

The *Sunday Times* was lying on the coffee table. I hadn't so much as glanced at it all day. As I sifted through the various bits, a headline in the business diary section caught my eye.

Clementine Montecute Quits over Storm in a D Cup

Lingerie tycoon Clementine Montecute, supplier of bespoke bras and corsets to crowned heads as well as Hollywood royalty, has shut up shop amid accusations that she lied to customers about her credentials as a lingerie designer. It would seem that before opening her atelier, she did not—as she had previously claimed—work as a designer for some of the best lingerie houses in France. The nearest she got was working as a junior PR assistant for La Perla. Moreover, her Mayfair atelier—which Montecute claimed employed some of the best lingerie makers in the world—was a sham. Instead of being "handmade in Mayfair," orders were outsourced to a women's co-op in Bulgaria. One customer, who asked to remain anonymous, said: "The quality of the lingerie was no better than average, but because she was meant to be the best, nobody dared question it. It was a case of the empress' new underwear. Clearly, the wealthy are easily deceived. What was more, she ripped us off shamelessly. Montecute was paying her workers pennies to make garments which cost her customers hundreds of pounds. This kind of profiteering almost amounts to fraud."

Clementine Montecute was a charlatan? I had to read the article three times before it sank in.

It seemed that in order to get away with her scam, Montecute had spent thousands of pounds buying people's silence. In the end one person had started demanding more money. When Montecute refused to pay up, the woman leaked the story to *Paris Match*. Kate and Pippa Middleton were thought to have withdrawn their patronage, along with several Hollywood A-listers, as yet unnamed. My heart was thumping. This changed everything. With Montecute gone, there was a chance. I had a chance.

I hadn't noticed Rosie come back into the room.

"Sarah, you OK? You seem miles away."

I turned to look at her. "Rosie, do you believe in taking risks?"

"Hang on, I thought we were going to talk about your bloke."

"We are. . . . It's all connected. . . . So, do you take risks?"

Rosie shrugged. "Depends what you mean by risk."

Twenty minutes and half a bottle of prosecco later I'd told her the whole story—about Aunty Shirley and the shop, Steve and his controlling behavior, the Clementine Montecute scandal. Rosie sat there, barely saying a word.

"So," I said finally. "What should I do?"

"About the shop or Steve?"

"Both."

"To be honest, I don't think anybody can tell you what to do—it has to be your decision—but if it were me, I would absolutely give the business a go. You're not keen on your job, Montecute's gone and you've got the aunties to help. I'd say you've got a hell of a lot going for you."

"Except money."

"OK, first you need to get your lawyer to put some pressure on the landlord. There must be some legislation that forces him to keep the building up to standard. Plus it's in his interest as well as yours."

I agreed. I said I would call him. "So you think it's a risk worth taking?"

"If you don't take it, I think you could live to regret it. You'll always be asking yourself 'What if?' "

"And if I fail?"

"If you fail, you'll always be able to say that you gave it your best shot. Life isn't about certainty. If it were, it would be very dull."

"Which brings me to Steve."

She topped up both our glasses. "OK, after Mike I can see why you fell for him, but from what you said, the man sounds like a bit of a bully."

"So you think I should dump him."

Rosie raised both hands in front of her. "I'm only telling you what I think. Ending it has to be your call."

Just then her cell rang. She took it out of the Moses basket and looked at the number.

"Sorry . . . it's a client. I really should take it. Maybe I should go. I mean it's one thing me doing this in my house. . . ."

"No, stay. I'm sure the kids are asleep. I'll go upstairs and check on them."

They were both dead to the world. Dan was cuddling his Monster Munch packet as if it were a soft toy. Ella was lying on her back with her mouth open, snoring gently. Her Monster Munch packet, still half full, was on her nightstand, propped up against the lamp. I kissed them both, straightened their covers and opened the window a crack to let in some air. "Sleep tight," I whispered.

Downstairs, Rosie was on the phone, going through her usual spiel. "Of course I'm wet for you, Brian," she said, chipping away at her nail polish.

I thought I might go and unload the dishwasher. When I'd finished, she was still on the phone.

"What? . . . . Your wife's back? . . . OK, but you've still got to pay me for the time you've had. . . . Brian, are you there? Brian, don't you dare hang up on me. You owe me money." Rosie looked up at me. "Brian's wife came home and he hung up."

"So I gather."

"Crap. I hate it when that happens."

Will was stirring. Rosie looked into the basket and then at her watch. "Time for his feed." She picked him up. "OK, noodle, your late-night snack awaits." A moment later he was guzzling happily.

"Of course," Rosie said, "if you decided not to take over your aunty Shirley's business, you could always do what I do."

"Me? Giving phone sex? You have to be joking. I wouldn't know where to start. Embarrassment wouldn't even begin to describe it. I'd be totally tongue-tied. And . . . don't take this the wrong way, but for me at least, it would feel really dirty."

"You soon get over that. Like I said, once you've memorized the script, it stops being real. It's more like doing some kind of kinky corporate presentation." She paused. "I could teach you if you like."

I burst out laughing. "No, you couldn't. I'd be useless. My mind would go totally blank."

"I bet you'd be brilliant." She picked up her phone. "Go on . . . take it."

"What? No." But I'd already taken it. "You do realize," I said, giggling, "that I'm only doing this because I'm drunk."

"OK, here goes . . . ring-ring . . . ring-ring . . ."

I knocked back some more prosecco. "Hello?"

"Right, let's pretend his name is Otto."

"Otto?"

"Yeah, he's German. . . . So, Sarah . . . vhat are you vearing?"

"Oh, I'm just in my bra and panties. I've been lying on the bed waiting for you."

"Excellent," Rosie said in her real voice. "See—you're really getting into it."

"So, Otto . . . would you like me to take my panties off?"

"Ach . . . Jawohl!"

"OK, I'm slipping them off now. . . ."

"Gott in Himmel!"

I snorted with laughter.

"Absolutely no laughing," Rosie said, barely containing her own. "You have to stay focused."

"OK, Otto . . . That's it, big boy. Take me! Take me!

"Mein Gott! Mein Gott!"

"Oh, Otto! Otto!"

"Sieg heil! Sieg heil!"

By now we were both in hysterics—me more than Rosie because I wasn't trying to breast-feed at the same time as laugh. Then, suddenly she stopped laughing. She was looking past me. I turned round to see Steve.

"You two seem to be having fun," he said, clearly not amused.

"Steve . . . what are you doing here? How did you get in?"

"The front door was open. Didn't you see it? Anybody could have walked in."

The catch had been sticking. I probably didn't close it hard enough after I let Rosie in. At the back of my mind I must have been thinking about not waking the kids.

Rosie was rearranging herself. "I think maybe I should be going." She looked at Steve. "I'm Rosie, by the way."

He gave her a sniffy look. "Yes, I'd guessed that much."

"Rosie, don't go. Stay and have another drink."

By now Will was back in his basket and she was tucking him in. I handed her back her phone.

"No, I really ought to get going. Speak to you tomorrow."

I nodded. "Sure."

She scooped up the Moses basket, said a quick good-bye to Steve and was gone.

"Did you have to be so bloody rude?" I said to Steve.

"Me rude? Correct me if I'm wrong, but it would appear that your new best friend is schooling you in the finer points of phone sex."

"Christ, why do you have to be such a jerk? We were messing around, that's all."

"And that's your idea of fun?"

"Yes, as it happens."

"What if one of the children had come down?"

"For your information, I'd just been up to check on them. They were both sound asleep."

"So, you won't sleep with me, but you're happy to act out this . . . filth." He spat out the word.

"It was a joke. Let it go. . . . Now why don't we sit down?"

He lowered himself into an armchair. I took the sofa.

"So you still haven't told me why you're here?"

"I came to apologize for last night. I was out of order. I'm sorry." He still sounded huffy. He wasn't about to forgive me for Otto anytime soon.

"Apology accepted, but I've made a decision. I'm taking over the shop."

"Fine. Do what you like. I've said all I'm going to say."

"Hang on. Hear me out. Things have changed. I just read this article in the *Sunday Times* and apparently Clementine Montecute has gone out of business. Now that she's no competition, I'm prepared to take the risk."

"OK, but for the record I still think you're crazy."

"That's all you can think about, isn't it? . . . The risk, the failure. Has it occurred to you that I might succeed? I can't live the way you do—like a permanently scared rabbit. I have to make something of my life."

He handed me a newspaper clipping. "It's a list of local government job vacancies. There are a couple in the town planning department I thought might suit you."

"Steve, we've had this conversation. For the umpteenth time, I'm not about to take a job in local government. I'm taking over the shop."

"Well, I hope you're not expecting any help from me."

"I'm not expecting anybody's help. I intend to do this on my own."

"Don't kid yourself. You need me. You'll never cope on your own."

"Of course I won't . . . because what I need is a pompous, condescending, arrogant son of a bitch undermining me and telling me what to do the whole time."

"OK, I've heard enough. You and I are through."

"What? You can't dump me. I'm the one doing the dumping."

"Fine. Whatever. You know what, Sarah, I've done my level best to help and look after you. What have you given me in return?"

He meant the lack of sex. He was right to be angry. I'd been cruel stringing him along, promising something that I knew deep down was never going to happen. Then just now, he'd come in and seen me messing around on the phone—being sexual and having fun. It was clearly more than he could bear.

"I'm sorry," I said. "I led you on. That's unforgivable. All I can say in my defense is that my head is still a bit of a mess. Nevertheless, I'm hugely grateful for everything you've done—the pro bono work, going over Aunty Shirley's accounts—and I will pay you back."

"I don't give a toss about the money. It was you I wanted."

"I know, but I can't be with somebody who wants to control me."

"Control you?" He sounded exasperated. "Not this again. Why is it that all the women I've ever dated think I'm out to control them? You're insane. My whole life, I've attracted insane women."

Still muttering to himself, he was out the door.

Chapter 7

"*M*ummy," Ella said, swirling Coco Pops around in her bowl in order to make the milk go brown, "do mummies have penises?"

Before I had a chance to say anything, Dan leaped in. "Of course they don't have penises, dummy. Mummies have beards."

Ella looked confused. I groaned inside. Seven thirty in the morning was way too early for discussions about female genitalia.

"You know—hairy vaginas?" Dan added helpfully.

"Yes, but Chloe in my class says they have tiny, teensy-weensy penises as well."

"No, they don't."

"They do. Chloe says."

"They don't."

"Do. They're called kit-risses."

Ella looked at me for confirmation.

"Actually, Chloe's quite right," I said. "Women and girls have something called a *clit-oris* and it is a bit like a tiny penis—except that you don't pee out of it."

"See. I told you I was right," Ella said to Dan. She poked her tongue out at him. "So," she said, turning back to me. "If you don't pee out of your clit'ris, what's it for?"

The death conversations had been so much easier than this.

"Tell you what—why don't you finish your cereal and we'll talk about this later when there's more time?" I could have added, "and I'm not so fantastically hungover from lack of sleep." I'd lain awake most of the night, furious with Steve for being a controlling jerk. At the same time I hated myself for stringing him along. I'd been dishonest and cruel. Deep down, Steve was a decent, kind man and he'd meant well. Maybe, instead of dumping him, I should have suggested he, slash we, see a counselor to help him work on his control issues. My brain had been so full of Steve that I'd barely thought about Clementine Montecute or my plan to reopen the shop.

Ella was getting down from the table.

"Where are you going?" I said. "You haven't finished your breakfast."

"I'll be back in a minute. I'm going upstairs to look at my clit'ris."

"Yuck. Gross. Mum, tell her that's gross."

Sarah . . . do not make a big deal of this. Girls should feel free to explore their bodies and not be made to feel embarrassed or ashamed of them.

"Dan, be quiet." I refrained from adding, "Like you've never played with your penis."

I called after Ella, "That's fine, sweetie, but make it quick or we'll be late for school."

I was in the middle of making the kids' packed lunches when the phone rang. It was Rosie, checking to see if I was OK after last night.

"Sorry to call so early, but Will and I are off in a bit. I've got this friend who works at T.J. Maxx and apparently they've just had a delivery of Vivienne Westwood. She's holding a couple of things back for me, but I need to get there for opening time."

"God, I miss clothes shopping," I said. "Even at T.J. Maxx."

I gave her a quick rundown of what happened after she left.

"Do you think I was too hard on him?" I said when I'd finished. "He seemed genuinely upset and confused when I accused him of being controlling."

"Hon—you had to end it. What choice did you have? And as for him being upset—it's not your fault he doesn't understand his need to dominate women. That's why in all these months you couldn't bring yourself to sleep with him."

"I know. I get that, but instead of dumping him, maybe I should have suggested counseling. I mean he wasn't a bad guy. Deep down, he meant well."

"You know why you didn't suggest counseling?"

"Why?"

"Because you spent years trying to mend Mike, and the sensible, sane part of you has no intention of taking on another project."

"You're right. And if I'm honest, I'm relieved that Steve and I are over . . . but at the same time I can't help feeling lonely."

"Of course you feel lonely. Steve filled an emotional vacancy and even though he was a jerk—OK, a well-meaning, generous jerk—you're going to miss him."

"I guess. . . . You know, I'm so cross with myself for not seeing through him sooner."

"Sarah, please don't start beating yourself up. We've all been there. I went out with this bloke Dennis for two years. He permed his eyelashes and hardly ever wanted to have sex. When he finally admitted he was gay, I couldn't believe it. All my friends had seen it the moment they met him, but the thought had never occurred to me."

"You're kidding. Never?"

"Not really."

"Huh."

"OK, I admit it was pretty dumb of me, but I just want you to know that I understand how you feel. OK?"

"OK . . . and Rosie . . . thanks."

"You're welcome."

She said she had to go because Will was squawking. I went back to the lunch boxes. As I started spreading egg mayo onto slices of granary, I found myself thinking about Steve again. God help me, I had fallen for a man who wore gray suits and parted his hair like a Mormon. I'd found him sexy. I still did. What was going on with me? What would Judy have said? She would probably have said that despite the feelings I still had for Mike, I felt a powerful compulsion to get as far away from him as possible. Steve had been about as far away as it got. What I actually needed was somebody who fell between the two extremes: a relaxed, happy-go-lucky, creative type, who made me laugh, preferably owned his own place, but definitely had savings and a pension plan. I didn't know for certain, but I suspected that happy-go-lucky guys with pension plans were pretty thin on the ground.

———

I'd dropped Dan and Ella at the school gates and was heading back to the car when Imogen Stagge moved into view. "Yoo-hoo, Sarah."

As she came trotting towards me, I couldn't help noticing that the hem of her skirt didn't quite cover her navy knee-highs. "Won't keep you—just wondering if you'd heard anything from Greg Myers."

"Not yet. I called my cousin Rupert and he promised to drop him an e-mail. I'm sure I'll hear something in a few days." I hated lying to Imogen. She was a bit hard to take, but she was a decent sort—the archetypal good egg. If I did the right thing and owned up about there being no cousin Rupert, she'd probably understand. But I couldn't trust her not to gossip. The chances were that any confession I made would get back to Tara and Charlotte.

"Jolly good. Jolly good," she declared. "Now then, you'll have to excuse me, but I must fly. I've got an appointment with the doc. I've decided that menopause-wise, hormones are definitely the way forward. My memory's got so bad, I'm practically having to write the boys' names on Post-it notes."

She laughed her hearty laugh and strode off, not before making me promise to keep her in the loop Greg Myers–wise.

I should have headed straight to work, but instead, almost without thinking I turned the car around and set off towards Aunty Bimla's. Having spent the night angry and troubled as I dissected my relationship with Steve, suddenly I was high with excitement. I couldn't wait to tell the aunties that I had decided to get the business up and running and they had their jobs back. I could have called them, but this was news that I wanted to deliver in person.

On the way, I called Don at the nonemergency helpline. "Don, I'm really sorry, but something urgent has come up. I'm going to be an hour or so late; can you possibly manage without me?"

"You all right, Sarah? Anything I can do?"

"Thanks, but I'm fine. Something I need to sort out, that's all."

"No worries. Everything's quiet here. See you when we see you."

"Thanks, Don. I owe you one."

Aunty Bimla's face lit up as she opened the front door. "Poppet, what are you doing here?"

"I have news."

"Good, I hope . . . Come in, come in. Sylvia's just got here. We haven't quite finished the corsets for *Così fan tutte*. Another day or so and we will be done. I don't want you to think we have been shilly-shallying."

"You honestly believe I'd think that?" I put my arm around her and gave her a squeeze.

Aunty Sylvia looked up from her sewing machine. "Bubbie, what are you doing here?"

"She has news," Aunty Bimla said. "But she hasn't said if it's good or bad."

"It's fantastic," I said.

Aunty Bimla clapped her hands. "In that case, I'll make tea."

"And there's still some of my homemade cheesecake left in the fridge," Aunty Sylvia said.

I explained that I didn't have time for tea as I had to get to work.

"I just popped in to tell you that things have changed and I've decided to reopen the shop after all."

"Really?" Aunty Sylvia said. I could hear the trepidation in her voice.

"Really."

"Sit, poppet, and explain. What has happened?"

Aunty Bimla pulled out a dining room chair. I sat. She did the same.

"It's Clementine Montecute," I began.

"What about her?"

I reeled off the story.

"So, her chickens finally came home to roost." Aunty Bimla was rubbing her hands with satisfaction.

"You know," Aunty Sylvia said, "there was something about that Montecute woman I never liked."

"What was that?"

"Skinny wrists. My mother-in-law had skinny wrists. Evil woman—God rest her soul."

"So here's the thing," I continued. "With Clementine Montecute out of the picture, we've lost our main competitor. I don't see any reason not to reopen the shop. What do you think?"

The aunties looked at each other.

"You know," Aunty Sylvia said. "There are competitors besides Clementine Montecute."

"Yes, but are you telling me their seamstresses are in the same league as you and Aunty Bimla?"

Aunty Sylvia shrugged. "Not quite as good maybe . . . But the shop is in such a terrible state. Where would you find the money to do all the repairs?"

"I agree. Poppet, I hate to say this, but you're living in cloud cuckoo land. Take my advice, let it go. There's no point in flogging a dead horse."

"OK, what would you say if I told you that Aunty Shirley is due a ten-thousand-pound tax rebate—which now comes to me? This means I can pay you both up to date and have some money left over to do some work on the shop. I'm also going to ask the landlord for a contribution."

"Good luck with that," Aunty Sylvia said with a sniff. "Old man Mugford's so tight, he wouldn't give you the steam off his piss."

"Sylvia, please. Do you have to be so crude?"

"I speak as I find. The fact is Shirley never got a penny out of him."

"Well, I thought I'd give him a call anyway. But that's not the main issue. The point is that you two are brilliantly talented seamstresses. If I'm to get the shop up and running again, I need to be able to offer the bespoke service. That's what the shop has always been known for. If I let it go, all I'll have is just another lingerie shop."

Aunty Sylvia turned to Aunty Bimla. "So what do we think?"

"Well, far be it from me to toot my own horn, but I think the child is right. We do know our stuff and I don't know about you, but the thought of retiring gives me the willies."

"Me, too."

"I'm thinking that maybe we should say yes."

"OK," Aunty Sylvia said. "It's a yes from me and it's a yes from her. Let's see if we can't make this work."

They said they wouldn't take a penny in payment until the business was on its feet. It appeared that money-wise their boats were about to come in. Sanjeev's big deal with the Paraguay people was on the point of going through and Roxanne had landed the part in the haunted refrigerator movie.

"That would appear to leave us at stalemate," I said. "Because I'm not prepared to even think about getting started until you're both paid up to date."

The aunties conferred and said that they would be more than happy with five hundred pounds each. I said that wasn't nearly enough and offered them two thousand each. They came back with a counteroffer of a thousand and we settled on fifteen hundred.

Aunty Bimla made us all high-five. Then she insisted I stay for tea and a slice of Aunty Sylvia's cheesecake.

*A*fter I left the aunties, I sat in the car, spooling through my e-mail. Viagra deals. Amazon offers. Twenty percent off on a funeral. The usual. I was about to hit "delete" one last time, when my brain did a double take. Marcus Winkworth Featherstone had replied—or at least Winkworth's PA had. Please God, please God . . . please let Greg Myers have said yes. I opened the e-mail.

Hi Sarah, Greg Myers asked me to thank you for your kind invitation to open your school fair. Sadly, due to his busy work schedule, he won't be able to attend. He thanks you for thinking of him and wishes you all the very best. . . .

Crap. Not that I was remotely surprised. Now what did I do? I thought back to my conversation with Steve during which we'd discussed what I would do if Greg Myers said no. Back then I'd been so full of bravado. Did I really have the balls to put my plan B into action and ambush him outside the theater? At any other time, I might have. But this wasn't any other time. I was at the point of opening a business. Even though it stood almost no chance of becoming a success, I wasn't entirely devoid of hope. I couldn't risk my future reputation by getting arrested for stalking Greg Myers.

On the other hand, what choice did I have?

I decided to hold that thought and call Mum and Dad to tell them my news about reopening the shop. My fingers were hovering over the keypad when the phone rang. It was Dad to say that he'd read about the Clementine Montecute scandal and wanted to know if I'd heard.

"I have . . . and I've made a decision."

"Let me guess. Now that she's gone, you're definitely reopening the shop."

"Dad, I can't let this opportunity go. Suddenly, it feels like all the planets are in alignment."

Dad laughed. "I suspect your aunty Shirley had a hand in that. I wouldn't put it past her."

"So you're not angry with me?"

"Of course I'm not angry with you and nor is your mum. We've been discussing it and we're both agreed that now you've got the tax money and there's no Clementine Montecute to worry about, reopening the shop doesn't sound like such a daft proposition. That's not to say we aren't worried, but there are times in this life when you have to take risks."

"Wow. I never thought I'd hear you say that. I really appreciate it. Having you and Mum behind me means such a lot."

"Hang on . . . your mother wants a word. I'll pass you over."

"Now then, darling, you're not to worry about a thing. Your father and I have decided not to go to Spain."

"What? No. You absolutely have to go. You need a rest. I won't hear of you staying."

"But how can we go and leave you with so much on your plate? For a start, you're going to need extra child care. . . ."

"Mum, stop fussing. I'll manage. I've made friends with my new neighbor, Rosie. She's lovely and I'm sure she won't mind helping out from time to time."

"But surely she goes out to work."

"No, she has a new baby—although she does do a bit of work from home."

"Oh, what does she do?"

Why had I opened my big mouth? "She's . . . um . . . She's in the hospitality business."

"Nice. Your cousin April works in hospitality. Maybe she knows her. You should get them together. It's always good for people in the same industry to network."

"Good idea."

"OK . . . Well, if you're absolutely sure you can cope . . ."

"I'm sure."

"And you promise you'll call if you need money. Remember, there's no shame in failing. You and the kids can always move in with us."

"Thanks. I appreciate that."

But there was no way I was going to let that happen. I wasn't a kid. I was a mother with two children. In a few years I'd be forty. I refused to fall back on my parents. I had to do everything in my power to make the business work.

"And you'll stay in touch?"

"When have I ever not stayed in touch? Mum, please, you have to stop worrying."

She said that asking her to stop worrying was like asking her to stop breathing.

Mum and Dad left for Spain two days later.

Chapter 8

"Great, so you're going to start stalking Greg Myers?" Rosie said after I'd told her the saga.

"I'm not going to *stalk* him. I'm merely going to ambush him. And I was wondering if you'd mind babysitting while I did it."

"No problem. And if you get arrested and sent to jail, I can adopt Dan and Ella if you like."

"Very funny," I said. "You sound like Steve. Why would I get arrested? All I'm going to do is hover outside the stage door after the show along with the autograph hunters and ask Greg if I can have a quick word with him. It's pretty straightforward."

"It sounds pretty straightforward. I still think it's a risk."

"This from the woman who is concealing from the entire neighborhood that she gets paid to do phone sex."

Rosie said she took the point.

I called the theater box office and was told that *Death of a Salesman* finished at ten. For no reason other than fear that I'd get there late and my quarry would get away, I got to the theater at nine. After I'd located the stage door, I went to sit in the bubble tea café around the corner. I ordered melon and vanilla. I calculated that it would probably be half an hour or so before Greg Myers emerged. If I were back at the stage door at ten, sharp, I would be in plenty of time.

When I got there, three girls—American, late teens, high on booze and anticipation—were already there.

"Omigod, do you think he's just as hot in real life as he is on TV?"

"Do you think he'd autograph my boob?"

"Are you crazy? Of course he won't autograph your boob."

"What about my panties?"

"With you wearing them?"

"Sure."

"Nah, he'd be way too embarrassed."

"What if I took them off?"

"Might work—but not in ballpoint. He'd need a Magic Marker."

"So when we meet him, what do we say?"

"The Brits all say 'how do you do.' "

"How . . . doo . . . you . . . doo."

"I think it's more 'how d'ya do'—and then you talk about the weather."

The stage door opened and Greg Myers appeared—tailored jacket, smart jeans, open-neck shirt. As he came down the steps to the pavement, he waved and smiled at the girls. I took in the blue-eyed chiseled symmetry, the little-boy grin. He was definitely as hot in real life. As he reached the pavement, the girls surged forward, and surrounded him, squealing "Oh, Greg we love you." They were stroking his hair, kissing him, reaching for his hands.

"Greg . . . Greg, please will you autograph my boob?"

"Will you sign my panties if I take them off?"

"Say something. We just adore your Briddish accent."

"Was the school you went to just like Hogwarts?"

Greg Myers was doing his best to keep smiling as he tried to make his escape. Every time he moved a few paces forward, the girls were all over him again. I could see he was flustered, but he kept smiling. Then he lost it.

"Madam," he yelled. "Will you please control your daughters."

I looked around for the girls' mother, but she was nowhere to be seen.

"They're completely out of control. Will you please take them and deal with them?"

What? He thought they were mine? That I was their mother?

"No . . . you don't understand. They don't belong to me."

By now he had barged his way through the girls, who were chasing him and still begging him to autograph their boobs and panties. "You call yourself a mother? These girls are drunk. Shame on you."

"No, no . . . You don't understand. They're not mine. I was waiting for you because I wanted to ask if you'd be available to open our school summer fair."

He ignored me, barged past and flagged down a taxi.

"I'll take that as a no, then," I called out after him. "And FYI, I'm only thirty-seven."

"He thought you were their mother?" Rosie said. "That is hysterical."

"No, it bloody isn't. It's terrible. OK, tell me honestly, do I look old enough to have eighteen-year-old daughters?"

"Of course you don't. But it was dark. He only got a glimpse of you and he just assumed you were their mother. But if you insist on wearing those long cardigans and Crocs . . ."

"Funee."

"OK," Rosie said. "So where do you go from here?"

"Nowhere. The show finished its run tonight. After Greg got in the taxi, I spoke to those girls. They seemed to know his every move. They said he's flying back to LA and he's not due back here until July thirteenth, when he starts shooting a period drama at Pinewood."

"Brilliant. So ambush him again."

"Two days before the fair? Plus he'll be busy filming. I don't think so."

"So that's that it?"

"Pretty much."

J gave a week's notice at the nonemergency helpline. It should have been a month, but the lovely Joyce in HR said she could see that I needed to get away as soon as possible and promised to pull a few strings.

On my last day, Maureen brought in a homemade coffee-and-walnut cake. She'd covered it in thick coffee-butter icing and piped "Good luck Sarah" on the top. That evening—having demolished the cake—we all went out for a curry. Tony the Fascist ordered egg and chips. We all got a bit pissed and Don put his arm around Maureen, which she didn't seem to mind.

When the waiter came with the bill, I took out my credit card to pay my share, but everybody insisted I put it away. When I protested, they shouted me down. By now it was nearly midnight and I'd told Rosie, who had offered to babysit again, that I'd be home by eleven. "I can watch your TV as easily as I can watch mine," she'd said. "Will's in his basket. It hardly matters where I am." Nevertheless, I'd insisted on ordering her Chinese takeout to say thank you.

"I'm really sorry, guys, but I have to get going. I should have been back an hour ago. I just want to say, thank you for a wonderful evening. Maureen, thank you for the fabulous cake."

I hugged everybody good-bye. They wished me luck with the shop and said how much they were going to miss me.

"And I'm going to miss you lot, too—not to mention all the daft callers." By now there were tears in my eyes. I promised to stay in touch and let them know how the business was going.

As I headed for the door, wiping a tear from my cheek, I heard Maureen say: "She's a lucky girl. What I wouldn't give to be twenty years younger and have the chance of a fresh start." The rest of them agreed.

Maureen was right. Risky as this project was, I was lucky to have been given such a great opportunity. Then, as I walked back to the car, texting Rosie as I went, the reality of what I was about to take on hit me. Until this moment, I'd been full of excitement and derring-do. Suddenly I was petrified. It was all I could do to stop myself racing back to Don, Maureen and the others, announcing that I'd been in the grip of some mental aberration and that I'd finally come to my senses and changed my mind.

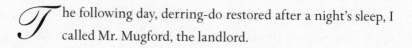

he following day, derring-do restored after a night's sleep, I called Mr. Mugford, the landlord.

"Mugford," he barked down the phone.

I was determined not to let this man intimidate me. I put my case politely but firmly. "Nothing to do with me," Mugford shot back. "Structural repairs are your responsibility."

"Mr. Mugford, you know as well as I do that's not the case. I've been over the lease with my solicitor and you are obliged by law to carry out all necessary building works."

He mumbled something about needing to speak to his own lawyer. "I'll get back to you."

The hell he would.

"With all due respect, Mr. Mugford, you can stall as much as you like, but the bottom line is that the lease is about to be transferred into my name. If you refuse to pay for the necessary repairs, I won't be signing. And I suspect that with the building in its present state, you won't find people queuing up to take it over."

Mugford grunted. "So how much are you looking for?"

Huh. I'd managed to reel him in.

"I won't know the exact figure until I've had a quote for the work."

"Two grand. That's my final offer."

"Three."

"Two-five."

"Done."

Yesterday I'd done a deal with the aunties, today with old man Mugford. I decided that I was getting rather good at this negotiation lark.

Mugford asked for my bank details, which I had to repeat several times because the sour old duffer was hard of hearing. Afterwards I panicked. How could I have been so stupid as to hand over that kind of information to a sleazeball like Mugford? But half an hour later, the money hit my account. When I called to tell Aunty Bimla, she could scarcely believe it.

"Sarah's got the money from Mugford," she called out to Aunty Sylvia.

Sylvia shouted back: "Tell her to make sure his check isn't made of rubber."

"Your Aunty Sylvia says—"

"I know. I heard. Tell her it's fine. He paid by cash transfer."

Aunty Bimla relayed the information.

"I still don't trust him. Shirley used to say that man was so cheap, he wouldn't spend Christmas."

*M*ugford insisted I sign a two-year lease. If he was paying out for repairs, he wanted to make sure it was worth his while. The good news was that I wouldn't be paying rent for the rest of the year, as Aunty Shirley had paid him up front. Where she had found the money, I had no idea. It was only after I'd signed that I told the children I had given up my job at the nonemergency helpline. If I'd let them know while things were still up in the air, Dan would have started fretting. Being that much older than his sister and more aware of our reduced circumstances, he would have worried about how I was going to earn a living. Now that the shop was officially mine, breaking the news seemed much easier. I told them over dinner.

"So do you have a new job?" Dan leaped in, before I'd had the chance to explain about the shop.

"I do and I start on Monday. It's going to be very exciting. I've decided to take over Aunty Shirley's shop. Do you remember the time I took you there? We'd been to Harrods to see Father Christmas and we called in at the shop to see Aunty Shirley . . . and you met the aunties."

The children nodded.

"They were nice and they gave us sweets," Dan said.

"That's right. Well, the plan is for the aunties and me to run the shop together. It needs doing up first, so we won't be reopening it straightaway."

"What does it sell?" Dan said. "I don't remember."

"Ladies' underwear."

"What, knickers?" Dan said, pulling a face. "Yuck."

"Actually it's mainly bras."

"Double yuck. I'm not telling anybody at school."

"One day," Ella said, "when I've got boobies, I'm going to have a bra. I want a pink shiny one with tassels."

"Excuse me?"

"Tara—you know, Cressida's mum—well, she's got one like that. I saw it on her bed. The tassels were black. And she's got these tiny knickers with fur on the front that's shaped like a heart."

Tara? Marc Jacobs' Tara was secretly a cheap slut? Good Lord. Who'd have thought?

"Can I have some like that?" Ella said.

"Some like what?"

"Knickers with a furry heart."

"What? No. Absolutely not."

"Why? They're pretty."

166

Until now, I'd been thanking God that my six-year-old daughter appeared—temporarily at least—to have lost interest in discussing her clitoris. Now this.

"I know, but they're meant for women."

"OK, so maybe I can have a pair when I'm bigger—like when I'm ten."

"No, you can't have a pair when you're ten."

"But why? Ten is practically grown-up. That's so mean."

"Jasper's dad runs a shop," Dan broke in, "and they're rich. Will we be rich?"

"I very much doubt it. And anyway, Jasper's dad doesn't run a shop. He owns a car dealership and he sells Jaguars. That's why they're rich."

"But could we be a bit rich?"

I couldn't help admiring his persistence. "You never know. It's possible, I guess."

Dan cheered up. "OK, then I don't mind you selling knickers and bras."

"Thanks, Dan. I appreciate that."

"So could I have a pair of furry knickers when I'm fourteen? That's really old."

"No, not even when you're fourteen."

"So when can I?"

"I don't know."

"What about when I'm thirty? Thirty's really old. I'll be almost dead."

This conversation was getting tedious.

"OK, you can have some when you're thirty."

"Cool."

With that, Ella jumped down from the table and disappeared. Ten minutes later she was back with her Hello Kitty notebook. Inside she had written: *I promis that Ella can have fury hart nikers when she is therty. Cross my hart and hope to di.*

"Right, go on, you have to sign it."

She handed me a pink glitter coloring pencil and I signed.

O n Saturday afternoon both kids had birthday parties. Once I'd dropped them off, I drove to the shop. I wanted to take another look around and remind myself what needed doing repairwise. I made a few notes and decided that since there was probably all manner of damp and decay lurking behind the old fittings and piles of junk, there was no point in getting estimates for the renovation work until the place had been cleared. I was capable of doing most of it on my own—all I needed was to hire a Dumpster—but the heavy stuff, desks, filing cabinets and whatnot, would be a problem.

When I got home, I Googled house clearance firms. Being Saturday, nobody was answering the phone. Eventually I found a bloke called Dave, who quoted me seventy-five quid.

"Ten o'clock Monday morning suit you?"

I said that it would suit me very well.

After speaking to Dave, I called a Dumpster company and arranged for a "five-yarder" to be delivered. This would take the rest of the junk, the stuff that was light enough for me to lift. I had no idea if a five-yarder was big enough, but the Dumpster guy said that as soon as it was full, all I had to do was call and he would arrange for it to be removed and replace it with a new one.

"So how many parking bays have you reserved outside the shop?" the Dumpster guy asked.

"Parking bays?"

"To park the Dumpster?"

"Ah. Right."

"A five-yarder needs three. I take it you've called Parking Services and got it all sorted."

"Parking Services . . . right. I haven't actually called them as such."

He muttered something about useless bloody women.

"So you're expecting my blokes to deliver a five-yard Dumpster first thing Monday morning and you haven't organized anywhere to park it?"

"I'm really sorry. I wasn't thinking."

The chap let out a sigh. "Call them now. They work until four on a Saturday. It's ten to now. You'll probably just catch them. Then get back to me."

"Brilliant. Thanks. Will do."

As I put down the phone, an image of Steve popped into my head. He was laughing at me and telling me how irresponsible I was.

*T*he good news was that Parking Services were still picking up. The bad news was the nice lady there charged me four hundred quid to park the Dumpster for the week.

Determined to avoid further cock-ups, I spent most of Sunday making a to-do list. This included calling the bank to set up a direct debit to cover the rent, buying heavy-duty refuse sacks to take all the paper rubbish, finding somebody cheap, reliable and competent to do the renovation work and calling my parents in Spain so that they wouldn't think I was neglecting them.

In the evening I cooked the kids' favorite dinner: roast chicken, roast potatoes and honey carrots. I bought strawberries and Ben & Jerry's for dessert. I meant it purely as a treat, but as we sat down, Dan announced that this was "Mum's good luck dinner." It was a sweet, lovely thought that brought tears to my eyes.

"Aw . . . thanks, hon."

"Yeah, good luck, Mum," Ella said. "Tomorrow when I'm in school, I promise to spend the whole day thinking about you. It might be hard in art 'cos I like art, but it'll be easy in humanities 'cos Mrs. Warboys is so bor-ing."

"Thank you, sweetie. All good luck thoughts greatly appreciated."

I didn't mention that despite my excitement about what the future might hold, I was praying that this good luck dinner didn't turn out to be my Last Supper.

O n Monday morning, after dropping the kids at school, I drove home, parked the car and walked the two minutes to the train station. There was no way I was driving into town on a weekday. Half an hour later, I was heading out of Bond Street station.

I picked up a latte and a Danish in Pret. I walked past Selfridges, took a left and headed towards Manchester Square. A couple of turnings later I hit Villiers Mews—its crested and brass-plated shops daring anybody without a title to cross their thresholds. It struck me what an idiot old man Mugford really was. If he'd been prepared to put his hand in his pocket and spend some proper money renovating the shop, he'd be getting five times the amount that I was paying him in rent. On the other hand, if he had decided to do up the shop, I couldn't have afforded five times the rent. I could only be grateful for his stupidity.

I unlocked the door of Shirley Feldman Found Garments and picked up the mail, which was scattered, along with a few dried-up leaves, over the shabby mat. As I sipped my coffee, I wandered around, tearing idly at bits of wallpaper and dislodging lumps of loose plaster. With only a few thousand pounds to keep me going, I needed to get the business up and running fast. For the umpteenth time that morning, I started to panic, but before the churning in my stomach had a proper chance to take hold, there was a tap on the door.

It was Dave, the house clearance guy. He had brought his mate Declan with him. They were a pair of chirpy, salt-of-the-earth types who spent an hour schlepping ancient storage units, filing cabinets and broken desks up from the basement. When he realized that there was no way that the Formica shop counter would go out through the front door in one piece, Dave obliged by going at it with a large hammer and a chisel. Dave and Declan even agreed to take down the shop awning and the sign. I was so grateful that I gave them fifty quid on top of the seventy-five we'd agreed. They seemed more than happy. "I bet they were," I imagined Steve snorting. "They saw you coming. Sarah—don't you get it? You're on a budget. You don't have money to throw away."

Not long after Dave and Declan had gone, the Dumpster arrived and slotted neatly into the three parking bays that I'd booked for the week. I paid off the delivery guys and spent the next couple of hours sifting through junk—in case there was anything worth keeping, which there wasn't—and lugging it up from the basement. There were battered box files spilling over with papers, stray mannequin limbs, roll after roll of stale faded satin, supermarket bags full of crisp, yellowing invoices and receipts. (The aunties had called me to say that they'd put recent ones in the safe.)

Everything was covered in dust, which rubbed off onto my clothes and skin. There were no windows in the basement. The more I gathered up junk, the more I disturbed the dust and the thicker the air became. Soon I was coughing and my eyes started to itch. I made the mistake of rubbing them with my hands, which only made it worse.

The current stock—the ready-to-wear range of bras, panties and corsets—was stored upstairs in the wall of "brown drawers." The overflow was packed into large, flat boxes. These were stacked to head height in one of the fitting rooms. Later in the week, I would load the boxes into the car and take them home. I couldn't risk leaving them to the mercy of drilling builders.

At three thirty I was back at the school gates, dusty, red-eyed and aching. All I wanted to do was get out of my filthy sweats and shirt and soak in a hot tub. I was in no mood for making mummy small talk. I was certainly in no mood for Tara and Charlotte, who were sashaying towards me.

"Sarah. Haven't seen you in ages," Tara cooed. "How *are* you?"

"I'm fine."

"Good. Good. Funnily enough, Charlotte and I were just talking about you. Weren't we, Charlotte?"

"We were."

"And we were wondering if your cousin Rupert has been in touch with Greg Myers." She put "cousin" and "Rupert" in heavy italics. The woman so didn't believe my story. When the truth came out, the summer fair committee would force me to be the target on the wet sponge stall.

"As far as I know, he's e-mailed Greg," I said. "And he's still waiting for a reply."

"Really?" Charlotte said. "Seems odd that he's still waiting, bearing in mind your cousin knows him."

"Oh, you know how busy these people are. Greg probably hasn't even opened Rupert's e-mail yet."

I was petrified that they were going to press the issue, but by now they'd noticed my clothes and were busy looking me up and down.

"Goodness, I had no idea you were into Dumpster diving," Tara said. If the woman were any more of a bitch, she'd have puppies.

Charlotte started to titter.

I glared at her and turned back to Tara.

"Not diving. Loading."

"Sorry, not with you," Tara said.

Noting her friend's confusion, Charlotte's dainty brow formed a supportive furrow.

I explained that I'd spent the day clearing out Aunty Shirley's shop. "She died recently and I inherited it. I'm hoping to have it open again in a few weeks."

"I'm guessing grocer's? Hardware store?"

Another titter from Charlotte.

"Actually it's a lingerie shop—specializing in bespoke bras."

"What? I don't think you'll find there's much call for bespoke bras where you live."

"Who said anything about it being where I live? Actually it's behind Selfridges."

"Really?"

"Yes. Villiers Mews."

"Villiers Mews? Are you sure?"

"Absolutely positive."

"Goodness. In that case, we might have to pay you a visit—don't you agree, Charlotte?"

"I do."

"OK—here's the thing," I said, looking straight at Tara. "Whereas I can see my little atelier being up Charlotte's street, I think you might be just a tad disappointed."

"Oh? Why's that?"

"Well . . . I'm not planning on doing a line of thongs with furry hearts."

I watched Tara's face turn the color of a furry heart. Then I caught sight of Dan and Ella running towards me.

"Sorry," I said, smiling at the two women. "I have to go."

"Omigod," Charlotte shrieked at Tara, apparently unaware that I was still within earshot. "I had no idea you wore tarty underwear for Hugo. But how on earth does *she* know?"

"One of her kids must have come into my bedroom and found it. Nasty snooping brats."

"So . . . come on . . . what else does Hugo like you in? Crotchless panties? Rubber? I bet you've got handcuffs and a whip."

"As it happens, I do. . . . But who said anything about them being for Hugo?"

"No!"

There was no point asking the mothers at school to recommend builders, because they all used people who cost the earth. Employing workmen from Kensington and Chelsea—gentlemen builders who'd quit working in the City for shorter hours and less stress—was just another way of outposhing one another. Smart vans with their understated lowercase lettering constantly dotted the neighborhood—especially in spring. Their arrival heralded the end of winter as surely as the cherry blossoms.

When Mike and I had been about to start renovating the old house, I'd inadvertently called several gentlemen builders to give me estimates. Umpteen Oscars and Benedicts had arrived in their striped rugby shirts with the collars turned up, their wrists covered in ethnic string-and-bead Shambhala bracelets, and demanded two grand just to paint and paper the boxroom. I was in no doubt that they would do an excellent job—I simply wasn't prepared to part with an arm, a leg and several bits of offal for the privilege. In those days I may not have been good with money, but I wasn't reckless. I told them I would let them know and started shopping around. I ended up hiring a small local firm. Although they didn't have pictures of Gwyneth Paltrow's loft extension in their glossy brochure— in fact they didn't even have a glossy brochure—they did an excellent job and charged a fraction of what the Oscars and Benedicts had wanted.

Battersby and Son may not have been fashionable, but even so, I got a kick having builders' vans parked on the drive for months. It gave me a sense of belonging, that I had a place in the neighborhood. The old me. I winced.

I must have spent an hour Googling builders and trawling through the customer reviews. In the end I made appointments with six, who appeared to be cheap and reliable.

They came with their notepads and bits of chewed pencil. Some had gone home first and changed into clean pressed shirts; others arrived in paint-spattered tees and jeans. They pulled bits of plaster off the wall, stuck the ends of their screwdrivers into architraves, prodded at damp patches. Heads were shaken. Air was sucked in between teeth. There was talk of new dampproof courses and ceilings, which sounded expensive. They all agreed that the place was rotten, subsiding, terminal. Had it been human, they would have instructed it to go away and get its affairs in order.

A few days later the estimates began dropping into my in-box. There wasn't one that came in below twelve grand. It struck me that they'd all bumped up their quotes because they reckoned that running a business behind Selfridges meant I was probably good for it.

By now I'd paid the aunties three thousand pounds, which left me with six or so. Mugford's two-and-a-half grand bumped it back up to more than eight—my total for the refurb and living expenses. I deleted the estimates.

I found Kandoo Building and Decorating on the notice board in my local newsagent's window. It was crammed with "situations wanted" postcards—mainly foreign au pairs and cleaners looking for work. Among them were a few landscape gardeners and carpenters offering their services. There appeared to be one builder, but his postcard was written in smudged pencil and full of spelling mistakes. I was about to give up when a printed card on the bottom row caught my eye: *Kandoo Building and Decorating—also basic plumbing and electrics. I am experienced, honest, hardworking. Reasonable rates. Excellent references.*

The moment I got home, I called the number.

"Kandoo. Hugh Fanshaw speaking." Posh name. Ditto the accent. Flashy gentleman builder. I could see little point in pursuing this conversation. Strange, though, that he was advertising in the newsagent's window. Maybe the recession was hitting high-end tradesmen harder than I'd thought. Even so, his prices would still be way out of my league.

Since I was too polite to put the phone down on Hugh Fanshaw, I had no option other than to describe the parlous state of the shop and gave him a rough outline of the work I thought was needed.

"The thing is, I'm on a very tight budget," I said. "I really don't have tens of thousands to spend."

Bound to put him off, I thought.

"And I'm a widow," I blurted. Great. Now he'd assume I'd just come into hundreds of thousands in life insurance.

"I'm sorry to hear that. Can't be easy. OK, why don't I come and take a look and we can take it from there?"

"Fine, but as I say, my funds are quite limited."

"Not to worry. These days everybody's being forced to cut corners."

I didn't buy his sympathy line. He was simply trying to snare me, but hell, I'd gone this far. What was the harm in letting him give me a quote? He could use all the strong-arm tactics he liked, but he couldn't make me spend money I didn't have. And there was always the chance—however slim—that his estimate might be reasonable. I gave him the address and we agreed that he would stop by around ten the following morning.

I expected a chinless toff in the regulation rugby shirt and Shambhala bracelets. Not only did Hugh Fanshaw turn out to have a rather well-defined chin, but he arrived wearing baggy cargo shorts—a spanner sticking out of one of the pockets—a discolored, misshapen tee and beaten-up Cat boots. Bog-standard builders' wear. Clearly I was out of touch. These days gentlemen builders were adopting a man-of-the-people image.

"Hi. I'm Hugh. Pleased to meet you." I was struck by his voice. It wasn't that posh actually—more BBC news anchor. He held out his hand. It was spattered in green paint.

"Sarah."

"Excuse the paint," he said as we shook hands. "I've run out of white spirit. In my defense, it is Chadwick and Dalton."

"Is that good?"

"The best."

I couldn't help laughing.

"Sorry, too, if I'm late." If he was, it was only by a minute or two. "I had a nightmare parking. In the end I found a loading bay, which should give me twenty minutes or so."

Two apologies in less than a minute. He was clearly trying to win me over with the self-deprecating charm that was so typical of the upper classes.

"Right, why don't I give you the tour?" I had no intention of engaging in unnecessary banter. The sooner he was out of here, the sooner I could get back to work. Today I was aiming to pack up all the stock and load it into my car.

I showed him round. "As I said on the phone, I don't have much cash. All I'm looking for is a cheap flash-up job."

"Piece of cake," he said when we'd finished.

"Really? Nobody else has said that."

"Look, I'm not going to lie to you . . . ," he said, rubbing his hand over the dark, well-tended stubble on his perfectly defined chin. OK . . . wait for it. Now for the hard sell.

"In an ideal world, you'd strip the place back to the brickwork, put in new internal walls and ceilings and pretty much start again, but I think I can patch it up for you. Should see you all right for a year or two."

"Seriously?"

"Can't see why not."

"OK, but what's it going to cost me? I need a new loo and hand basin—plus a sink and a couple of cupboards in the kitchen area."

"Well, I can't say off the top of my head. I need to go away and work out the figures. . . ."

Of course he did.

"But as far as the loo and kitchen area go, I've got a mate who's a plumbers' merchant. He's always getting in units that are a bit chipped or damaged. I'm sure he'll give you a deal."

"Really?" I hadn't been expecting that. Experience had taught me that gentlemen builders weren't in the business of offering customers cheap deals. I thought I had the cut of Hugh Fanshaw's jib. Now I wasn't so sure. "That would be great," I said. "Maybe you could give him a call?"

"Will do."

I noticed he was looking down at the worn carpet.

"So," he said, "what are you planning to do with the floor?"

"I don't know. Get new carpet, I suppose."

"You'll need heavy-duty commercial quality. That'll cost you."

He bent down and lifted a corner of the old broadloom. "Hello . . . Have you seen what's under here?"

"Uh-uh."

"Parquet flooring. And it looks like it's in pretty good shape."

I knelt down to take a look. He wasn't wrong. "Wow. I wonder if the whole floor is in the same condition."

"If it is, I'd be more than happy to sand and varnish it. Save you a fortune."

"That would be brilliant." We both got up. I was starting to change my opinion of Hugh Fanshaw.

"Don't suppose you're any good at carpentry, are you? I'm in need of a shop counter. The old one was in such a bad way, I had to get rid of it."

"Woodwork's not really my forte," he said, "but I tell you what would look great in here, an antique shop counter. Something heavy and Victorian, to match the mahogany shelves. Oh, and what about one of those ancient silver cash registers?"

I laughed. "You read my mind, but antiques are way beyond my budget."

"You should try looking around junk shops. I've picked up loads of stuff: original film posters, a nineteenth-century phrenology head, the James Bond Aston Martin DB5—the one from *Goldfinger*—with the original suitcases in the trunk."

"Hang on—you found James Bond's Aston Martin in a junk shop?"

He started grinning. "No. I found the Corgi model."

"The model. Of course . . ." He must think I'm bonkers or dumb. "I used to love wandering around junk shops and flea markets," I said in an effort to convince him that I hadn't lost the plot. "These days I don't have the time."

My mind went back to when I was decorating the old house and the kick I used to get out of combing Conran for a pair of antlers or a tacky Murano glass clown.

"Maybe take a look online," he said.

"You're right. I should."

He looked at his watch. "Right—I need to get back to the van before I get a ticket. I'll e-mail you with a quote in a couple of days."

I thanked him for coming and we said our good-byes. With that, Hugh Fanshaw headed to the door.

*T*hree days later he e-mailed me a quote for seven thousand pounds. It was well below all the other estimates, but still beyond my budget. It didn't help that by now I'd been onto his Web site and checked out his references. Everybody I spoke to sang his praises. He was honest, was hardworking and did a good job. One woman—who lived round the corner from the newsagent's where he'd placed his ad—was so full of praise that she insisted I come round and see her newly decorated flat. I took one look at her perfectly hung, lump-free wallpaper, her immaculate grouting, and agreed that Hugh Fanshaw's work was excellent. I was loath to turn him down.

"Well, if you ask me," Rosie said after I'd explained my predicament, "I still think your first instinct was right. He's just another one of those flash toffs who thinks he can charge the earth."

"To be honest, I don't think he is charging the earth. You haven't seen what needs doing."

It was a sunny Sunday afternoon—the weather had just started to warm up—and Rosie and I were sitting on kitchen chairs, taking tea on my strip of crazy paving that passed for a patio while Will napped in his basket and my children played upstairs.

"You sure you haven't simply been taken in by his public school charm?"

"Maybe, but by the time he left, I'd kind of changed my mind about him. He seemed really genuine. He even said he could get me a good deal on a loo and a sink . . . and he likes looking round junk shops."

"Wait. You're telling me he seems genuine because he likes looking round junk shops?"

"You had to be there. We sort of connected."

"Of course you did." She clearly thought I was a lost cause. "So what are you going to do?"

"What can I do? I don't have time to shop around for more quotes. Every day the shop is shut, I'm losing money. I'll just have to find the cash. Maybe I could find a bar job a couple of nights a week."

"Are you crazy?" Rosie said. "First you'll exhaust yourself and second, everything you earn will go to child care."

I took the point.

We sipped our tea in silence. "OK . . . hang on . . . I've got it,"
Rosie said. "I know how you can get his bill down."

"How?"

"Well . . . I'm betting it's his labor costs that are hiking up the bill.
What if you helped with the work?"

"What? Don't be daft. I don't know a thing about plumbing or
plastering."

"I'm not suggesting you help with the major stuff—just the painting and decorating. Anybody can work sandpaper and a paint roller."

"I guess. . . ."

"In fact, even better—we could make it a group effort. I could
help and you could even ask those aunties of yours. I know they're
getting on, but they might be up for it, and we'd have fun. If we need
to work on the weekend, my sister could take your kids and Will. She
adores children—always got a houseful."

Just then Rosie's cell started ringing. "Crap. Do men really need
to jerk off on a Sunday? It's the Sabbath. You'd think that on the
Lord's Day their sexual urges wouldn't have to take priority."

"Yeah . . . surely even the penis needs a day of rest."

I loved our banter, the way we made each other laugh. I'd felt a
connection with Rosie from the get-go, but over weeks that was becoming much stronger. I was in no doubt that I'd found a new best
friend. "Stop moaning and answer the phone," I said. "You seem to
forget that this job pays the bills."

"I know. I know. I'd better take it inside. Don't want the neighbors earwigging."

Finally, she hit "connect." I picked up the Moses basket and followed her into the kitchen.

"Harry . . . how are you? How are things in the corridors of Whitehall?"

I went upstairs to check on Dan and Ella. They were absorbed in a game of Connect 4 and shooed me away. As I left, I closed the bedroom door behind me. I wanted to be certain they could hear nothing from the kitchen.

I decided that while everybody was occupied, I might as well give Hugh Fanshaw a call and put Rosie's plan to him. Still worried that the kids might come downstairs and barge into the kitchen, I thought it best to call him from the hall.

"Hugh—Sarah Green here . . . Look, thanks for sending the quote, but the thing is . . ."

"It's more than you can afford."

"It is. Five grand is my absolute limit."

"Jeez . . . I couldn't do it for that. That would mean slashing my labor costs and I simply can't afford it. I'm really sorry."

"No, I get that. Please don't apologize. The thing is, I've had an idea—or at least a friend of mine has. . . ."

I explained.

He didn't hesitate. "Brilliant. Having help with the painting would shave off a week or more."

"So you could do it for the five grand?"

"Absolutely. I've got another job lined up after yours, and the sooner I can start, the better."

We agreed that he would get going on the structural work in a couple of days. As soon as he reached the decoration stage, Rosie and I—and the aunties if they were up for it—would join him.

When I came off the phone, Rosie was still pleasuring Harry, her

Whitehall mandarin. I was about to check on the children again when the doorbell rang. It was Betty from across the street.

"Hello Sarah, dear. Sorry to disturb you on a Sunday, but I was just wondering if you could spare a couple of tea bags. I've run out and I'm not sure my legs are up to a walk to the shops."

"Of course. I'll fetch you some."

"I don't suppose you heard the goings-on at number forty again last night. Music blaring until five in the morning. I didn't get a wink. The guy next door to me was there. Between you and me I think he's carrying on with her."

"What, the woman at number forty?"

"Yes. Apparently she's got a boyfriend as well. Heaven only knows what they get up to. Some kind of *ménage à trois* if you ask me. It's not right—not when there are kiddies."

I had to agree that it wasn't.

It was rude of me not to invite Betty in, but I couldn't risk her hearing Rosie in full sexual rapture. If Betty discovered what Rosie did for a living, the news would be around the neighborhood before you could say "phone sex."

"You don't mind if I come in, do you? I haven't seen the inside of this house since the last people did it up."

"What? Er . . . no, of course not. Come in."

The next moment she was standing on the hall mat. "Rosie still here? I just happened to be at the window dusting the ledge when I noticed you letting her in."

If there were ever a burglary in this street, the perp would stand no chance.

"Actually, she is."

"Been having a nice cup of tea and a bit of a gossip, have you?"

I couldn't help feeling sorry for Betty. For all her faults, she was a sad, lonely old soul who just wanted some company. On the other hand I simply couldn't let her any farther into the house.

"Hasn't the weather been glorious today?" I said, still standing my ground. "Wonderful after all that rain we've been having . . ."

"So, have you been sitting in the garden, Betty?"

"Not really. The heat doesn't agree with me. Brings me out in hives."

"I'm taking off my panties now. . . ."

Please. Make it stop.

Even though Betty's hearing wasn't great, I knew that she would eventually cotton on. I had to get her out.

"Betty, have I shown you my new lavender plant in the front garden?"

"Actually I noticed it as I came up the path. Nice, but not much scent."

I tried to think of another excuse to get her out the door, but by now my brain had frozen in a panic.

That was when the shrieks started—followed by the thuds. I turned around to see Ella lying at the foot of the stairs, her entire body—including her face—swaddled in several layers of Bubble Wrap. She looked like some weird modernist mummy. By now her brother was standing next to her and they were both laughing hysterically—Ella through a sizable hole in the Bubble Wrap.

"Again. Again," Ella cried.

"What the . . . ? Good God. Ella, are you all right?"

"Now it's my turn," Dan said to his sister.

"What? No! It's nobody's turn. What on earth do you think you're doing?"

"Falling down the stairs," Ella said. "But it's OK. Dan wrapped me in this special stuff so that I wouldn't break my bones. Can Dan have his turn now?"

"No, he absolutely can't."

"Why not?" Dan said.

"Because it's dangerous."

"Not if I wrap myself up," he pleaded.

"I've said no and I mean no."

"Your mum's right," Betty said. "You can't be sure you won't break something. When I was a little girl, my brother and I used to slide down the banisters. Then one day I fell off and broke my arm. I was in plaster for six weeks."

"Cool. Did everybody sign their names on the cast?"

"Dan, stop it. For your information, breaking your arm isn't remotely cool."

"That it isn't," Betty said. "I remember it being very painful and itchy. Especially at night when I tried to sleep."

While I got down on my knees and started to unwrap a protesting Ella, Betty reached into her cardigan pocket and produced two KitKats. She handed one to each child. I wasn't happy about her rewarding my children's reckless behavior, but I didn't have the heart to stop her.

As they thanked her and tore into the foil, I listened for sounds coming from the kitchen. Nothing. Rosie and Harry were done. Rosie had been saved by all the commotion.

"Now off you go—back to your room," I said to the kids. "I'll be up to talk to you about this later."

As they trudged upstairs, Dan turned to glare at me. He was clearly furious with me for refusing to let him have a go at rolling down the stairs.

Betty turned to me. "You're lucky," she said.

"In what way?"

"The Lord may have taken your husband, but he left you with a house that's filled with children's laughter. Be thankful for that. One day they'll leave home. If you're anything like me, you could be a long time on your own."

"I know, Betty. You're right. Come on, I'll find you those tea bags. Tell you what—why don't you stay and have a cuppa?"

"Oh, that would be lovely. I'd like that."

*H*ugh said he could start work on the shop straightaway. Meanwhile I went in search of an antique shop counter. Even the one or two I came across in junk shops were way out of my price range. *Affordable* and *antique* seemed like a contradiction in terms. Then I found one online. It was a Victorian, seven-foot-long haberdasher's counter—oak with wooden shelves and glass panels at the front. It would have been unaffordable had it not been covered in pea green gloss paint. The dealer said I could have it for three hundred pounds. We agreed on two twenty-five, so long as I came to his shop in Surrey and picked it up. I hired a van. Another fifty quid.

The dealer—an old hippie called Ken—helped me load the counter, which came apart and divided into three just about manageable sections. When I got back, Rosie was waiting to give me a hand.

We lugged the parts into the house and leaned them against the living room wall.

Rosie chipped off some of the green paint with her nail. "Wow, have you seen how many layers you've got here? I can see blue and white under the green. It's a magnificent beast, but I reckon you'll have your work cut out trying to restore it."

That night I ordered a couple of books on restoring antique furniture.

When most of the paint came straight off with paint stripper, I decided that Rosie had got it wrong. This was going to be easy. That was before I noticed that the paint stripper hadn't worked at all well on the areas of the counter that were carved. And there were a lot of heavily carved areas—particularly along the base. I set to work with wire wool and a putty knife, but getting into all the crevices took forever. In the end it took five days to strip off all the paint. Then came the sanding. The crevice issue again. Another three days. By the time I got to the best bit—the staining and varnishing—my fingers were stiff and the skin on my hands was raw and cracked. I'd tried wearing rubber gloves, but the thickness of the rubber got in the way and meant I had less control over the sandpaper.

When I showed Rosie the fully restored counter, she said it looked magnificent.

"What a transformation. It looks so elegant and grand."

"Oh, come on. It still looks pretty beaten up."

"But that's part of its charm. You said you were going for hipster chic."

"But the stain's all patchy. And what about the varnish? Look how thick and streaky it is. I know I should have sanded it down

189

between coats, but in the end I got so tired and bored that I couldn't be bothered."

Rosie told me to stop obsessing and insisted the counter was going to look just the ticket and that nobody would notice.

I wasn't convinced.

"Hon, you OK? You seem to have got yourself really worked up about this counter. It's not like you. Is there something else going on?"

I let out a long breath. "I guess I'm just worried about money and getting the shop ready."

"Nothing else?"

"Well, I suppose this Greg Myers thing is still at the back of my mind. I feel so bad about leaving Imogen hanging on like this, not knowing the truth. She's a lovely woman. It's not fair to her. I've got to come clean."

"OK, but if you ask me, now isn't the right time. You're battling against the clock to get the business up and running, you're worried about money and you've got the kids to think about. You've got too much on your plate. Imogen can wait another week or so. Send her an e-mail to say you're still chasing Greg Myers. Then when the shop's open and everything's calmed down a bit, pop round and see her."

"I dunno. Putting it off feels mean and cowardly. I really should bite the bullet."

"OK, go ahead, but do you really think you can cope with the fallout from that along with everything else you've got going on?"

I thought for a few moments. If I confessed to Imogen, she would be sad and disappointed, but she wasn't the type to get angry. "Chin up, chest out and carry on" was her motto. Tara and Charlotte were the important issue. I could only guess at the humiliations they would unleash.

"OK. Maybe you're right," I said. "I'll e-mail Imogen and hold off telling her the truth for a bit longer."

The following day Rosie and I loaded the counter into another hired van and I drove it to the shop. This time it was Hugh who helped with the lifting.

"Wow," he said when we'd reassembled and positioned it. "You've done a really good restoration job."

I was forced to admit that the counter did look rather magnificent against the parquet floor and the "brown drawers." But however good my restoration job had been, it didn't compare with what Hugh had achieved in ten days. The man was certainly no slacker. He'd replastered the walls and ceilings, stripped and varnished the parquet floor. In the basement there were new spotlights, kitchen units and a loo. Painting the floorboards in the basement was pretty much the last job. Then we could start decorating.

"All it needs now," Hugh said, regarding the counter, "is that antique cash register. I actually took a look on eBay for you."

"You did? That's so thoughtful. . . . So go on—how much?"

"I found a couple in the US. They were both around a thousand dollars."

"I suppose I could always try an offer of twenty-five quid."

"Don't worry. You won't always be this hard up."

"I wish I had your faith," I said, offering him a weak smile. "By the way, I just want to say again how amazing the place looks and how much I appreciate the effort you've put in. You've worked like a demon."

"Protestant work ethic," he said. "My parents thought shirking was the eighth deadly sin."

"Wow, sounds jolly."

"It was." He grinned.

"Shame you weren't born Jewish. We have a nap ethic. You work; you take a nap. You eat; you take a nap. You smite the Philistines; you take a huge nap. Then you eat again . . . colossal amounts of fried food that killed more Jews than Hitler. And so it goes. . . . You nap, you eat, you die."

Hugh Fanshaw laughed. I couldn't help thinking how cute he looked.

"Well, I'd better get back to work," he said eventually. "That basement floor isn't going to paint itself."

What I wanted to say was: "Sod the floor. Let's go over the road and get a coffee and swap notes about our crazy parents."

"I'm sorry, I've been holding you up," I said. "The kids finish school at half past three. I'd better get a move on, too."

Chapter 9

"*I*'m pretty sure Viagra's kosher," Aunty Sylvia said in answer to Aunty Bimla's inquiry. She carried on steering her paint roller back and forth along the tray of Jasmine White emulsion. "Except maybe at Passover when nothing's meant to rise."

The aunties hooted. So did Rosie and I. It wasn't just the joke the pair of us was laughing at. It was more the sight of two respectable ladies of a certain age, one of whom was dressed in a *salwar kameez*, behaving like a couple of six-year-olds reveling in a poo joke.

It was Saturday, our first painting and decorating day. Rosie, the aunties and I were getting on with our assigned jobs, while Hugh, Dan and Ella were out doing a tea and coffee run. All week I'd been trying to persuade the kids to spend the day with Will at Rosie's sister's place, but they'd refused point-blank.

"No way," Dan declared. "We don't want to be with a boring baby. Painting walls will be fun. We promise we'll be good—don't we, Ella?"

"Yep. Cross my heart and hope to die."

They wanted to feel part of the action. I couldn't say no.

The aunties, who by now had finished the order for *Così fan tutte*, had been equally enthusiastic about helping. When I suggested that at their age they might find the work a bit too much, they were most offended. "I'll take it easy when I'm dead," Aunty Sylvia informed me.

Grateful as I was that they wanted to help, I was still concerned. Aunty Bimla admitted she'd never held a paintbrush in her life. Aunty Sylvia said that the closest she'd ever come to decorating was painting her nails. "But how hard can it be?"

"Oh, I nearly forgot," Aunty Sylvia was saying now. "Great news. Roxanne didn't get the part in the haunted refrigerator film."

Aunty Bimla asked her why not getting the part was such great news.

"Because she's landed a much bigger part in something else." Aunty Sylvia began rolling paint over a section of newly plastered wall. "She's so excited. It's a children's film. It's all about this centipede. And each section of the centipede is a person."

"Oh, that is so cute," Aunty Bimla cooed.

"The centipede is good, but apparently there's this very naughty doctor who wants to hurt it."

"But why on earth would anybody want to hurt a centipede?" Aunty Bimla said.

Rosie, who was kneeling beside me, helping to sandpaper a length of skirting board, stopped sanding and gave me a nudge.

"Are you thinking what I'm thinking?" she whispered.

"I dunno. What are you thinking?"

"That this so isn't a kids' film."

"I'm not with you. Why wouldn't it be?"

"God, Sarah—you really need to get out more. . . . So, Aunty Sylvia . . . what's this movie called?"

"*Human Centipede 4.* Apparently it's just like the *Teletubbies*."

"Huh. Is that right?" Rosie dug me in the ribs. "Are you with me now?"

"Ouch. Yes. Thank you. I get it."

"Tell you what," Aunty Sylvia went on. "As soon as it comes out on DVD, you should get it for William. By then he'll be just the right age to appreciate it."

"I'll bear that in mind," Rosie said.

"Bloody hell," I whispered to Rosie, "the poor woman is going to be mortified when she finds out. How could Roxanne be so stupid? If she wanted her mother to think it was a kids' film, why go and tell her the actual title? Take it from me, this isn't going to have a happy ending."

"And Sanjeev is also doing exceedingly well, too," Aunty Bimla piped up. "His big business deal has gone through and he is now the proud owner of five thousand acres of land in Paraguay. He plans to start building holiday villas."

"And he's seen this land?" I said, quicker on the uptake this time.

"Only photographs, but it looks most picturesque. It's right by the sea."

"Wow. Sounds lovely." I turned back to Rosie and whispered, "That nephew of hers is such a schmuck."

"Why?"

"Duh. Paraguay's landlocked. He's been conned. God knows how much money he's lost."

"Mazel tov," Aunty Sylvia said. "He's going to be a rich man, that nephew of yours."

"This is what I am thinking, so when Sanjeev asked me if I would like to invest some of my own money, I didn't hesitate. In business, the early bird catches the worm. You have to strike while the iron is hot. Sarah would agree with me on that, wouldn't you, Sarah?"

"So how much did you invest?" I said, evading her question.

"Ten thousand. Sanjeev says I will triple my money by the end of the year. He says it's a surefire slam dunk."

"Shit," Rosie muttered.

I felt sick.

Just then Hugh walked in with Dan and Ella. Hugh was holding the cardboard drinks tray while each child clutched a carton of juice and a sticky bun. "OK, elevenses, everybody. Come and get it." Hugh put the tray down on the pasting table.

We'd been working since half past eight. Nobody needed telling twice. A moment later we were all gathered around the table. While Aunty Bimla passed around chunks of carrot halva, Aunty Sylvia tempted us with her homemade honey cake. I'd made it clear to Rosie and Hugh that in order to avert hard feelings, they should accept whatever foodstuffs the aunties offered them and rave about them in equal measure.

"Fabulous honey cake," Hugh announced. "And this halva—wow—just melts in the mouth."

"Doesn't it?" Rosie said. "They're both to die for."

"Have some more," the aunties cried in unison.

Rosie and Hugh protested that they were full. Like that was going to put the aunties off.

"But sugar is good for your breast milk," Aunty Bimla informed Rosie.

"Come on, Hugh, another piece won't hurt you," Aunty Sylvia said. "You're skin and bone. You could do with fattening up."

"And you're still growing," Aunty Bimla added.

Hugh grinned. "I'm thirty-eight. I think I probably stopped growing a while ago."

"Well, for your information," Aunty Bimla said, "that's not entirely true. I read in the *Reader's Digest* that a person's nose and ears continue to grow throughout their life."

Clearly realizing there was no escape, Hugh helped himself to more halva and honey cake. Rosie did the same. I followed their example. Normally the aunties would have tried to force-feed Dan and Ella, too, but they were still busy chomping their way through their sticky buns.

"So, Hugh," Aunty Bimla said, "you're thirty-eight. You're handsome. You run your own business. . . . Why aren't you married?"

"Don't embarrass the boy," Aunty Sylvia hissed. "For all you know he might be gay . . . or pansexual. That's a thing now apparently."

I shot Hugh an apologetic look, but he was smiling. "Actually I'm not gay or pansexual."

"I knew you weren't," Aunty Bimla said. "You have such broad, masculine shoulders. So do you have a young lady?"

"Not at the moment."

"Ree-ally," the aunties cried, looking at me.

They could have looked at Rosie. By now they knew all about Simon and how he'd walked out on her, but they'd known me all my life, so matchmaking-wise, I was top of their to-do list.

"You know, Hugh," Aunty Bimla said, "Sylvia and I are most highly impressed by the work you have done. What a transformation. It is nothing short of a miracle."

"She's right," Sylvia said. "Look at this beautiful floor. I had no idea there was parquet under that tatty old carpet. And what about the antique counter? My father had one just like it in his tailor's shop."

"And the toilet. You're forgetting the toilet."

Aunty Bimla hadn't stopped marveling at the new loo. It had one of those electronic flush buttons that was activated by the slightest touch. Aunty Sylvia said she wasn't sure about the color—turquoise. I explained that the color was the reason I'd gotten it half price.

Like everybody else I was thrilled and amazed by what Hugh had done to the interior, but my pride and joy was the new sign that hung outside. I'd splurged and hired a signwriter, who'd removed SHIRLEY FELDMAN FOUND GARMENTS and put up a new sign. I hadn't been able to make up my mind whether to go for minimalist lowercase lettering or something swirly and over the top. Hugh reminded me that since I'd just bought four rolls of knockoff French wallpaper depicting bucolic scenes from le Petit Trianon, maybe minimalist lettering wouldn't be in keeping. I agreed. Ostentation was required. Gold swirls and curlicues were so much more Marie Antoinette.

The sign read: SARAH GREEN LINGERIE. The aunties and Rosie had persuaded me to add "UK" in brackets to encourage me to think big. The day it went up, I took a photograph and sent it to Mum and Dad, who called back straightaway to say how proud of me they were and that they'd forwarded it to all the family.

"And you're looking after yourself?" Mum said. "You're eating properly?"

"Yes, I'm looking after myself. Yes, I'm eating."

"And what about the children?"

"They're eating, too."

"And money?"

"I'm fine for money."

"You sure? Sarah, if you need money, you mustn't hesitate to ask. I can't bear to think of you and the children suffering."

"Mum, I promise you we're not suffering. We're absolutely fine. I'd tell you if we weren't. . . . So how are things in Marbella?"

The sun was glorious. Uncle Lou's flat was fabulous—although there had been a significant grease buildup on top of the cooker hood. The complex had not one but two pools. On the downside, it was next to a main road, but you couldn't have everything. All in all they were having a great time and, despite the main road, Mum was getting lots of rest.

I'd been worried that today was going to turn into chaos. The children were my main concern. Once they got bored with painting—which would take about fifteen minutes, if that—they would start charging around the place demanding to be entertained.

As well as fretting about the children, I'd been worried about Hugh and Rosie. I was convinced that they wouldn't hit it off. By now I didn't have a single doubt about Hugh's integrity, but Rosie was still suspicious.

"I'm just worried that when he presents you with his bill, it's going to be full of hidden extras."

On top of that, the aunties' lack of decorating skills still bothered me. I was in no doubt that they would do their best, but neither of them had any experience. I imagined their streaky, patchy paintwork and how it would make more work for Hugh instead of less.

I shouldn't have worried.

Both aunties proved to be remarkably proficient with a paint roller. Earlier this morning, Aunty Bimla had caught me watching her. "Don't worry, poppet, it isn't rocket science, you know." She stood back so that I could get a look at her handiwork as well as Aunty Sylvia's. "We are cutting the mustard, wouldn't you say?"

"Definitely. Not that I ever doubted you."

"Of course not," Aunty Sylvia said, grinning.

I felt like an idiot. These women were two of the most talented seamstresses in the country. Manual dexterity was in their genes. As if they wouldn't be able to handle a paint roller.

As I predicted, the children did get bored. To their credit they lasted over an hour helping Rosie and me sandpaper the skirting board, but by about ten o'clock they'd had enough. It was Hugh who suggested I give them a break and take them for a quick wander around Selfridges' toy department. "Later on they can come with me when I do the tea and coffee run. Do you guys like sticky buns?"

It went without saying that the children strongly approved of both ideas. Under normal circumstances I would have shot down the Selfridges suggestion. Taking children to look around a toy department when neither they nor their mother had any money wasn't my idea of fun. But since Dan and Ella were each in possession of a twenty-pound note—going-away money from their grandparents—Selfridges seemed like a plan.

We returned—Dan with a robotic crab, Ella with a Fairy Dough Cookie Kit . . . *the dough turns magically pink*—to find that Hugh had sketched a huge seascape across one as yet unpainted wall. The idea was that the kids could color it in and add boats and sea creatures, using the sample paint colors that Hugh just happened to have in his van.

The moment they saw it, Dan and Ella began jumping with excitement. They couldn't wait to get started.

"Hugh, thank you. This is really brilliant. It's so going to keep them occupied. . . . Dan, Ella, what do you say?"

"Thankyou-thankyou-thankyou."

"Can we start now?"

"Hugh, please, please open the paint?"

Hugh crouched down in front of them. "OK, if you could just calm down for a moment, there's one thing you have to understand. I know that your picture is going to be fantastic, but eventually we will have to paint over it."

"That's not fair," Ella said, arms folded—offended that anybody would want to paint over her artwork.

"But why can't you keep it?" Dan said. "It could be a murial . . . you know, like the Romans had."

"I'm not sure," Hugh said, "that a seascape would be quite right for this sort of shop."

"Yeah, dummy," Ella shot back, seizing the opportunity to get one over her older brother, even if it meant relinquishing her own case. "It sells knickers. You'd have to have a knicker murial."

Time for me to butt in. "Ella, don't speak to Dan like that. He was making a perfectly reasonable suggestion."

She mumbled her apology. Normally she would have argued rather than apologize, but the last thing she wanted was me confiscating her Fairy Dough Cookie Kit.

"I know what we'll do," Hugh said, clearly anxious for this not to turn into a full-scale bickering match. "Before we paint over the wall, we'll take some photographs of your art and you can take them to school. How does that sound?"

They both shrugged, aware that they had no choice.

"Right," Aunty Bimla was saying now, "break over. Time to get back to work. A rolling stone gathers no moss." She opened a plastic trash bag and began collecting cups. When she headed downstairs to the kitchen, I followed her.

"Aunty Bimla. Can I have a word?"

"Of course, poppet," she said, shoving the plastic bag into the trash can. "What is it?"

"It's just that I'm a bit worried about all this money you've given Sanjeev. Ten thousand pounds is a great deal of money. Don't take this the wrong way, but you're not getting any younger. It's money you're going to need."

Aunty Bimla laughed. "You worry too much, poppet," she said, stroking my arm. "Sanjeev is a bright boy. Very switched on. He knows you have to speculate to accumulate."

"I know but . . ."

"No buts. It's all going to turn out fine. Better than fine. Just you wait and see."

She shooed me back upstairs.

"Don't suppose any of you are good at hanging wallpaper?" Hugh was saying. "I could do with an extra pair of hands."

"I wallpapered Will's nursery," Rosie said. "I think I did an OK job of it."

"That works for me," Hugh said.

The one thing that still worried me was Rosie and Hugh not getting along. When I introduced them, Rosie had been polite, but until now she'd kept her distance. I was surprised at her volunteering to help Hugh.

"Mum, Mum," Dan cried, interrupting my thoughts. "Before you go back to sandpapering, you have to come and see our murial."

I went over to their wall, followed by the aunties.

"Wow, that is awesome," I said, taking in the pea green man-eating sharks and giant, matte black beady-eyed squid.

Aunty Bimla declared it to be "truly magnificent." Aunty Sylvia said she wouldn't fancy meeting Mr. Squid on a dark night.

I knelt down beside the skirting board and got back to work. Every so often I glanced at Rosie and Hugh. I was waiting for Rosie to launch an attack, but none came.

As they stood cutting and pasting wallpaper, they appeared to be getting along fine. More than fine, in fact. They were chatting away like old mates. Hugh was making her laugh and she was reciprocating by touching his shoulder.... Hang on? Were they flirting? I watched as Rosie threw back her head and let out a great gale of laughter. Another shoulder touch. They were so definitely flirting. I'd been so worried about Rosie disliking Hugh that it hadn't occurred to me she might find him attractive. And from what I could tell, Hugh was definitely taken with Rosie. Why wouldn't he be? Those green eyes that made Angelina Jolie's look meh, the pouty lips, the magnificent breasts. What's more, in her outsize painting shirt, skinny jeans and bare feet, her head scarf tied in a big floppy bow, Rosie gave every impression of being the epitome of feminine vulnerability. Any man would fancy her.

When Hugh disappeared to get more wallpaper paste from the van, Rosie came sidling over. "OK—hands up. I was wrong. He's great—nothing like I expected. And do you know what, he didn't bat an eyelid when I told him what I did for a living."

I stopped sandpapering. "Blimey—talk about being up-front."

"He asked me," she said. "I wasn't going to lie."

"But you've only known him for two minutes. How do you know you can trust him with information like that?"

"You trust him, don't you?"

"Yes, I do."

"Well, that's good enough for me. Hugh's a good guy, you can just tell. Plus he loves babies—always a good sign in my book. Turns out his sister has a little girl the same age as Will. He was telling me about her christening and how she disgraced herself by pooing all over the vicar. He's such a funny bloke. We really clicked."

"Yeah, I could see that."

"And he's rather cute, don't you think?" she said. "Lovely smile."

"Do I get the sense that somebody's smitten?"

Rosie's eyes widened. "Me? God, no."

"Oh, come on. I've just been watching the pair of you. You've both been flirting like crazy."

"You couldn't be more wrong. I was laughing at his story about his pooing niece, that's all. I don't fancy him. He's not remotely my type. In case you hadn't noticed, I go for dark, brooding men like Simon who end up letting me down." She paused. "For your information, I was actually thinking that Hugh might be more up your alley."

"Mine?"

"Oh, come on. He's gorgeous. Don't say it hasn't occurred to you."

"OK, perhaps I have thought about it, but it's you he fancies. He was definitely coming on to you."

"No, he wasn't. There wasn't a hint of a sexual vibe. We were just laughing about babies."

"Well, that's not how it came across."

"Sarah, I do telephone sex—you have to trust me on this."

"I dunno. . . ."

"So you do like him, then," Rosie said.

"Possibly."

"Do you want me to ask him if he fancies you?"

"What? No! How old are you, fifteen? Don't you dare say any-thing."

Rosie grinned. "OK."

"No, seriously. I mean it."

"Take it easy. Of course I won't say anything."

"Good."

"So, come on," Rosie said, "when are you going to make your move?"

"Me? It's up to him to make the first move."

"Sarah, stop being so damned conventional and get in there. Men like Hugh—they're like Louboutin heels on the first day of the Har-rods sale. They don't hang around for long."

Rosie rearranged herself so that she was sitting on the floor with her back against the wall. "Oh, by the way, getting back to Simon.

He's moving to France—with the actress-model. Says he thinks the Côte d'Azur will inspire him. Truth is her dad's got a yacht moored in Cap d'Antibes."

"So that means he'll see even less of Will."

"Yep. But the child support's arriving regularly now, so I suppose I should be grateful."

"Meanwhile he's missing out on being a father and Will's missing out on having a dad."

"Simon's loss, but Will's going to be fine. I'll make sure of that."

By now Hugh had returned with more wallpaper paste. "Better get back," Rosie said, smiling. "Don't want to get on the wrong side of the boss."

An hour later they had finished papering the wall behind the counter. Hugh said he had some paper left over and asked me if I was certain I didn't want to put some in a couple of the alcoves. I said I was sure. An excess of bucolic romping would have been overwhelming— particularly as I'd bought the matching fabric, which the aunties had already made up into curtains for the fitting rooms.

"Looks really great," Hugh said, using a wallpaper brush to smooth over a couple of areas that had started to bubble.

Everybody stopped work to look at the romping nymphs and garlanded milkmaids.

"Fabulous," Rosie said.

"You don't think it's a bit flamboyant?" Aunty Sylvia asked.

"Ah, but that is the entire idea," Aunty Bimla said. "It's what's known as ironical ostentation. I read all about it in my *Sunday Times* Style supplement. When you look at this wallpaper, you have to put speech marks around it."

"Speech marks?" Aunty Sylvia repeated.

"Yes. Isn't that right, Sarah?"

"It is."

Aunty Sylvia waved a hand in front of her. "Ach, what do I know from speech marks around wallpaper? I'm sure it's all very modern. Very nouvelle cuisine."

"Oh, by the way," Hugh said, looking at me, "I nearly forgot. We still need to discuss what type of locks you want for the basement window."

I suggested we go downstairs to take a look. In the end, we agreed that locks alone wouldn't be enough. The window was just about big enough for a person to crawl through. It needed bars. Hugh said he would order some. "Shouldn't cost too much." He slid his metal tape measure from its housing and laid it across the window.

"So I guess that's it," I said. "The work's pretty much done."

"Yep. We should have the decorating finished by the end of the week."

A few more days and he would be gone. I was suddenly aware of how much I was going to miss him.

"I know I keep on thanking you," I said, "but I don't know what else to say. You've been an absolute lifesaver."

"A decent review is all I ask."

"Five stars. Guaranteed." I paused. "There's something else I've been wanting to say. I've been feeling a bit guilty."

"Guilty? Why?"

"When you came here that first time to look at what needed doing, I was a little rude. I want to apologize."

"You were? I didn't notice."

"Now you're just being polite. The truth is I had you down as one of those flashy gentlemen builders. You know the sort: ex–City boys who think they can charge an arm and a leg."

He frowned. "Really? Why would you think that?"

"Oh, come on . . . Fanshaw has to be one of the top ten poshest surnames. Then there's the BBC voice. You don't exactly come across as your average builder."

He smiled. "Point taken. And, er, actually it's Fanshaw with two *f*'s."

"No. You mean you're actually *F*-fanshaw? That has to be the most aristocratic thing ever."

"Yeah, but the first *F*'s silent."

I couldn't help laughing. "Next you'll be telling me that you're awfully good chums with Bertie Wooster."

"No, but my great-grandmother used to invite Noël Coward to her house parties."

Of course she did.

"So what happened? How does an *F*-fanshaw end up as a builder?"

"I need to earn a living."

"And you chose the building trade as opposed to the law or going into the City."

"OK—I admit that building isn't my primary career."

Now we were getting somewhere. "Oh, I get it. You're studying."

"Nope. I'm actually an actor."

"An actor?" The voice. I should have guessed. "I can't believe that I've known you for nearly a month and I've only just discovered this crucial piece of information."

"Sorry. I tend not to mention it because people lose interest when they find out I'm not famous and I don't know Claire Danes."

I laughed. "So I guess that means you don't know Greg Myers either."

"Uh-uh. Why?"

I told him the tale.

"Bloody hell, you've really got yourself into a pickle."

"Just a bit."

"But it's really funny—Greg Myers thinking you were the girls' mother."

"You're as bad as Rosie. It's not funny. At the time, it really hurt."

"But thank God you managed to get over it."

I poked his arm. "Stop teasing. I was severely traumatized."

"Maybe you should have thought about counseling."

"Behave."

We fell about laughing.

"So where do you go from here?" Hugh said.

"Eventually, I'll have to come confess, but I'm such a coward, I keep putting it off. Meanwhile I keep praying for a miracle—like I bump into Greg Myers in Starbucks, we fall into conversation, he just happens to be free on July sixteenth and has spent his entire life dreaming of opening a school summer fair."

Hugh laughed. "Stranger things have happened."

"Not to me they haven't." A beat. Then: "So, you do the building and decorating between acting jobs?"

"I do. Everybody thinks I've got some huge trust fund to fall back on, but I haven't. I need to work."

"So the *F*-fanshaws aren't landed gentry, then?"

"I actually dropped the double *F* when I left school," he said. "People kept taking the piss. As far as being landed gentry goes, until the seventies the family was one of the biggest landowners in the country. Right now there isn't one of us with—as my mother so delightfully puts it—'a pot to piss in.' Actually Mum and Dad aren't that hard up, but that's not how she sees it."

"What happened?"

"My paternal grandfather gambled it all away—the manor house, works of art, thousands of acres. Mum and Dad worked on the estate and lived in one of the houses rent free. They lost their home, their income and Dad's inheritance."

"I guess that must have been hard for your dad, particularly when you've been raised with that sense of entitlement."

"Actually it wasn't that bad. After my grandfather went bust, but before the receiver marched in, he gave Dad a painting. It was a Turner seascape. Grandpa had been hiding it in the wine cellar. With the proceeds, Mum and Dad were able to buy a small farm in Sussex and pay for my education and my sister's. So we didn't suffer too much."

I asked him how his parents felt about his becoming an actor.

"Dad's OK, but Mum isn't keen. She kept nagging me to go into banking. She feels that Dad's family let me down and that I was deprived of my birthright. She's desperate for me to get back to what she sees as my rightful position in life."

"And you?"

"Well, suffice it to say I don't give a damn about my 'rightful position.' My mother, bless her, is a terrible snob and that's her problem. When I was at RADA, I decided I needed a trade to fall back on, so I got a part-time job with a building company. Mum was furious when she found out. Apparently people like us should never stoop to going into trade."

"She's right. When gentry fall on hard times, they're meant to become governesses or go into the church."

Hugh said he didn't think he was cut out for the church. "I'm not sure they take atheists."

"Actually I have a fair idea what your family must have gone through with your grandfather," I said. "Mike, my husband, was a heavy gambler. When he died, we were on the point of going bust—not that we stood to lose a stately home or great works of art—just a regular house."

"Bloody hell . . . And you had kids. It must have been terrifying."

"It was. Then he died. And along with all the other emotions, I felt this huge sense of relief."

"Funny . . . my grandmother said the same after the old man died." He paused. "So, what happened? I mean how did your husband . . . Oh, God, sorry, I'm prying. I have no right to ask. It's none of my business."

I told him I didn't have a problem talking about it and gave him the bullet points.

"The thing that made the grief almost unbearable was that I'd been about to divorce him."

"Because of the gambling."

"Yes. I was at my wit's end. I couldn't take any more."

"I don't know how you coped as long as you did."

"I think a bit of you just goes on automatic pilot. . . . So what about you? You ever been married?"

He smiled. "No, but I've come close a couple of times." He paused. "So come on, finish telling me your story. . . . What made you decide to open a bra shop?"

I told him about Aunty Shirley dying and leaving me the business, how it had been failing for years, and the Clementine Montecute saga.

"It was Clementine Montecute folding that gave me the final push, but I'm still scared stiff. I keep wondering if I've made the most terrible mistake."

"I feel the same about acting."

He explained that he'd been in the business for fifteen years. "I'm luckier than most. I get quite a bit of work. I've just finished a stint in *Richard III* at the Globe. I get the odd soap, the occasional half-decent role in the West End. I've even done odds and sods in Hollywood—playing dastardly Brits mainly, but I'm still a working actor. Actually I'm doing something right now. I'm in a revival of *The Producers*."

"I love *The Producers*. My mum and dad took me to see it in the West End years ago when it first came out. But hang on—you mean after putting in a full day here at the shop, you've been doing a night shift at the theater? You're really serious about this Protestant work ethic thing."

He laughed. "It's only two nights a week."

"Still, that's enough."

I asked him where it was showing.

"Way out of town, I'm afraid . . . the Croydon Empire."

"Who do you play?"

"Franz Liebkind, the mad Nazi pigeon fancier."

"I remember. . . . He has that line about Hitler being a great painter."

Hugh immediately snapped to attention, clicked his heels and raised his arm in a Nazi salute. "Hitler, zer vas a painter! He could paint an entire apartment in VUN afternoon! TWO coats!"

I burst out laughing. "That's it. And what was his other famous line? Something about the Queen."

"I swear my eternal allegiance to Adolf Elizabeth Hitler. . . . *Ja!* Not many people know this, but the Führer vas descended from a long line of English qveens."

His Franz Liebkind was priceless. I couldn't remember the last time I'd laughed so hard. "Brilliant."

"You're most kind."

"No, I mean it. So when can I come and see the show?"

The words were out of my mouth before my brain could process them. Now he'd think that I was coming on to him.

"Really?" he said. "You'd seriously like to see it?"

"I'd love to. But don't worry, I'll come, I'll see the show and then I'll go. I don't want you to feel you have to look after me."

"Oh." He seemed disappointed. "Will you at least let me sort you out a complimentary ticket?"

"Only if you're absolutely sure. I'm more than happy to pay."

"Don't worry," he said. "There are always a few freebies knocking around for friends and family of the cast."

"OK . . . that would be great. Thank you."

"And perhaps afterwards we could have a drink . . . or a bite to eat maybe . . . but it's fine if you'd rather not."

"No. I mean I would. I'd like that."

A moment later the kids were calling down the stairs to say they'd just finished painting a giant sea monster and wanted us to come and take a look.

Chapter 10

*L*eo Bloom got wet and hysterical. Max Bialystock had a rhetorical conversation. Ulla flaunted it. The audience roared. By the end of the show they were on their feet whooping and applauding. *The Producers* at the Croydon Empire may have lacked famous names—or even vaguely well-known ones—and the sets may have looked like they'd been supplied by the local drama societies, but there was no lack of talent and energy. Hugh's Franz Liebkind was magnificent. The moment he appeared onstage in his Nazi helmet and lederhosen, I was laughing. I carried on until I wept and my ribs ached. After the show, as the audience piled out of the theater, I was still wiping my eyes and humming "Springtime for Hitler."

Hugh and I had arranged to meet in the pub down the road. I went to the bar, ordered a glass of house white and, since I knew that Hugh would be another ten minutes or so because he had to take off his makeup and get changed, I called Rosie. She'd been thrilled that I'd "got in there" and yet again had offered to come and mind the kids before I had a chance to ask. She picked up on the first ring.

"Hey, how's it going?" I said.

"Great. The kids are fast asleep. And I've just managed to get Will down. He's in his basket, so I'm having a cuppa and watching *Parks and Recreation*. . . . How was *The Producers*?"

"Fab. I'm in the pub waiting for Hugh."

She asked me what I'd decided to wear in the end. "One of the posh dresses I still have from when Mike and I had money." There were three or four. I hardly ever wore them, partly because I never went anywhere fancy enough and partly because I didn't want them to wear out. This one was my favorite—black Lycra, scooped neck, three-quarter sleeves, clung in all the right places. I'd set it off with a wide patent belt and heels.

"I bet you look fab."

"I don't know about that, but I think I still scrub up OK."

"So, are you going to make a move on him?"

"No way. I'm just going to wait and see how things pan out. These things need to happen organically."

"I agree. So accidentally spill a drink into his lap and brush past his organ."

"Great idea. Why didn't I think of that?"

"OK. Maybe it's not very subtle."

"You think?"

Just then Hugh appeared in the doorway. "Sorry, hon, gotta go."

"He's there?"

"Yep."

"Bet he scrubs up well, too."

"He sure does," I said, taking in his tailored jacket and posh jeans. I'd never seen him in anything other than shorts and a tee. "OK, bye, see you later."

"Text me if you're not coming home."

"Will you behave?" I hissed. Then I hit "end."

"Wow," he said. "You look amazing."

"Wow, yourself," I said. "Nice jacket."

"Shucks. This old thing? I've had it for ages."

I was already laughing.

He sat himself down on the stool next to mine. "The show was fantastic," I said. "I loved every minute and you were absolutely brilliant. I cried with laughter. Look . . . my mascara's all gone streaky."

"Thank you. I'm glad you enjoyed it. It's actually had a couple of decent reviews in the nationals. It's not often that the papers take an interest in a small out-of-town production."

"Maybe you're about to hit the big time," I said.

Hugh laughed. "I'm not holding my breath."

He ordered a pint and another glass of wine for me. We looked around for a table, but they'd all been taken. The entire audience appeared to have rolled out of the theater and into the pub. I asked him how long the show had left to run. He said another three weeks.

"So, what then?"

"I don't know, but I try not to let it bother me. Something usually crops up. No point becoming an actor if you're going to panic every time a job ends. I've got the building work to fall back on, but I have to admit that since the recession, jobs have been harder to come by."

"But don't you worry about how you're going to pay your bills?"

"I've never actually been broke . . . although there was a time, a couple of years back, when I lived on baked beans for a month."

"And it didn't worry you?"

"Not really. It's different when you've only got yourself to think about."

"So when did you decide to become an actor?"

"I was five."

"Five?"

He nodded. "Our class was performing 'The Three Little Pigs' as part of the school's end-of-year concert. I was asked to play straw."

"What, all of it?"

"Yup. I think it was because the teacher knew we had rather a lot on the farm and that my mum would have no trouble making me a costume. Anyway, after that I was hooked. All the other kids got stage fright, but I loved getting up and performing in front of an audience. Then, much later on—when we did *Oh What a Lovely War* at secondary school—a couple of my teachers said they thought I had real talent and suggested I think about applying to drama school after uni. So that's what I did."

"And you stuck with it. Unlike me. I wanted to be a fashion designer. After art school I even opened my own business. I was just starting to make a name for myself when the kids came along."

"So you gave it up?"

"Being a mum was more important . . . but I've often thought about . . ."

". . . what might have been."

"Yes . . . Then after Mike died, having a career was the last thing on my mind. All I could think about was putting food on the table. I eventually found a job with the police—working on the nonemergency crime helpline."

"Not exactly a bundle of laughs."

I said it had its moments.

When we'd finished our drinks, Hugh asked if I fancied a curry. "Don't know about you, but I could murder a saag chicken." He said that there was a place around the corner that wasn't at all bad. I hadn't had a curry since my party after leaving the helpline. "Lead on," I said.

We were both starving, so we made the mistake of ordering far too much: onion bhajis, samosas—meat and vegetable—saag chicken, lamb passanda, chapatis and two giant peshwari naan packed with coconut and sultanas. Hugh insisted we order rice as well. It turned out we both had a thing for sweet Indian rice.

"You do know it's meant as a dessert," Hugh said.

I said that I did. Aunty Bimla had set me straight years ago.

"And you know that the waiter will snigger when we order it."

"I do and I don't care," I said.

"Great. Nor do I."

As we tackled the mountain of food and downed pints of Cobra, the conversation turned to the traditional first-date topics. For me at least, this seemed a bit odd since we already knew so much about each other's personal lives. But there were still gaps that hadn't been filled. So we talked about our favorite books, films, places we'd been, places we wanted to go. It turned out that Hugh had done a lot of traveling—India, China, South America, the Australian outback. He said that every time he finished a long run in the theater or a big building job, he rewarded himself with an adventure. Trekking in Morocco was next on his to-do list.

I discovered that he loved tinned spaghetti sandwiches and that his pet hate was building Ikea furniture. I told him about this kid in third grade called Deborah Lukover who used to bully me, and how I got her back by sneaking into the cloakroom and squirting my mother's Miss Dior over her salt beef sandwiches.

"And what's more, none of the teachers found out and my mum never discovered that I'd *borrowed* her perfume. I think it's still my proudest moment."

Hugh said his proudest childhood moment was beating his grandmother at Scrabble with a seven-letter word.

"What was it?"

"Farting."

I laughed so hard I nearly choked on my sweet rice.

Eventually the conversation went back to films—him trying to convince me that *2001* was a masterpiece and a work of genius, me saying I'd seen it twice and each time it had bored me stupid. "The music was nice, though."

He rolled his eyes.

"Tell you one film I absolutely love," I said. *"To Kill a Mockingbird."*

"Great film," he said.

"Scout has this line that always makes me smile. . . . 'There was to be a pageant representing our county's agricultural products. . . .'"

" 'I was to be a ham,' " we said in unison. Then we started laughing.

"No . . . I can't believe you know that line," I said.

"Of course I do. It's wonderful. It's the way she says it—like it's perfectly normal to dress up as a ham."

Precisely.

We talked more about our families. My Jewish parents who plutzed and kvetched and monitored my childhood bowel movements. His Protestant ones who didn't.

"Mum and Dad weren't big on affection or showing their emotions," he said. "But heaven forbid I flunked a test or was dropped from the rugby team. Then all hell broke loose. The pressure was unbearable."

"Rosie's mum was the same," I said. "She gave Rosie hell. And in the end she rebelled, just like you. You have a lot in common."

"Sounds like it." He took a mouthful of beer.

"And she's very beautiful," I went on. I was testing him. Even though Rosie had insisted that there was no chemistry between them, I needed to find out for myself. "I really like Rosie and you have to admire her—doing what she does to put food on the table."

"You really do. She's got more balls than most men I know."

"But to look at, she's like a lot of those model types."

"I dunno. I always think there's something a bit sexless about physical perfection."

"Really? So you're telling me that you prefer a woman with a broken nose and a squint."

"Squints not so much," he said, grinning, "but I'm a sucker for a unibrow."

I slapped him playfully on the hand. "Idiot."

"And dark, almond-shaped eyes," he said, holding my gaze and making me blush.

At half past eleven we were still in the restaurant, drinking coffee. "You know, I really should get going," I said. "Rosie's babysitting. She said she doesn't mind what time I get back, but I don't like to take advantage of her. She's still getting up in the night to feed Will."

Neither of us had brought a car, so we decided to share a taxi home. It would drop me off first, and then take Hugh on to his place in Tooting, a mile or so farther on.

"Dan and Ella must miss their dad," Hugh said at one point.

"They do, but these days their emotions aren't quite so raw. They struggled in the beginning. I felt so useless. I couldn't make it better. All I could do was love them."

The next thing, there were tears streaming down my face.

"Sarah. Are you all right? I really didn't mean to upset you."

"It's OK. You haven't. I'm just tired, that's all, and I've had too much to drink. It's made me maudlin. I'm sorry." I rummaged in my bag for a tissue and began dabbing my eyes. "The thing is, it was so awful . . . the gambling, our marriage, his death."

I kept apologizing, but the words and tears refused to stop. Unlike Steve, who was always uncomfortable around my emotions, Hugh didn't seem at all fazed.

"After my grandfather died," he said, "my grandmother was desperate for somebody to talk to. She tried opening up to my parents, but they weren't interested—told her there was nothing to be gained by raking over the past. So she tended to turn to my sister and me. I got to be quite a good listener."

"Steve was like your parents . . . always telling me not to 'dwell' and to 'move on.' "

"Steve?"

"This guy I started seeing after Mike died. It's been over a while."

"Well, Steve sounds like a jerk."

"He meant well," I said. "I'm sorry. I've made a complete fool of myself. I don't know what you must think of me. I'm not usually this needy. Honest."

He smiled. "I've seen you in action these past few weeks. You don't have to tell me."

Finally, the taxi turned into my street. "I've really enjoyed tonight," Hugh said. "How would you feel about doing this again?"

"I'd love to and I promise faithfully not to blub."

"I don't mind. Feel free to blub away."

"That's very kind of you, but I think it would make for a pretty miserable evening."

"Never," he said. "So, I'll see you at the shop tomorrow?"

"Sure."

As I reached for the door lever, he leaned towards me. Before I knew it, his lips were on mine and I was kissing him back.

"Sleep tight," he said.

"You, too."

"And stop worrying about Greg Myers. Something will work out."

"I doubt it. I'm a dead woman walking."

He laughed. I thought how sweet it was of him to be concerned about my stupid problem with the summer fair.

I took off my jacket and went into the living room. Rosie was sitting on the sofa, feeding William.

"Sorry to be so late," I said. "Hugh and I were talking and we lost track of time."

"So, it went well, then?"

"Really well. The show was great. We went out for an excellent curry. Oh . . . and I got maudlin about Mike and wept most of the way home."

"Smart move."

"I couldn't help it. It was the booze."

"How did Hugh take it?"

"He was great—didn't seem remotely perturbed."

"Huh—lucky for you. Some men would have run a mile. He's clearly a sucker for a vulnerable woman. So was there any kissing?"

"There was. And he's asked me out again."

"See—he finds you irresistible. Blubbing is your superpower."

"Mummee, is that you?" It was Ella calling from upstairs. "Can I have a glass of water?"

I went out into the hall. "OK, hon. Give me a moment. I'll be right up." I picked up a bottle of wine that I'd left on the hall table.

"This is for you," I said to Rosie, "to say thank you for sitting with my kids."

"Come on . . . you really didn't need to. It was a pleasure to sit with them—honest. They're great kids."

"Well, thank you anyway."

By now William was back in his Moses basket. Rosie tucked the wine under her arm and took hold of the wicker handles. "I'd better get going. If I'm lucky, I might get a few hours of sleep before his next feed." She turned to go. "Oh, by the way, you're out of Marmite. And crumpets. And cheese. Oh, and marshmallows. The kids and I snacked."

Cue disapproving look from me.

"Ah . . . you don't like the kids to snack at night?"

"No, no—I'm fine about them snacking, but Marmite and marshmallows? Really?"

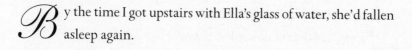

*B*y the time I got upstairs with Ella's glass of water, she'd fallen asleep again.

I put the glass on the nightstand, kissed her forehead and glanced over at Dan, who was snoring, mouth wide-open. Enlarged adenoids, the doctor had said. Apparently he would grow out of it.

It must have been the kiss that made Ella stir. "Mum, did you bring my water?" she said, her voice thick with sleep.

I held the glass to her lips. She took the tiniest sip and fell back onto her pillow.

"Did you enjoy Hugh's show?"

"Yes, it was great."

"I like Hugh. He's nice and he makes me laugh."

"He makes me laugh, too," I said. "Night-night, darling."

Ella replied with a soft grunt. Dan let out another snore.

*B*y lunchtime on Friday the painting and decorating was finished. I took everybody to Pizza Express to celebrate and made a tearful speech, thanking them all for their hard work. Afterwards I presented Rosie and the aunties with a bunch of flowers each. I gave Hugh a bottle of Macallan. He said that I shouldn't have, since I'd already paid him. "Yes, but you've done a great job and you put in so many extra hours. I wanted to let you know how much I appreciate it."

"Hear, hear," said the aunties.

"I just don't know what I would have done without you all," I went on. "I'm so lucky to have you all as friends. As you know, I can't afford to pay you, but it goes without saying that none of you will ever have to pay for another bra."

"Wow . . . I don't know what to say," Hugh said.

After lunch Rosie went home. Hugh came back to the shop and went into the bathroom to take a look at a dripping tap. The aunties came, too. They insisted on giving the place one final going over with dusters and Lemon Pledge.

"OK, you've done enough," I said eventually. "Go home and take it easy this weekend. See you on Monday. Don't forget, we open at ten."

"Like we're going to forget," Aunty Sylvia said. "We've been working here for forty years. And make sure you show up knowing how to fit a bra. We don't want you all fingers and thumbs on your first day."

I assured them that their instructions were burned into my brain. "First you measure around the woman's trunk, directly under the bra."

"Yes, but make sure she's exhaled first," Aunty Sylvia said. "That measurement needs to be as small as possible."

"OK . . . then you measure over the fullest part of the bust. To calculate the cup size you subtract the first measurement from the second. A one-inch difference means the client is an A cup, two inches means a B cup and so on."

"Bravo, poppet," Aunty Bimla said. "By Jove I think she's got it."

Aunty Sylvia didn't seem so sure. "And what are the signs of a badly fitting bra?"

"Easy, Aunty Shirley taught me this. First—there's the quadra-boob where the breast spills over the top of the cup. This was something I suffered from, but have since corrected. Oh, and even worse is when there are two extra side boobs."

"And what does it mean if the bra is riding up at the back?"

"It's too big."

"And if the cups are wrinkling?"

"They're too big."

"Not bad," Aunty Sylvia conceded. "You're getting there. We'll make a bra fitter of you yet."

The aim of course was to be able to work out a woman's bra size just by looking at her. I could hear Aunty Shirley's voice. "I can take one look at a woman and tell her bra size—even when she's wearing a coat."

After the aunties had gone, I finished loading the rails with bras and panties. Then I turned my attention to the glass display cabinet under the counter. I covered the floor of the cabinet in a length of scarlet velvet that Aunty Sylvia had found, ruched it up a bit and arranged a selection of black satin basques and boned corsets on top. I'd just finished when Hugh reappeared.

"Tap's all done," he said, wiping his hands on a rag. "Washer needed tightening."

I thanked him and he began loading his tools into his toolbox.

"Do you think the black and the red looks too tart's boudoir? Perhaps I should tone it down a bit?"

Hugh said he thought it looked great.

"Typical bloke," I said. "The sluttier, the better."

His face turned red. He was so cute when he was embarrassed.

"What can I say?" he said.

There was a moment of high-octane silence. The next thing I knew, I was taking his hand and praying that this wasn't too much too soon. After all, so far we'd only exchanged one kiss.

"Where are we going?"

"Shh."

I led him into one of the fitting rooms and pulled the curtain across.

"OK, I get it," he said.

"Too slutty?" I said.

"I thought we just established that I love slutty."

With that, he started kissing me. Then he reached under my sweater and unfastened my bra.

As he ran his hand over my breasts, I pulled him closer. I felt his erection hard against me. "Wow," I said, rubbing my hand over his crotch. Our kissing was deep and urgent. I was about to reach for his jeans zipper when . . .

"Poppet! Are you there? It's only me, Aunty Bimla."

The pair of us froze. Then I started fumbling with my bra fastener, which refused to work.

"OK, stay there," I whispered to Hugh, finally getting a single hook into an eye. "Don't move."

I pulled the curtain to one side and stepped out.

"Hi Aunty Bimla. What's happened? What are you doing back?"

"I got all the way to the station before I realized I didn't have my scarf. . . . Ah, here it is."

She picked her pink silk scarf up off the counter.

"Poppet, you looked flushed. Are you all right?"

"Yes. Yes, I'm fine."

"You sure you're not coming down with something? Apparently there's a nasty bug doing the rounds. Maybe you should take some vitamin C and some zinc. I read this article in *Daily Mail* and apparently, it works wonders."

"OK, perhaps I'll give it a go."

"Make sure you do. All right, poppet, see you Monday. Bright and early."

"See you Monday."

The door closed and Hugh poked his head round the fitting room curtain. "You coming back to finish what we started?"

I went back into the fitting room and we tried to get back into the mood, but the moment had passed.

"But we will do this again, right? . . . Not necessarily here."

"Oh, you bet," I said, planting a kiss on his lips.

We stepped back into the shop. Hugh finished packing up his tools. I looked around for anything else that needed doing.

"You know what this place could do with?" Hugh said.

"Whatever it is," I said, wiping an imaginary speck of dust off the countertop, "please don't tell me. I'm practically skint. I can't afford anything else."

"Fine. I won't say another word." He snapped his toolbox shut.

"OK, go on. What is it? . . . What have I forgotten?"

"A couple of chairs, that's all—where people can sit while they're waiting to be fitted."

He wasn't wrong. "I know. A couple of dainty filigree chairs would be perfect. But it's too late now. The pot's practically empty and I haven't got time to schlep round more junk shops."

"No need. I know the very place. I bought loads of stuff there when I was fixing up my flat. But we need to be quick. It starts at three."

"What does?"

"The furniture auction."

Apparently it was held every Friday afternoon in an old warehouse behind Waterloo station. "I promise you'll be able to pick up a couple of chairs for fifty quid."

"OK, but that's literally all I can afford. And I have to be at the school by five to pick the kids up from singing practice." Thirty or so children had been selected—Dan and Ella included—to perform "Hits from the Shows" at the summer fair in front of residents from a local old people's home.

Hugh didn't have his van today as it was being fitted with new tires. I had my car—because I'd had to bring in all the stock that I'd been storing at home—so I drove us across town. For once the traffic was fairly light and we made it in twenty minutes. The saleroom was dingy and dark. It smelled of damp and hot dogs. That hadn't put the punters off, though. There were at least a hundred people there.

We just about had time to inspect the furniture before the auction was due to start. Most of it was junk. Eighties plastic sofas; government-issue office furniture, complete with gray filing cabinets and stained chairs; beds that looked like they had been recently occupied by corpses. He must have seen I was looking a bit crestfallen.

"OK, yes, most of it's crap, but there are usually a few gems lurking."

"Really?"

I was all for giving up. It was Hugh who spotted the chairs—three reproduction French "fauteuils" with rickety legs and stuffing falling out of the mauve, polyester satin seats. "Don't panic, I know a bloke who can restore these. They're modern repros. Play your cards right and you'll get the three of them for seventy-five quid."

"You told me I wouldn't have to spend more than fifty. And then how much will your guy charge to restore them? With the shop opening on Monday, I won't have time to do the work myself."

"Yes, but what you're forgetting is that you should soon have an income."

I grunted.

I noted down the lot number—111. Hugh reckoned it would take half an hour or so for the auctioneer to reach that far down his list, so we decided to get a cup of tea from the hot dog van outside.

We sat drinking our tea on grubby plastic chairs, me suddenly a bundle of nerves about Monday. Would anybody show up? If only I'd been able to afford to take out an ad in the *Standard* to announce the shop's relaunch. Would the theaters still come to me with their bespoke orders? I'd e-mailed them to explain that I had taken over from Shirley, reassured them that the aunties (of course I didn't refer to them as "the aunties") would still be providing the same impeccable service.

"It's going to be fine," Hugh soothed. "I promise."

"You don't know that. It might all end in disaster."

"Sarah, you have to calm down. You've done your absolute best. Nobody could have done more. You need to have faith. And if it does all go pear-shaped, you'll always be able to say you gave it your best shot."

I let out a sigh. "I know. You're right. I need to stay focused."

Just then I heard the auctioneer announce lot 111.

"How did that happen?" I said. "I thought we had half an hour." Then I looked at my watch. We'd actually been sitting having tea for more than twenty minutes. "Come on . . . the bidding's about to start."

We legged it back into the hall—me still holding my half cup of tea. People were already bidding. The auctioneer—a roly-poly bloke in a leather bomber jacket and sovereign rings—couldn't have been less Sotheby's. "OK, ladies and gents, what am I bid? Right you are— I have fifteen pounds from the gent here in the front row."

This was my first ever auction. I turned to Hugh. "How much should I bid?"

"With cheaper items, you shouldn't need to go up more than two quid at a time."

"Seventeen," I called out.

Somebody put in a bid for twenty.

My hand went up again. "Twenty-five."

"Careful," Hugh said. "You're pushing the price up too fast."

"Thanking you," the auctioneer said, waving his hammer at me. But somebody was already making another bid. "Thirty from the luvverly lady on my left."

I came back with thirty-three. The "luvverly lady" offered forty. I countered with forty-three. The woman immediately went to fifty.

"Sixty," I cried.

"Whoa, steady on," Hugh said.

"But I really want those chairs."

The woman shook her head. She was out.

"Sixty. Sixty pounds I'm bid. Are we all done at sixty pounds? Yes?" The auctioneer brought down his hammer. "Sold to the lady holding the paper cup."

"Yess!" I hugged Hugh. "I got them! That was so exciting. I can't believe I haven't done this before."

"Well done," he said, laughing. "But you do need to work a bit on your bidding technique."

I told him to stop being a killjoy. I'd gotten them. That was the main thing—and for less than we thought.

"If you'd care to make your way to the back of the room," the auctioneer said, "my assistant will sort you out."

I finished my cold tea, dropped my cup in the trash and got out my wallet. The auctioneer's assistant—a plump, fifty-year-old Goth with purple hair and a tattoo of a bat on her upper arm—was standing behind a counter, saying "cheerio" to her previous customer.

Finally she turned to me. "Sorry to keep you waiting, love. Will you be wanting them wrapped?"

I said I didn't think that would be necessary.

"Your call, but they're pretty fragile." A moment later a young lad—another assistant, this time in a long green apron—came ambling over, presented me with three porcelain bedpans and ambled off again.

"You did very well there," the woman said. "As you can see, they're genuine Victorian—none of yer repro rubbish. Look at the decoration—all hand painted and not a mark or a chip to be seen."

"Excuse me?"

"So will that be cash or card?"

"Neither. I mean . . . I'm not with you. . . . These are bedpans."

The woman looked confused. "Yes, you just bought them."

"No, I didn't," I said, putting them down on the counter. "I was bidding for the reproduction fauteuils. I wasn't bidding for bedpans."

"Yes, you were." She produced the sale list. "See . . . lot one hundred and seven—one set of Victorian bedpans. The chairs are lot one hundred and eleven."

"Oops—I think we misheard," Hugh said.

"You think? Bloody hell, what am I supposed to do with a set of bedpans?"

"But surely," the woman said, "you saw the bedpans on the table next to the auctioneer?"

"No, our eyes were fixed on the chairs behind him."

"Sorry, love, but we can't take them back unless there's some damage that wasn't disclosed. It's saleroom policy."

"That's OK. I understand," I said. "It's my fault."

"Would it help if I threw in a set of men's antique urinal bottles?"

I said that I wasn't sure that it would. She slipped a pair into the top pan anyway.

I paid on my card. Hugh picked up the bedpans and the urinal bottles and we headed to the car. Behind us, the auction was still in full swing.

"And we're done at forty-five pounds. Sold to the gent on my right—three reproduction fauteuils."

"Shit, Hugh. Did you hear that? They just went for forty-five pounds."

We got into the car. Hugh sat in the passenger seat with the bedpans and urinals piled up on his lap. There was no room in the boot because it was packed with empty lingerie boxes that needed to be put in the recycling.

"This is all my fault," he said. "I'll refund you the sixty quid."

"What? Don't be daft. How on earth is this your fault?"

"I suggested we come to the auction."

"Yes, and I agreed. Plus it was me who misheard the lot number. If it's anybody's fault, it's mine. There is no way I'm taking any money from you. Now please, let's just forget it."

"OK, if you say so," he said, but I could tell he wasn't happy.

"You look really daft with all those bedpans on your lap . . . daft but sexy."

That made him laugh. "I suppose you could always put them in the garden and use them as planters."

"Maybe."

"Or you could use them as giant outside ashtrays. Or maybe you could string them with guitar wire and we could start a band. We could call it the Urinators."

"Or the Jingle Smells."

"I don't believe you just said that," he said.

In the end we were laughing so hard that I had to pull over. Of course one thing led to another, but since it was broad daylight and we had to be at the school by five, we made no attempt to venture beyond first base.

We made it to the school with ten minutes to spare.

"Come for dinner," I said, turning off the engine. "I made lasagna and there's way too much. And the kids really enjoy your company. In fact the other night Ella told me she really likes you."

"Really? Well, in that case I'd love to come."

I left Hugh and the bedpans in the car and went to wait for the kids in the playground.

"What ho, Sarah!"

Imogen.

"Hi Imogen. I haven't seen you in ages."

She said she'd taken a part-time job in a friend's bookshop. Apparently she'd been desperate for something to keep her occupied. Clearly her roles as PTA chair and troop rallier in chief weren't enough. "Woman just came in and asked me if Anne Frank wrote a sequel. It's so hard sometimes not to lose one's patience with the general public. . . . So, Sarah, all tickety-boo your end?"

"Yep, my end's pretty good."

"Excellent. And Greg Myers . . . I'm assuming he's confirmed?"

OK, this was it. The time had come. I couldn't lie to the poor woman any longer. "Actually, Imogen, I need to have a word with you about Greg."

"Oh, God, he's not demanding traveling expenses, is he?"

"No, no. Nothing like that. It's just that . . . Well, you see the thing is . . ."

"Sarah! Imogen!"

Crap. Tara and Charlotte. They were both dressed from head to toe in black.

"Goodness," Imogen said. "You chaps look like you've been to a funeral."

"We have," Tara said. "My father-in-law died. The booze finally got him."

"And you were so brave," Charlotte cooed, "keeping a stiff upper lip and not crying."

"Darling, there was no way I was going to cry. Have you any idea what I pay for mascara?"

"Your poor mother-in-law couldn't stop weeping. I have to say, she looked dreadful."

"Yes, but she was no oil painting to start with. I always think that plain people are lucky in many ways. Ugliness lasts so much longer than beauty. Wouldn't you agree, Imogen?"

I found myself thinking how dreadful it was that we lived in a world where it was socially unacceptable—not to say illegal—to slap women like Tara.

But Imogen hadn't been listening. She was too busy reading a text.

"Good Lord, they're releasing Mummy from Grantanamo Bay

while they refurbish. She's coming to stay for a whole month. I love Mummy to bits, but the old dear is completely batty. . . ."

"Darling, just book her in at the Ritz," Tara said. "Let them take care of her. It's what Margaret Thatcher's family did, so they're clearly used to looking after old trouts."

Imogen said she wasn't sure she and her husband were quite up to the five hundred quid a night it cost to stay at the Ritz. Tara said she was sure Imogen would think of something.

"So," Tara said, turning to me. "How is your little bra shop coming along?"

"Very well, thank you. We open on Monday."

"You're opening a bra shop?" Imogen said. "I had no idea. Well, good for you. The country needs more female entrepreneurs. Let me be the first to wish you the best. I'd come along for a fitting, but it isn't really worth it since I don't possess much more than a couple of fried eggs."

Tara grimaced and turned back to me. "So, Greg Myers all signed up for the summer fair?"

Whereas I'd been prepared to tell Imogen the truth, there was no way I was about to admit my failure to Tara and Charlotte, who would take such delight in tormenting and ridiculing me.

"Absolutely," I heard myself say.

"We're so looking forward, aren't we, Charlotte?"

"Oh, definitely."

By now the children were coming out of school. Tara and Charlotte took their leave and went in search of their offspring, who—naturally—had also been chosen to sing for the old people. I could see Ella and some friends. I could also hear them. They were belting out "Hello, Dolly!"

"So," Imogen said, "you said there was something about Greg Myers that you needed to discuss."

"No, it's fine. It was just to firm up timings on the day, but it can wait."

"Good, good."

The kids clambered into the car and demanded to know what the weird things were on Hugh's lap.

"Victorian bedpans," he said.

"What are bedpans?"

I turned to Hugh. "Maybe I should take this," I said. "OK . . . sometimes if you're ill in hospital and can't get out of bed, you have to poo and wee into a bedpan."

"Aaargh. Gross. Stink."

When she'd got over being grossed out, Ella burst into, "I'm Gonna Wash That Man Right Outa My Hair."

"Those songs are stupid," Dan said. "I wish I hadn't been chosen."

"Aw, don't say that. You got chosen because you have a nice singing voice."

"Yes, but why can't the boys put on a football match for the old people?"

"Because most of them would probably prefer a sing-along."

Dan grunted. Ella kicked off with "Edelweiss."

"Ella, shuddup."

"You shuddup."

"No, you shuddup."

I started yelling, which only made things worse.

"I suggest you both calm down," Hugh said. "Otherwise, I'm not going to show you my surprise."

"What surprise?" Dan said.

"If I told you, it wouldn't be a surprise. Now, just sit quietly and wait until we get home."

There wasn't another word from either of them.

*W*hen we got home, I put the lasagna in the oven and started on the salad. Hugh asked the children to come and sit at the kitchen table so that he could show them his surprise.

"OK, here you go," he said, handing them each a paper wallet. "I printed off the photographs of your *murial*. Each of you has a set to keep."

"Wow. Cool. Thanks."

"You know, the *murial* really was very good," Hugh said.

The kids sat examining the photographs.

"My shark was the best."

"My octopus was better."

The only thing they agreed on was that they would both take the prints to school for show-and-tell.

"So, Hugh," Dan said eventually. "What board games do you like? We've got Monopoly, checkers, Operation, Scrabble."

"I have to admit that I'm rather partial to a game of Scrabble," Hugh said.

Dan didn't need any more encouragement. He disappeared and came back with the Junior Scrabble box.

"I should warn you," Hugh said. "I'm rather good."

"Not as good as me," Ella piped up.

They drew lots. Ella went first with a three-letter word.

"Bum," Dan said. "That is so lame."

"OK . . ." She added an *E* and an *R*.

"I think you'll find there are two *M*s in bummer," Hugh said.

"Yeah, *ignoranus*," Dan piped up.

"Has it occurred to you," I said to Hugh, "that there's been a definite arse theme running through today?"

Before we sat down to eat, Hugh nipped out to buy some wine. He also got candy bars for the kids.

"Wow, Mum never lets us have chocolate," Dan said.

"That is so not true. I just don't let you have it every day."

"Yeah, Dan," Ella said. "You're such a liar."

"Well, at least I'm not an *ignoranus*."

*O*nce the kids were asleep, Hugh and I took our glasses and a second bottle of wine into the living room and snuggled up on the sofa.

"This is a lovely house," Hugh said. "And you've managed to make it really warm and comfortable. It's a proper home."

"I've done my best. After everything the kids have been through, I needed to provide them with some kind of a sanctuary."

"And you have. Right now they probably don't appreciate what you've done for them, but one day they will and they'll thank you."

I laughed. "You reckon?"

"I know it." He took a sip of wine. He didn't say anything for a moment or two. There was clearly something on his mind. "So," he said eventually. "Are we dating, then?"

"Yes. I think we are."

"Good . . . how's about you come to my place tomorrow and I'll cook for you?"

"Oh, Hugh, I'd love to, but there's nobody to mind the kids. I can't keep asking Rosie. She's been great, but I don't want her to feel like I'm using her."

"No, of course not. I get that."

"Sorry," I said, kissing him on the cheek. "You could always come here again."

"I know, but I was thinking that we could do with some time alone with no risk of interruptions."

"That would be nice," I said.

He moved in to kiss me. "Stop it! The children might come down." But his lips were already on my neck, the tops of my breasts. I heard myself letting out tiny moans of delight.

"I thought you wanted me to stop."

"No . . . please don't stop. . . ."

But he pulled away. "Maybe we should. Before we really get carried away. Listen, are you sure you can't make tomorrow?"

"I don't see how. Right now I can't afford proper babysitters."

He looked at me. "It's OK. We'll sort something out."

"Sure."

"Sarah, you sure there isn't something else bothering you? You've slumped all of a sudden."

He was right, I had. Just when I thought I'd shoved it to the back of my mind, the summer fair issue was haunting me again.

"I know I'm being a coward, but the thought of Tara and Charlotte reveling in my failure is just too much to bear."

"In which case, I'd say you have only one option."

"What's that?"

"Blackmail."

"Brilliant. Why didn't I think of that?"

"Come on—the playground bleeds gossip. You must have something on one of these women."

"Hugh, stop it. I'm being serious."

"So am I," he said, grinning. "I bet one of them's playing away."

"Funnily enough, it just so happens that Tara is cheating on her husband. . . ."

"Aha!"

"What's 'Aha' supposed to mean?"

"OK, here's what you do. . . ." He was laughing now. "You go up to her, tell her straight out you couldn't get Greg Myers and that if she dares to even think of making trouble, you'll tell her old man that she's cheating on him."

"Yeah and maybe I should put a couple of bullets in her kneecaps as well, just to make sure she keeps her mouth shut."

"Good idea. Where do you keep your sawed-off shotgun?"

"Idiot. Come on, you've had too much to drink. I'm calling you a cab."

I was watching him climb into the cab when the thought occurred to me. I ran into the street and got him to wind down his window. "Tell you what, maybe there is a way I could come to your place tomorrow. Leave it with me. I'll call and let you know."

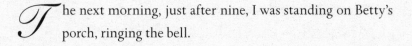

he next morning, just after nine, I was standing on Betty's porch, ringing the bell.

"Hi Betty . . . Look, you'll probably think this is a huge cheek, but I don't suppose there's any chance you could do me a massive favor?"

When I asked if she could babysit, she looked at me as if she'd just won the jackpot at bingo. At one point I thought she might hug me. "Me? You'd like me to look after the children?"

"If you wouldn't mind?"

"Mind? I'd be delighted. Did I ever tell you that when I was younger, I was really good with kiddies? They seemed to really take to me. Heaven knows why."

"Yes, I think you did mention it. But my kids can be little blighters. You might not be so delighted if they give you a hard time."

"Oh, I'm sure they won't. They're lovely children—a real credit to you. . . . So where are you going?"

"Well . . . actually . . ."

Betty smiled. "I know. . . . You don't need to say another word. You've got a young man, haven't you?"

"Actually, I have."

"Good for you. Don't make the mistake I made and end up a lonely old widow. Now then, what time do you want me?"

"Seven if that's OK, and I'll leave you all dinner in the oven."

She said that sounded perfect.

I told the children to promise not to give Betty a hard time. "She's getting on and old people tend not to appreciate pranks and jokes."

"Why?"

"Because they don't always see the humor."

"Why?"

"Because they've slowed down."

"Why?"

"Because older brains don't produce as many new cells as young ones."

"Why?"

"OK . . . that's enough. Just do as I tell you. Be kind and polite and tidy up after yourselves. Do not expect Betty to run around after you."

Ella said she would sing her some songs from *My Fair Lady*. I said that sounded like an excellent idea.

"So is Hugh your boyfriend?" Ella said. She and Dan were sitting on the bed, watching me get ready.

"Well, it's early days yet, but I think you could say he's my boyfriend."

"Is he going to be our new dad?" Dan said.

I sat on the bed and put an arm around each of them. "Listen, there might come a day when I decide to get married again, but believe me, nobody will ever take the place of your dad."

"No, but Hugh's great. He'd be a good dad. He even supports Chelsea."

Just then the phone rang. Dan reached over and picked up. "Hi Grandma . . . Yeah, we're fine. . . . Mum's got a boyfriend."

"Dan! Give me that phone."

"What?"

"Just give it to me."

"Hello Mum. How are you? . . . Yes, I have started seeing somebody. His name's Hugh. He's an actor. What? No, of course it's not Hugh Grant. Don't you think I'd tell you if I'd started dating Hugh Grant? . . . Yes, he's done a bit of TV. No, he doesn't know Claire Danes. . . . His surname's Fanshaw. . . . OK, good idea, you Google him and get back to me. Actually, Mum, I'm getting ready to go out.

Can we speak tomorrow? . . . OK . . . fine, when you and Dad get back from your flamenco class . . . Hang on, you're learning flamenco? . . . No, of course I'm pleased you've got a hobby. It's just that neither of you ever had one before and you've certainly never shown an interest in any kind of dancing. I'm just a bit surprised, that's all. . . . What? Yes, of course I've got somebody to mind the children. Look, I really have to go. Speak soon . . . Yep, love you, too."

*T*here was no polite way of saying it. Hugh's flat was a dump. Clearly all his furniture—the tatty leather sofa, the orange Formica table and chairs, the office swivel chair plonked in front of the TV—had come from the Waterloo auction house. But it wasn't just the worn-out, bad-taste furnishings that depressed me. There was stuff everywhere—books, CDs, newspapers and magazines. Then there were his collections: his James Bond cars, the eighties cell phones that looked like bricks, his reel-to-reel tape recorders, some of which were really big and were taking up floor space because there was nowhere else for them. Then there were his work tools. I found two spanners on the sofa, a set of drill bits on top of the toilet cistern.

When I arrived at Hugh's place, he was in the middle of making chicken risotto. We stood in his kitchen drinking wine and taking turns to stir the risotto.

"Sorry the place is such a mess," he said. "I did clean the bathroom in your honor, though, and gave the kitchen a going over." It was true. He had made an effort. I'd noticed fresh towels in the bathroom. Plus the basin had been freshly cleaned and green toilet gel had been squirted into the lavatory bowl. Lined up against the wall was a pile of at least two dozen loo rolls.

"It's just a bit blokey," I said, noticing a crusty, charred oven glove. It was lying next to the gas stove—a model that I was guessing went out of production in the seventies.

"Which is a polite way of saying it's the town dump."

That made me laugh. "You could try getting some blinds and a few plants to brighten the place up a bit."

"The only thing that would brighten this place up is a flame-thrower."

"Oh, stoppit. You're a builder and decorator for crying out loud. Knowing how hard you work, you could sort it out in a couple of weeks."

"I know. It's just that since the place isn't mine, I can't really be bothered."

He explained that he rented the flat from a mate of his who now lived in Manchester.

"Pete gives me a great deal on the rent. He even threw in the van. All I had to do was furnish it—which I did from the place in Waterloo. Don't think I spent more than a hundred quid."

"Huh—as much as that?"

"OK, I know I should make an effort—maybe give it a lick of paint—but I prefer to spend my spare cash on traveling. I just use the flat as a base."

I was aware of making a mental note: doesn't own flat or even his van. And this bothered me because? It wasn't like I owned my house. And my car probably wasn't worth more than five hundred quid. But bother me, it did.

Hugh's risotto was excellent—creamy, but with just the right amount of bite. When we sat down to eat at the orange dining room table, he was at pains to point out that he'd laid it with matching plates and napkins.

"Should I feel honored?" I said, laughing.

"You bet."

"I don't get you," I said. "Until now I've been under the impression that you were really into style and decoration. You were always coming up with great ideas for the shop."

"I am interested, but I'm on my own and I spend so much of my time working. Like I say, this place is just a base."

It was only after we'd eaten that I noticed that one of the living room walls was completely covered in framed photographs of Hugh's travels.

I got up to take a closer look.

"Hugh, these are fantastic." I was studying a black-and-white photograph of a group of elderly Chinese men playing cards in a smoke-filled basement.

"My new Hasselblad can take most of the credit. See, I do own some stuff . . . my laptop, my iPad, my iPhone, my posh music system . . . my season ticket to Chelsea."

"Where did that come from?" I said. "I don't care what you own or don't own."

"Really? Back there in the kitchen I thought you seemed a bit surprised when I told you that I didn't own the flat."

"Don't be daft," I heard myself say. "That would be pretty hypocritical of me, bearing mind I don't own my place. Now come over here and talk me through the rest of these photographs."

There were Icelandic landscapes, portraits of Nepalese monks—images of the Mumbai slums, which managed to be both brilliant and gut-wrenching.

"You've never seen such levels of poverty. India has its own space program and yet it isn't tackling the poverty. And countries like the UK and the US still give them aid. Shit—I still give them aid."

"You do?"

"Yeah, thirty quid a month. God knows what it gets spent on."

"But you wouldn't stop giving it?"

"Of course not. I mean, you can't, can you?"

"You are a good man, Hugh *F*-fanshaw."

"I do my best," he said. "I even went out and bought new bed linen for tonight. Want to see?"

"Absolutely."

He took my hand and led me to the bedroom. A dozen candles, dotted around the room, were flickering in the moonlight. Hugh wrapped his arms around me and began planting kisses on my face.

"Are you sure you want to do this?"

"I've never been surer."

I was experiencing something that I'd felt once before, many years ago: the knowledge and certainty that I was coming home.

Chapter 11

I was loading the kids' lunch boxes, reliving how Hugh had undressed me, told me how beautiful I was, with particular reference to my breasts, how he had opened me, caressed me, causing me to whimper in ecstasy—when Dan and Ella came rushing into the kitchen and presented me with a good luck card made from the back of a Cheerios box. It had a picture of a pink frilly bra and panties on the front. "Aw—thank you, guys. That's fabulous. I will keep it forever." I gave them both a hug. While Ella was clearly delighted that I loved the card, Dan didn't say anything. I was pretty sure that Ella had drawn the bra and panties and her brother had just signed the card—no doubt going, "Yuck . . . this is so gross" as he did so.

Mum and Dad sent a huge bunch of white lilies to the shop. The note read: *All the luck in the world, darling. So proud of you. Love and hugs, M&D. xxx* There was a PS from Mum: *BTW Googled Hugh and noticed he's been in several episodes of* Miss Marple *and* Downton. *Why didn't you tell me he was famous? So excited. Can't wait to meet him.*

I didn't have the heart to tell her that he'd only had bit parts in both and that he really wasn't very famous at all.

There was a possibility, though, that this could be about to change. When Hugh phoned early that morning to wish me luck, he had news. His agent had called a few moments before to say he'd just discovered that auditions were being held today for a new production of *The Importance of Being Earnest* and that Hugh should go along and try out for Algernon Moncrieff. "He thinks because I'm posh and was brought up among 'those' people, I'd be perfect and that it would hardly involve any acting. Blasted cheek."

"Absolutely. The man is clearly a cad and you should dispense with his services henceforth and forthwith."

Hugh laughed. "You're on good form, bearing in mind it's opening day."

I assured him that I was feeling sick with nerves and this was only gallows humor.

He said to stop worrying and I'd be fine. I told him to break a leg.

"And I'll see you later," I said. We'd arranged that he would come round that evening with Chinese food and we'd have dinner with the kids.

"Great. Oh, and there should be a surprise waiting for you at the shop."

Along with Mum and Dad's lilies, there were red roses waiting for me when I arrived. These, along with my having been to see Hugh in *The Producers*, left the aunties in no doubt that the two of us were "courting."

"OK, yes, we are dating," I said, "but it's early days yet. I don't want you two getting carried away."

The aunties couldn't have looked less carried away. There were no overexcited hugs, just troubled faces. What was going on? A couple of weeks ago they couldn't wait to get us together.

"What is it? Why the long faces? I thought this was what you wanted."

"Poppet, Hugh is a lovely boy. Your aunty Sylvia and I think the world of him, but are you sure you're doing the right thing? Acting is such an unreliable profession."

"It's true. Look how my Roxanne struggled until she got her big Hollywood break."

"Come on, don't you think you're both overreacting? Hugh and I are dating, not planning our future together."

"I know," Aunty Sylvia said, "but suppose it gets serious? Granted, Hugh is a sensible boy and he has a trade to fall back on, but at the same time, an actor's life is so haphazard. He probably doesn't know what he's doing from one week to the next."

"After everything you've been through, poppet, we want you to find a man you can rely on, who will look after you and provide for you."

I could only imagine what they would say if they discovered that Hugh owned little more than his laptop and a fancy camera and spent all his spare cash on traveling. As far as the aunties were concerned, when it came to a relationship, savings and owning property counted as foreplay.

Aunty Sylvia was nodding. "Bubbie . . . you need to find a banker with a big bonus."

"Look," I said, offering them a smile. "I know how much you both worry about me and I really appreciate it, but to be honest I'm done with relying on men. If life has taught me one thing, it's that I have to start relying on me. That's one of the reasons I need the business to work."

"But suppose it doesn't?" Aunty Sylvia said. "What then?"

"Please—this is opening day! I will not have defeatist talk today of all days. I have to make it work. I have no option."

Aunty Sylvia looked sheepish. "Sorry, that was wrong of me. Of course you're going to make it work."

"Absolutely, poppet. Chin up, chest out, best foot forward. That's the spirit."

With that, the aunties disappeared to their workstation in the basement. A few minutes later they were back again. "Guess what," Aunty Sylvia said. "We've just had an e-mail from the Duchess of Kent Theatre. They're putting on a production of *Pygmalion* and they want half a dozen boned corsets. It's not a huge order. . . ."

"No, but it's definitely a start."

"Indeed it is, poppet. To quote my father: 'A journey of a thousand miles starts with a single step.'"

"You sure it was your father who said that?" I inquired. "And not some famous Eastern philosopher?"

"No, no. My father definitely said it first."

At ten on the dot, I unlocked the front door. Then I went to check the fitting rooms—for what, I had no idea. After that, I tidied displays that didn't need tidying. Once or twice I stood at the window and watched the people on the street—some scuttling, some strolling, but none of them stopping. Then one of them did. The door opened. My first customer. I was gripped by the sudden urge to celebrate her entrance with a trumpet fanfare.

"Excusing me," she said. "Which is truthful position for Victoria's Albert Museum?"

I directed her to the number 10 bus stop. For this she offered me many thankings.

The second customer only wanted to buy a pair of Spanx, but what the heck, I thought as she left—I'd made my first sale. We'd only been open for half an hour and already we'd received an order from one of the West End theaters and I'd sold a pair of Spanx. The next customer wanted to know if we stocked breast pads for nursing mothers. I said we didn't and directed her to Boots. After that, one of the workmen who'd been repairing a burst water main down the street came in and asked if we stocked edible undies.

"I'm afraid we don't."

He scratched his head. "OK, what about crotchless panties? Bras with tassels?"

" 'Fraid not."

"You see, I'm looking for something for the wife's birthday."

"OK—let me show you some of our pretty lace lingerie."

"Nah. I was thinking of something a bit more racy. Not to worry. She probably wouldn't wear it anyway. Maybe, on second thought, I'll get her a giant jigsaw."

Around lunchtime a harassed thirty-something woman came in. "I've been to all the department stores for a bra and they have absolutely nothing in my size. I need cleavage. For tonight. Can you help me?"

I said that I was sure I could and led her into a fitting room.

When the woman got undressed, I could see the problem. Two teensy torpedoes. My breasts hadn't looked like that since I was thirteen. I didn't need a tape measure to tell me she was no more than a 30A—if that. I asked her what sort of dress she was wearing. Strapless. I left her for a few minutes while I went to check out our strapless bras.

I came back with three—all of which were padded. Each time she tried one on, her face fell. "You see, this is what happens," she said after I had fastened her into the last bra. "They give me a bigger bust, but no cleavage." She placed her hands under the cups and hiked up her breasts. A passable cleavage appeared.

I needed something to prop up her breasts so that they sat higher in the cup. "OK, I have an idea." I asked her if she'd mind slipping off the bra.

I could see what was needed. The cup needed to be three-quarters filled with a solid piece of foam. This would rest against her chest wall. Her breast would sit on top of the foam and some of it would spill over the top of the cup to make cleavage. I took the bra over to the counter, found some tissue and stuffed it hard into the cups.

"But I couldn't wear it like this," the woman said when I presented her with the bra. "It's stuffed with tissue. It would be terribly uncomfortable."

I explained that if the idea worked in principle, we could make something permanent to fill the cup. She tried on the tissue-filled bra. Presto. Cleavage.

I went down to the basement, explained the woman's problem to the aunties and how I thought it might be solved.

"I am most impressed," Aunty Bimla said. "You are spot-on. This modification is known as the 'étagère.' It means shelf. We've actually been doing it for years. Most women just shove tissue or stockings underneath the breast to give it a lift, but it isn't satisfactory—always ends up lopsided."

The aunties came upstairs and went into the fitting room. To make more space, I stood outside. I watched as they fussed over the customer and flattered her, told her how much they envied her handspan waist. Where was she going this evening? Claridge's? How grand. As pins were pinned and tucks and folds made, the woman began to relax.

"OK," Aunty Sylvia explained, "what we're going to do is fill the cup with foam, which we will cover in satin. Nobody will see it and you can wash the bra as normal."

"Fantastic. When can you have it ready?"

Aunty Sylvia asked if three o'clock would be soon enough.

"Absolutely. You can really have it done by then?"

"No problem. And when you come, bring your dress, so that we can check everything is perfect."

Aunty Bimla worked on the bra and had it finished by half past two. The woman returned with her dress. When she tried it on with the bra, some of the lace cup was peeking over the top. Aunty Bimla returned to her sewing machine with the bra. In a matter of minutes she had fixed the problem.

Before she left, the woman hugged both aunties and me and promised faithfully that she would be back and that she would recommend us to her girlfriends.

We agreed that a celebratory cuppa was called for. I put the kettle on and Aunty Bimla produced some halva from her bag.

At four o'clock I called to see how the kids were doing. A few weeks ago, I'd asked Fiona—she of the pitying looks whose son, Tom, had taught Dan how bodies rot—if she could possibly help me out. I explained about the new business and that I didn't have anybody to pick the children up after school or on a Saturday.

"Say no more," Fiona said. "It would be my pleasure. After everything you've been through, you poor soul, it's the very least I can do. I'll pick them up and give them tea, so they'll be fully fed and watered when you come to collect them." She was also up for having them on a Saturday. "When the kids have friends to play, it keeps them occupied and they stop nagging me."

"Are you absolutely sure?" I stressed that it would only be for a few weeks until my parents got back from Spain. (My mother had made it clear that she couldn't wait to get back to her role as deputy carer.)

"Positive. But I do worry that the stress of setting up a new business might be too much for you. Tell me, did you ever get around to trying Zumba like I suggested?"

I confessed that I hadn't.

"Well, you must. Grief . . . stress . . . They say it works for everything."

"In that case, I really must give it a go. . . . Now, as far as money is concerned . . ."

"Sarah, please. I wouldn't dream of asking you for money. I know you'd do the same for me if the situation was reversed."

It was true. I would in a heartbeat. Fiona could be irritating, but, like Imogen, she had a good heart.

*N*ow Fiona was telling me how Dan and Ella had just demolished a huge helping of textured protein nuggets and turnip fries and that all was fine.

My kids had "demolished" textured protein and turnip fries? I wanted to ask Fiona how, exactly, she defined "demolished." Instead

I thanked her again for stepping into the breach and said I'd be there just after six thirty to pick them up.

No sooner had I put the phone down than Rosie called. "Hey, how's it going?"

"Well, we're not exactly overwhelmed with customers, but I guess it's only the first day."

"You have to give it time. Let the word get out."

"I know. I just wish I'd had some money to spend on advertising, that's all."

"Don't worry. It'll happen. I have every faith in you, Sarah Green. This business is going to be huge."

I laughed. "Just keep telling me."

"Listen, I need to talk to you about something. You got a moment?"

I said that I would have to ring off if the Duchess of Cambridge appeared, but for the time being I was all ears.

"OK, here's the thing. . . . I bumped into Betty across the street and she says you've been asking her to babysit your kids."

"That's right. I have."

"OK, but up to now you've asked me and I was wondering why you'd stopped. I promised I wouldn't take calls from punters at your place and I didn't. Honest. I don't want you to think that you can't trust me."

"Of course I trust you! It's nothing like that, really. It's my fault. I should have explained. I asked Betty to babysit because I didn't want to keep taking advantage of you, that's all. I don't want our friendship to be based on me constantly asking you to help out with my kids. It's also why I asked one of the mums from school to pick the kids up each afternoon until Mum and Dad get back."

"But you know I would have them. I love your kids. They're no trouble and I'm right next door."

"I know, but Fiona from school has two kids, Tom and Grace, who are the same ages as Dan and Ella. It probably works better for them."

"OK, I suppose that makes sense."

"I really didn't mean to upset you. I'm so sorry."

Rosie said there was no need to apologize and that she was sorry she'd jumped to conclusions.

"So how are things going with you and Hugh? Have you done the deed yet?"

"We have."

"Brilliant. So come on, dish. How was it?"

I told her how Hugh had lit candles, how gentle and tender he'd been, how right the whole thing felt, that I hadn't felt this way since Mike. "Worries about the business aside, I can't remember the last time I felt this happy."

"So you think you could be falling for him?"

I said that I thought I might.

"OK, can we change the subject now? I don't do well with jealousy. I might have to kill you."

"I'd rather you didn't, if it's all the same to you."

"I'll do my best. Oh, before I go—I have news. Simon called. Seems he left the Antibes tart and he's back in London. He wants to see me tonight and God knows why, but I've said yes. He says he's got something important to discuss. I might be wrong, but I think he wants us to give it another go."

"Bloody hell. What are you going to say?"

"I don't know. To be honest, I'm all over the place. He's the father of my child and—bottom line—I've never really stopped loving him. A bit of me has always hoped that one day he might change."

"Maybe he has."

"Yeah, well, I'm not holding my breath."

"Listen—I could babysit Will if you like."

"Really? That would be amazing, but you've been at work all day. Are you sure you're up to it?"

I said it wasn't a problem as Hugh was coming over tonight and bringing Chinese, so I wouldn't be busy cooking.

"You absolutely sure?"

"Positive. I'd love to have him."

She said she'd be there around seven. I pressed "end" and looked up. Standing in front of the counter was a woman in her seventies with a Jackie Stallone face-lift and underarm poodle.

"I'm so sorry," I said, "I didn't see you come in."

She dismissed my apology with a haughty wave. "I need to be fitted for new bras." No greeting. No "I wonder if you could help me." Just the announcement.

"Well, you've come to the right place. I should tell you, though, that we don't allow dogs in the shop."

"This isn't a *dog*. This is Jeremy."

"And what a beautiful color he is, too. The lavender really shows off his brown eyes."

"Thank you. I had him dyed to match my bedroom curtains."

"Tell you what, why don't I take Jeremy into the basement and one of my seamstresses could give him a drink."

"All right, but he only has Evian."

"Of course."

She passed the dog to me. I took him downstairs. He was a docile chap. Smelled of Coco Mademoiselle.

"Sorry to be a pain," I said to the aunties, "but would you mind guarding the mutt for a few minutes?"

"Poodle duty again," Aunty Bimla said, laughing. "Forty years and nothing changes. Oh, this one's purple. Very nice."

"And maybe you could give him a drink. Apparently he only has Evian."

"Of course he does." With that, Aunty Sylvia poured some cold tea out of her cup and into a saucer. She lowered the saucer onto the floor. The poodle lapped it up in seconds and then made big "more, please" eyes at Aunty Sylvia.

"Evian, my tuchas," she said, reaching down to refill the saucer.

Jackie Stallone woman insisted that there was no need to measure her. "I'm a perfect 34B. Have been all my life."

"Excellent. Makes my job all the easier."

Even with her jacket on, I could see that the woman was huge. Instead of two breasts, she had a single, enormous ledge. I'd have put money on her being at least a 34F.

Once we were in the fitting room, she took off her top. Her bra was several sizes too small. It was riding up at the back and she had the usual quadraboobs going on: two extra at the top, two at the sides.

"You know what," I said. "I suspect that the bra you have on has shrunk in the wash. It really isn't a great fit."

She stared into the fitting room mirror. "Hmm . . . you could be right. It's my housekeeper's fault. She washes everything at sixty degrees. Ruins everything—silk, cashmere, you name it."

I brought her three bras in a 34G, but didn't mention the size. She tried them on. Her crepey quadraboobs were no more.

"Oh, these are perfect. I'll take two of each."

"Excellent. Tell you what—I can see that the labels are rubbing you. Why don't I cut them out?"

"Good idea. I have very sensitive skin and they do tend to irritate."

A few moments later, she left the shop, Jeremy under one arm, her Sarah Green Lingerie bag over the other, a contented smile on her face.

"So, how did it go?" I said to Hugh as I let him in.

He shook his head. "I didn't even get to audition. By the time I got there, they'd already chosen somebody." He handed me the bag of Chinese food and we headed into the kitchen.

"That's a bit bloody mean. Not even giving you the chance."

"Way it goes," he said.

"Oh, hon," I said, putting my arm around him. "I'm really sorry. I was sure you were going to get it."

"Actually, I'm OK about it. I've got plenty of building work lined up. It pays far better than the theater."

"I know, but that's hardly the point." I put the bag of food down on the kitchen table.

"Maybe not, but what can I do? I'll get over it. . . . Now come on . . . tell me about your day."

"Not a lot of customers," I said, "but I made a couple of decent sales. I guess it's going to be slow until the word gets around."

"And it will get around. You just need to be patient."

I'd just cracked open a couple of bottles of Chinese beer when Rosie and Will arrived. For once Will wasn't asleep. He was wide-awake and kicking in his little bouncy chair.

"Hey, you guys," Rosie said. "Thank you so much for agreeing to look after Will."

I hadn't actually mentioned to Hugh that we were watching Will, but he didn't seem remotely perturbed.

Rosie put Will's chair down on the kitchen floor and handed me a plastic carrier bag. I glanced inside: nappies, wipes and a bottle of formula. "Sorry, I have to get going. I'm running late. I shouldn't be more than a couple of hours."

"No rush," I said as she gave Will a good-bye kiss.

After Rosie had gone, Hugh and the kids laid the table and opened the cartons of food while I played with Will.

"Look at you," I cooed as I watched his chubby hand make a grab for one of the plastic animals strung across his chair. "You are such a clever boy. Yes you are." Will beamed back at me. "Look, he's smiling. He's smiling. I need to take a picture for Rosie. Quick, where's my phone?"

It was on the table. Hugh handed it to me and I started snapping. "There's a lovely smile! There's a lovely smile."

By now Ella was playing peekaboo with him. "Look, Mum . . . look. He's actually laughing. Get another picture."

Dan groaned. "Why do girls get so goofy around babies?"

"It's called hormones," I heard Hugh say. I was pleased that he was bonding with Dan.

"What are they?" Dan said.

"Chemicals. They're what make girls girls."

"Well, I'm glad I haven't got them."

"Actually, you do."

"What?"

"Don't panic," Hugh said, laughing. "They're special man hormones. Speaking of which, how do you fancy coming with me to see Chelsea next week?"

"Yeah! You bet!"

"Right," I said. "Since Will's happy playing, why don't we all sit down and eat?"

I watched Dan and Ella pile food onto their plates.

"You two still hungry?" I said.

"God, yeah," Dan said. "Fiona gave us this stuff that tasted like poo."

"Yeah. And these disgusting fries."

"Well, she told me you loved it and that you both ate loads. So thank you for being polite. I really appreciate it." I paused. "Listen, something's worrying me. . . . Are you guys OK with me farming you out to Fiona? I feel really guilty about not being there to pick you up from school. But I'm not sure what else . . ."

"Don't worry," Ella said. "Fiona's is great. Grace and I practiced our songs for the old people. We did 'Edelweiss' and Fiona joined in. She's good fun."

"Yeah and Tom's got Gross Science."

"What on earth is Gross Science?"

"It's brilliant. You can make this life-size wobbly brain, and stomach vomit and wounds with maggots and zits that you can actually squeeze . . . with real pus."

"Stoppit," Ella yelled. "I'm eating." She turned to me. "Him and Tom chased Grace and me with the vomit and we told Fiona and she yelled at them."

"Good for her. The whole thing sounds disgusting."

"I disagree," Hugh said. "I think it sounds great. Why didn't we have toys like that when we were kids? So, Dan, how do you actually make the pus?"

Dan was about to explain, but Ella punched him on the arm.

At this point I decided that a change of subject might be in order. "Oh, by the way, a woman came into the shop today with a purple poodle."

"Our maggots were purple."

Great. So much for changing the subject.

"Kids, tell you what, why don't you take your plates into the living room and watch a DVD?"

They didn't need telling twice.

Hugh poured me another Chinese beer.

"By the way," I said. "Thank you for inviting Dan to football. I really appreciate it. It's the kind of thing boys miss out on when they don't have a dad around."

"My pleasure," he said. "He's a great kid. We'll have fun. In fact, they're both great kids."

"They are, but then I am biased." I drank some beer. "Oh, FYI, I've decided what to do about the school fair." The idea had come to me last night as I was dropping off to sleep.

"Go on."

I got up and closed the door so that the kids wouldn't hear.

"To compensate for the lack of Greg Myers I'm going to hire a rockabilly band."

"That's a great idea. Everybody loves rockabilly."

"That's what I thought."

"OK, so how are you going to explain the lack of Greg Myers?"

I'd worked that out last night, too.

"I've decided to come clean. I'm fed up with lying. It's too stressful. I loathe Tara and Charlotte and they're going to be crowing for years, but I got myself into this mess."

"So when will you tell them?"

"As soon as I've got the band sorted. I'll send a group e-mail and then wait for the brickbats to come flying."

"Don't do that. Wait until the actual day of the fair."

"Why? What would that achieve?"

"Once they see what a great band you've got and everybody's bopping and having a great time, they won't be so angry. The flak might not be so bad."

"But I did a bad thing. I deserve the flak."

"Yes, but you don't deserve the vitriol you'll get from the likes of Tara and Charlotte. Damage limitation is what you should be aiming for. Take my advice and hold off saying anything until the actual day. Do it for me."

"For you? Hugh, why are you so worked up about all this? It's kind of you, but I can take care of myself."

"I know, but I hate the idea of you being bullied by these bitches."

I reached out and took his hand. "Thank you for worrying, but if

I know Tara and Charlotte, it won't last long. They'll soon get bored and go in search of somebody else to pick on."

"Maybe, but I'd still rather you didn't own up right now."

"I need to. I can't go on being dishonest." I stabbed a kung pao prawn. "Unless of course I made a public statement on the day. Then I'd really be falling on my sword. I suppose an e-mail is a bit cowardly."

"Exactly. Getting up in public is going to take a hell of a lot of guts. But in the end it could work out for the best."

I wasn't entirely convinced, but I decided to take Hugh's advice on the grounds that it was probably the lesser of two evils. "OK, I'll hold off making the announcement."

"Excellent. And let me lend you the money to pay for the band. Anybody decent is going to cost the best part of a grand."

I leaned across and kissed him on the forehead. "That's a lovely gesture and thank you, but I'd rather stick it on my credit card. I got myself into this mess. It feels better if I take responsibility."

"And how will you pay it back?"

"I dunno. Work hard, I guess."

Since Will had nodded off and the kids were in the living room glued to *Back to the Future III*—which was going on way past their school night bedtime—I got out my laptop and Googled "rockabilly bands." There were loads, all with names like the Hound Dogs and the Alley Cats. We listened to half a dozen or so playing "Tutti Frutti," "Blue Suede Shoes, "Great Balls of Fire." They were all pretty good. In the middle of the Milkshakers' "Be-Bop-a-Lula," Hugh grabbed my hand and we went jiving around the kitchen. He was terrific. I was terrible. I had almost no idea what I was doing, but pretty soon we were turning and spinning—me yelling at him to be careful of Will—who somehow remained fast asleep in his bouncy chair. When the music finished, we stood in front of each other laughing and breathless, me complimenting him on his great moves.

"I have others," he said, drawing me towards him.

"Really? Why don't you show me?"

"Well . . . I have this," he said, slipping my dress strap off my shoulder and kissing my neck. "And I have this." His hand was under my skirt, stroking the inside of my thigh. "Oh, and this . . ." He pulled away the crotch of my panties and pushed two fingers hard inside me.

"Hugh! Stop! The kids. They're next door."

"Sorry. I totally forgot. But I can't keep my hands off you. I suppose it's too early for me to start sleeping over?"

"I think so. The kids aren't ready. I'd need to sit down and explain about us. And I don't know what I'd say. It's not like we're planning to get married or live together. We've only just started dating. We need to give it time."

"Fine, but can you enlist Betty's services a bit more?"

I promised that I would. The kids seemed to really like her. The night she'd come to babysit, she'd brought a pack of cards and taught them gin rummy and pontoon. Dan loved it. Ella insisted that she did, too, but I knew she was still far too young for games like rummy and pontoon. Further investigation revealed that what she'd really enjoyed was playing with Betty and beating Dan.

"So, which band do you think was best?" Hugh was saying now. "The Milkshakers were pretty good, but like I said, they're going to cost you."

I said that I'd get the bedpans appraised by an antiques expert. "You never know. One of them might be worth a fortune."

"I promise you, they're not. They're worth what you paid for them."

"Well, sixty quid's better than nothing. I'll just have to put the rest on my credit card. Not a great idea, I grant you, but I don't have a choice."

I sat down and e-mailed the Milkshakers, asking if they might be available to open the school fair and perform a two-hour set.

*R*osie got back just after ten.

"So, how did it go with Simon?" I said.

She flopped into an armchair. "He says he loves me, that he always has, that he's sorry for the way he's treated me and wants to move back in. Plus some production company or other has bought his screenplay, so he can afford to pay his way."

"Wow. So what did you say?"

"I said no."

"Why?"

"I'll tell you why. We spent two hours in the pub and he barely mentioned Will. I think he asked after him once. He's simply not interested in being a dad. Even though he's making money, he just wants somewhere cheap to hang out. He hasn't changed."

"That must have been hard."

Rosie was close to tears. "Come on," Hugh said. "Have a drink." He took a Chinese beer out of the fridge.

For once, Rosie didn't hesitate. She took a sip and tears began streaming down her face.

"On the upside," Hugh said, "Sarah's solved the Greg Myers problem by hiring a rockabilly band."

"Great idea," Rosie said, between sobs. "Everybody loves a rockabilly band." She sniffed. The tears kept coming.

I whispered to Hugh that maybe this wasn't the right time to be discussing rockabilly bands.

"Sorry, I was just trying to lighten the atmosphere, that's all."

"I know, but it isn't working."

"The thing is, I never stopped loving him," Rosie sobbed. "I always lived in hope that one day he might change."

I put my arms around her. "I know, hon, but hard as it was, you did the right thing."

"I guess. I'm just so bloody sad, that's all. I'm starting to think that nobody's ever going to want me."

"Stop it. For starters you're a new mother and you haven't exactly been on the dating scene. Second, you're gorgeous and funny. Of course somebody will want you."

"Hear, hear," Hugh said. "Now, how's about I make you a plate of Chinese? There's loads left."

"That would be nice." Sniff. "Thank you."

In the living room, Ella burst into song: "Matchmaker, matchmaker, make me a match. . . ."

Chapter 12

Two weeks later, Mum called to say that she and Dad were missing the kids and me so much that they were coming home as soon as they'd finished their flamenco course. She was at pains to point out that the decision to finish the course was Dad's, not hers. They'd been away the best part of two months and she was anxious to get back, but apparently Dad had almost mastered the *jaberas*—a tricky Málagan fandango—and wanted to see it through to the end.

By now, Hugh and I were spending a lot of time together, either in bed at his place or—since the kids were always around—not in bed at mine. He was working hard at making friends with them: "OK, Ella, I think you've finally nailed 'Edelweiss.' Why don't we take 'Supercalifragilisticexpialidocious' again, from the top?" He'd taken Dan to football twice now. "We had such a great time," he said one night over dinner at his place. "I think the two of us are really bonding." He paused. "You don't mind, do you? I mean, I'd hate it if you felt I was treading on your toes."

"Mind? I couldn't be more delighted. I love it that he's got some-body to take him to a game. Dad takes him occasionally, but he's never been a huge football fan."

"Excellent. So you'll be pleased to hear that I've decided to buy Dan a season ticket to Chelsea. So now we'll both have one."

"Hugh, that's incredibly generous and Dan will hero-worship you until the end of time, but season tickets cost a fortune, as you well know."

Hugh shrugged. "I can afford it. Plus I'm going to do that trekking-in-Morocco trip I've been talking about."

"When?" *The Producers* had finished its run, but as far as I knew, he had months of building work lined up.

"November. Things always go quiet in the run-up to Christmas. Why don't you come with me?"

"I'd love to, but I've got the kids to think about, and I couldn't even think about leaving the business."

His mouth turned down at the corners. "I don't want to go on my own."

"Brilliant, so don't go and put the money into a savings account."

If I was honest, it wasn't just the thought of him spending the money that troubled me. Maybe I was jumping the gun, but I couldn't help thinking that if we decided at some stage to make our relationship permanent, he would still want to take these trips abroad—leaving me, not to mention the children, who already thought the world of him, alone for weeks or even months at a time. When it came to men, I'd never been the needy, clingy type and I had no problem with Hugh—or me, for that matter—taking short breaks. The occasional week apart could be good for a relationship.

Months were different. I'd lost Mike to the next world. I didn't want to lose Hugh to this one.

"Why should I put the money in a savings account?" Hugh said. "I've got all I need."

"Yes, for now, but suppose you got ill and couldn't work."

"I'd be entitled to benefits. I don't need much to live on. I own a few nice boy toys. I could always sell them. Plus I'm used to eating potatoes and beans."

"But what about other things . . . clothes, shoes, haircuts?"

He shrugged. "I'd get by."

"OK, but what about now? If you had money saved, you could think about buying a flat or a car. I definitely want those things. I want to be in a position where I can buy the kids new clothes without having to stop and think if I can afford it. And I always want to have money in the bank—something to fall back on."

"Fair enough, but just make sure you don't end up the richest corpse in the cemetery."

"That's a mean thing to say. You make it sound like I'm obsessed with money."

He reached out and touched my arm. "I'm sorry. I shouldn't have said that. Of course you're not obsessed with money. It's just that I see too many people hoarding cash instead of getting pleasure from it."

It was the first time we'd had anything approaching a cross word and it left me feeling troubled. There was no doubt in my mind that I was falling for Hugh, but I was worried that his attitude to money—not to mention his long absences—might become a thing.

A month after the shop opened, business wasn't picking up and I was starting to panic. Bills were piling up that I couldn't pay. I'd used my credit card to pay the Milkshakers a hundred-quid deposit. I was making sales, but not enough. Theater orders were trickling in, but not flooding. I decided to hold a strategy meeting with the aunties to discuss our next move. I asked if they could come in half an hour early on Monday morning.

When I arrived, Aunty Sylvia was in tears. Aunty Bimla was doing her best to comfort her with platitudes, which didn't appear to be working.

I put my arm around her. "Aunty Sylvia, what on earth is it? I know business is slow, but you mustn't let it get to you. If we put our heads together I'm sure we'll come up with a plan."

"It's not that."

It turned out that Roxanne's cute little centipede movie had been canceled and she was back working on the checkout in Target.

"I keep telling her that Roxanne will be fine," Aunty Bimla said. "And that God never gives us more than we can handle."

"It's the second time this has happened to her," Aunty Sylvia said, dabbing her eyes and ignoring Aunty Bimla. "A few years ago she got a part in a cable show that got canceled. She was so happy to have finally got her big break and now it's all gone. I'm just beside myself."

Yes, but nothing like as beside herself as she would have been if she'd discovered the true nature of *Human Centipede 4*. Now Aunty Sylvia wouldn't have a stroke from the shock and drop down dead. As far as I was concerned, the film being canceled was a miracle.

"That's Tinseltown for you," Aunty Bimla said. "It builds you up and then it steals your dreams."

Aunty Sylvia dabbed her eyes. "Did your father say that?"

"No, Heath Ledger."

"It'll work out, you'll see," I said to Aunty Sylvia.

"It won't. Roxanne's talking about leaving LA and coming home."

"Is that such a bad thing?" I said. "Maybe it's time she made a fresh start. And if you're honest, I think you'd like nothing better than to have her home."

"Yes, but not if she's going to be unhappy."

"And how happy has she been working in a supermarket? When she gets home, maybe she could go take a course, retrain maybe."

A sniff from Aunty Sylvia. "You could be right. Perhaps she could work with animals. Roxanne's always loved animals. When she was little, she kept stick insects. The other kids were really scared of them, so Roxanne would take them to school and put them in their lunch boxes."

Part of me was glad that when I was growing up, my path and Roxanne's had never crossed.

"You know," Aunty Bimla said, "not a day goes by when I don't thank the Almighty for giving me Sanjeev and turning him into such a successful entrepreneur."

"Yes, well, not all of us can be as lucky as you," Aunty Sylvia snapped back.

In an effort to ease the tension, I said I would put the kettle on.

"Just half a cup for me," Aunty Sylvia said.

I got up and flicked the switch on the kettle. "Oh, guess what, I finally got those bedpans appraised by a dealer."

"And?" Aunty Bimla said.

"He said they were worth the sixty quid I paid for them. I put them on eBay and they ended up going for seventy, but I forgot to ask the buyer to pay the postage. So I ended up exactly where I started."

"Such a putz," Aunty Sylvia said.

We all started laughing. The mood had lifted.

So, I said, "If we could focus on the business for a moment. Have either of you got any thoughts on how we could give it a bit of a kick start?"

There was no getting away from it; the big mistake had been my failure to set aside any money for advertising.

"Plus your Web site isn't top-notch," Aunty Bimla said.

Aunty Sylvia blinked at her. "What on earth do you know about Web sites?"

"Nothing at all, but I showed it to Sanjeev before he went to Paraguay. He said—and I quote: 'The problem is you have no back end.'"

"Stop it, Sarah has a perfectly nice back end."

I said that I knew what Sanjeev meant. My cheapo Web site was nothing more than a shop window. There was no way for customers to look at the products or buy online. "It was all I could afford. I can't improve it until there's some spare cash."

"What about twittering?" Aunty Bimla said. "Sanjeev says that in business it is most important to . . . now let me get this right . . . *to hone your social media savvy.* He also mentioned something called *visibility.* We should think about a mission statement and post it on Facebook. And what about giving customers loyalty cards—you know, like they do in coffee shops?"

Aunty Sylvia said the idea was far too down-market and I was inclined to agree.

"You know what I think we should be doing?" I said. "Checking out the opposition. I've just realized that now Clementine Montecute is out of the frame, I've no idea who our main rivals are or if they're doing any better than us. If they are doing better, I need to find out why."

"Obviously there are the department stores," Aunty Sylvia said, "but none of them does a bespoke service. Then there are few small lingerie shops dotted about the West End. Oh, and of course . . . Valentina di Rossi."

I knew the name at once. Valentina di Rossi owned La Feminista. She had a branch in Kensington and a few more in the well-to-do suburbs. The business went back decades and was hugely successful. Gossip had it that Valentina di Rossi had been the only thorn in Clementine Montecute's side.

"I think I should pay La Feminista a visit," I said.

"Poppet, don't. The place is so chic and glamorous. It will only make you depressed."

"Probably, but I need to take a look. I should have done it months ago."

"OK," Aunty Sylvia said, "but whatever you do, don't announce yourself."

"Why not?"

"It's a long story."

"Go on. I'm listening."

It turned out that way back, Aunty Shirley and Valentina di Rossi had been good friends. They'd managed this despite being business rivals. Then they had an enormous falling-out.

"It was back in our heyday, poppet—when we had so much work

we were rushed off our feet. We didn't know if we were coming or going."

"When we were really up against it," Aunty Sylvia broke in, "we would subcontract work. Shirley would give work to Valentina and vice versa. So one day Shirley asks if Valentina's seamstresses can take on a big theater order that we can't manage. They say yes. They do the work and Shirley refuses to pay up."

"But why on earth would she do that?"

"Shirley said the work wasn't up to standard, but it was. It was crazy—Bimla and I had to sit and remake all those corsets."

"But that's crazy. Aunty Shirley would never do something like that."

The aunties explained that it had happened around the time that Uncle Harry was dying.

"Shirley went a bit crazy," Aunty Sylvia said. "Actually she went a lot crazy. It was the stress of running the business and watching Harry die. She started having terrible panic attacks. She was on tranquilizers and antidepressants. Round about the time she refused to pay Valentina the money she owed, her doctor diagnosed a breakdown and she finally agreed to go into a psychiatric hospital. Bimla and I went to see Valentina to try to explain what was happening, but she didn't want to know. She was too angry. When Shirley came out of hospital, Valentina threatened to take her to court, but in the end she gave up because her legal costs would have amounted to more than she was owed. Valentina never forgave her."

"How much was involved?"

"Five thousand pounds," Aunty Sylvia said. "And that was a long time ago. Apparently Valentina was desperate for the money. She needed it to pay for her mother's eye surgery in Switzerland."

"But surely she could have gotten it from the bank? What about her husband?"

"He was an architect struggling to make a go of his new business. The bank refused her a loan because she'd just borrowed thousands to renovate the shop. Shirley—who was still loopy—accused her of making it all up, but a few months later her mother went blind and committed suicide. Once Shirley recovered, she realized what she'd done and wanted to repay her, but she could never afford it. Business had started to slow down and Harry left her with a mountain of debt. I think not being able to repay Valentina haunted her for the rest of her life."

I thought back to the day before Aunty Shirley died and what she'd said to me about having regrets. This was what she was referring to.

"That's awful. What a mess. Mum never told me anything about this. I suppose you can't really blame Valentina for being angry. On the other hand, Aunty Shirley was a basket case."

"You've no idea how ill she was," Aunty Bimla said. "Your poor mother was beside herself with worry."

It was typical of my mother that at the time she had shielded me from her distress.

"So, like I say," Aunty Sylvia said. "Go if you must, but don't introduce yourself. You won't be welcome."

I had no intention of making myself known to Valentina di Rossi. I imagined her yelling and swearing at me in Italian and chasing me out of the premises.

I asked the aunties to mind the shop and took the bus to Kensington. La Feminista was just off High Street.

The shop still had its original Georgian bow window. There were no mannequins in the window. Clearly Valentina thought that models draped in lingerie—no matter how expensive—looked trashy. It occurred to me that my window display could be turning customers off.

Outside, deep window boxes were bursting with garish geraniums and petunias. Gray marble steps led up to the door. A perfectly manicured bay tree stood at either side. I opened the glass door and felt my heels sink into the carpet. Assistants in black skirts and white blouses hovered. Women with impossibly young faces sat reading the glossies as they waited to be fitted.

One of the black-skirted assistants approached me and asked if she could be of help. "Oh . . . um . . . yes, I'd like to look at your swimwear."

She directed me to the rail. I browsed the swimsuits and bikinis, which turned out to be far less exciting than mine and much more expensive. But I guessed that the kind of women who shopped here expected to pay a fortune. It was reassuring, made them feel that they were in safe, dependable hands.

I had just picked up a swimsuit and spotted that the stitching on one of the straps was coming loose when I saw a woman coming down the thickly carpeted staircase, half a dozen bras draped over her wrist. She was carrying a few extra pounds around her middle. Her face was heavily lined. There was no evidence of "work," no attempt to disguise her age, which at a guess was north of seventy. But she wasn't lacking in elegance. Her gray hair had been cut into a soft chin-length bob. Her simple gray shift had been set off with a jazzy scarf and a long string of pearls. She must have seen me staring at her. "Can I be of assistance?" she said, smiling. Hint of an Italian accent. This was definitely di Rossi.

"Thank you, but I'm just looking."

"Well, if you need any help, just shout."

She turned to go, but by now curiosity had got the better of me. I wanted to talk to her, find out more about her relationship with Aunty Shirley, but I couldn't think of a way in.

"Actually, I'm in the lingerie business," I blurted.

"Really?"

"*Y*es . . . I'm Sarah Green . . . Shirley Feldman's niece. You probably heard that she died recently. I've taken over her shop."

The smile vanished. "Yes, I knew she'd passed away."

I waited for her condolence, but none was forthcoming.

"If you will excuse me," she said. "I am very busy. We're getting ready for the National Lingerie Awards."

The National Lingerie Awards. I hadn't heard those words in years. Better known as the Bra Oscars, the NLAs—which was a competition rather than a simple awards ceremony—used to be a huge deal. When I was a child, Aunty Shirley entered every year. Contestants—who had to work in the industry—were asked to design a piece of lingerie, usually a bra, basque or corset. There was always a theme. I remember once it was "itsy-bitsy teeny-weeny." Every year, in the weeks leading up to the competition it was the same song and dance at the shop: Aunty Shirley and the aunties flapping, fussing and fighting and staging all-nighters at the sewing machines. Shirley Feldman Foundation Garments won the itsy-bitsy teeny-weeny award. I could still see that half-cup black and pink polka-dot bra. In fact she won the competition a few times. There was no cash prize, just a tacky bronze statue of an impossibly thin and busty woman in her bra and panties. The real prize was coverage galore in the upmarket glossies, which had the A-listers flocking. Winning the Bra Oscars was one of the reasons that, back in the day, the business did so well. Then Shirley stopped entering. I had assumed the competition had been dropped. Clearly it hadn't.

"Of course," I heard myself say. "I understand how frazzled you must be. I'm the same. It's always so stressful in the weeks leading up to the competition."

What was I saying? I was clearly having another Greg Myers moment.

"You're entering the competition?" Valentina di Rossi arched an eyebrow.

I swallowed hard. "Yes. Why wouldn't I?"

I could think of several reasons why I wouldn't. I hadn't the foggiest notion what this year's entrants were being asked to make or if I was capable of making it. . . . On the other hand, I did have the aunties. Finally, I had no idea of the closing date for entries. For all I knew, it could be tomorrow.

"By the way," Valentina said, "I don't know what you are doing here, but please don't come again. You are not welcome. Please leave."

"I'm sorry you feel that way. After what happened between you and Aunty Shirley, I was curious to meet you, that's all. It was wrong of me. I apologize."

Having asked me to go, she wouldn't let me.

"Do you know what Shirley did to me?"

"I do and I'm so very sorry."

"Your aunt killed my mother. I hope her soul burns in hell."

"Shirley was very ill. She didn't know what she was doing."

"My mother was ill. And she committed suicide. Now, please leave."

I did as she asked.

Chapter 13

The first thing I did when I got back to the shop was Google the National Lingerie Awards. It appeared that the competition had been struggling for a long time—mainly due to Clementine Montecute. She won the competition nearly every year, and the gossip was that she had the judges in her pocket. Last year, when fewer than a dozen people entered, there had been talk of the competition being dropped. All this explained why it had been off my radar for so long.

This year, though, things had changed. Clementine Montecute was no more, and for the first time, *The British Lingerie Review*—the dull but important trade magazine—was sponsoring the competition, with all new judges.

I went in search of the online entry form. This year's theme was "a gap in the market." The judges wanted entrants to design and make a piece of lingerie that women wanted but struggled to find in the stores. The closing date was July 2.

"Crap."

"What is?" Aunty Sylvia had appeared, carrying a tray of tea.

I turned my laptop screen towards her. She put the tray down on the counter and started reading.

"The closing date's in two weeks," I said. "We'd never make it."

"And why would we want to? Nobody goes in for the Bra Oscars anymore. It's a fix. We haven't entered for donkey's years."

"I know, but carry on reading. Now that Clementine Montecute's gone, everything's changed."

By now Aunty Bimla had appeared with a plate of digestive biscuits.

"Bimla, take a look at this," Aunty Sylvia said.

Aunty Bimla looked. "Well, I never . . . all new judges . . . And you're really thinking of entering?"

"I don't know. Maybe. You have to tell me honestly. Do you think we'd have a chance?"

"It's possible," Aunty Sylvia said. "Back in the old days, we won it three or four times. But you're forgetting Valentina di Rossi."

"Come on . . . who has the best seamstresses—me or Valentina? And you've beaten her before, right?"

"We have."

"Right, then surely it's a no-brainer."

Aunty Sylvia said that she wasn't so sure. "I admit that her most experienced seamstresses have retired and that perhaps the younger women she's got working for her aren't as good, but this competition isn't simply about cutting and stitching. It's about design. Sarah, you'd have to design a bra or a corset and make a pattern—something you have never done. Something Valentina has been doing for decades, and you can take it from me, the woman is extremely gifted."

"She's really that good?" It was a stupid question. Of course she was.

Aunty Sylvia nodded. "Every bit as good as Shirley was."

"Crap," I said again. I reached for a digestive and started munching.

"On the other hand if we came up with the right thing," Aunty Bimla said, "something that really filled a gap in the market . . . who knows? Anything's possible."

That's when the idea hit me. "OK, got it. What about the étagère bra? That's never gone into mass-market production."

Aunty Bimla was shaking her head. "Everybody who makes bespoke lingerie does a version of the étagère. I would bet you a pound to a penny that nearly all the contestants will try their hand at it. We need to find something different."

"Great. But what?"

Nobody spoke. The aunties stood sipping their tea. I suggested we go away and think about it.

"Aunty Bimla's right. With the right idea, we could actually win this competition. . . ."

"I didn't quite say that. I said it might be possible."

"OK, but even if we don't win, it would be a chance to put the business on the map. I'd be more than happy to settle for that. I think we have to enter if we possibly can. Agreed?"

The aunties looked at each other and shrugged as if to say, "What do we have to lose?" "Agreed," they said.

We clinked teacups. Then, for some reason, Aunty Bimla started checking out the entry form again. "Poppet, look. It says that on the night of the awards ceremony, there is to be a fashion show so that the audience can see all the entries and after that, the judges will make their final decision. Apparently contestants are expected to provide their own models."

"Well, that's easy," Aunty Sylvia said, waving a digestive. "Rosie. She's gorgeous and with her top half, she'd be perfect."

Aunty Bimla agreed. "Rosie has the most perfect boobies."

"I wonder if she'd do it," I said, draining my teacup.

We all agreed that there could be no harm in asking. "I'll pop in and see her tonight."

Aunty Bimla began gathering up empty cups.

"By the way," I said, "I called in on Valentina di Rossi."

"Poppet, what on earth possessed you? Didn't you listen to a word we said?"

"Of course I did, but curiosity got the better of me, that's all."

"With all the aggravation we've got," Aunty Sylvia said, "we need this like a hole in the head."

"Need what?"

"Look, don't get me wrong," Aunty Bimla said. "We all feel sorry for Valentina, but she's always had a temper. By crossing her you have reignited the dragon's fury. I wouldn't put anything past her."

"Oh, please. Maybe I should point out that this is not an episode of *Game of Thrones*."

"Game of what?" Aunty Bimla inquired.

"Thrones," I said. "It's a fantasy drama on TV."

"About dragons?"

"Dragons do appear, but it's mainly about war and power struggles."

"Oh, I know," Aunty Sylvia piped up. "It's the one with the sexy midget."

Aunty Bimla was waving her finger. "You know it's not at all politically correct to refer to somebody as a midget. The *Guardian* recently printed a glossary of the latest socially acceptable terms and I think they prefer dwarf or little person."

"Midget, dwarf, whatever. I'm telling you he's really sexy. I'm not kidding. If I was thirty years younger and three feet shorter . . ." Aunty Sylvia cackled. Then she stopped. "So what's an elf, then?"

When I got home, I called Mum in Spain to tell her about the Bra Oscars and to find out if she could throw any more light on the Valentina di Rossi affair.

She thought entering the competition was a marvelous idea. She agreed that we didn't need to win and that getting noticed would be enough.

As far as Valentina di Rossi went, Mum knew about as much as the aunties. "Dad and I went to see her, too—you know, to explain that Shirley was in a terrible way and in hospital. Later we even offered to pay her the five thousand pounds, but by then her mother had died. She didn't want to speak to us. She just told us to get out."

"Yes, she showed me the door, too," I said.

"I know for a fact that she still holds a terrible grudge and, to be honest, who can blame her? I came across her a few years ago. We happened to be standing next to each other in the taxi queue outside Waterloo station. I was in front of her, but the moment my cab appeared, she barged past me with such force that I almost fell backwards. As she got in, she let out some curse in Italian. I would have given anything just to sit down and talk to her. But she's still too angry. Even though she was crazy, my sister did a terrible thing. You have to feel sorry for Valentina."

"Of course you do. The woman is clearly tormented, but at the same time she's all mouth. Seriously . . . what's she going to do?"

*H*ugh popped in after dinner on his way home from work. He'd been fitting a kitchen in a house a few streets away. I offered to put something in the oven for him, but he said he'd already grabbed a pizza.

"Listen, hon," I said before he'd even taken off his jacket, "can you watch the kids for a bit while I go next door? There's something I need to ask Rosie. Oh, and don't let them eat any more ice cream. They've already had loads. I don't want them to get stomachaches. And Dan needs to finish his homework and they need to start getting ready for bed in twenty minutes or so."

"Sure. Anything else? Move the house a little to the left, maybe?"

"No, that's it," I said, grinning. I gave him a quick peck on the cheek. "Thanks. I won't be long. Promise."

Rosie answered the door, cell clamped to her ear.

"There's clearly been some confusion," she was saying. "I don't do lesbian sex. . . . Why not? . . . I don't know. Maybe it's because I'm straight and I can't get into it. . . . Look, if you think I'm betraying the sisterhood, that's up to you. If I could do it, I would. Believe me, I could use the money. . . . Maybe you're right and I should be more bi-curious. . . . I'm sorry if you think I'm not doing enough for dyke visibility and yes, I will read Ellen DeGeneres' autobiography. In fact I will do it now . . . as soon as I get off the phone. Yes, and *snatch the day* to you, too . . ."

Rosie hit "end" and pulled a face at the phone. "God knows how she got hold of my number."

I told Rosie she looked like she could use a drink.

"Too right." She said that now she'd started weaning Will onto solids, she was buying wine again and that there were a couple of bottles of sauvignon blanc in the fridge.

She led the way into the kitchen. "I'm so knackered," she said, opening the fridge. "William's rebelling against his new big-boy cot. He was just screaming for an hour. No sooner had I got him down than this bloke rang who wanted me to pretend I was Björk and kept complaining because I couldn't do an Icelandic accent. He was followed by the crazy lesbian."

She handed me a glass of wine and went over to the oven. "Hope you don't mind watching me eat," she said, removing a foil container, "but I'm starving."

We sat at the kitchen table, Rosie eating lasagna out of the container. I asked her how she was feeling about Simon. She said she was finally starting to let go, albeit slowly.

"You know what I need?" she said.

"What?"

"A new start. I have to ditch this bloody job. It's so tedious and depressing."

"Actually, that's why I'm here. I have a job for you. It's only a one-off, but I think it could lead to other things."

"You know what, I'm not great at shop work. Plus the posh women customers you have to deal with would really piss me off. I'd end up telling them where to go."

I said it had nothing to do with working in the shop and explained about the competition. "Before the prizes are handed out, all the bras are going to be modeled and I thought—with your fabulous chesticles—you could model mine."

"So you're asking me to get up in front of hundreds of people in my bra and knickers?"

"Oh, come on. You of all people can't have a problem with that."

She held her fork in midair. "I do when I know that the audience will be full of ogling men. I mean why would any man who wasn't an A-list creep decide to go into the lingerie business? It's the same with male gynecologists. I find the whole thing a bit pervy."

I said that sounded a tad harsh.

Rosie said she thought I was being a tad naive.

"OK," I said. "If you're not comfortable with it, that's fine."

"And let's face it, I'm way too old to start modeling. And you know I have all these self-esteem issues. . . ."

"Oh please. You're stunning and you know it. Despite what your mother did to you, I'm guessing that deep down you always knew it. Come on, Rosie, you're looking for a new start and this might lead to something really big."

She didn't seem convinced. "It'll lead to a load of pervs gawping at my tits, that's where it'll lead." She paused, clearly mulling. "OK, do I get to keep the bra?"

"You bet. It will have been specially made for you."

"And somebody would do my hair and makeup?"

"Absolutely."

"In that case . . ."

"You'll do it?"

"I admit I'm warming to the idea."

I got up and hugged her. "Thank you so much. You have no idea what this means to me."

"You're welcome. I just hope I don't fuck up."

"Don't be daft. Of course you won't fuck up."

I said that the theme was "a gap in the market." "What are women looking for that they can't find in the stores?"

"Oh, come on. That's easy."

"It is?"

"Of course it is. What women want but can't ever find is a decent nursing bra. It simply doesn't exist. The things you buy in the shops are more like mammary hoists. No real support. Your breasts just jig around. Why is it so hard to make something that fits?"

This rang a loud bell. Why hadn't I thought of it? How often had I moaned about the nursing bras I bought when I was breast-feeding Dan and Ella? In fact they'd been so useless support-wise that I stopped wearing them. I told Rosie how I'd ended up modifying my ordinary bras. By cutting away part of the cup, I made a flap, which could be unhooked for feeding and reattached afterwards. Nursing bra manufacturers used the same method. The only difference was, I was starting with a decent bra. (At least I thought I was. At that stage I hadn't had the benefit of being fitted by Aunty Shirley.)

"Brilliant," Rosie said. "So all you have to do is design me the perfect bra with an inbuilt breast-feeding modification."

"I wish it was that easy. The problem I've got—as the aunties keep reminding me—is that I've never designed a bra before, let alone made a pattern."

She asked me why the aunties couldn't make the pattern. I said they'd never been taught.

"But you studied fashion. Surely you've made patterns."

"Yes—for dresses and pants. Have you any idea how complicated a bra pattern is? I've seen them. They look more like blueprints for a suspension bridge."

"Well, I have every faith in you. I know you can do it. And when you do, all the mothers out there are going to love you, and the bra manufacturers will be offering you a fortune to roll it out. Take it from me, this is a real winner."

"I wouldn't bank on it—not when I'm up against the likes of Valentina di Rossi."

"Isn't she the woman who owns La Feminista? I've read about her. She's a really talented designer."

"She is and that's what scares me, but I know I have the better seamstresses. So we'll just have to see. . . ."

By the time I got back, having told Rosie the entire Valentina di Rossi story over the rest of the sauvignon, the kids were in bed and Hugh had dozed off in front of the football. He woke as soon as I switched it off.

"Hey, I was watching that."

"No, you weren't," I said, going over and planting a kiss on his forehead. "You were snoring."

"I was?"

"Yep." I sat down next to him on the sofa. "Sorry I was so long. Rosie and I got talking."

"No worries. I read to the kids. Oh, and Dan asked me if worms bleed."

"What did you say?"

"I told him that according to the *Boys' Book of Facts* which I was given for Christmas circa 1989, they most definitely did."

"I bet he was impressed."

"He was. The only problem was that Ella got stroppy and insisted the book should have been called *The Children's Book of Facts*, since it wasn't just boys who were interested in knowing if worms bleed."

I laughed. "Good for her. She's got real spirit for a kid her age."

"I know. Like her mother."

We snuggled up. Hugh began playing with my fringe.

"I've got something to tell you," I said. "I'm afraid you won't be seeing much of me over the next couple of weeks."

"How come?"

I explained about the competition and why I'd gone to see Rosie.

"I can certainly see why she'd be the perfect model. And just imagine if you won. How amazing would that be?"

"I know, but we have a serious rival." I told him about Valentina, how talented she was and the story of how she and Aunty Shirley had fallen out.

"The woman's clearly still furious. But you can see why she's pissed off."

"I know. Don't get me wrong. I feel really sorry for her."

The following morning, Mum texted me from the tarmac at Heathrow: *Wheels down. All come for dinner tonight and bring Hugh!!!*

I texted back: *Tonight? You'll be exhausted. Come to me instead.*

She replied: *No effort to put chicken in oven. See you at seven.*

I called Hugh and said that if he wasn't ready to meet my folks and in particular my crazy starstruck mother, I would understand.

"On the other hand, her roast chicken is of the gods."

"Say no more. And since I have a crazy mother of my own, I'm sure I'll manage."

*M*um and Dad looked better than I'd seen them in years. Dad said it was just the tan and his blood pressure was still up and down. "But mostly down," Mum was quick to point out. She'd put on weight and she was laughing and full of bustle. The light that had gone out was shining again.

We managed to get all the hugs and missed-yous out of the way before Hugh got there. He arrived with flowers for Mum, which hit just the right note. Dad pumped his hand and immediately started giving his views on the acting profession, opining that it wasn't what it was, particularly since the likes of Gielgud, Olivier and Redgrave were no more. This hit slightly less than the perfect note, but to his credit Hugh didn't seem remotely put out and even had the good grace to agree.

Mum, who was taking Dad's remarks in slightly less good humor, suggested it was time to give everybody their presents from Spain.

There were sombreros, maracas and painted fans for the kids— olive oil and cured ham for me. Dad presented Hugh with a bottle of sherry. "Now, this isn't any old sherry," Dad said, as if he were presenting Hugh with some ancient Egyptian artifact. "It's a Manzanilla. While we were in Spain, I became something of a Jerez aficionado. The Manzanilla is a jewel among sherries. You'll find it's quite yeasty with woody and roast almond top notes and a nutty finish. Very different from the oloroso, which has an almost cheesy aroma and a more complex finish."

Hugh thanked him and said he couldn't wait to try it. Meanwhile Mum was giving Dad a look that said, "Enough with the tutorial already."

"Hugh, do help yourself to another Gruyère spiral," she said. "So, tell me about *Downton*. What was Dame Maggie like to work with? They do say she can be a bit prickly."

"I was only playing a footman. We didn't actually have any scenes together, but people said she could be pretty demanding."

"She's got such a presence and such an amazing face—those steely eyes that look everybody up and down. And of course when you were in *Jane Eyre*, you got to meet Dame Judy."

"Again, I played a footman, so I only saw her from a distance."

"I'm never too sure about her short hair. I can't help thinking that at her age, it might soften her features if it were a bit longer."

I was in no doubt that Mum was capable of carrying on like this for hours, and we hadn't even sat down to dinner yet.

"And when you were in Hollywood, I don't suppose you got to meet Claire Danes. I love her."

"Actually, no, I didn't."

"So, come on, Dad," I piped up. "Aren't you going to show us your fandango?"

"What's a fandigo?" Ella said.

"It's a fan-dango," Dad explained. "And it's a kind of dance they do in Spain."

"Yes, come on, Granddad, do your dance. We want to see."

"No, I haven't practiced for days and I'd need to get changed."

"Go on, then," Mum said. "Go and get changed."

"All right, but it isn't going to work very well on the carpet."

Mum said he could perform in the kitchen, which had a wood floor.

Dad disappeared upstairs and returned five minutes later wearing a puffy-sleeved shirt, a waistcoat and a black hat with pom-poms. A red sash was tied around his potbelly. Then I noticed the stacked heels. A small, corpulent Jewish man of a certain age on his way to a fancy dress party. Dan and Ella were beside themselves.

We got up and moved into the kitchen.

"Right, what you need to understand," Dad said, "is that a fandango is meant to be a dance for two people and there should be a guitar accompaniment. . . ."

"Come on . . . just get on with it." Mum started clapping out a rhythm—the *palmas*, she called it.

Dad pulled himself up to his full five foot seven and a half—eight and a half if you included the heels. Hands on hips, he lifted his triple chin in an effort to reveal a chiseled jaw. This didn't materialize on account of it being cloaked in jowl. "The stance needs to be proud and self-important," he said.

Mum said he looked more like somebody had just shoved a poker up him.

More hysterics from the children.

Dad began stamping his stacked heels so fast that I was blinking in amazement. Then he started strutting and clapping with such skill and poise that I actually felt my mouth fall open. The rest of us started following Mum's clapping rhythm. Dan and Ella were yelling, "Go, Granddad!" More exotic hand flourishes, swaggering and prancing from Dad. Then he fell backwards over a kitchen stool and managed to knock a cup of cold coffee off the counter.

Hugh rushed to his aid, but the rest of us were paralyzed with laughter. All except Mum, who was tutting because the coffee had gone over the cream roller blind. While she made an emergency dash for the biological detergent, the rest of us told Dad how brilliant he was. "Tell you what—we should get you to do a turn at the school summer fair."

"No way," he said. "This is strictly for private consumption."

Over dinner Mum continued to interrogate Hugh about the actors he'd worked with. On the rare occasions she paused for breath, Dad held forth about the latest DVD he'd acquired—the BBC's *World at War*. It turned out that Hugh was a bit of a Second World War buff and had watched it, too—all twenty-six hours. I could tell that Dad was delighted to be able to talk to somebody to share his enthusiasm. After dinner Dad and Hugh continued to debate whether Churchill should have bombed the concentration camps. The children went to watch TV and Mum and I loaded the dishwasher.

"He's lovely," Mum said. "So handsome, and that voice! I could listen to him for hours. And he's clearly smitten with you."

"You think so?"

"Have you seen the way he looks at you? Of course he is."

I suspected that she might be right about Hugh being smitten. He wasn't the only one. But I wasn't about to tell Mum that. At least not yet.

Chapter 14

The aunties and I agreed that I should work on designing Rosie's bra at home. There were too many distractions at the shop and since trade was slow, they said that they could manage perfectly well on their own.

I began by studying the old, yellowing books on bra design and patternmaking that the aunties had given me. I also bought a couple of more up-to-date manuals. Gradually I began familiarizing myself with bra vocabulary: the wings, the cradle, the bridge, the strap platform. I got acquainted with terms like *cup grading* and *cup apex point*. I also studied the darted-bra grading rules—reason being, I was planning to design Rosie a simple full-cup, darted bra, which I would modify into a nursing bra.

Since I knew what I wanted and I had some experience in changing an ordinary bra into a nursing bra, the design part didn't take long. The bit I was going to struggle with was making the pattern. In preparation, I made space in my bedroom for my old technical drawing board, which I'd got down from Mum and Dad's attic. I bought packs of squared paper, a flexi-curve—a protractor-like device that made it possible to draw curved lines—a flexible ruler to measure curved seams and two sets of compasses, large and small.

I read and reread the manuals, tried to follow the instructions and intricate diagrams. Bra patternmaking seemed to be a cross between origami and trigonometry. Much of the time I was baffled and bewildered, but not as baffled and bewildered as I would have been if I hadn't studied fashion design.

It took a few days, but once I'd decided that I sort of vaguely knew what I was doing, I called Rosie and asked if she could come round so that I could take some measurements. "No probs. Betty just popped in to see Will. I'm sure she wouldn't mind taking him for a walk."

I could hear Betty in the background. "Wouldn't mind? I'd love to. Why don't I take him to the park to see the ducks?"

"So Betty's finally stopped looking down her nose at you for being a single mother?"

"It's Will. Now that he's a bit older, she's started taking a real interest. Every time she sees him, she goes completely gaga. She can't get enough of him. I tell you, what with her looking after your kids and spending the odd hour or two with Will, she's a new woman."

I agreed. Betty was a judgmental old gossip, but now that she felt needed and didn't feel so lonely with us and the children around, the real Betty was coming out.

Rosie showed up a couple of minutes later.

"OK," she said, pulling her T-shirt over her head. "I'm thinking emerald satin with a black lace trim." She raked her hair with her fingers.

"For a nursing bra?"

"Too slutty?"

"A bit," I said. "I think we should probably stick to cream or ivory."

"Yeah, I guess emerald and black doesn't quite say Madonna and baby."

I picked up my tape measure.

"OK, so first I have to get your 'over-breast' measurement." I explained that this involved starting at the "breast root" at her side and taking the tape over her breast to the breast root at the center front.

"Then I have to measure you around the back from breast root to breast root. After that, I can start on making the cup block."

"The what?"

"The pattern."

"Well, you certainly seem to know what you're doing," Rosie said.

"If only you knew," I said, giving her a thin smile. "OK, I need you to raise your arms to your sides."

She lifted her arms and I started taking measurements.

"So how are things with you and Hugh? You do know he's in love with you, don't you?"

"Mum said the same. Except she described him as being smitten. Said she could tell from the way he looks at me."

"Yeah, I've noticed. It's sort of all gooey and doe-eyed—but sexier than that sounds."

I wrote down both over-breast measurements on my pad.

"OK, if you turn round, I'll take the band measurement."

She turned.

"So are you in love with him?"

"I think I am."

"God, I'm so jealous."

"Oh, come on, Rosie. I did have a husband go and die on me and leave me with two kids."

"You're right. I'm sorry. I'm just fed up with months of broken nights and having nobody to share it all with."

"I know, hon. But your time will come. I promise. You just need to get back out there." I wrote down the final measurement and told her we were done.

"Now that Will's older and taking a bottle, you should let Betty look after him more. Plus I'm around. You're hardly short of sitters."

"I know. I need to make more of an effort." Rosie sat on the bed and pulled on her T-shirt. "I'd be lucky to find somebody like Hugh, though. He's gorgeous, reliable, loves your kids."

"Yes, but we still have our issues."

"Oh, come on . . . like what?"

"His attitude towards money, for a start. He doesn't own his flat, or even his van, and he spends all his spare cash on travel. He doesn't have anything set aside for emergencies. Plus this traveling bug worries me. I'm not the needy clingy type, but I really don't fancy being abandoned while he goes off on foreign jaunts for months at a time. I know I'm jumping the gun, but it's not impossible that a year from now we could be living together. I don't want to be spending great chunks of it on my own. And getting back to the money issue—I was married to a gambler. I know what it's like being with a man who refuses to take any financial responsibility."

"OK, the travel thing I get. But surely that's something you can discuss and negotiate. As far as the money thing goes, I think you're way off. Hugh might be a spender, but he isn't a gambler."

"Maybe not, but he's a jobbing actor who earns most of his money working as a builder . . . in a recession. Granted he has an admirable work ethic, but that doesn't guarantee he won't end up out of work and in debt. Then he'll expect me to bail him out—assuming I have the money. I can't do it. I will not live like that."

"But if the bra business takes off and you're earning . . . and you love him—what's the difference? What's mine is yours and all that."

"Rosie, you lived with Simon. You know 'what's the difference.' You know how it feels to have a man sponge off you."

"Hugh really doesn't strike me as the sponging type, and second of all, there's a difference between somebody sponging because they are genetically idle and a person in genuine need."

"I get that, but the fact remains that Hugh is making no attempt to protect himself financially if he gets ill or the work dries up."

"So," Rosie said, "you dumped Steve because he was too boring and safe and too obsessed with financial security and now you're turning into him. That man had more of an effect on you than you care to admit."

"Rubbish. I dumped Steve because he was a control freak."

"OK, whatever. Have it your way." She paused. "Look, forgive me if I'm a bit confused here, but it seems to me that it's fine and dandy for you to take a colossal financial risk by taking over a business which has been on its knees for decades. It's OK for you to have zero savings, but when it comes to Hugh, you judge him by a completely different standard."

"You're right. Yes, I'm taking a huge risk, but the difference is that my risk is a one-off. For Hugh, living hand-to-mouth is a way of life. He will always be like that. I can't live like that. The stress would be to much."

"But you're getting stressed about something that might never happen. You're panicking because one day, Hugh might, possibly, if things go very, very bad, need to borrow some money from you."

She had a point. I didn't say anything.

"You need to take a step back here. Tell me honestly, do you love Hugh?"

"Of course I do. I'm crazy about him."

"Right. If you guys love each other, you have to work this out and come to some sort of compromise. You cannot let this issue be a deal breaker."

I sat fiddling with my flexi-ruler. "Maybe."

"There's no maybe about it. You need to sit down and have a proper discussion."

I let out a long breath. "You're right. Maybe I am panicking un-necessarily. I'm sure we'll be able to sort it out, but you have to un-derstand that after Mike I'm so scared of making a mistake. . . . Anyway, as you so rightly say, Hugh hasn't even said he loves me yet."

I bent down, put my arms around Rosie and gave her a hug. "Thanks for being there, hon. Love you."

Rosie grinned. "I love you, too. And thank you for the bra. So, you're absolutely positive we can't go for the emerald and black?"

I laughed. "Absolutely."

Just then we heard Betty calling up to the window. "Hellooo, we're back."

Rosie left and I went back to my drawing board. I sat reading my next set of instructions:

From point of bust, arc out a line 11.57 cm, an arc 13.6 cm (this line will become the "Neckline Hem" of the bra cup) and an arc 7.13 cm (this line will be curved to become the "underarm" hem of the cup). See diagram for start points of the arcs/lines.

Piece of cake.

*T*hat night, I lay in bed thinking about Hugh and how much I loved him. Rosie was right, I would be a fool if I let this money issue become a deal breaker. We were intelligent adults, perfectly capable of talking this and the traveling issue through and coming up with a solution. It was nonsense to think otherwise. So confident was I that we would work it out, I made a decision. It was time to move our relationship to the next level. If Hugh was too chicken to tell me he loved me, then pretty soon I would have to take the initiative.

*O*n Sunday afternoon, Dan had a playdate and Ella had a birthday party at the zoo. Hugh and I decided to go for a walk in Richmond Park. We headed for the Isabella Plantation. This time of year it was bursting with rhododendrons. Arms around each other, we strolled past the dazzling purples and fuchsias, remarking on the beauty of it all. After five minutes or so, we reached the lake. A group of children were throwing chunks of bread in the direction of a mother swan and her half dozen cygnets. Hugh and I sat on the grass, watching the gobbling and laughter. "By the way," Hugh said. "Your Mum's right."

"What about?"

"I am smitten."

"You heard that?"

"I was coming into the kitchen to get a glass of water." He turned to face me. "In fact I'm more than smitten. I'm in love with you."

Call me old-fashioned, but I couldn't help thinking how much more heart-leapingly romantic it felt, him taking the initiative rather than me.

"You are?" I said.

"I'm crazy about you."

"I'm crazy about you, too."

Hugh's face was one huge smile. He cupped my face in his hands and kissed me on the lips. When we finally drew apart, we sat—me with my head resting on his chest—watching the sunbeams dancing on the rhododendron bushes. Couples went past, shouty children charged by on scooters, but we barely noticed.

"Come back to my place?" he said.

I looked at my watch and nodded. We still had a couple of hours. We practically ran to the car park.

He was pulling off my top before we got into the bedroom. In seconds we were naked. He pushed me back onto the bed, spread my legs and gently, slowly glided his fingers over my wet clitoris. Soon I was floating, feeling only half-present. I heard myself let out soft moans of delight as he increased the pressure. I cried out, begging him not to stop when he eased off again. Finally, he let me come. Afterwards, my hand guiding him inside me, I looked into his eyes and told him how much I loved him.

We lay in a sweaty breathless heap.

"Wow," he said.

"Wow, yourself." I glanced over at the bedside clock. "Crap. I need to get going."

"Aw, stay . . . you've got ten minutes or so."

"What if there's traffic?"

He told me to stop fretting. "So if you're late, what are the parents going to do, throw your kids out?"

"I guess not."

For a few moments we lay there, me with my head in the crook of his arm, playing with his chest hairs. "You happy?" Hugh said eventually.

"Happier than I've been in years. In fact I can't remember the last time I was this happy."

"Same here. By the way," he said. "I booked that trekking holiday in Morocco."

"Great," I said, aware that my tone was pretty flat.

"You don't mind me going without you, do you? I'm going to miss you like crazy—not to mention the kids—but it's something I've really been looking forward to."

"No, of course I don't mind. I told you. I couldn't come anyway."

"What's the problem, then? You seem sort of discombobulated."

"I'm not remotely discombobulated."

"Sarah, I've known you long enough to know when you're discombobulated. What's going on?"

I sat up. "OK. I'm angry."

"You're angry because I've booked a holiday?"

"I'm angry at the way you spend money. Doesn't it ever occur to you to put something aside? What would you do if you got ill? What are your plans for your old age?"

"Sarah, we've had this conversation. I've explained all this. It's important for me to enjoy the money I earn. People save all their lives. They end up with a great pot of cash in the bank. Then it hits them that they've been so busy squirreling money away that they haven't traveled or allowed themselves any real pleasure and now they're too old and frail to start. I don't want to end up as one of those people."

"I'm not suggesting you save every penny, but you need something to fall back on."

"I don't get it. Why are my spending habits so important to you? I don't want to appear unkind, but the bottom line is, it's none of your damn business."

"OK, suppose we decided to live together. Would your finances be none of my damn business then?"

"I don't know. I haven't given it much thought."

"No, of course you haven't. Well, I have. Hugh, we're in a recession. I know things are going well for you right now, but suppose for some reason your work dried up or you got ill, God forbid. What would you do?"

"By the same token, suppose your business goes tits up. What would you do?"

"I don't know," I said. "But at least I'm thinking about the future. You're not."

"That's just the way I am. I can't get obsessed with what might possibly happen one day."

"But suppose you hit on hard times and meanwhile my business is on the up. You might be forced to come to me for money. Let me be clear. I'd have no problem helping you out if you'd already made some financial provision—taken at least some responsibility for yourself. It's the fact that you refuse to do anything at all that gets me. I can't face having to support somebody who hasn't made the effort—somebody who has squandered all his money. It has too many echoes of Mike. I can't do it."

"Sarah, I am nothing like Mike. I don't gamble. I've never been in debt in my life."

"But if you carry on like this—living for today, not giving a toss about tomorrow—you might end up in debt, and that scares me." I paused. "And the money isn't the only thing."

"Go on."

"OK . . . I'm worried that this is going to be our future—you swanning off abroad for weeks or months at a time the way you always have. Maybe I'm being melodramatic, but it just feels like another kind of widowhood."

He looked genuinely shocked. "Christ. I hadn't given it a moment's thought. I've been on my own so long that it hadn't occurred to me how you might feel about me going away."

"Well, maybe you could start thinking about it . . . all of it."

I looked at the clock again. "I really do have to go. Can we talk about this another time?"

"Sure . . . but you do still love me, don't you?"

"Don't be daft. Of course I still love you."

I was due to collect Dan first. On the way, I called Rosie.

"It all just came pouring out," I said. "I don't know what came over me. I couldn't stop it. I thought I'd be able to compromise, but I'm not sure that I can. The man lives like there's no tomorrow. On the other hand, he did get thoughtful when I told him I didn't want him leaving me for weeks on end. I suppose that's something."

"You're right. It means he really loves you and cares about you. Look, I understand how his attitude to money upsets you, but maybe one of the reasons he's so relaxed is that he's assuming he'll inherit when his parents go."

"He might—assuming the money isn't swallowed up in care home bills. And even if it's not, I don't want to be with a man who's relying on his dead parents to support him."

"Does it really matter where the money comes from?"

"Yes. To me, it does."

I could practically see Rosie shaking her head in frustration.

"I know you think I'm being too hard on him, but . . ."

"It doesn't matter what I think. I never had to live with Mike. That experience clearly had a profound effect on you. And why wouldn't it?"

The tears started falling down my cheeks. "Shit, Rosie, help me. I don't know what to do."

"Sweetie, love you as I do, you know I can't make this decision for you. It was the same with Steve. It has to be your call. All I'd say is this: think very carefully before you do anything you might come to regret."

I'd just gotten the kids to bed when Hugh called.

"I really think we need to talk. Can I come over?"

He arrived ten minutes later. I took a couple of beers out of the fridge and suggested that as it was such a warm night, we take them into the garden.

"Since you left, I've been doing some thinking," Hugh said. "First of all I want to say I had no idea how you felt about being left while I went away. I wish you'd said something. I can't promise that I'll stop traveling, because apart from my relationship with you it nourishes me more than anything else I know. But I promise I'll never ever go away for long stretches. How does that sound?"

"That sounds great. Thank you. That means a lot to me."

"And as for long trips—we could do them together, with the kids. We can go away for a couple of months during the summer, the best part of a month at Christmas. . . ."

"What are you talking about?"

"I'm talking about us having fun."

"Look, first of all it will be years, if ever, before I can leave the business for more than a couple of weeks. And second, have you any idea what these trips would cost?"

"Sarah, I don't know what you want from me. My business is doing well; I'm not in debt. From where I'm sitting it feels like you want to change me simply because you've got some hang-up about having loads of cash in the bank."

"It's not a hang-up. I've told you before, all I want is for you to start thinking about the future. Just put *something* aside for the future. Christ, it's not asking the earth. It's what most people do."

"OK, fine. So where are your savings?"

"I don't have any. I know you think I'm being a hypocrite lecturing you like this while I have nothing, but I promise you that the moment I have any spare cash, it will go straight into the bank. I will always make sure I have money for the children, money for me if I get ill or the business goes down."

"I can't help it. I just feel like you're bullying me. I had enough of that with my mother. She wanted me to become a banker and I stood up to her. My last relationship broke down because the woman I was with wanted me to give up acting and get a proper job. Being a builder didn't work for her either, because the way she saw it, building was a trade, not a profession, and she wouldn't be able to hold her head up among her banker friends. I had no choice but to walk away. I'm fed up to the back teeth with people trying to get me to do what they want. What about what I want?"

"Hugh, read my lips. I'm not asking you to give up anything. All I'm asking is that you start putting some money aside."

He took a mouthful of beer. "Sarah, have you any idea how many hours I work in an average week?"

"Of course I do. I also know that you drive yourself way too hard. I have no idea how you coped working on the shop during the day and doing *The Producers* in the evening. I don't know how you didn't get ill."

"I never get ill and that's because I'm always planning my next trip. I can't live without it."

"Then you'll have to live without me." I couldn't believe what I'd said, but I made no attempt to take the words back. It didn't feel like I was being irrational, but if I was, then that's what being married to Mike had done to me and I felt powerless to fight it.

"What? That's it? You're breaking up with me because I enjoy traveling?"

"No, I'm breaking up with you because you refuse to compromise."

"Why does it all have to be about me? I don't see you compromising. Shit, Sarah. Are you crazy? We love each other. We should be sitting here planning our future. Please don't do this. . . . Look, I understand what you went through with Mike, but . . ."

I was on my feet now. "You know what? You don't understand. You don't have the remotest idea. If you did, you wouldn't be so dogmatic."

"Here we go again. It's me who's refusing to compromise. I'm the one being dogmatic. What about you? . . . OK, what do you want? Tell me what you want me to do and I'll do it."

He stood up, took a wad of fifty-pound notes out of his wallet and threw them onto the garden table. "Right, first thing tomorrow, we'll take this lot to the bank and open me a savings account."

I shook my head.

"Not enough? You want more? OK, I have more." He found some more notes and slammed them down on top of the others.

"Can't you see? I want you to *want* to do it. I refuse to be the one forcing you, constantly nagging."

"I'm sorry, but that just isn't me. It's not who I am."

"I know."

"Christ. This is just so fucking stupid."

"Maybe to you."

"I need to get out of here." He headed back into the kitchen. "I cannot believe this is happening."

Nor could I.

———

*P*art of me thought—or hoped—that he would call the next morning, admit that I was right and that he was living like an overgrown student. Then we'd sit down, have a sensible talk, the whole thing would be resolved and we'd have jungle makeup sex on the living room floor. But he didn't. He didn't call the next morning either. Or the one after that.

I couldn't sleep. Missing him was unbearable. The ache was almost physical. I lost count of the times I almost picked up the phone to say that I was sorry for being such an arse and please could we just go back to where we were. But I couldn't do it. Rosie accused me of being impossible and stubborn and suggested I go back into therapy to deal with this anxiety over money that Mike had left me with. I took the point, but at the same time I didn't think what I was asking of Hugh was outrageous. If we got back together, we'd be arguing again in minutes.

I decided to say nothing to my mum. I couldn't cope with all her angst. I suspected she was already fantasizing about her wedding outfit.

My most important task right now was to finish the bra pattern. There was less than a week to go to the competition deadline. I would sit at my drawing board, compasses in one hand, flexi-ruler in the other—staring at my instruction manual. *Next, extend the lines that "radiate" from the Point of Bust point to the edge of the cup and beyond. Number the lines 1 to 7 clockwise starting at the "cup apex," as in the diagram.*

And now in English if you please. I would screw up another sheet of graph paper, aim it at the bin and miss. I was wading in paper balls. Then I would make coffee, open another KitKat and start thinking about Hugh.

There was no room for error. It needed to be perfect. Given that this was my first attempt at making a bra pattern, perfection or anything close to it was unlikely. The aunties kept telling me not to panic. They were sure that my pattern would be perfect, and if it wasn't, they would modify things. "Don't forget, poppet, that Rosie will need two fittings. That gives us plenty of room to adjust."

Finally I handed over the pattern. The aunties insisted it would be perfect. I told them not to count on it. I was losing faith and enthusiasm, partly because I was tired and frazzled and partly because I was missing Hugh.

"For crying out loud," Aunty Sylvia said. "Get off your high horse and phone him."

I'd thought twice before telling the aunties what was happening with Hugh and me. They liked him—that was never in doubt—but they still didn't approve of my dating an actor. I wasn't sure I could cope with all the we-told-you-sos. But seeing me so miserable, they'd had had a bit of a rethink.

"No. He needs to grow up."

"I agree," Aunty Bimla said. "He does need to grow up. That means you will need to give him time, but I promise you he will come around. He isn't going to let a wonderful girl like you slip through his fingers."

I said it felt like I'd already slipped.

Of course Dan and Ella wanted to know why they hadn't seen much of Hugh lately. When I told them we'd had an argument, they got cross and said it was bound to be all my fault. Even though he had no idea what the argument was about, Dan called me "a fat bossy poo head." Ella burst into tears and demanded to know what she was going to do now that she'd been chosen to sing a solo and had nobody to help her practice. Of course, I offered to help her, but she said she wanted the song to be a surprise.

"A surprise for me?"

She nodded. "Oh, darling, that's so sweet. I don't know what to say. Tell you what—maybe Grandma could help you."

"No. I want Hugh."

I didn't want to tell Mum and Dad about breaking up with Hugh. The inquisition would be endless, but if I kept quiet, I risked their hearing it from the kids. So one night after they'd gone to bed, I made the call.

Mum picked up on the first ring. "Hi darling. I've just been sitting here thinking about you. I'm just so excited about the bra competition. I've got this feeling you're going to win. You're so gifted. Plus you've got two of the most talented seamstresses in the country helping you. What shouldn't you win?"

"Because I know almost nothing about how to make a bra pattern and Valentina di Rossi is entering as well."

Mum wasn't having it.

"You'll be fine. You've got your aunty Shirley looking over you. She's probably collaring the Almighty right now and having a quiet word in his ear."

The image made me smile. For a moment I forgot why I'd called.

"Mum, there's something I need to tell you. Hugh and I have stopped seeing each other."

"Oh, darling. No . . . I'm so sorry. The pair of you seemed so together. What happened?"

"It's complicated."

"Don't tell me. He's found somebody else. Funny, though. He didn't strike me as the type. Mind you, I suppose all actors are the type. I mean when you move in those glamorous circles. It's a different world. There's temptation at every turn."

I assured her that there was nobody else.

"Then what is it?"

The rest of the story came tumbling out. "I love him," I said finally, "but after Mike . . ."

"I know, darling. You don't have to tell me."

"So what do I do?"

"Keep talking. Keep yelling and fighting if needs be. Thrash it out. If you love each other, you'll work it out."

"I thought we could do that, but it's just not happening."

"Then one of you has to climb down."

"But which one?"

*T*he following morning there were more tears. This time, from Aunty Bimla. Rosie had just arrived for her fitting and she and I were sitting in the basement having a cup of tea with Aunty Sylvia. It was well after nine thirty and Aunty Bimla hadn't arrived.

"It's so unlike her," Aunty Sylvia said. "Maybe I should give her a call."

"She'll be fine," I said. "She's probably stuck on the tube."

But she wasn't fine. A moment later, Aunty Bimla appeared, her eyes red from crying, her face puffy with exhaustion.

"What on earth is it?" Aunty Sylvia said, putting her arm across Aunty Bimla's shoulders.

"It's Sanjeev."

"Has something happened to him?"

"No. Nothing like that. He's fine, but it is all such doom and gloom."

It seemed that Sanjeev's business deal had gone south. I looked at Rosie and rolled my eyes. "So, the excrement has finally hit the air-conditioning," I muttered.

"He arrived at my place late last night," Aunty Bimla sobbed. "He was in a terrible state. He's lost everything. It turns out he's been back from Paraguay for weeks, but he's been too scared to say anything to me or his parents back in Pakistan. He's been sleeping on friends' floors. Now he's asking if he can move in with me."

"So what happened?" Rosie said. Like we didn't know.

"It turns out that Paraguay has no coastline. The land he was sold wasn't on the beach. It was an unusable swamp by a filthy lake. By the time he found out, he'd already handed over the money. He tried to get it back, but the people who sold him the land have disappeared. He took out a huge loan. The bank is chasing him for money. He's sold his flat and his sports car to keep them off his back for a while, but beyond that, he has no idea what to do. And nor do I. We are up the creek without a paddle."

"And what about the ten grand you gave him?" I said. "Is that gone, too?"

"Yes, but it doesn't matter about me. Sanjeev worked so hard. These people are evil. He was like a lamb to the slaughter."

"What? No, he wasn't," Rosie piped up. "He was a bloody idiot and part of me wants to say he deserved all he got."

"What? How can you say that?"

"I can say it because he didn't do his homework. What fool parts with his money before checking out the land he's buying? He got greedy and fell flat on his face."

"If you ask me, that boy is too flash by half," Aunty Sylvia said. "He needs a smack on the tuchas, not you weeping all over him." Aunty Sylvia was so enjoying this. She clearly hadn't forgotten how Aunty Bimla had gloated when Roxanne lost her part in *Human Centipede 4*. Now it was her turn.

"So what should I do?"

"He needs to go out and get a job," I said. "It's time you stopped indulging him."

Aunty Sylvia had her arms folded across her chest. "You've been killing that boy with kindness and look where it's got him. It's time to give him an ultimatum. He either gets a job or you tell him he can't stay with you."

"I couldn't do that!"

"What choice do you have?" I said. "It's for his own good, and one day, when he's a bit older and wiser, he might even thank you."

Aunty Bimla looked thoughtful. "I don't know. It won't be easy. But you're right. It's time for me to start playing the bad cop. I just hope I can do it."

"You will," I said. "Because you know how important it is."

"I hope so."

"So," Rosie said, brightening up. "Come on . . . where's my bra?"

Aunty Sylvia took it out of her desk drawer. The sections of ivory satin were roughly tacked together.

"Well, it certainly looks like a bra," I said, laughing. I could only pray that it would fit.

The four of us trooped upstairs and squeezed into one of the fitting rooms.

"OK, Rosie," Aunty Bimla said, "what you do is lean forward and just let your boobies fall into the cups. Excellent." She fastened the back.

The aunties got busy with their pins, discussing darts, tucks and seam allowances as they went. Whether or not the bra fitted was down to my pattern. From what I could tell, it didn't look too bad, but that didn't stop me digging my nails into my palms as I waited for the aunties' verdict.

"You have done an excellent job, poppet. It's going to be beautiful."

"She's right," Aunty Sylvia said through a mouthful of pins. "Shirley would have been proud of you. You're a chip off the old block."

"Really? You actually think I did OK?"

"You did more than OK," Aunty Sylvia said.

"But it was such a struggle. I don't feel like I'm anything approaching a natural at this."

"You mustn't let that trouble you, poppet. When the going gets tough, the tough get going. You learn and suddenly you turn into a natural."

Later in the week, Rosie came in for a second and final fitting. After that, the aunties disappeared into the basement for two days to finish the bra. The sewing machine chattered. The kettle boiled. Deliberations turned into loud disputes. "OK, have it your way. I'll unpick it. No, of course I'm not offended. Why should I be offended?"

I stayed upstairs, served the few customers who wandered in and kept out of the way.

Rosie's bra was finished with time to spare. There were still twenty-four hours before we had to deliver it to the offices of *The British Lingerie Review.*

Rosie insisted on being there when the aunties unveiled it.

"Oh, this is outstanding," I said, lifting it from the tissue-filled box. I ran my fingers over the seams, the satin cups, trimmed in Belgian lace, the bow and tiny diamond nestling on the bridge between the cups. "It's sensational. To call you two 'gifted' is an understatement."

Rosie said she'd drink to that. "Will you just look at this? It's beyond beautiful. It's a work of art."

Rosie tried on the bra. It was a perfect fit. I tested out the breast-feeding modification. It worked perfectly. We high-fived, Aunty Sylvia burst into "Happy Days Are Here Again" and Aunty Bimla cracked open a plastic container of chocolate halva.

Chapter 15

I heard the commotion before I saw it.

"Stop her! Somebody stop her!"

I turned into the street. People were pausing to stare at the crazy old ladies—one in a pink overall, trying to run in patent sling-backs, the other in a *salwar kameez*, hair falling down around her face, her scarf billowing as she gave similarly ineffective chase—on account of her bunions. But nobody else made any attempt to go after the young woman escaping down the road.

The aunties were maybe twenty yards in front of me. I sprinted towards them. "It doesn't matter," I hollered. "Let her go." I had macabre visions of the aunties' hearts giving out and them collapsing in the street—all because they'd tried to stop some two-bit shoplifter.

As the woman's lead increased, they were forced to give up. We stood on the pavement and watched her get into a taxi. The small crowd that had gathered started to melt away.

"My God," Aunty Sylvia wailed. "What have we done? We let her get away."

"It's OK," I said. "Don't worry. These things happen. You did your best."

The aunties were both so breathless that they could barely get the words out.

"You don't understand, poppet. It's gone. She took it."

"Took what?"

"The bra."

"OK . . . when you say *the* bra . . ."

Tears were tumbling down Aunty Bimla's cheeks. "The competition bra. She came in and stole it."

I felt sick. "What? How? We've had it locked in the safe. Only the three of us know the combination."

"Poppet, we are so sorry."

"But how could this happen? How?"

Then I thought about the aunties and all their exertions, how they could still collapse from heart attacks and didn't need me adding to their stress by yelling at them.

"OK," I said. "The first thing we need to do is get you two back inside."

I put up the CLOSED sign, sat them down and got them each a glass of water. "Tell me exactly what happened."

Aunty Sylvia said that the woman had come in about twenty minutes ago and asked to be fitted for a bra. "She tried on a few. In the end, she decided on the Prima Donna—the gunmetal gray with the pink trim. Looked lovely on her. She seemed like such a nice young woman. Polish. I told her about how my family had come over from Poland before the First World War. . . ."

Aunty Bimla was rubbing her bunions and rolling her eyes. "So to cut to the chase . . . after she paid for the bra, she brought up the subject of the Bra Oscars. She said she was interested because she was a fashion student and that she was taking a bra-making module. She wanted to know if we were entering."

"Of course we said yes," Aunty Sylvia said. "Then she said that she would love to see our entry. She said she'd heard that the Queen wore bespoke bras and that she could only imagine the workmanship that went into one."

By now my head was in my hands. "You showed her? You actually showed her?"

"It was stupid, poppet, but we were flattered. We allowed our vanity to get the better of us."

"I don't believe this. How could you be so foolish? So naive?"

"Anyway, she stood admiring it for a few moments," Aunty Bimla went on, "and the next thing we knew, she was running out of the shop with it and tearing down the street."

It was all my fault. If I hadn't gone to Ella's "Everyone's a Hero" assembly this morning, I would have been at work on time. I would have been behind the counter, not the aunties, and none of this would have happened.

"Poppet, what are we going to do? The bra has to be delivered to the *BLR* offices by two."

"What *we* do is *I* pay a visit to Valentina di Rossi."

"She's behind this?"

"Oh, come on. Who else? You said yourselves that I'd reignited the dragon's fury. That woman stole the bra because Valentina put her up to it."

"Not necessarily," Aunty Sylvia said. "Maybe she's another one of our competitors and she wanted us out of the competition. Valentina isn't our only rival."

"Maybe not, but Valentina is the only one with an added agenda. She's out for revenge. I just know it."

I marched into La Feminista, interrupted a saleswoman who was busy with a customer and demanded to know where I would find Valentina.

"She's upstairs in the office, but you can't go barging . . ."

I took the stairs two at a time and burst into her office.

Valentina was at her desk, on a call. She looked up, startled. A moment later her face had become a glare.

"Something's come up," she said into the phone. "I'll call you right back." She hit "end." "Who the hell do you think you are, barging into my office like this?"

"Let's dispense with the fake indignation. Just hand over the bra."

"What bra?" She seemed bewildered. I had to give it to her—the woman was a good actress.

"The bra I'm entering for the *BLR* competition—the one you just stole—or hired somebody to steal."

"I haven't stolen anything." More self-righteous fury. "How dare you accuse me. You're crazy. Now get out or I'm calling the police."

"I'll be more than happy to leave, as soon as you return the bra."

"I have no idea what you're talking about."

I leaned on the desk, brought my face close to hers.

"An hour ago, a woman came into my shop and stole my entry. You are the only person with a motive to do something like this."

"How dare you accuse me! I would never stoop to something so cheap."

"Of course you would. This is your way of getting your revenge on Aunty Shirley."

"Rubbish. If I'd wanted revenge, I would have got it in her lifetime."

"OK, so why did you steal it, then? Is it just because I'm a threat and you want me out of the competition?"

Valentina leaned back in her chair and laughed. "Sweetheart, do you really think I feel threatened by an upstart like you? I was designing bras and making patterns while you were still in nappies. I intend to win this competition—but I also intend to win it honestly. I am not the sort of person who gets pleasure from eliminating the opposition. I've heard enough of this nonsense. Now, do as I say and get out."

I stood there, shaking with fury. "I'm not leaving until you give me the bra."

She picked up the phone. "I'm calling the police. They can escort you off the premises." She began stabbing the keys.

I realized that leaving was my only choice. I had no evidence that Valentina had stolen the bra. The police wouldn't be interested in hearing my side of the story. They would inform me that it was a civil matter and that if I wanted to pursue it, I should consult a lawyer.

"Don't worry. I'm going."

I slammed the door shut behind me and stood on the small landing, weeping with rage. This woman had ruined my chance of success, of even getting noticed in the industry. There was no way I would come back from this. I was about to head downstairs when I noticed the loo across the landing. It occurred to me that I could hide out in there until Valentina left her office. Then I would go back and search it. I was so angry that I didn't give a damn that I was about to commit burglary—or close to it.

Fifteen minutes later I heard her door open. I prayed she didn't need to pee. I opened the door a crack and watched her disappear down the stairs.

There wasn't much furniture in the office. There was Valentina's desk, a couple of old-fashioned metal filing cabinets and a floor-to-ceiling cupboard in the alcove. I started with the desk drawers. Laptop, hand cream, folders, a couple of packets of tights. The filing cabinets were open, but empty. Probably due to be thrown out. The alcove cupboard turned out to be a wardrobe. There was a black cocktail dress hanging up, a pair of evening shoes, a clutch bag and a pashmina. Presumably Valentina was due at some kind of glitzy gathering tonight. I stood on a chair to get to the top shelves, but all I found were more files. No bra.

I snuck down the stairs and darted out of the shop, praying that nobody noticed me. After a few seconds I looked back to see if anybody was coming after me. No one was. I crossed the road, turned into a side street and called the shop. Aunty Sylvia picked up.

"Valentina's denying she stole it," I said. "I managed to search her office, but it's not there."

"It could be in the workroom downstairs or in the shop itself—maybe in a drawer."

"I doubt it. Not secure enough. I think that the woman who stole it might have had instructions to take it to Valentina's home."

"Unless of course she hasn't handed it over yet and still has it."

"In which case we're totally screwed. We have to just pray it's at Valentina's place. Don't suppose you know where she lives?"

Aunty Sylvia knew her address from years ago, but couldn't be certain she was still living there.

"Give it to me anyway."

Bayswater. Just up the road. I flagged down a cab. It was nearly midday. Two hours left.

The cab dropped me outside a Victorian mansion block. Aunty Sylvia hadn't been sure of the actual number. I checked the brass plate. Trellforth/di Rossi. Number seven. I pressed the buzzer. A man's voice. Elderly.

My turn to speak. I hadn't the foggiest what to say. Crap. I didn't have a plan.

"Hello . . . er . . . Is Valentina at home?"

"No. I'm afraid she's at the shop."

"The thing is, I'm one of her business associates. I was just passing by with a selection of samples. Would you mind if I dropped them off?"

"Not at all. Come on up."

He buzzed me in.

The only thing I had in my bag that could pass for samples was a Marks & Spencer carrier containing Dan's dirty PE kit, which he'd given me to wash. I removed the sneakers and flattened the plastic.

The man standing in the doorway had to be in his seventies, but he was tall and slim. Still striking. I took in the cropped gray hair, the charcoal cashmere, the well-cut jeans.

I needed an excuse to get into the flat. I decided to ask if I could use the loo.

"Don't suppose you fancy a cuppa," he said, making my plan redundant. "I've just made a pot of coffee."

"Thank you. I'd love one."

"I'm Charles by the way—Valentina's husband."

"I'm Lacy," I blurted. "Lacy Cagney."

"Lacy—that's not a name I've come across."

He led me along the passageway: white walls, abstract paintings, expensive wood floor. Fancy, schmancy kitchen. German. A grand for a tap. I only recognized it because Tara had the identical units and fittings. Charles invited me to sit down at the granite breakfast bar and asked me how I took my coffee.

"So, what are these samples you have for Valentina?"

"Oh . . . right . . . they're backless bras. The company I work for has come up with a revolutionary new design."

"And you'd like her to stock them."

"That's the idea."

We drank our coffee and chatted. Charles told me that before he gave up work, he'd been an architect—which I already knew from the aunties. He hated being retired, he said. There were only so many films to watch, books to read. The days dragged. He wished that Valentina would give up the shop and then he would have some company. "But she refuses. I think being at home with me all day would drive her dotty, but I'm working on her."

The next moment we heard the front door open. "Surely that's not Valentina," Charles said. "At this time of day."

A moment later she walked into the kitchen. She put her bag and keys down on the countertop.

"I knew you'd come here," she said, ignoring her husband, who was looking more than a little startled. "What were you planning to do? Search my home like you just searched my office? You left all the drawers and doors open. Not very professional."

"Of course I was going to search here. Do you think I wouldn't?"

"Pardon me," Charles said, "but could one of you please tell me what's going on? I have to confess to being completely baffled."

"This woman is Sarah Green—Shirley's niece."

Charles looked at me. His face had gone white. "You're Sarah? But you told me your name was Lacy."

"I'm sorry. I came into your home under false pretenses, but only because your wife stole the bra I was about to enter into the *BLR* competition."

"And I'm telling you," Valentina broke in, "that I did not—repeat—did *not* steal it. I will not stand here and be accused. Why are you persecuting me like this?" She had started to cry.

"I'm persecuting you?" I cried, tears in my eyes now. "I don't believe I'm hearing this. Have you any idea what you've done to me? I'm trying to rescue a business that has been dying on its feet for years. I've sacrificed every penny I possess. My husband died. I've got two kids to support. This was my last hope of making a success of my life and you've taken it from me. Whatever Shirley did to you, you have no right to do this."

"I didn't do it. Do you hear me? I didn't do it."

Charles sat down. "No," he said, his voice barely audible. "I did."

To put it mildly, that took the wind out of my sails.

Valentina swung round. "You did? Don't be ridiculous. Why on earth would you even say a thing like that?"

"Because it's true."

"Charles, I understand if you're trying to protect me, but there's really no need."

"I'm not trying to protect you. I stole the bra. Or at least I paid the au pair downstairs to steal it."

"But why?" Valentina and I said in almost comic unison.

"You'd been going on for so long about how much you wanted to win this damned competition, and how you'd discovered on the grapevine that Sarah was entering and that she had Shirley's seamstresses working for her. You said that winning the competition would be your last hurrah and that then you might think about retiring. This was going to be my secret gift to you—to us—making sure you had no real opposition."

I should have been just as furious and outraged with Charles as I'd been with Valentina, but he looked so pathetic sitting there, I couldn't find it in me.

Valentina sat down next to him. "How could you do such a despicable thing? Do you honestly think that's how I would want to win?"

"No, but I wasn't thinking. I was being utterly selfish. I've been feeling so alone these past few years. You have no idea. I thought it would be a way of getting you back." Charles turned to me. "What I did was inexcusable. I'm deeply ashamed. You have every right to report the matter to the police."

Maybe. On the other hand, here was a lonely old man, crying out for his wife's attention. He knew that he'd done a bad thing and I was pretty sure he wouldn't shake off the guilt any time soon. Assuming I could get the bra to the *BLR* offices in time, no real harm had been done.

"I can't see any need to involve the police," I said.

Charles looked close to tears. "I don't know what to say."

"You don't need to say anything. Please, just give me the bra."

He stood up. "It's in my study."

"I'm so sorry for this," Valentina said. "All I can say is that what Charles did is completely out of character. He's right, though. I have neglected him. It happens when you're running a business. It swallows you up. I had no idea quite how badly it was affecting him."

"I can see that," I said.

"Thank you for not going to the police. I cannot tell you what that means to me. My reputation would have been destroyed overnight."

"That's OK. And I guess I owe you an apology, too. I shouldn't have accused you. It was very wrong of me."

"I would probably have done the same in your position." She paused. "Of course, under the circumstances, I will call the organizers and withdraw from the contest."

"No. Don't do that. After all, no real harm's been done."

"But I couldn't possibly take part now. It wouldn't feel right."

"Look, this wasn't your fault. You deserve to be in the competition."

"That is very generous of you. I don't know what to say other than thank you."

It occurred to me that Charles' act of madness meant that Valentina and I were now even. She'd been hurt by Aunty Shirley. Charles had hurt me. We were never going to be friends, but it felt like we could call a truce.

Charles came back with the bra. Valentina found me some tissue paper to wrap it in and a box.

J stood on the pavement and looked at my watch. I had twenty minutes to reach the *BLR* offices. I saw a black cab with its light on and stuck out my arm.

"I don't care what it costs," I said to the driver. "But I need you to get me to Piccadilly in twenty minutes."

"You 'avin' a laugh? 'Ave you seen the roadworks along Bayswater Road? You'll be better off tubing it."

I sprinted to Queensway station. At the barrier I discovered my Oyster card needed reloading. Then there was a queue at the ticket machine. Finally I made it to the platform. I probably waited no more than three minutes for a Central line train, but it felt like thirty. I needed to pick up the Bakerloo line at Oxford Circus. As usual the station was thick with shoppers and tourists. I pushed and barged my way through. "Sorry. Excuse me. Emergency." A Bakerloo line pulled in as I reached the platform. I made it to Piccadilly Circus with five minutes to spare. The *BLR* offices were on Shaftesbury Avenue. Another mad dash. I arrived at reception, a sweaty, breathless beetroot.

"Bra competition," I said, virtually slamming the box on the desk. I grabbed a pen and began scrawling my details across the box lid.

The commissionaire looked at the clock. "I'm afraid it's two minutes past," he said. "I have strict instructions. . . ."

"Please," Wheeze. "I'm begging you." Wheeze. "Some woman

stole my bra and then when I got it back, I tried to get a taxi, but there were roadworks and my Oyster card needed reloading. . . ."

I was one batshit crazy, beetrooty woman. "Tell you what," the commissionaire said. "Why don't we say, for the record, that it's five to two?"

"You could do that? Thank you. Thank you so much."

"No problem," he said. "If you can't help a fellow human being from time to time, what's the point of it all? That's what I say."

I leaned over the desk and planted a huge smacker on his cheek.

*T*he awards ceremony was due to be held the following Friday. It was a convention going back decades that the judging shouldn't be long and drawn out. I felt grateful and terrified at the same time.

Aunty Sylvia decided she was going to stop worrying about the competition—because it was giving her acid—and plutz about something else instead: what to wear. Aunty Bimla had no trouble making up her mind—a formal occasion always called for her embroidered silk *salwar kameez*. Aunty Sylvia couldn't decide. "Maybe I should go for my navy two-piece. But I'm just not sure it quite says dinner at the Savoy. Perhaps my emerald would be better. It's got a bit of sparkle. Unless I went for my cream silk. Then of course I'd have to buy new shoes."

While the aunties and I plutzed, Rosie spent dozens of hours practicing her catwalk strut. She'd taken to doing it in her back garden—using the long stone path as a runway. I would coach her over the garden fence.

"No, as you walk, bring your knees up more. You need to look more like one of those dressage horses. . . . That's it." Then she'd go and ruin it all by getting a stiletto caught in a crack in the crazy paving and falling on her face.

Troy—the hair and makeup artist who'd been recommended by Sylvia's next-door neighbor's daughter who worked as a fashion assistant on one of the glossies—came to Rosie's to do a tryout. "OK, so I'm thinking that right now, ethereal is like majorly on trend." His look of choice was bird's nest hair, white lips and no eyebrows. Rosie was all for it and said we should dump the heels and go for army combat boots.

"Fabberlous," said Troy. "You know I was at a show in Gowanus last week and Kate Moss was wearing them—in herringbone."

I said that inspired as the concept was, maybe it need toning down, just a teensy bit.

"You see, Rosie's going to be modeling a nursing bra and I'm looking for a look that's more . . ."

"Say no more. I'm already in your headspace. OK, I'm thinking Madonna and child. . . . How's about we forget the hair and cover her head with a nun's veil? Then you juxtapose that with cheap hooker makeup and a giant crucifix."

"Help me out here," I muttered to Rosie.

"I think what Sarah's trying to say is that she's thinking more suburban chic."

Troy took a moment to process this. "I . . . am . . . loving . . . it. That is like so übercurrent. We'll keep it understated and natural—peach tones, hair long and loose, a few soft curls maybe."

I patted his shoulder. "Troy, I think you've got it."

———

I dug out one of my taffeta rockabilly party dresses. It was dark green with a black shimmer. I'd worn it for my engagement party. It had always been one of Mike's favorites.

I tried it on, along with the fat black net petticoat. Not only did it still fit—with all the stress of the last couple of weeks I must have lost weight—but although I said it myself, it didn't look at all bad. I got it dry-cleaned and treated myself to a pair of peep-toe heels.

On the day of the ceremony I closed the shop early to give us time to go home and get ready. Mum and Dad were collecting the kids from school and taking them back to their place for the night.

I was sitting on the bed doing my makeup and enjoying the peace when the phone rang. "Mum, we're just calling to wish you good luck and Dan wants to know if he sits on his hand all day, will it fall off and will he die? Oh, and Grandma says that you should break a leg, but I don't want you to break a leg."

No sooner had I gotten off the phone from my children and both parents than it rang again. I looked at the caller ID. Hugh. I felt a great surge of happiness and hope. He'd phoned to apologize, to tell me he'd rethought his crazy adolescent way of life and that he'd come up with a strategy. I hit "answer."

"Hugh!"

"Have I caught you at a bad time?"

"No, not at all . . . I mean apart from the fact that it's the Bra Oscars tonight and I'm in the middle of getting myself all dolled up."

"That's actually why I called. I just wanted to wish you good luck."

"Aw, that's really kind. Thank you."

"So how you doing?"

"I'm good."

"Kids?"

"Yep, they're good, too."

"Your mum and dad?"

"Both fine. So how are you? Anything going on?"

"Not really. Just the same ol' same ol'. Working hard. You know me."

"Sure."

"Right, well . . . I should probably get going. . . ."

"Yep, me, too. Still got to dry my hair."

"Anyway, good luck again."

"Thanks. And thanks again for calling. I appreciate it."

I fell back on the bed. Disappointment didn't begin to describe what I was feeling.

"*B*ut you could have made a move," Rosie said as we waited outside for the taxi. "Told him how much you were missing him. He'd made the effort to call and wish you luck—the least you could have done was meet him halfway."

"I can't. That's all there is to it. Now can we let the subject drop? Please?"

"You're such an idiot, do you know that?"

"Thanks."

"You're welcome."

"You look beautiful by the way," I said. "Your tits look amazing."

"It's the scaffolding," she said, referring to the seriously boned Vivienne Westwood she'd picked up at T.J. Maxx.

"And you're clear about what time you're due to go and get changed?"

She said she'd had a call from one of the competition organizers and apparently the toastmaster would announce it during dinner. A meeting room had been set aside for the models, where they could get ready and do their hair and makeup. The plan was for Troy to join her there.

"And I love that pink you've used on your nails," I said. "It's perfect."

"You're not going to get round me. I still think you're an idiot."

"OK, I'm an idiot. I'm also really, really nervous. Do you think we could have this conversation another time?"

"Sure." She reached into her bag, pulled out two miniature Scotch bottles and handed me one. "Get this down you," she said. "Oh—and you look gorgeous, too."

We headed to the River Room, where predinner drinks and canapés were being served.

Everyone and anyone in lingerie was there, milling and mwahing and sipping Sea Breezes as the evening sun poured through French windows and a cellist played Bach in the background.

Rosie said the place had to be full of journalists from the glossies and that I needed to start working the room.

"What? I can't just march up to people and barge in on their conversations."

"Of course you can. You just introduce yourself and let them know that you're this new hot-shit kid on the lingerie block."

"You want me to say that?"

"Well, maybe not those exact words."

"Hang on," I said, noticing a blond woman in heavy tortoiseshell specs. "Isn't that India Fitzroy?"

"Who?"

"You know. Writes for *Elle*. I recognize her from her byline picture."

"OK, you have to go over and speak to her. Play your cards right and she might give you some publicity."

India appeared to be on her own. What did I have to lose? I made my way over. Rosie was a couple of paces behind.

"India, how do you do. I'm Sarah Green. I'm one of the contestants."

"Oh, right, yah." She offered me a limp hand.

"I'm such an admirer of your work. I'd just like to say that I absolutely adored your piece on the return of denim."

"It went away?" Rosie said. I dug her in the ribs.

"Thanks. Glad you liked it."

"I really did. Anyway, I run Sarah Green Lingerie. It's a new business—well, not totally new—my aunty Shirley used to run it. Then she died. . . ."

"Really. Great. Fabulous." India was looking past me, clearly scanning the room for somebody more interesting to speak to.

"And this is my friend Rosie. She's going to be modeling my entry."

India gave a vague nod in Rosie's direction. "Great tits," she said.

Before Rosie had a chance to say anything, India was off. "Valentina, darling! How are you?"

"That went well, then," I said.

"Brilliant . . . She liked my tits, though. So is she gay or what?"

"No, she's just in the fashion biz. It's how they are."

*T*he aunties had stationed themselves near the bar—not that they were drinking anything stronger than orange juice.

"Here they come," Aunty Sylvia cried. "Oh, will you just look at the pair of them. Aren't those dresses stunning?"

Aunty Bimla agreed and said that we were both the belles of the ball.

"And look at you two," I said, giving them hugs. "Don't you look gorgeous?"

Aunty Sylvia had gone for her emerald. Aunty Bimla was in peacock blue. There were dozens of bangles at her wrists. Dark blue crystals set in gold cascaded to her collarbone.

"Tell me honestly," she said. "You don't think it's a bit too Aladdin's mother?"

Rosie and I sipped Sea Breezes while the aunties oohed and aahed over the canapés, the flowers, the thickness of the carpets, the politeness of the waitstaff, the cellist and the difficulties of fitting such an enormous instrument between her legs while still managing to look ladylike. If they disapproved of anything, it was some of the women's outfits. Aunty Sylvia was particularly vocal on the subject. "What does she look like? I wore more to give birth."

"So, do we know how many contestants there are?" I said.

Aunty Bimla thought she'd overheard somebody say there were around sixty.

"There are so many unknown quantities," I said. "It won't just be Valentina we're up against."

"You know, poppet, not many people would have let that husband of hers get away with what he did. He's a bad egg."

"Hear, hear," Aunty Sylvia muttered.

"Come on, Valentina did offer to take herself out of the competition. It was me who insisted she stay in. Charles isn't bad. He's just old and lonely."

"So what?" Aunty Sylvia said. "I'm old and I get lonely. Do I go around stealing? No, I don't."

"Well, for what it's worth," Rosie said, "I'm with Sarah. I would have done the same. He's just a pathetic old man."

Aunty Sylvia grunted.

"Well, one thing is for certain," Aunty Bimla said. "My poppet has charity in her heart. If you haven't got charity in your heart, you have the worst kind of heart trouble."

"Who said that?" Rosie asked. "The Prophet?"

"Bob Hope."

The toastmaster was inviting everybody to take their places for dinner. We headed to the banqueting room, where the aunties continued to marvel. This time at the giant silver candelabras, the intricate cake-icing plasterwork on the walls and ceiling, the lavish centerpieces.

I was sitting between Rosie and a plump, jolly curator from the V&A named Pru. It turned out that her main area of interest was the history of women's underwear.

"Did you know," she said, helping herself to sparkling water, "that women didn't wear drawers until the very end of the eighteenth century?"

"Must have been drafty," I said.

The aunties were sitting on the opposite side of the big circular table. At one point they called me over to meet their companion, an elderly trimmings manufacturer called Sid, who it turned out lived a couple of streets away from Aunty Sylvia.

*B*y now, Pru, my nice lady curator from the V&A, was describing a pair of Victorian bloomers she'd just acquired. I assumed she meant for the museum rather than herself, but I couldn't be certain. "You know my favorite word?" she said. *"Gusset."*

A loud screech of feedback. The red-liveried toastmaster was on his feet. "Ladies and gentlemen, I'm pleased to introduce your host, Mr. Malcolm Healey. . . ."

Malcolm Healey was the CEO of the company that owned *The British Lingerie Review.* A Yorkshireman whose tone steadfastly refused to undulate, he proceeded to welcome us to this, the forty-seventh Bra Oscars ceremony. For the next twenty minutes, he outlined the history of the competition, its contribution to the lingerie industry, and thanked by name each member of "the team" without whose sterling efforts this event wouldn't have been possible. "And let me say that despite the bean counters' predictions of doom and gloom, it looks as if, moving forward, it's going to be another banner year for the industry. . . ."

"How much longer?" Rosie muttered. "I'm aging here."

"And so, in conclusion, just to remind you that tonight's theme is 'a gap in the market.' Our hope is that by the end of the evening that gap will have been identified and successfully closed. Thank you, everybody, and good luck."

Because most people had zoned out, the applause took several seconds to kick off.

Dinner was gazpacho, roast lamb and lemon tart with berries. Of course it was sublime. This was the Savoy. Only Aunty Sylvia had reservations. "You don't expect to come to the Savoy and be given cold soup. And such a small portion."

Rosie just about managed to finish her lemon tart before the toastmaster asked if all the models would collect their pieces of lingerie from the judges' table and make their way to the dressing room.

I said I would come with her, but she insisted that I would only make her more nervous.

"Good luck," I said, giving her a hug.

"You, too."

She blew a couple of kisses at the aunties and was gone.

*T*he six female judges, each of whom worked for one of the major lingerie companies, sat at a table beside the runway. The models seemed to fall into two categories. First there were the six-foot, long-of-leg professionals who probably spent their days doing photo shoots on industrial sites in Gowanus. These girls tucked out their chests, lifted their knees and did their pony walk to "Barbie Girl" and "Girls Just Wanna Have Fun." The other models looked distinctly more down-market.

"And next up is Jade," said the lady with the microphone. I took in the fake tan and trout pout. "She's modeling an innovative backless bra, which comes courtesy of the Booby Trap in Manchester. . . ."

Lights flashed as the snappers snapped.

"Next we have Natalie from Accentuate the Positive in Bristol. . . ."

And so it went on. Sitting so far away in the audience, it was impossible to tell how well made Jade's and Natalie's bras were. The good news was that nobody else had attempted to make a nursing bra. Mostly it was new takes on old themes: corsets that created waists like no other, bras that lifted and separated like never before.

"And now . . . from Valentina di Rossi—an example of the étagère or shelf bra."

Not only did Valentina's model look like Naomi Campbell's younger sister, but the black bra gave her the most sensational cleavage. The cameras clicked faster than ever. I watched the audience, men in particular, exchanging glances. The aunties had warned me against entering an étagère on the grounds that everybody else would do it, but so far only Valentina had.

Rosie came on second to last. Troy had outdone himself. Her hair fell to her shoulders in soft loose curls. Her makeup was positively chaste. The bra looked great. Her strut was perfect. More clicking and flashing. The photographers couldn't get enough of her.

When the show was over, there was a half-hour interval. So far I'd only glimpsed Valentina when India Fitzroy had raced off to speak to her. Now Valentina was crossing the room towards me. "I just wanted to come over and say hello," she said. "I didn't want you to think I was ignoring you. By the way, your bra looked wonderful. I wish I'd thought of something so clever."

"Thank you, but yours looked amazing."

She shrugged. "Maybe. Who knows?"

Valentina returned to her table. A moment later, Malcolm Healey was back onstage. He was holding the familiar, tacky trophy.

"Ladies and gentlemen, we have a winner." The room went silent. I was standing between the aunties, gripping each of their hands. "I feel like my heart's about to burst," Aunty Bimla said. I just felt sick.

"In third place . . . it's the Booby Trap." Loud applause. A slightly crestfallen owner of the Booby Trap. "In second place, with her innovative nursing bra, Sarah Green." I shouldn't have been shocked—I'd always known that Valentina was the better designer and patternmaker—but I couldn't help it. I'd worked so hard and prayed so much. "And the winner, with her magnificent étagère bra, is Valentina di Rossi." People who weren't already on their feet stood up. The room was filled with applause and whistles, which weren't for me. I watched Valentina walk onto the stage to claim her prize. I looked around for Charles, but he wasn't there to share his wife's victory. I assumed that, knowing I was going to be at the event, he had felt too embarrassed to show his face.

Laughing, tears streaming down her face, Valentina held her trophy high in the air. "Ladies and gentlemen, I have been waiting over four decades to do this. Thank you to the judges. Thank you to my wonderful seamstresses and all my staff at La Feminista . . ."

Meanwhile I was wiping away tears. Aunty Bimla noticed and was quick to point out that I had no right to feel disappointed. "Listen to me. A journey of a thousand miles begins with a single step, and you have covered nine hundred and ninety-nine of those miles. You came in second. That is good news. It is wonderful news."

"She's right, darling," Aunty Sylvia said. "This is a victory."

"But I let you down."

"How on earth did you do that?" Aunty Sylvia said.

"You are the best seamstresses, but the judges could tell that my pattern wasn't good enough."

"You know what, maybe it wasn't. But it was your first attempt. And even then you came second. You just wait and see what effect this has on the business."

Rosie came tearing across and threw her arms around me. "Yay—second place. That is magnificent. From now on, you are so on the map."

I called Mum and Dad and the kids. They all said the same. Second place was wonderful. I had every reason to be proud. First would have been great, but I was young. It would come.

They were right. With more hard work, it would come. Suddenly I did feel proud. Not so long ago, I'd been a grieving widow, a sad lost soul with no idea which way to turn. Look how far I'd come.

I called out to Rosie and the aunties. "OK—group hug . . . thank you for all your support and love and for being there . . . for everything. I don't know what I would have done without you. I love you all."

I texted Hugh, letting him know that we'd come in second and that we were extremely happy with that. I guess I could have called him, but I couldn't face speaking to him again. He replied straightaway. *Result!!!! What a star. Hope you're cracking open the bubbly.*

I went over to congratulate Valentina. She was surrounded by a thicket of journalists, well-wishers and photographers. She caught sight of me and edged her way through the crowd.

"Well, the best woman won," I said, shaking her hand. "Congratulations."

"Thank you. This means so much to me. But I will never forget what you did to make it possible. It was the kindest, most generous thing anybody has ever done for me."

"You're welcome."

"Listen, would you mind if I called you next week—when all the fuss has died down? Maybe we could meet for a coffee."

"Sure. I'd like that."

Chapter 16

I reached out from under the duvet and began fumbling for the ringing phone.

"Hey—it's me."

Rosie.

"OK—you have to guess what just happened."

"Wha' time is it?"

"After nine. Wake up. Listen—guess who just called me at half past eight on a Saturday morning."

"I dunno."

"Oh, come on. You have to guess. It's no fun otherwise."

"Fun for you maybe. I'm still asleep."

"OK . . . you won't believe this. I just got a call from Delphine."

"Delphine who?"

"What do you mean, Delphine who? Delphine. *The Delphine.* The lingerie company. They want to meet me."

I sat up. "No."

"Yes. They're looking for new models, apparently."

"See. I told you last night would lead to something. I didn't think it would be this quick, but I could tell the photographers loved you. Oh, Rosie, well done. So what's the deal?"

"I don't know exactly. I've got a meeting with a couple of their people next week. . . . So have any of the companies called you about the maternity bra?"

"No, but I'm guessing that after all that champagne we put away last night, most people are still asleep."

"Yeah, you're probably right. Listen, I gotta go. Will's bawling."

" 'K . . . and congratulations again. It's brilliant news."

"Thanks, hon . . . and don't worry, your phone will start ringing."

But it didn't. Nobody called over the weekend—not that I was expecting them to. Monday and Tuesday came and went. Still nothing.

"I don't get it," I said to the aunties. "Why isn't anybody calling me? Women are crying out for decent nursing bras. Surely the manufacturers can see that."

"You'd have thought so," Aunty Sylvia said.

"Well, if they can't or won't see it, then we're totally screwed. We may as well pack up and go home."

"It will happen, poppet. These things take time. The most important thing is not to panic."

But I was already panicking. On top of that, I was still pining for Hugh. Everybody kept telling me to call him, but I couldn't see the point.

"Look at you," Rosie said. "You're depressed and miserable and still you won't pick up the phone. I just hope you don't live to regret this."

"He needs to make the first move."

Rosie said she gave up.

If that wasn't enough, it was the school fete on Saturday. I was due to get up in front of the entire school and confess that I had lied about Greg Myers. This would result in my becoming a pariah, and I would probably have to take the kids out of school. It didn't help that Ella was getting more and more nervous about performing her solo and was still blaming me because Hugh wasn't around to coach her.

On Wednesday the phone did ring. It was Valentina. She wanted to know if I was around the following afternoon for a cuppa and a chat. I said that I was. We arranged to meet at the Old Tearooms in Kensington.

"I don't know about you," she said as we sat down, "but I'm still celebrating. Why don't we go for the cream tea? My treat."

"You're on."

"Actually it's wonderful just to take the weight off for five minutes. We've been running around like headless chickens since the competition. Just between you and me, this morning, I had a call from Buckingham Palace. The Queen and the Duchess of Cambridge both want me to come and fit them for bespoke bras. The business has always done well, but winning this competition is going to launch us into the stratosphere."

"Valentina, that's fabulous news. I'm really pleased for you." If I'm honest, my delight was tinged with more than a modicum of jealousy.

The waitress arrived with scones, homemade raspberry jam and golden clotted cream.

"Right," Valentina said, spreading strawberry jam over half a scone, "I don't believe in beating around the bush, so I'm going to come straight to the point. Charles and I have been discussing our future. I've finally decided that the time has come for me to call it a day. I've neglected Charles terribly. I'm seventy-five. It's time for me to retire and for the two of us to spend whatever time we've got left having some fun. So we've decided to kick off with a world cruise. That's where you come in."

"Me?"

"How would you feel about running the business?"

"You mean while you're away?"

"No. I mean forever."

"You want me to run La Feminista?"

"You'd be brilliant. You're young, gifted, ambitious. You work hard. I can't think of anybody's hands I would rather leave it in."

"It's a wonderful offer, Valentina, but I couldn't give up my own business. I've put so much time and energy into it. I can't walk away now. I need to make something of it."

"I'm not asking you to walk away. I'm not looking for a shop manager—I'm looking for a partner. An equal partner. We would merge the two businesses."

"You're kidding."

"Sarah, one thing you need to know about me is that I never kid. I'm deadly serious. I want us to go into business together. We'll rename it Green di Rossi. How's that? We'll even put your name first."

"I don't know what to say."

Valentina smiled. "*Yes* would be a start."

"What about Aunty Bimla and Aunty Sylvia?"

"Believe me, I'm not about to let them go. They're a major asset. I know that towards the end, Shirley was struggling to pay them a decent wage. I also know how dedicated and loyal they were, so how's about they come in as equity partners? And when they finally retire, we'll provide them both with a generous pension."

"That's more than generous," I said. "I couldn't argue with that." But I was aware that I still wasn't saying yes. "The thing is, I've been waiting for somebody to show some interest in the nursing bra. If I sell the idea, it's going to be worth a lot of money. Then I'd have enough to go it alone."

Valentina didn't say anything for a few moments. Then: "I'm not sure you're going to sell it."

"What do you mean? Whyever not? Women are crying out for nursing bras that fit properly."

"You don't have to tell me that. The point is that the bra manu-facturers don't need you to make a version of their own. Now you've given them the idea, there's nothing to stop them producing a de-cent, well-fitting nursing bra. It's the same with the étagère bra. I identified the gap in the market and put it out there, but nobody needs me to manufacture it."

"So people will just steal the idea?"

"Yes, but you and I know that the high-street version won't be up to snuff. My plan is to roll out the étagère bra myself—along with the best-fitting nursing bra on the planet."

"Are you serious?"

"I just told you, Sarah. I don't kid."

"But what would we use for capital?"

Valentina grinned.

"You have that kind of money?"

"Absolutely. We'd need to acquire a factory, set the whole thing up, but I'm sure that's not beyond you. The point is, Sarah, the business would be effectively yours. You'd get to sign off on pretty much everything. I would just show up for the annual board meeting and advise on the really big decisions, but otherwise it would all be yours."

"But how do you know you can trust me? This is huge. I don't even know if I can trust me."

"I trust you because you're a good person. Your kindness and generosity—the way you let Charles off the hook after what he did—will stay with me forever. We will always be in your debt. Charles still hates himself for what he did to you. I'm not sure he will ever get over it."

"Please tell him I don't hold a grudge. I know it was just a moment of madness."

"Maybe you would speak to him?"

I said that I would.

"Valentina, I'm truly bowled over by your offer, but it's just so sudden. I need time to think."

I could see the disappointment on her face. "Let me tell you the other reason I want us to be partners. I want to make amends. I carried all that hate inside me for too long. It's time to let it go, rebuild. Can you imagine how your aunty Shirley would feel—the two of us in partnership?"

The thought brought a smile to my face. "I think I probably can," I said.

"Please . . . Do it for her. . . . Now, tell me we have a deal."

I let out a long breath. "OK . . . we have a deal. And thank you. I'll do my best not to let you down."

"That's all I ask," Valentina said. "Now come on and let's finish these scones."

"*G*ather round," I said to the aunties. "I have news." I expected them to be beside themselves with delight, but Aunty Sylvia's reaction in particular was surprisingly muted.

"It all sounds wonderful," she said, "but I don't know how I feel about working for Valentina. She hated Shirley. I don't know if I can forgive her for that."

"On the other hand, she has reached out to us," Aunty Bimla said. "She wants to make peace. All that mutual loathing and animosity isn't good for the soul. We must forgive and forget, let bygones be bygones. This is the chance for a new beginning."

"I don't know. It's not that easy. It feels like we're being disloyal to Shirley."

"I disagree," Aunty Bimla said. "If anybody wanted to make peace, she did. She tried so hard."

"That's true. . . ."

"And you get a share of the profits during your lifetime," I said. "As well as a hike in salary and a pension."

"Really?' Aunty Sylvia said. "Valentina agreed to that?"

"She didn't simply agree to it. It was her suggestion."

"Who'd have thought? I can't believe it."

By now they were both welling up. Their money worries were over—and so were mine. Valentina had offered me a large lump sum on signing the deal. I had already earmarked some of it for Steve—

for all the work he had done. I left the aunties in the shop and went downstairs to drop him an e-mail. He answered straightaway.

What wonderful news. So happy for you. Honestly you don't need to pay me back and especially not with interest, but since you absolutely insist, see calculations below. And if you need an accountant, you know where to come. All good here. Have been dating lovely tax inspector. Planning to get engaged at Christmas.

Much love, Steve

A tax inspector. Perfect. I couldn't have been happier.

I went back upstairs with a tray of tea. "I've been thinking," Aunty Bimla said. "We should celebrate. What about lunch at my place on Saturday? Sanjeev is staying with me, Roxanne's back home. It would be great for us all to get together."

I said that it was a lovely idea, but I wouldn't be able to make it because it was the kids' school summer fair.

"I've got it," Aunty Sylvia said. "Why don't we come along to the fair and get together for tea?"

No! I didn't want the aunties hearing my confession. The humiliation would be too much. They couldn't possibly come.

"You're more than welcome," I heard myself say, "but will Sanjeev and Roxanne be up for it? I'm not sure that spending the afternoon at a school summer fair is exactly their thing."

"Of course it is," Aunty Sylvia said. "Who isn't a sucker for cotton candy and the hook-a-duck stall?"

Oh, let them come, I thought. What the hell. Another few people discovering how feeble and dishonest I'd been wasn't going to make much difference.

I'd just given the kids supper and finished long phone conversations with my mum and Rosie, who were both delirious at my news and convinced that Aunty Shirley had orchestrated the whole thing from above, when the phone rang again. It was Valentina's lawyer to say that he would have all the papers drawn up by the end of the week. I was learning something else about Valentina. Not only didn't she kid around; she didn't waste any time getting things done.

That night, on the spur of the moment, probably because I was feeling so upbeat, not to mention ever so slightly merry on supermarket bubbly, I decided to cave in and call Hugh. One of us had to come off their high horse. It might as well be me.

"Hugh, it's me."

"Sarah. That is so weird. I was literally just about to pick up the phone to you. How's it all going?"

I told him the Valentina saga—including the bit about Charles stealing the bra—and how it had ended with her offering me a partnership in the business. He couldn't have been more delighted.

"You are so on your way now. Everything you worked for is bearing fruit. This is sensational news. I am so proud of you."

"Thank you. I'm not sure it's quite sunk in yet. . . . Anyway, the thing is, I've been doing some thinking. . . ."

"So have I."

"You have?"

"Yes and there's something I need to tell you. Listen, is there any chance we could meet?"

"When?"

"Have you eaten?"

"Not yet."

"OK, so how about now?"

Betty was only too glad to come and mind Dan and Ella. They were even gladder because it meant a game of gin rummy. "Mum," Dan said. "Please don't say anything to Grandma. I mean, we like it when she and Granddad come to babysit, but Betty teaches us card games and she's said when we're older, she'll even teach us poker."

Hugh and I met at a pizza place in Tooting. The moment I saw him, I could see he was bursting to tell me something. I'd barely sat down when he said:

"I have news. I've got a job. Not an acting job. A proper job. It even comes with a pension. What do you think of that?"

"I don't understand. Why would you get a proper job?"

"Because I love you and I want to spend the rest of my life with you and if this is what it takes—"

"Whoa. Stop. We've been here before. You're doing it again— putting all the responsibility on me. If you get a job, it has to be because that's what you want—for you. I don't want you doing it for me. That would make us both unhappy."

"But I am doing it for me. This is a great job. It's teaching theater studies at Guildford University. I think I'm going to love it. In fact, I know I will."

"You're absolutely sure."

"Absolutely. I know I'm doing the right thing. It pays well. I'll be able to start putting money aside. I've realized that I'm finally ready to grow up."

Just then the waitress appeared with menus. "Hugh! Oh my God. What a surprise. How are you?"

Hugh made the introductions. The waitress' name was Lucy. She and Hugh had been in *The Producers* together.

Of course. Now I recognized her. "Ulla!"

She laughed. "And as you can see, I'm still flaunting it." She turned to Hugh. "But I hear on the grapevine that life's looking up for you. Congratulations on the job."

"Thank you," he said.

"So Hollywood finally came knocking, eh? Good for you. You deserve it."

Hugh looked like he wanted the wooden floor to swallow him up.

"Hollywood?" I said. "I don't understand. You just told me you got a teaching job."

"Lucy—do you think you could bring us a couple of Peronis?"

"Sorry, did I say something I shouldn't?"

"No. It's fine," Hugh said. "If you could just get us the beers?"

"Sure thing." She disappeared.

"OK," I said. "Do you mind telling me what's going on?"

"It's nothing."

"Since when is Hollywood nothing? Tell me what happened."

"OK . . . This producer at a small independent film company in LA called me and asked me if I'd like to read for the lead in a crime caper they're making. Apparently he'd seen me in *The Producers* when he was over here visiting relatives. Anyway, they're looking for a psycho but sunny German villain and thought I'd be perfect. I went over, did the audition, and they called last week to offer me the part. In the meantime I got offered the teaching job."

"And you're taking that instead of the movie?"

"Yes."

"Are you out of your mind?"

"What? But I thought that's what you'd want."

"Hugh, have you listened to anything I've said to you? I've always been clear that I'd never want you to give anything up—least of all acting. Being an actor is who you are. I can't believe you'd think I'd want you to turn down an offer from Hollywood. It's a truly amazing thing to have happened. Of course you must go for it. This is going to be your launchpad. I just know it."

"Hang on. I'm really confused here. I thought you wanted me to stop living like an overgrown adolescent."

"I do, and to that end, all I've ever wanted is for you to stop spending thousands on gallivanting around the globe and start putting some money away."

"Actually, that was the next thing I had to tell you. I've opened a savings account."

"What? You have to be kidding."

"Nope. And there's already money in it. I realized that now your business has hit the big time, you'd be putting money aside. I couldn't let you be the only grown-up in our relationship."

He reached into his jacket pocket and produced a deposit slip.

"Wow. I don't know what to say. A thousand pounds. I'm impressed . . . not just with the amount, but the fact that you did this. It means such a lot to me. Thank you."

"I just want you to know that I'm serious about us and that I want to start planning the future—our future."

I reached out and squeezed his hand. "Well, you can start by taking this job in Hollywood."

"But it's a huge risk. There are no guarantees the movie will even get made."

I said that I didn't care. "I haven't been fair to you. I've spent the last few months putting my future and my children's futures at risk. And it's paid off—not quite in the way I expected or hoped, but it has paid off. I have absolutely no right to prevent you from doing the same."

"But suppose the movie's a flop. Suppose I end up penniless."

"Then you'll do something else. If you think for one minute I'm letting you give up on this opportunity, you can think again."

"You know I love it when you take control."

Lucy came back with our beers and took out her notepad. "So have you decided?"

"Yes," I said. "I think we have."

*H*ugh slept over that night, not that we did much sleeping. As the sun came up, we were still lying awake, in each other's arms. "I don't half love you, Hugh *F*-fanshaw."

"I love you, too, but would you mind if we got some shut-eye now?"

We dropped off. What felt like ten minutes later, but was probably a couple of hours, Ella came running into the room, demanding a morning cuddle. She saw Hugh and stood at the foot of the bed, head tilted.

"Have you been doing your sex on my mummy?" she said by way of greeting.

"Hi Ella," Hugh said. "And good morning to you, too."

"Ella, do you have to say stuff like that?" I said.

"But it's what grown-ups who love each other do in bed. You told me about it and you said that it was normal. . . ."

"Yes, but there are times when it's OK to discuss it and times when it's not so OK."

"Like in front of Betty or Grandma and Granddad?"

"Exactly."

"Goddit."

Then Dan appeared and started bouncing on the bed.

"So have you two made up?" he said.

I told him that we had.

"So, Hugh, are you going to be our new daddy now?"

"I'm going to be around a lot more, but I don't think you'd want anybody to take the place of your real dad, would you?"

"No, but we could call you Dad Two. That would be OK."

"So can you help me with my solo now?" Ella said. "It's the summer fair this afternoon and I need to have one final practice."

I made toast and put on some coffee. Hugh and Ella went into the living room to practice. They made me switch on the radio so that I couldn't hear.

I was listening to some tedious report on fiscal deficit when the phone rang. It was Rosie.

"Hey—how did the Delphine meeting go?"

"Really well. They want to use me on a freelance basis to start with. After that, assuming they're happy, I'll be given a year's contract. The two women who interviewed me said that unofficially they were looking for the new 'rack of Delphine' and that I could find myself in the running."

"You're kidding."

"I am so not kidding. I mean, me as the rack of Delphine. Can you imagine? It's funny, isn't it, how life can be crap for ages and then suddenly everything changes?"

"Tell me about it."

"How do you mean?"

"I have news, too. Hugh and I are back together."

"Noo! So you finally came to your senses."

"Yeah. But he compromised, too. He's opened a savings account. But the really massive news is he's got a film gig in Hollywood."

"Get out of here."

"Listen, I'll give you all the details when I see you, but suffice it to say things are looking up."

"Sarah, you have no idea how happy I am for the both of you. Give Hugh a kiss from me and say hi."

"I will."

"You know, all I need now is a bloke in my life and things would be perfect."

I told her that modeling was going to bring her into contact with loads of men.

"Yeah, gay ones."

"Oh, stop it. You're back in the outside world, that's the important bit."

"Yeah, I know. You're right. I need to keep the faith. So anyway

I'm off to Rome on Monday to do my first photo shoot. I've got it all organized—Betty's going to come and look after Will."

"Listen, why don't you come to the summer fair this afternoon and celebrate with a cream tea. The aunties will be there. They'd love to hear your news."

She said she couldn't because she was going to see her sister. She asked me to pass on her news to the aunties. "I'm really sorry I won't be with you to give you moral support."

"I'll be fine. I'll have Hugh there. And what's the worst that can happen?"

"You have to flee the country?"

"That's not going to happen."

"But that Tara woman is going to hound you wherever you go. I think Mexico might be your only answer."

"Thanks for that. I needed cheering up."

"*Y*ou know, Ella's actually got a great little voice," Hugh said later, as we sat at the kitchen table, drinking coffee. "And she certainly belts it out. I think you're going to be dead chuffed when you hear her." He took a mouthful of coffee. "So how do you feel about the summer fair?"

"Crap, thank you for asking. But it has to be done. I owe it to everybody to confess my sins. Rosie thinks I should run away to Mexico."

Hugh laughed. "Stop panicking. It's going to be fine."

"No, it isn't. It's going to be terrible and I'm going to be a laughingstock and everybody will refuse to speak to me. The kids will probably have to leave the school."

"Stop it. Nothing like that is going to happen."

"How do you know?"

"I just do, that's all."

I said I wished I had his confidence. "So anyway . . . changing the subject, how do you feel about becoming the children's daddy?"

"Great, but I'm thinking it might feel a bit odd if we're not actually married."

"Yeah, I can see that."

"So what do you think?"

"About what?"

"Getting married?"

I started laughing. "Hugh, is this a proposal?"

"Yes . . . Look, I know it's not very romantic, but how about I do a repeat performance tonight over a posh, candlelit dinner? You know, get down on one knee. . . ."

"That might work."

"But for now, what do you say?"

"Er . . . let me think. . . . OK, I guess that would be a yes."

With that, he reached over and pulled me towards him.

Just then Ella appeared.

"Dan, quick," she called out. "They're snogging."

For days, I'd been praying for the fair to be rained out, but it wasn't to be. The sun shone out of a cloudless sky, the school playing field had been mowed and rollered to perfection and bunting had been strung between the trees. Women were out in their Tommy Padstow Breton tees; kids were white with sunblock; daddies had dug out their brown sandals and Panamas. The stalls were ready to go. Dan and Ella had gone off with Fiona and her kids. Dan was busy telling Tom that he had already worked out the order in which he was going to visit the stalls: guess-the-number-of-sweets, the tombola, coconut shy, hoopla, lucky dip and finally, leaving the best until last, the throw-a-wet-sponge stall.

Imogen came charging across in her giant floppy hat and Crocs. "All ready for the off? I have to say everybody's absolutely dying to meet Greg Myers. We're all so grateful to you for persuading him to come. And as for you organizing this rockabilly band. What can I say? It's incredibly generous."

"It's nothing. My pleasure . . . Imogen, before things kick off, there's something I need to—"

"Sorry—must dash, the donkeys have just arrived and apparently one of them has just wandered into the hall and taken a gigantic dump."

I was aware that Hugh was looking at his watch. "You got a bus to catch?" I said.

"No, it's nothing. Nervous habit."

"Really? I've never noticed it before."

He said he needed to go to the car park to check on something. "What?"

"I think I may have left my wallet in the glove box." With that he was gone.

Just then Tara and Charlotte appeared. They looked like they were on their way to Woodstock, but had taken the wrong exit. Tara was in a cheesecloth maxi-dress and platform sandals. Charlotte was sporting flowery flares and big round shades.

"It's almost three," Tara said, all faux smiles. "Greg Myers is cutting it a bit fine, wouldn't you say?"

I managed a thin smile, but said nothing. Knowing that my personal Armageddon was no more than a few minutes away, I felt tears forming behind my eyes.

Just then, the aunties appeared—along with Roxanne and Sanjeev. Tara and Charlotte offered everybody perfunctory smiles and took their leave.

As I wiped my eyes, I realized that I wanted nothing more at this second than to throw myself into the aunties' arms and tell them that Hugh and I were getting married, but I couldn't. We'd agreed that nobody could know until we'd told the children and our parents.

"Sarah—you remember Roxanne," Aunty Sylvia said.

"Of course. How are you? Long time no see. I was sorry to hear your film didn't work out."

Roxanne hadn't changed. She was just as skinny and orange with a fake tan as ever. "I think the film not happening was probably for the best," she said.

"I agree," I said, lowering my voice and pulling her a few feet away so that Aunty Sylvia couldn't hear. "I'm guessing that sadistic horror isn't your mum's genre of choice."

"But I told her it was a kids' film."

"Yeah, but the rest of us worked it out."

"God . . . if Mum had found out . . . Holy crap . . ."

"Well, luckily for you, she didn't."

"So," Aunty Sylvia piped up, looking at Roxanne. "Have you told Sarah that you got into the veterinary nursing course?"

"You did?" I said. "Congratulations. Are you happy about that?"

"Of course she's happy. Mark my words, it's going to be the best thing she's ever done."

"I just need to get my own place," Roxanne whispered. "And sooner rather than later."

"Aunty Sylvia driving you crazy?" I whispered.

"Doesn't even begin to describe it."

Aunty Bimla had been hovering, desperate to break into the conversation. "And this is Sanjeev," she said. I only knew Sanjeev by reputation. I'd never met him. He had to be in his thirties, but standing there in his hoodie, head down, hands in his jeans pockets, he looked like a truculent seventeen-year-old.

"Sanjeev, I want you to meet Sarah. Now, Sarah is a real entrepreneur."

"Oh, I wouldn't quite say that. Hey, Sanjeev."

He shook my hand, but it was clear he would rather have been anywhere but here among the stupid fairground stalls and donkey rides.

"I just wanted to say thank you for what you've done for my aunt. Believe it or not, I was hoping to provide for her in her old age."

"There's nothing stopping you. You make it sound like this is the end."

"It certainly feels like it," he said.

"Sanjeev is going to live with his uncle in Bradford, aren't you, Sanjeev?"

"Apparently."

"He's going to work in his convenience store, until he's paid me and the bank the money he owes."

"Do your time," I said. "And then start over, but when you do, remember to keep your wits about you."

"That is good advice," Aunty Bimla said. "You be sure to take it."

"I will," Sanjeev said, but I doubted he meant it. He might be down on his luck now, but I couldn't help thinking that once a player, always a player.

"Right now let's all go and find some toffee apples," Aunty Sylvia said. "I haven't had one in years."

They invited me to go with them, but I said that I had to wait for the Milkshakers. They arrived a quarter of an hour later, all quiffs and drainpipes, and started setting up on the small stage—the stage from which, any minute now, I was due to make my announcement.

Hugh had returned from the car park—apparently he'd found his wallet—and was starting to pace. "What on earth is it?" I said. "I'm the one who's meant to be nervous."

"I'm fine. I'm just a bit jittery on your behalf."

"Please don't be. You're actually making me feel worse."

By now the field was packed with mums, dads and kids; the organ-grinder music was playing; the smell of barbecue filled the air.

"I do hope he hasn't got stuck in traffic," Imogen said, cropping up again. "Do you think you ought to try his cell?"

Sod it, I thought. I might as well just get this over with. Without offering Imogen a reply, I climbed onto the stage, where the Milkshakers were still sorting out cables and speakers, and picked up the microphone. I gave it a couple of echoey taps. "Good afternoon, everybody. If I could have your attention. I just want to welcome you all to our annual summer fair. For once the weather has been kind, so let's hope that this will be a bumper fund-raising event. Now, I did promise that we would have Greg Myers here to open the fair, but I'm afraid . . ."

The sudden tap on my shoulder made me swing round. "May I?" the voice said. I watched silently, blinking as Greg Myers took the microphone from my hand.

"Hello, mums and dads, boys and girls," he hollered into the mic. "So, are you all having a good time?"

"Yess!"

"Are we going to raise loads of money this afternoon?"

"Yess!"

"Are we all going to buy lots of raffle tickets?"

"Yesss!"

"OK . . . in that case I would like to declare this summer fair well and truly open. I'll be here for a while—I'm starting off on the wet sponge stall, so if any of you would like to come and throw a sponge at me, feel free."

Applause, whistles, whoop-whoops. The Milkshakers got going with "Be-Bop-a-Lula." I could see Dan and Ella boogying with Tom and Grace.

Greg Myers extended his hand. "Hi, I'm Greg. You must be Sarah."

"Yes. I mean . . . hello . . . and thank you so much for coming, but can somebody please explain what's going on? You're not meant to be here. Not that I'm not glad you are here—it's just that I'm really confused."

Hugh was looking down at the ground, smiling.

"You're responsible for this, aren't you?"

He held up his palms. "Guilty."

"So that explains all the weird behavior. It also explains why you were so anxious for me not to make my big confession until today. But why on earth didn't you tell me?"

"That was down to me," Greg said. "I asked Hugh not to say anything because I was filming this morning and right up till the last minute I wasn't sure I was going to make it."

I turned to Hugh. "But I remember asking you if you knew Greg and you told me you didn't. You said you didn't know any famous actors."

"I don't. But it just so happens that Greg went to drama school with an old mate of mine. So I gave him a call."

"I don't know what to say. I'm just so grateful to both of you. You've saved my reputation and stopped me from having to flee to Mexico. Thank you. Thank you so much." I gave Greg a hug and a big kiss.

"Oh, and I'm sorry I was so rude to you that night. You don't look anywhere near old enough to be the mother of teenage daughters."

"Hugh told you about that? Honestly, I barely gave it a second thought."

"Don't I get a kiss?" Hugh said.

"Maybe later. I'm still pissed off with you for not telling me you'd arranged all this."

"Mr. Myers! Welcome!"

It was Imogen. A dozen thrilled and excited mothers hovered in the background. Tara and Charlotte stood to one side of the group, looking neither pleased nor excited. I smiled and waved at them. They looked down their perfect noses and walked off.

Greg Myers extended his hand and insisted that Imogen call him Greg.

She introduced herself. In his presence, Imogen was blushing and stuttering like a smitten schoolgirl.

Greg and Hugh disappeared with Imogen and the hovering mothers to the wet sponge stall. Hugh and I arranged to meet later in the hall where the children were due to perform their show tunes.

I wanted to find Tara and Charlotte to gloat some more, but they seemed to have disappeared. I spent ten minutes or so wandering around. Finally I caught sight of Tara. She and her husband were at the refreshment stall. I couldn't hear what was being said, but judging by all the gesticulating, they were having one hell of a fight. Charlotte was hovering in the background with her kids and Tara's.

"Hell hath no fury like a man cuckolded." Imogen was standing beside me. She'd clearly tired of the wet sponge stall, although I suspected not of Greg Myers. She was holding two glasses of Pimm's. She handed me one. "Between you and me, I think somebody might be wishing she'd signed a prenup." Imogen started to cackle. "Bottoms up," she said.

*T*he school hall had been cleared of donkey dung, although it had to be said, and indeed a number of people were saying it, that a certain aroma still lingered. It didn't help that the children were accusing the old people who, along with their wheelchairs, walking frames and nurses, had packed out the hall.

The performance kicked off with "My Favorite Things," followed by "Singin' in the Rain" and "Sunrise, Sunset." The old folks clapped and sang along and passed around boiled sweets and Tums. Finally it was Ella's turn to perform her solo. Grinning all over her face, she marched to the front. The piano struck up.

Ella took a deep breath. "The sun'll come out tomorrow. . . ." She was bellowing more than singing, but it was still the most beautiful sound in the world. Tears poured down my face.

"She wanted to sing that for me?"

"Especially for you," Hugh said. "She chose it and her teacher said yes."

The rest of the kids joined in the final chorus. Dan, who was singing with particular gusto—even though he would probably have given anything to be outside playing football—spotted me and gave me a tiny wave as if to say, "This is from me, too."

"If I think back to how they were after their dad died. Now look at them—two happy, confident kids. They made it through."

"They wouldn't have done it if they hadn't had such a great mum. If I were you, I'd be really proud of them."

"I am. You have no idea."

"So when are we going to tell them our news?"

We agreed to postpone the romantic dinner we'd planned for the night and take the kids to Puccini's instead. We would tell them over pizza. Afterwards we'd all pop round to my parents' to give them the news. Then I would call Rosie and the aunties. I couldn't wait to see how the aunties changed their tune about Hugh once I told them that he was about to become a Hollywood actor. Hugh made the point that, bearing in mind Roxanne's Hollywood experiences, they might not be that easy to convince, but I said I'd work on them. "Deep down, they adore you. They'll come around. Just you see."

"I hope so. . . . Oh, and tomorrow I should call my parents. Or better still we should go and see them, so that I can introduce you."

"God, how's your mother going to feel about you marrying a cabdriver's daughter with two kids?"

"Are you kidding? Valentina just told you she got a call from Buckingham Palace. You are about to become purveyors of lingerie to the Queen. My mother is going to adore you."

"You sure?"

"I'm certain."

A few hours later, as we finished our Napoletanas and Pepperonis, Hugh turned to Dan and Ella and said there was something important he needed to ask them.

"What?" Dan pincered a black olive off a slice of pizza and dropped it onto his sister's plate.

For once she didn't notice, so for the moment ructions had been averted.

"Well, I'm sure you've both realized by now," Hugh said, "that I'm very much in love with your mum, and I'm delighted to say that she loves me, too. So I was wondering if you would consider giving me your permission to marry her."

Even if it was a tad Baron Von Trapp, I thought it was a lovely gesture to involve Dan and Ella and make them feel they had an important part to play in our decision.

"Really?" Dan said. "You're going to get married?"

"Only if you agree," I told him.

"That is so cool. I hated being the only kid in the class without an alive dad. Permission granted."

"Me, too," Ella joined in. "And I want to be a bridesmaid with a pink fairy dress, with wings and sparkly shoes and a crown and glitter all over. . . ."

"We'll see what we can do," Hugh said, grinning.

"So, do we get hugs?" I said, arms open.

The kids leaped off their chairs and launched themselves at us.

"I'm not going to call Hugh 'Daddy' yet," Ella announced, climbing onto my lap. "Maybe first I'll practice on my own, just to see what it feels like."

"You do anything you like," Hugh said. "It's fine with me."

"And Mummy has to have a white dress, with all diamonds and sequins and a train and shoes and flowers and a Cinderella coach, and Hugh and Dan have to wear suits, with a flower. . . ."

Hugh winked at Dan. "Football on Saturday?"

"You bet."

Photo © Jonathan Margolis

Sue Margolis was a radio reporter for fifteen years before turning to novel writing. She lives in England with her husband.